HIGHLAND ROSE

CELESTE BARCLAY

OLIVER HEBER BOOKS

0 9 8 7 6 5 4 3 2 1

Published by Oliver Heber Books

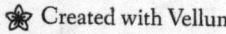 Created with Vellum

The ones we love and lose live always in our hearts and souls.

Happy reading, y'all,
Celeste

Subscribe to Celeste's Newsletter

Subscribe to Celeste's bimonthly newsletter to receive exclusive insider perks.

Have you read *The Highland Ladies Guide*? This FREE first in series is available to all new subscribers to Celeste's monthly newsletter. Subscribe on her website.
Subscribe Now

The Clan Sinclair Legacy

Highland Lion
Highland Bear
Highland Jewel
Highland Strength (Coming March 2023)

Sinclair Family Name Guide

Liam Sinclair m. Kyla Sutherland

b. ***Callum Sinclair*** *m. Siùsan Mackenzie* (SH-IY-oo-san)

b. Thormud Seamus Magnus Sinclair (TOR-mood SHAY-mus)

b. Rose Kyla Sinclair

b. Shona Mary Sinclair

b. ***Alexander Sinclair*** *m. Brighde Kerr* (BREE-ju KAIR)

b. Saoirse Sinead Sinclair (SEER-sha shi-NAYD)

b. Nessa Elise Sinclair

b. Mirren Louise Sinclair

b. ***Tavish Sinclair*** *m. Ceit Eithne Comyn* (KAIT-ch En-ya CUM-in)

b. Ailish Elizabeth Sinclair (A-lish)

b. Tate Henry Sinclair

b. William "Wiley" Matthew Sinclair

b. ***Magnus Sinclair*** *m. Deirdre Fraser* (DEER-dreh FRA-zer)

b. Maisie Blair Sinclair

b. Blake Magnus Sinclair

b. Torquil Lachlan Sinclair

b. ***Mairghread Sinclair*** (Mah-GAID) *m. Tristan Mackay*

b. "Wee" Liam Brodie Mackay

b. Alec Daniel Mackay

b. Hamish Kincaid Mackay

b. Ainsley Maude Mackay

Preface

Welcome to *The Clan Sinclair Legacy*, a spinoff from my *The Clan Sinclair* series. As you join the second generation of this remarkable family, you may recognize heroes and heroines from the first series. For some of you, it may be a chance to become reacquainted with old friends. For those who haven't read *The Clan Sinclair*, take heart: all of my books can be read as standalones, so you don't have to read the earlier series to enjoy this one. Many readers of the original books wondered what would become of the couples from my *The Highland Ladies* series. Fear not. The children of several of those couples will have their chance to find love with the younger Sinclairs and their Sutherland relatives over the course of my next twenty books.

The Clan Sinclair Legacy takes place roughly twenty years after *The Clan Sinclair* and about ten years after the final installment of *The Highland Ladies*. In my first series, I never explicitly stated who ruled Scotland at the time; however, King Robert the Bruce and Queen Elizabeth de Burgh appear throughout *The Highland Ladies*. By the time this new series would take place, the Bruce is dead, and his son, David II, is on the throne. You will discover more about King David's complicated reign in later books in this new series.

As I plotted this series, I realized that I'd already paired much of the Highlands with the Sinclairs and Sutherlands, so it was a challenge to find clans with whom none of our heroes or heroines would be directly related. I figured it out, but it took a couple maps, and making charts and family trees. That's how I devised our hero, Blaine Keith, since the Sinclairs haven't interacted with Clan Keith yet, but they were neighbors. It also put them in proximity to the Sinclairs and Sutherlands, which created more opportunities to revisit old friends from *The Highland Ladies* series. While they have cameos, Blair and Hardi Cameron, Lachlan and Arabella Sutherland, and Hamish and Amelia Sutherland appear in this story.

If you aren't familiar with the complicated family tree that is the Clan Sinclair, I shall endeavor to give you an overview to hopefully prepare you for this story. Liam Sinclair, patriarch and laird, married Kyla Sutherland in *Their Highland Beginning*. This ended a long-time feud, and Hamish Sutherland, Kyla's brother, is introduced for the first time. The foundation for the mightiest alliance in the Highlands was born. This is a product of my imagination, even though there were periods in history when they were both enemies and allies.

Mairghread Sinclair married Laird Tristan Mackay in *His Highland Lass* (my very first book). This created an alliance that laid the foundation for the entire *The Clan Sinclair* series. The bond that this marriage, and Liam's to Kyla, secured the Sinclair-

Sutherland-Mackay trifecta. Mairghread and Tristan had four children, "Wee" Liam being the first grandchild for Laird Liam Sinclair. We met "Wee Liam" in *Highland Lion,* when he traveled to Orkney and met Elene Isbister.

Liam and Kyla's oldest son, Callum, married Siùsan Mackenzie in *His Bonnie Highland Temptation.* This allied the two clans in *The Clan Sinclair.* The alliance was redoubled in *Highland Jewel* when Saoirse (Alexander and Brighde's oldest daughter) married Siùsan's younger half-brother Magnus. It was during *His Bonnie Highland Temptation* that I laid the foundation for the ongoing strife with Clan Gunn. Siùsan's family, through her mother, were the MacLeods of Assynt. This formed another alliance for the Sinclairs.

Alexander and Brighde's marriage in *His Highland Prize* didn't create an alliance with her family, the Kerrs. When Blake (Magnus and Deirdre's oldest) meets Cerys Kerr in *Highland Bear,* the rivalry flares again. While they find their happily ever after, the Sinclairs and Kerrs don't form an alliance. However, it was during *His Highland Prize* that things with the Gunns come to a head for that generation.

In *His Highland Pledge,* Magnus reunites with his one great love, Deirdre Fraser. I don't specify from which Fraser branch she haled. That didn't come until this series. Her relationship with Magnus created a rift between the Sinclairs and Frasers that I don't resolve until a brief mention in this book. This implied reconciliation brings yet another clan into the fold.

Tavish Sinclair fell in love with Ceit Comyn while at Robert the Bruce's royal court in *His High-*

land Surprise. They were supposed to be an arranged marriage, but they fell in love before any contracts were formally signed. We've only heard mention of their children so far in *The Clan Sinclair Legacy*, but their loves stories are coming. The Comyns weren't allied with anyone for the most part since they were one of Robert the Bruce's primary rivals. While there was no animosity with Ceit's family, no alliance formed between them and the Sinclairs.

The original Sinclair siblings' cousin Maude married Kieran MacLeod of Lewis (*A Wallflower at the Highland Court*), forming an alliance with the Sutherlands and, therefore, the Sinclairs and Mackays. They were distant relatives and the head branch of the MacLeods that included the MacLeods of Assynt. This marriage linked the Sutherlands to the MacLeods of Assynt indirectly. The Sinclairs were already tied to the MacLeods of Assynt through Siùsan's mother.

Blair, Maude's sister, married Hardwin Cameron (*A Saint at the Highland Court*), creating an alliance to the Sutherlands which meant an indirect alliance to the Sinclairs and Mackays. Blair and Hardi are visiting Blair's family at Dunrobin during this story, so we briefly reunite with them.

Lachlan, Maude and Blair's brother, married Arabella Johnstone (*A Beauty at the Highland Court*), but Arabella's refusal to marry the man her father chose created an irreparable rift between the Sinclairs and Johnstones. The man Arabella was supposed to marry was, lo and behold, a Gunn. This brought the Sutherlands, Mackays, and Sinclairs into conflict with their nemesis once more.

Edgar Gunn, the villain in this story, was introduced in *A Hellion at the Highland Court*, when he entered into the ill-fated wager against Brodie Campbell and Laurel Ross, who was Hamish and Amelia Sutherland's niece since Amelia was originally a Ross. He is now an experienced laird who continues the ongoing feud between the Gunns, and the Sinclairs, Sutherlands, and Mackays.

If you're completely confused, I understand! Check out the family tree that appears after this Preface. This will help you understand the Sinclairs' enormous family. If you're curious about the alliances and rivalries mentioned from *The Highland Ladies*, I recommend subscribing to my newsletter and receiving a free copy of the series guide. This gives you a behind the scenes view of the entire series.

As I usually strive to do, I included as much accurate history as possible. For the sake of including these events, I did take some creative license and shortened the time between some of them, so they would happen relatively close to when this book took place. Strife did exist between the Keiths and Murrays, and the Battle of Keith's Muir was a real event, as well as a Keith leader being killed at Keith's Pot, or Keith's Stone. However, this would have taken place well before Blaine was born.

Several Keiths served as the Great Marischal of Scotland. There was a Keith who, as Marischal, did murder a number of children with boiling wort, the liquid that comes from brewing ale and whisky. I couldn't find any specific details about how this came to pass, which is likely a good thing, since it could only have been gory. One Keith accompanied Robert the Bruce's heart back to Scotland, which I mention in this story. Another Keith, who I made Blaine's father, accompanied King David II and Queen Joan to France and remained there throughout the young king's exile. This situation gave me a convenient excuse to have Blaine seek support from the Camerons, one of their allies. As I've pointed out already, the Camerons were closely allied with the Sutherlands through marriage, so that meant an alliance between the Camerons, and the Sinclairs and Mackays.

To end a feud between the Keiths and Irvines, a Keith woman did marry into an Irvine laird's family. I considered making it Blaine's sister, but that seemed to add a level of complexity that I didn't need. Instead, I made him an only child and created a much more dire situation.

The rivalry between the Keiths and the Gunns did take place, but once more, I took liberty with the dates, just as I did when the Sinclairs feuded and allied with the Mackays and Sutherlands.

I tackled eating disorders and body dysmorphia in Maude's story (*A Wallflower at the Highland Court*). This story has a connected theme where our heroine, Rose Kyla, develops more fully than most of her family and friends. While she's grown comfortable in her own skin, certain events have made her aware that some men would pay her unwanted attention. I wanted to create a realistic character who had moments of what might seem like conflicting self-confidence and low self-esteem. It's my goal to show these aren't mutually exclusive characteristics. That sometimes the reasons for low self-esteem seem entirely reasonable to the person in question despite how it might not make sense to anyone else. And sometimes, it masks even deeper self-doubt and senses of inadequacy.

While Blaine missteps at the beginning of this story, I think you'll find that he values Rose Kyla for all that she brings to their relationship. He wishes for a relationship between equals and admires Rose Kyla's resilience and resourcefulness, even if some of her actions might make him go gray at an early age. He seeks Rose Kyla's council from the beginning, which creates a quick but strong basis for how their relationship progresses so rapidly.

I hope you enjoy Rose Kyla and Blaine's journey as much as I enjoyed crafting it.

Happy reading,
Celeste

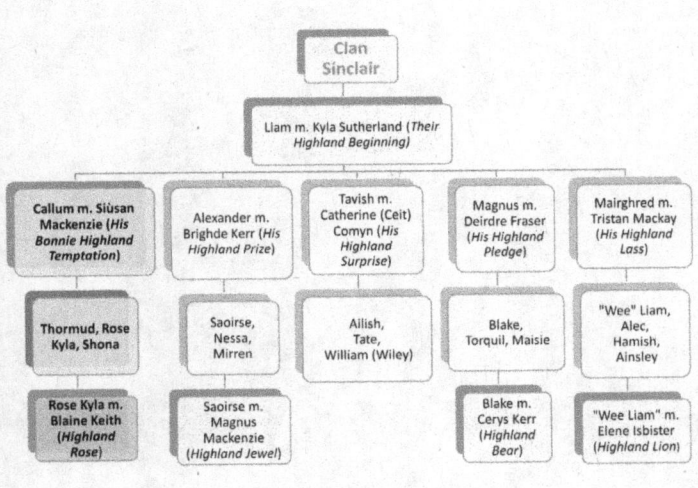

Clan Sinclair

Liam m. Kyla Sutherland (*Their Highland Beginning*)

Callum m. Siùsan Mackenzie (*His Bonnie Highland Temptation*)

Alexander m. Brighde Kerr (*His Highland Prize*)

Tavish m. Catherine (Ceit) Comyn (*His Highland Surprise*)

Magnus m. Deirdre Fraser (*His Highland Pledge*)

Mairghred m. Tristan Mackay (*His Highland Lass*)

Thormud, Rose Kyla, Shona

Saoirse, Nessa, Mirren

Ailish, Tate, William (Wiley)

Blake, Torquil, Maisie

"Wee" Liam, Alec, Hamish, Ainsley

Rose Kyla m. Blaine Keith (*Highland Rose*)

Saoirse m. Magnus Mackenzie (*Highland Jewel*)

Blake m. Cerys Kerr (*Highland Bear*)

"Wee Liam" m. Elene Isbister (*Highland Lion*)

Chapter One

"Who's that?" Rose Kyla Sinclair asked as she leaned toward her younger sister, Shona.

"I dinna ken, but he is a braw mon." Shona drew her lips in to keep from laughing as she watched her sister. She'd barely glanced at the entourage of Clan Keith men approaching Dunrobin's front gates. She'd felt more than seen her sister nearly trip and darted her gaze at Rose before looking at the ground. There was nothing there that would make her stumble, so she knew it must be the men riding before them.

Rose and Shona stopped as the horsemen crossed their path. The group's leader sported sandy blond hair and at least a three-day old beard. But it was his luminescent gray eyes that entranced Rose as they met her whisky-brown ones. They were the only feature she'd inherited from her father. She'd tucked her strawberry-blonde locks beneath a St. Birgitta's cap that morning before venturing to the village beyond the barmekin. The white linen coif hid all of her hair and made her eyes more prominent. Rose shifted the basket of fish from her right hip to her left, bumping into the basket of leeks Shona carried.

"Ow. Those are ma fingers ye're squashing." Shona's elbow jabbed Rose, but her sister merely took a step ahead before they continued along the path. They passed beneath the portcullis just as the men dismounted. As she walked around a wagon with a towering load of hay, she came to an abrupt stop.

"Ma pardon. I didna see ye there." Rose smiled as she stepped back from the handsome man she'd nearly plowed into, her basket now resting against her belly.

"Nay harm done, lass." The deep, rich voice wrapped around her like a seal-skin cloak on the coldest Highland night. But her brow twitched at the address. She hadn't been called a lass in years. Normally, people addressed her as "ma lady."

"Welcome to Dunrobin." Rose could think of nothing else to say as she titled her head back to meet his gaze.

"Thank ye. Do ye ken where I'd find the laird?"

"Keith, I'm here." Laird Hamish Sutherland hurried from the lists and stuck out his arm as he approached. The Earl of Sutherland and the younger warrior clasped forearms in a warrior handshake. "I dinna ken if ye've met ma tánaiste and son, Lachlan. Lach, this is Blaine Keith, his clan's tánaiste and son of Sir Robert de Keith."

"Welcome to Dunrobin." When Lachlan repeated Rose's welcome, Blaine glanced back at her before turning his attention to the Sutherland men.

"Thank ye. It's been a longer ride than it should've been, and I didna ken if I'd make it in one piece."

"Come to ma solar. We can talk there. Ma guess is the Murrays."

2

"Ye'd be right." Blaine walked beside Hamish, who positioned himself between Blaine and Lachlan. He didn't wish to walk away from Rose, but he had little choice. The buxom woman with the sun-kissed and freckled face continued to watch him. He wondered if she was a serving woman within the keep and if he might catch her attention that night. He wouldn't mind her company.

It surprised him when she and the dark-haired woman beside her followed the men up the keep's main steps. He assumed she would make her way to the kitchens rather than enter through the main doors. There was no reason for her not to, but he'd seen the fish within the baskets. When they entered the Great Hall, she set her basket on top of the other woman's and smiled at Hamish.

"I'll find Thormud and send him to yer solar."

"How'd ye ken?" Hamish grinned.

Rose shrugged her shoulders before gathering her skirts and taking the stairs to the second floor. With the material pulled tight across her backside, Blaine had a view that made him glad his sporran covered the front of his plaid. Her generous curves and ample bottom left him doubly wishful that he'd see her at the evening meal. He would ask her to dance, and perhaps more. He dragged his eyes away from the young woman to watch where he walked lest he run into a wall or door. When he sifted his attention forward, he found Lachlan staring at him, eyes narrowed. It was Blaine's turn to shrug before they entered the solar.

As Blaine took a seat at the massive oblong table in the center of the room, he forced himself to remember why he'd ridden with such haste to Dunrobin. "Ye're right, Laird. Even with our defeat, they continue to burn our land and our crops. With ma father away, they believe they can roam freely without consequence. I must admit I'd hoped to find Laird Cameron here."

Before Hamish could respond to Blaine, a light knock sounded at the door. He called out, "Enter."

Blaine turned in his seat, hoping Laird Hardwin Cameron would join them, but it was a man in his early twenties who entered. It shocked him that the woman he'd seen outside the gates and in the bailey stepped into the solar behind the young man.

What is a peasant woman doing in the laird's solar? There is nay way she's Hamish or Lachlan's leman because they're both too besotted with their wives to ever stray. The women would have their bollocks if they did. Lachlan doesnae have daughters, and his sisters are married. It's Lachlan's sister Blair who's married to the Cameron, and that's why they're here. Is she this mon's leman? They look vera comfortable together. But he looks like a noblemon. Bah. All the more reason that she must be. Bluidy hell. That would be ma luck.

Blaine stood as he greeted the younger man, extending his arm for another warrior's handshake. Before he could say anything, the woman retreated and left the solar. Blaine remained completely confused as to why she'd come until he noticed she'd placed a tray with food and mugs on a table near the door. She was a servant.

"Blaine, do ye remember ma grandnephew, Thormud Sinclair? He's Callum's son and second in line for the lairdship to Clan Sinclair. Though with the way Liam is, I doubt that line shall move anytime

4

soon." Hamish grinned as he clapped Thormud on the shoulder.

"I'm in nay hurry, Uncle. Grandda can take his time. Nay one is ready for him to leave us." Thormud grinned, thinking about his grandfather, who, like Hamish, neared his seventh decade and still looked like a man half his age.

"Aye." Lachlan snorted. "Yer da's in nay hurry to give up his time chasing yer mama."

"Wheest, lad," Hamish chortled. "Ye learned from yer cousin."

"I did nae. I learned from ye." Lachlan rolled his eyes at the same time Hamish did. They could have been twins rather than father and son.

"Blaine didna come to Dunrobin to hear aboot our family's randy nature."

"Nay one needs to come here to hear aboot it, Uncle." Thormud shook his head in mock disgust. As though his parents, aunts and uncles, great-aunt and great-uncle, and his father's cousins weren't bad enough, he had his own cousins Wee Liam, Blake, and Saoirse to ignore. While he hoped to find the same marital bliss his relatives had, he was in no hurry to join them. "What brings ye here, Blaine? I havenae seen ye in at least two years, and that was at court, in passing."

"The Murrays are causing more trouble. I hoped to see Laird Cameron aboot the matter. What are ye doing here?"

"Ma sisters and I came to visit. Dunbeath's a wee crowded these days. We've been here a sennight and plan to stay another moon." Thormud grinned as he thought about just how crowded the family of nearly forty made the keep.

"Just how badly are they giving ye grief?" Hamish leaned forward to accept the cup of whisky Thormud handed him before the younger man gave one to the others.

"They canna accept their victory with grace. After winning the Battle of Keith's Muir, ye'd think they'd be content to let us lick our wounds and take their time to gloat. But they're still laying waste to our sundry land and burning villages. I ken they're testing me, and they ken that if I rally, I will defeat them. But they also ken it'll be at an expense I dinna want to pay. With Father in France with King David, this isnae the time to have a war, but that's what they're counting on. I hope Laird Cameron might be a mediator for us."

"And if nae a mediator, then lend ye some sword arms," Thormud surmised. Blaine's lips turned down as his left eyebrow rose.

"Laird Cameron and Blair went for a day's sail. Blair's used to being landlocked these days, but she doesnae miss a chance to be on the water," Hamish explained. "They should be back in a few hours. The tide'll change and make it hard for them to come ashore if they wait too long. Amelia will send a bath to yer chamber, and ye can refresh yerself before the evening meal."

"Thank ye, ma laird."

"It's Hamish. With God's grace, it'll be a long time before ye become a laird in yer own right, but one day ye will. Ye may as well call me Hamish as we're allies."

"Thank ye." Blaine swallowed his last gulp of whisky, enjoying the way it heated every inch it passed. He followed Hamish and Lachlan from the solar, Thormud leaving the room last. "Good afternoon, Lady Sutherland."

"Welcome to our home, Blaine." Amelia Sutherland was only a couple years younger than her husband and still looked more like her daughters' sister than their mother. She had laugh lines that bracketed her mouth and crinkled beside her eyes. Her smile was easy and genuine as Blaine bowed to her. "I have a chamber for ye, and the bath is on its way up. Ye have aboot three hours before the evening meal, so there's time for a rest if ye wish."

"Thank ye, Lady Sutherland."

"I'm certain Hamish has already told ye to call him by his given name. I'm Amelia." She led Blaine abovestairs to the third floor, where the guest chambers were. As they passed the second floor, he thought he heard women's voices, but he assumed it was the maids. It surprised him when Amelia laughed.

"That's Hardi and Blair's Tira with her cousins. Ye'll meet them at the evening meal. Dinna be fooled by any of them. They're rowdier than any of the lads." Amelia showed Blaine to a spacious chamber where he was soon alone and soaking in his tub.

"She nearly fell on her face staring," Shona hooted.

"Wheest." Rose's lips pursed as she scowled.

"Is he really that braw?" Tira Cameron looked between her second cousins and waited. She giggled as Rose's fair skin flamed bright red.

"Aye. I think so."

"He was naught special to me." Shona elbowed Rose as they sat with Tira on the bed. Amelia knew

Rose preferred solitude at the end of each day, so her great-aunt assigned Rose a smaller chamber on the third floor while Shona shared one with Tira. Thormud shared a chamber with Tira's brothers on the second floor. The keep was full with Blair and Hardi in her old chamber and Lachlan sharing his chamber with his wife, Arabella. Their three sons each had their own room, too.

"Do ye think he found ye bonnie?" Tira whispered.

"I dinna ken what he thought. We didna really speak."

"But how did he look at ye? Like Da looks at Mama? Like Uncle Lach looks at Auntie Arabella? Like—"

"Nae like any of them. Uncle Hamish and Lachlan would run him through if he looked at any of us lasses like the men look at their wives." Rose glanced toward the door as though she could see through it to where the men were likely back in the lists.

"That's probably true. Yer da would skewer Uncle Lach if he thought some mon was making eyes at ye." Tira exaggerated as she fluttered her eyelashes.

"Then he'd come after yer da next." Rose's eyebrows shot up, knowing how protective her father was of her and her sister. She only partially jested that Callum would have words with Lachlan and Hardi if either of them let a man be too brazen with his daughters. "After everything that happened with Saoirse and Magnus Óg, I dinna ken that Mama and Da will be so quick to disagree with me marrying. But I dinna think they're looking forward to me leaving Dunbeath for good either."

Rose and Shona's uncle Alex and aunt Brighde objected to their daughter Saoirse's love match because they couldn't face Saoirse leaving Dunbeath. They used the age difference between Saoirse and Magnus Óg as an excuse, but it didn't last long when it became obvious how in love the couple was.

"It may nae even matter. Mayhap he's married."

"If he is, he shouldnae have been looking at ye like that." Shona's chin tipped down as she gave her sister another pointed look.

"So, he was looking at Rose!" Tira hooted.

"He was?" Rose appeared shocked. She thought Blaine hadn't paid her any attention once she wasn't about to knock him over with her basket.

"Och, aye. I dinna ken how ye couldnae tell. Men have looked at ye like that before."

"Nay, they havenae, Shona."

"Ye havenae noticed, but they have."

Rose stared at her sister before she shook her head. "Only men who dinna ken that our da is Callum Sinclair. They think me a wench or maid because I dinna look like a lady."

"What do ye mean, ye dinna look like a lady?" Tira's brow furrowed. "Ye speak like one and move like one. How could anyone nae think ye are?"

Rose looked down at herself, then back up at Tira. "I'm nae elegant like ye two."

"Of course, ye are. Ye're the best dancer I've ever met. Ye practically float." Tira shook her head before her lips flattened. "Do ye mean because ye're built the way we all wish we were? I have nay chest. I may as well be one of ma brothers for all ye can tell I'm a lass. It's only ma hair that gives it away."

"And I never got an arse." Shona giggled as she

stood, turned away from Tira and Rose, then wiggled her hips. "Ma backside is as flat as the Pax Board during Mass. Ye have the body of a woman, and we're still wee lasses."

"Men like to have something to hold on to." Tira pulled her kirtle away from her chest, looked down at her breasts, and shook her head.

"Aye. When they're with a tavern whore, nae when they're with their lady wife."

"Dinna let Kieran hear ye say that aboot Maude." Shona put her finger to her lips as she glanced at the door, trying not to giggle again. "Ye're built like her and Auntie Amelia. She and Uncle Hamish have been married more than two score, and he canna keep his hands off her. Rose Kyla, ye're named for our grandmama Kyla, and Auntie Mairghread says ye're built just as she was. We ken Grandda hasnae looked at another woman since he met Grandmama, and she's been in Heaven for nearly a score-and-a-half years."

Rose sighed and nodded. Shona and their cousins told her similarly reassuring things as they grew into womanhood, and Rose no longer thought much about her appearance. But there were still times when she wished she were petite, like Shona and their cousins. She didn't regret having an ample bust and backside, but she didn't like to think people compared her to a whore for something she couldn't control. She was just as active as any of the other women in her clan, and she didn't eat more than an average woman either. There was just more of her.

"They'll serve the evening meal soon. Blaine will sit at the dais, so ye'll ken whether or nae he noticed

10

ye." Shona stood again and straightened her skirts. "I wager the dirk that he stares at ye most of the meal."

"Ye canna bet the dirk. The others arenae here." Much like her father, uncles, and aunt shared a dagger they'd used to wager since they were adolescents, the cousins had a dirk that passed among them whenever someone won a bet. Shona won it from Rose three weeks earlier when she swore Thormud could out drink Kirk Hartley. Rose wagered Blake would drink the most. Thormud was the only one who could stand by the end of the night. Rose wouldn't mind getting it back since, like her Auntie Mairghread with her brothers, she was the one who held onto it the longest and most often among the cousins.

"They'll understand. I wager ye the dirk that he looks at ye at least five times during the meal." Shona stuck out her right arm as she held out the dirk in her left. Rose grasped her sister's arm in a warrior handshake.

"Let's go before we're late. And nay cheating, Shona," Rose warned. "Dinna do aught that will make him look in ma direction."

"I dinna cheat." Shona grinned, then whispered, "Often."

Chapter Two

Blaine followed the three young women, but he couldn't hear what they said since they'd lowered their voices as they moved across the passageway from a family chamber to the stairs. He recognized the woman from the path to the keep, who nearly walked into him in the bailey and mysteriously appeared in the laird's solar. He wondered why she walked with two ladies, clearly friends with them. She no longer wore the white linen St. Birgitta's cap. Her strawberry-blonde hair tumbled down her back in soft waves. She was even more stunning than she'd been when all he could spy were her deep brown eyes.

"Can ye find Lach and Hardi?" Amelia approached Rose as the women entered the Great Hall. "Shona, Tira, round up yer brothers."

"Are Blair and Hardi back from sailing?" Rose looked toward the keep's doors.

"Aye. They came back a couple hours ago, but then the lads went to the village to check a few crofts for damage after the last rains. I dinna think they realize how late it is."

"All right, Auntie Amelia." Rose hurried toward the door as Thormud entered alone.

"Where are ye going?"

"To find Lach and Hardi. Shona's looking for ye." Rose hurried through the door Thormud held open for her. It wasn't until she reached the bottom of the steps that she realized she had another shadow. She spun around and found Blaine hurrying after her.

"The meal's aboot to be served. Ye should find a seat before ma cousins leave ye in the far corner." Rose smiled and turned toward the postern gate.

Blaine's brow furrowed. Her cousins? "I heard Lady Amelia say ye were going to find Lachlan and Laird Cameron. I hoped to speak to the laird before the meal. Do ye ken where I can find him?"

"Somewhere in the village." Rose smiled, and Blaine nearly fell off the last step as his heart hammered behind his ribs. Her brilliant white teeth seemed to sparkle as a dimple deepened in her right cheek. A breeze wafted her heather and violet scent toward him, and he inhaled deeply. The pleasant scent calmed the anxiousness he felt about speaking to Hardi.

Rose waited for Blaine to step beside her once they passed through the postern gate. She waved at children running home from playing near the loch. She petted the miller's dog as it brushed past her, before wishing its owner a good evening. She'd traveled to Dunrobin so many times over her three-and-twenty years that all the villagers knew her as well as they did any of the Sutherlands. It was her second home.

Blaine wished to know about her, but he realized he didn't even know her name. He still wondered if

13

she might be Thormud's leman. He no longer thought it likely, but he didn't want to misstep and make advances toward another man's woman. As he watched her ease with the surrounding people, and how even the animals ran to see her, he marveled at the strength of his attraction toward her. She seemed far more like the type of woman a man married rather than just bedded. But he was a laird's heir, and she was a peasant. It wouldn't matter how attracted he was, the best he could hope for was a tryst or two.

"Lass, I dinna ken yer name." Blaine blurted.

"Och, I suppose nay one's introduced us properly." Rose stopped and turned toward Blaine. His height allowed him to block the dazzling early evening summer sunlight from shining in her eyes. "I'm Lady Rose Kyla Sinclair. Laird Hamish is ma great-uncle."

"Ye're a lady?" Blaine wished to swallow his tongue. Rose's chin came up, and her spine straightened, yet she appeared to shrink at the same time. He knew he insulted her, but there was something more to her reaction; however, he couldn't tell since he barely knew her.

"Aye. I'm Callum's daughter. He's our clan's tánaiste and heir to the Clan Sinclair."

"I've heard of ye, but I dinna think we've ever met. I should have kenned from yer hair."

Rose's eyes narrowed as she spun on her heel, her skirts swishing around her ankles. "I canna say I've heard of ye before today. Hardi should be over here." She released a piercing whistle. A moment later, Lachlan and Hardi stepped out of a croft's shadow and looked toward her. She waved, then turned back to the keep. "He's the one on the right."

Blaine wished to reach out and catch her arm as she walked past, but he couldn't do that with two men from her family watching. They would run him through, then ask questions. But he watched until she disappeared through the postern gate.

"What did ye say to Rose Kyla?" Lachlan asked as he and Hardi came to stand with Blaine.

"Naught. I just didna realize who she was."

"With that hair? How could ye nae ken? Ye saw Thormud earlier. He and his twin have the same coloring." Lachlan glanced toward the keep before looking back at Blaine. He tried not to laugh when he watched Rose shoot daggers at him before stalking away, leaving Blaine looking lost.

"She had that coif covering her hair earlier. I thought—I insulted her because I didna realize she was a lady. And instead of keeping that to maself, I said as much."

Hardi clapped Blaine on the shoulder and squeezed. Hardi didn't mean it to intimidate, Blaine realized. It felt fatherly. He couldn't remember the almighty Lord Robert de Keith ever doing such. "Apologize to the lass. She isnae one to hold a grudge. How was the journey here?"

"Long, hot, and dusty." Blaine chuckled, but he still wondered if he would have a chance to dance with Rose. Instead of seducing her, he had an apology to offer.

"What have the Murrays done now?" Hardi walked to Blaine's left while Lachlan was to his right. They were all of a similar height and build, but gray strands peppered the older men's hair, and deep lines weathered their faces. Blaine wondered if people thought he was as mature as the men with whom he walked or if they thought Hardi and Lachlan were as young as him. He realized he hoped for the former. He didn't want to come across as a boy running to tattle because he couldn't get along with his neighbor's children.

"They're still harassing us. They're burning fields and villages and reiving cattle. They burned the keep at Hall-forest. I've sent men on successful hot trots to get our animals back, and ma patrols have prevented several raids. But they keep pushing. If I use enough force to stop them, then it'll be a war. I'd rather nae send any men to die, but I will if they dinna stop."

"Why'd ye come here?" Hardi knew, but he would hear it from Blaine.

"Ye ken ye can mediate this since yer clan is stronger than mine or these Murrays. I'd rather try diplomacy first. If that doesnae work, then I will rally ma men and slaughter them. They were lucky at the Battle of Keith's Muir. They pushed us back across the River Dee, drowning many of our men before an arrow killed ma father's second, who was also ma aulder cousin. That was years ago. A war with us looking like the aggressors will only darken our reputation with the king. It'll look like ma father shouldnae have left me in charge."

"It'll look like ye arenae to be pushed around and will defend yer clan when ye need to," Hardi countered.

"And more men will die. If we can come to some type of peace without blood, isnae that the better choice to try first?" Blaine wondered if Hardi and Lachlan thought him cowardly.

"Aye. It is," Hardi conceded. He'd lost much of his family during a battle. Between that, an illness, and a snowstorm, he moved from sixth in line to inherit to being the laird. He knew better than most what happened when diplomacy failed. "Do ye really have the force to defeat them?"

"Barely. But if I can choose where we fight, then I believe we can win."

"Ye came for more than to ask me to be yer go-between."

"If ye canna mediate, then ye can threaten to join with us."

"Ye wish me to do more than threaten. The threat is me intervening to have the conversation." Hardi looked at Blaine and considered his choices. "I ken ye werenae the one to start this. It wasna even yer father. When yer cousin, as the last Great Marischal of Scotland, burned children in wort, it wasna easy to ignore."

The liquid that came from the mashing process while brewing whisky and ale had scalded them as badly as tar poured from the battlements onto an enemy. Keith knew the history and knew how detrimental his cousin's actions were when the man was still alive and the Marischal. It escalated a long-standing feud, and little had calmed since.

"Blaine, what do ye wish me to offer them to create this truce?"

"It's nae what I wish. The king is pressuring ma father to marry ma cousin to the Murray's auldest son."

"Would that be so horrible?"

"For me? Nay. For Clara? How can I trust them nae to mistreat her? I dinna want ma cousin to be a lamb to the slaughter."

"She wouldnae be the first woman in an arranged

marriage to bring peace." Hardi held the door open as Blaine, then Lachlan, entered the keep.

"Will ye use yer daughter to keep the peace with the Chattan Confederation?" Blaine stopped and stared Hardi in the eye. He wouldn't move until he made his point. Everyone knew the Sutherlands married for love. By extension, that meant the Camerons too.

"We arenae talking aboot ma clan or me." The edge to Hardi's voice warned Blaine, but he stood his ground.

"If ye arenae willing to do that to yer daughter, then ye canna fault me for protecting ma cousin."

"I'm laird. Ye are nae. It's yer father's decision, and ye will have to obey him as yer laird." Hardi pointed out.

Lachlan had remained quiet until this point, but he didn't want an argument in the Great Hall just before the meal. There were far too many ears listening. "We will solve naught this eve. Everyone is waiting for us to begin the meal. We can figure this out in ma da's solar tomorrow."

Blaine exhaled and nodded. Lachlan was right, and antagonizing Hardi wouldn't convince the man to help Blaine. They continued to the dais, and he looked for an open seat. There were three, and he knew he couldn't take two. One was beside Blair, saved for Hardi, and the other was beside Arabella, which was for Lachlan. The only open seat was next to Rose. Considering how she remained turned toward the dark-haired woman he'd seen, even as he sat, he knew she wasn't eager to spend the meal so close to him.

Once the priest blessed the food, Blaine seized his opportunity before Rose began talking to someone else. "Lady Rose, I apologize for earlier. I didna mean offense. I was under the wrong impression."

Rose turned her head to look at Blaine, and he felt her assessing him. When her eyes narrowed, he knew he'd failed. "Thank ye." She turned back to the food a servant placed before her in a trencher.

"I mistook ye for a servant."

"I gathered that or—" Rose snapped her mouth shut.

"Or, ma lady?"

"Are ye trying to prove a point now by calling me that?" Rose felt the flush rise in her cheeks, and she loathed her fair complexion for the umpteenth time.

"It's how I should have always addressed ye. I erred, and I'm trying to make up for it."

"Thank ye."

Blaine stifled his sigh. He made no headway with Rose, and he could tell that, if he pushed, he would only make it worse. He turned to the adolescent next to him and discovered the young man was one of Lachlan's sons. They discussed everything from horse breeding to battle strategy during the meal. It engaged Blaine, but it didn't stop his awareness of everything Rose did.

Rose tried to pay attention to her conversation with Shona, but every time Blaine moved, she curled her toes. He'd shaven before the meal and was even more attractive than when he arrived. It disappointed her that he held her in such low esteem. She didn't believe for a moment that he thought her a servant, but she couldn't bring herself to say it aloud. He smelled of fresh pine, and his voice rumbled, sending a vibration straight to her core. When their hands brushed as they reached for their chalices, she could feel its heat. She'd glanced at him, and his gray eyes appeared curious. By the end of the meal, Rose wanted nothing more than to escape to her chamber.

"Will ye dance with me, ma lady?" Blaine spoke just loud enough for the surrounding people to hear, without everyone at the table noticing. Rose gritted her teeth, knowing he'd put her in a position where she couldn't easily deny him. He helped her move back her chair after she nodded. He offered his arm as they walked off the dais to join the other dancers.

St. Columba's bones. She feels even better in ma arms than I imagined. This was a mistake. If ma sporran moves even a wee, she'll ken what she does to me. She moves like an angel. How could I have imagined she was anyone but a lady? It's clear someone taught her properly. I should have kenned from her graceful walk, but that ruddy cap and basket distracted me. It was her eyes, then her hair, nae her walk. Dinna be daft. If I'm being honest, it was that lovely arse too.

"Lady Rose, I still feel like I owe ye an apology. I'm sorry for insulting ye by nay realizing yer station."

"Mayhap if yer eyes hadnae been on ma arse each time they werenae on ma breasts, ye might nae have thought I was a tavern wench."

"I never thought that. I told ye. I thought ye were a servant."

"But ye dinna deny why ye thought that." Rose tried to pull away, but Blaine wouldn't let go. She scowled and looked toward Lachlan and Arabella, who danced next to them. She turned her gaze back to Blaine and cocked an eyebrow in warning.

"Lady Rose, it was the bluidy St. Birgitta's cap and the basket of fish that made me think that. I never took ye for—" Blaine lowered his voice to a whisper. "—a whore. I thought ye worked in the kitchens or were a maid."

"I saw the way ye looked at me, then, ma brother. Ye wondered if I was his leman."

"How could ye ken that?"

"Again, ye dinna deny it."

"That I canna. But I still wish to ken how ye knew."

"Ye looked confused when ye saw me, then ye looked at Thormud, and it was as though it made sense."

"Mayhap I realized ye were his sister."

"But ye still thought me a servant. It canna be both." Rose leaned back. "At least, nae in ma family. Dinna give me excuses."

"Are ye always so astute at reading people?"

"Only when they're obvious. Even if ye thought me a maid, ye still looked at me for a tumble."

Blaine steered them out of the crowd and toward a passageway. Sconces lit the darkness, but it was still far too private for an unmarried couple.

"Lady Rose, I never once thought ye were a tavern wench. I believed ye a servant. I did wonder if ye might be interested in more after the evening meal, but it wasna merely because I thought ye a maid."

"Aye. I told ye, I ken what ye were looking at."

"Eyes that remind me of aged whisky, and hair like fine strawberry wine."

"Quite the bard. Ye were looking at ma tits and arse, and ye assumed I was a maid who'd wanted a tupping."

Blaine sighed as he ran his hand through his hair. "Ye're astute, but ye're also stubborn. Ye are set on nae believing me. It was the coif that confused me. It was yer eyes that intrigued me, and I willna lie that I find all of ye vera attractive. But ye seem convinced that it's yer body that made me think of ye as aught but a lady. It's what attracted me, but what fooled me was that hideous thing covering the bonniest hair I've ever seen."

"Thormud has the same hair as me," Rose whispered. She wanted to let go of her conviction that it was her curvaceous body that allured him, but she feared being made a fool. She didn't know exactly how he would do that, but the anxiousness nipped at her.

"Color, mayhap. But I dinna care aboot him or his hair. Besides, I hadnae seen yer hair then. It was still covered. I wish ye would believe me."

Rose stared at Blaine for a minute before she nodded. "I can see how it would be confusing. The last rains damaged some of the crofts. I went to help the women tidy their homes. I didna want to get dust in ma hair, and it was too hot to have it down, so I covered it. Shona wore one too, but she took hers off when we left the last croft. The husband and sons of one family we helped are fishermen. They gave us their catch to give to the kitchens. They insisted on paying us, but I refused. I said I'd accept the fish kenning it would already come to the keep because I didna want to hurt their pride."

"That's vera thoughtful. Ma lady, could we have a new start? I dinna want to make a bad impression on ye."

Rose tilted her head. "Why does it matter?"

"Because I'm a guest in yer family's home. I dinna want ye to be uncomfortable with me here. I dinna want ye to think I will insult ye again."

Suspicion once more clawed at her. She wondered if he wished for her good opinion, so he could try for a tryst after all.

"Lady Rose, mayhap others canna tell what ye're thinking, but I believe I can. I am nay flattering ye to convince ye to do aught improper. I respect ye as a lady and as ma host and hostess's grandniece. Even if ye were a servant, if ye'd said nay, I would have respected that too. I am nae trying to play ye for a fool."

"All right."

"May I ask ye something?"

"Aye." Hesitation filled her tone.

"Have other men made improper advances? Is that why ye believed I assumed ye were a wench?"

"A few. But I ken I'm—" Rose looked away, but Blaine gently turned her face back to him with his thumb and forefinger on her jaw.

"What do ye ken, ma lady?" Blaine's soft voice once more sent a vibrating ache to her core. His expression was so earnest that she couldn't help but believe he cared what she said.

"I ken I'm built more like a whore than a lady." Rose wanted nothing more than to bolt to her chamber. She couldn't believe she'd said that aloud. Not only to a man, but to a stranger.

"I can guess what those men said, but a woman's body isnae what makes her a whore or a lady. Even if I thought ye a servant who might like a tryst, I never imagined ye were loose. Aye, ye have a body that any mon would want, but that doesnae mean ye're a wanton with every mon ye meet. It just means ye're beautiful."

Blaine kissed her cheek before offering her his arm. She glanced down at it and shook her head. He was slow to lower it.

"Nay one must have seen us come down here because ye're still breathing. But if anyone sees us coming out of this passageway, ye'll be dead or wed before dawn. Go first. They're far less likely to believe ye trysted with someone if the mon goes out first." Rose's hands gripped her skirts. "Thank ye for the kind words. Ye did ken what I was thinking, even if I tried nae to show it. I'm usually nae so bothered aboot how I look, but—" she shrugged "—I didna want ye to think that of me."

"I hope ye'll see I'm honorable."

"I believe ye are. I didna expect such a frank conversation aboot this, but ye were blunt enough for me to believe ye spoke the truth."

"And I'm glad ye felt ye could trust me enough to tell me the truth." Blaine kissed her cheek again, wishing he could do far more. But if he gave even a hint of what he wanted, she would paint him a liar and never believe his misunderstanding was honest. "Goodnight, Lady Rose."

Blaine slipped down the passageway and looked in every direction before entering the Great Hall again. He joined Thormud and Lachlan's sons by the fireplace, but he watched the passageway. He grew worried when Rose didn't appear, but he spied her entering the Great Hall from the keep's main doors. No one would know they'd spoken together or that he'd kissed her cheek twice.

If she's nae a servant, then mayhap there's a

chance to see if we suit. And if we do, then mayhap she could be ma wife after all. With the way she understands people and the way she's so candid with me, she would make any mon an excellent helpmate when he leads a clan. It doesnae hurt that I've never wanted a woman more.

Chapter Three

For the next three days, Blaine observed Rose but kept his distance. He watched her with her siblings and extended family. He saw how she laughed often, and from her expressions, deduced she had a sharp sense of humor. He watched how she never hesitated to help a servant if she saw something that needed doing, whether it was wiping tables, cleaning wax from sconces, or carrying in baskets of laundry. He watched her leave the kitchen one afternoon while she wiped flour off of her hands, clearly having baked bread.

They sat together at dinner Blaine's third night at Dunrobin, but he wondered if it was a coincidence. Rose sat between Blair and Arabella the other nights. While he didn't ask her to dance, they partnered often as the music made people switch. He caught her glancing at him several times because he was already looking at her, but he never found her looking at him. He wondered if it was disinterest or if she was more subtle.

"Why dinna ye just ask ma sister to dance?" Thormud asked as they entered the Great Hall on

Blaine's fourth evening with the Sutherlands. He and Hardi were still discussing possibilities and hadn't come to any agreement.

"What do ye mean?"

"Dinna play daft. She's ma twin. Mayhap others havenae noticed yet, but I have. And I can sense how ye are when ye're near each other. Just ask her again. Ye did on the first night."

Blaine weighed whether to tell Thormud the truth about why he gave her distance. Clearly, Thormud could already tell Blaine was attracted to Rose, and his encouragement was some type of consent. He tilted his head toward a wall away from the tables where people already sat.

"We had a wee misunderstanding. I thought she was a servant, and I had a different impression aboot her."

Thormud straightened from leaning against the wall and crossed his arms. "Ye thought ye'd toss her skirts while ye were here. I'll tell ye now, dinna dally with any of the servants here. Uncle Hamish willna have it. Nay woman is to feel like she must bed a mon because he's a noble, and she isnae. If she offers, still dinna do it. Go to the village and find a whore or a widow."

"I'm nae dallying with anyone while I'm here. I'm nae running off to tup a woman when I'm interested in yer sister."

"To tup her?"

"To marry her," Blaine snapped before he clenched his jaw and pushed his shoulder away from the wall. "I'm nae going whoring, so everyone can ken that I'm lifting ma plaid at night while chasing Lady Rose during the day. If she'll have me, those days are done. Why would I wish for someone else if she agrees to marry me?"

"So ye only want to marry her because ye wish to tup her."

"Bluidy hell. Ye *are* twins."

"What's that supposed to mean?"

"It means she thought I assumed she was a tavern wench when I didna. I told her I thought she was a servant because of that cap she wore. Aye, I thought I might have a tryst or two with her before I kenned she was a lady. But she assumed it was because of her—" Blaine exhaled a puff. "I didna think her body had aught to do with ma confusion. I willna lie to ye or her because there's nae point. I think she's the bonniest lass I've ever seen, so aye, I'm attracted to all of her."

"Ye walk a fine line telling a mon that ye've been ogling his sister."

"Ye already ken that I am, since ye told me to dance with her."

"When did ye have this conversation? And more importantly, where did ye have it?"

"The first night."

"Where, Blaine?"

"Privately, Thormud. We didna do aught but talk, I swear. I've kept ma distance because I dinna want her to think I lied and that I'm after only one thing."

"Well, if ye avoid her much longer, she's going to think ye arenae interested because ye didna get that one thing."

"How do ye ken? Did she say so?"

"Calm yerself, mon. I told ye, she's ma twin. We've kenned how each other thinks since before she pushed me out of the way and came into the world first."

"She's aulder?"

"Aye, by three minutes. Apparently, I was impatient to catch up. I didna take as many pushes." Thormud grinned as he looked toward Rose. His expression made Blaine look over his shoulder to find Rose staring at them. "Skip the dancing tonight and go for a walk with her."

"Are ye giving me consent to court yer sister since yer da isnae here?"

"I'm wishing ye luck with her. She's stubborn, but she's reasonable. She's like our mama. I'm just stubborn. I get that from our da. But let me warn ye, if she turns ye away, and ye dinna respect that, I will hurt ye." Thormud's chest and biceps flexed as his gaze bore into Blaine.

"I dinna doubt that. I dinna wish to do Lady Rose any harm. There's one more thing."

"Aye?"

"Ye ken I think she's beautiful. But I'm nae so shallow nae to realize that looks fade with age. It's obvious Hamish believes Amelia is still a bonnie woman, but he respects her for far more than that. I dinna want a wife who is a bonnie face but hasnae a mind to help me lead. I've seen how hard she works. I ken how she understands people. It's obvious people like and respect her. If I just wanted a bonnie woman in ma bed, I'd find maself a leman. I want more than that."

"Find yerself one? So ye dinna have one."

"Nae for nearly five years. I'm nae a monk, Thormud. But they're too much trouble. She wanted all ma attention and wouldnae accept the clan must come before aught I want and definitely ahead of aught she wanted. A wife is different."

"I'm glad ye understand that. I've seen ye in the lists and heard ye speak with Hardi and Uncle Hamish. Ye dinna leer at ma sister either. That's why I'm willing to encourage ye. Ye may as well call me Thor."

"I'll remember that ye swore to rain down thunder and lightning on me if I dinna treat yer sister right."

"Aye. And dinna confuse me for ma cousin Tor. He's just as protective of Rose as I am. All the Sinclairs are protective of our women."

"I've heard." Blaine grinned as he looked back over his shoulder as Rose took a seat on the dais. "Do ye think Lady Rose will ever be as protective as I've heard the Sinclair women are of their men?"

"Aye. She's ma mother's daughter."

The men walked to the dais, and Blaine was certain Thor reached the steps first, so he could choose a seat next to Shona, leaving the seat next to Rose for him.

"Good evening, Lady Rose."

"Good evening."

They fell silent as the priest blessed the meal and the first round of servants brought out heaping platters. Once the servants left everyone to enjoy the first course, Blaine pressed his elbow against Rose's.

"Would ye walk with me this evening? Please?"

"I dinna have a chaperone unless I ask Shona."

"We dinna have to go anywhere but the bailey. Willna people see us there if we wait until after the meal? They'll be returning to their crofts and see we arenae doing aught improper."

"Aye. But—"

"Dinna ye want to be seen with me?"

"It's nae ye as Blaine. It's ye as a mon. I dinna want people whispering."

"Then ask Shona to come if ye'd be more comfortable, but I'd hope to speak to just ye."

Rose looked around at her family before she nodded. "As long as people can see us, but nae where we're going to draw too much attention."

"That makes sense."

Blaine hadn't just observed Rose during the previous meals when she spoke to others. He'd noticed what she preferred and avoided. Throughout the meal, he signaled to servants he saw carried platters of what she might like. After the third time, she looked at him.

"How do ye ken ma favorites? And how do ye ken to say 'just for me' to the things I dinna like?"

"Ye ken I watched ye."

"Enough to care what I ate?"

"I wish to ken ye better."

Rose nodded. When a servant brought a platter of pheasant, she shook her head. "Nae for either of us. Thank ye."

"Ye noticed too." Blaine grinned, and Rose's toes curled. She noticed she did that a lot when Blaine did something that affected her, but she wanted no one—especially him—to know.

"Aye. Mayhap a few things. But, Blaine, ye canna do this anymore. The servants will talk. I dinna usually care aboot gossip, but I dinna want Uncle Hamish to get the wrong impression."

"And what impression is that?"

"That ye're courting me. He willna assume we're just friends."

"Are we friends, Lady Rose?"

31

"Getting there, I suppose."

"And if it's both? I wish to be yer friend and to court ye?"

Rose's gaze swung from one end of the table to the other. "Then we should wait to talk aboot that until we're outside."

By silent mutual agreement, they turned their attention to other people sitting near them and struck up conversations with them. When the servants pushed the tables and benches toward the walls, and the musicians tuned their instruments, people moved to the center of the Great Hall for a country reel. Most of the people on the dais left their seats to join the clan members. Rose looked around but saw no one paying attention to her until she spied Thor. He nodded, which made her brow furrow.

Once she and Blaine stepped outside, she stopped. "Does ma brother ken?"

"Aye. He suggested I dance with ye tonight. We talked, then he suggested we should take a walk together, so there arenae any more misunderstandings."

"Ye told him what I thought? What ye thought?"

"Aye. I didna see any reason to lie."

Rose nodded, unsure how she felt about Thor giving permission to something over which he had no control. He didn't decide who could court Rose any more than she controlled who he might want to court.

"Lady Rose, he's yer brother. He just wanted to be sure of ma intentions."

Rose walked down the steps. "And those are?"

"Are ye always so direct?"

"Aye."

Blaine chuckled, but he followed her as she strode toward the garden. He realized she hurried to move them away from the main doors. When they reached the garden, she turned away from the gate. He understood that would be too private, too incriminating.

"Ye ken I've been watching ye. It's obvious I've paid attention. If I just wanted a roll in the hay, would I care that much?"

"I dinna ken. Nay one's ever offered me a roll in the hay to ken if that's what a mon does beforehand."

"I appreciate how practical ye are. Ye dinna blather. I hope that's because ye're comfortable around me."

"I suppose I am. I suppose I have been from the beginning, even if I didna realize it."

"If ye kenned I dinna like pheasant, does that mean ye noticed aught else aboot me?"

Rose nodded. When Blaine said nothing else, she supposed she would have to give in a little. "I noticed that yer men like ye, but there's the right amount of formality between ye. I've seen ye in the lists with Lach's sons. All three of them think highly of ye. Callen and Alasdair have both ridden out a few times now, and Gavin is eager to join them. Ye dinna treat any of them as weans, but ye ken they still need plenty of guidance. I've seen ye work with them."

"Ye've watched me?"

"Ye tend to spar near the entrance. I see ye when I pass by. Ye spend a lot of time with them, so ye must be teaching them something. If they wish to spend so much time with ye, they must be learning something."

"I confess I almost lost an ear yesterday because I saw ye walk past and got distracted."

"And Alasdair boasted he got ye across yer ribs."

"Aye. Left a bruise, too. I wish to court ye, Lady

Rose. But if ye dinna want that, then I'd like to be yer friend."

"We dinna ken each other that well. Why do ye wish to see if we suit?"

"Think of how many arranged marriages there are. Yer parents were arranged, but I've heard the stories how they fell in love before they even wed. Yer grandda believed they would be a love match. That's why he arranged it. Yer grandparents were arranged, and they fell in love too. But there are so many couples who dinna ken aught aboot each other. Wives who dinna ken if their husband will beat them or love them. Husbands who dinna ken if their wife will run the keep or run their clan into the ground. We have a chance to get to ken each other before aught is arranged or signed. If we dinna suit, then we go our separate ways. If we do, then we decide if we wish to marry. I'm nae going to insist that because I wish to pay ye court, ye must marry me."

"And ye believe I will run yer keep and nae run yer clan into the ground."

"Lady Rose, I believe nae only will ye run our keep, but I can see ye as a close confidante to help me run our clan."

"Our? Ye already sound convinced."

"I am. But I would give us time in case I'm wrong or ye dinna want me."

Heat flared in both sets of eyes. Rose knew what he meant, but the only type of want she could think about was physical desire. Blaine took a step closer before he looked around. When Rose didn't move away, he reached past her and lifted the latch to the garden gate. He made no attempt to walk into it until Rose took several steps backwards. He followed, shutting the gate with his foot. Rose continued to walk with her back to much of the garden, now watching for anyone who might spy them. When they moved into the keep's shadow, she took Blaine's hand and led him into a darker corner where no one could see them in passing.

Blaine pulled Rose against him, wrapping an arm around her waist as the other hand wrapped around her neck, his thumb resting on her jaw. He leaned forward, bringing their mouths close, but he paused. His thumb swept over her jaw several times as Rose's hands moved from where they'd grasped his biceps to his chest. Heat radiated through his leine, making her palms and fingers tingle. She tilted her head back further as she watched him.

"Lady Rose—"

"Just Rose or Rose Kyla."

"Have ye ever gone by just Kyla?"

She shook her head. "Never. I ken some think Kyla Rose would sound better, but ma parents named me for ma mother's mother. She was ma other grandmama's best friend. Ma grandda didna just ken ma parents would fall in love. He wanted to protect his wife's best friend's daughter from the horrible life she had. Mama never knew her mother, but she was what truly brought ma parents together."

"And Kyla is for yer da's mama?"

"Aye. Ma parents always meant for both names to be ma given name, but it's been shortened over the years."

"Would ye mind if I called ye Kyla?"

"Why?"

"Because it would only be mine."

Rose's eyes widened before she nodded. He could

have sounded possessive, instead, his tone was reverent. It touched her that he wanted something that only they would share. Her soft smile flashed a hint of her dimple. Blaine's thumb brushed over it.

"But I like the name Blaine. I dinna ken anyone else by that name."

"Ye may call me whatever ye wish, as long as ye call me."

Rose giggled and shook her head. It was a cliché, but his lopsided grin appeared boyish and hopeful. She slid her hands up to wrap around his neck before he lowered his mouth to hers. Blaine intended merely to feather his lips against hers, giving her a hint in case she was as inexperienced as he now suspected. She meant only to see what it was like to be kissed. But the moment their lips met, a fire erupted between them.

Blaine flicked his tongue against her lips until she opened. She'd seen plenty of couples kiss with their mouths open, but she never imagined how it would feel to have their tongues touch. Her fingers flexed around his neck, and he knew he'd surprised her. That only intensified his desire. Now he felt possessive, knowing no man had kissed her before. He preferred to keep his hair short, so it didn't fall in his eyes while fighting. He didn't think she would enjoy tunneling her fingers through it, but she sighed as her fingernails grazed his scalp. Her body fully relaxed against his.

"Kyla, I want to touch more of ye. But I dinna want to frighten ye or make ye think that I've lied."

"The parts of me I assumed ye wanted."

"For now, aye. If we marry, so much more."

"May I touch more of ye, too?"

"Dear God, I hope so."

As their mouths fused once more, Blaine's hand slid from her waist to her bottom. He inched down, letting her adjust and predict what he would do. Once he cupped her backside, his fingers spreading to grasp most of it, he groaned. He didn't notice how tightly he held her until she moved restlessly against him. The fingers that cupped her neck trailed over her collarbone and over her chest until he palmed her breast. He did little more than hold the mound until Rose arched her back. He kneaded it while he reveled in sensations she elicited as her hands roamed over his back and chest, then down his ribs, and around his waist until both pressed against his buttocks.

She squeezed much like he did to her, marveling at how hard the muscles were beneath his plaid when she knew how soft her own backside felt. It was like chiseled rock hiding beneath wool. Her hands explored his hips and waist before returning to his arse. She held on as Blaine moved them until Rose's back brushed the stone wall. One hand abandoned its resting place and moved to glide over his rippled abdomen. She found she enjoyed both parts of him. She fisted his leine when he nipped at her lip. She flicked her tongue and drew him into her mouth before she lightly sucked.

"Lass, do that again, and I'll drag ye before the priest before sunrise."

"Does that mean ye liked it?"

"Vera much. I ken ye dinna have experience doing any of this, but I can tell ye ken aboot it."

"Mama and ma aunts are honest with us aboot what marriage can be, both inside and outside the bedchamber. They have to be since they canna keep their hands off their husbands, and Da and ma uncles arenae any better. I have three married cousins too. I've talked to Saoirse and Wee Liam's and Blake's wives. I probably ken even more from them than from Mama. But I havenae done aught before."

"If ye wish to kiss again, I willna say nay. But if I ever do aught that's too much or that ye dinna like, ye tell me, Kyla. I dinna want ye to ever feel like ye have to accept everything just because ye're the lass."

"I ken that because Mama's explained that, but I already sensed it aboot ye. And I definitely wish to kiss again."

Blaine watched her and knew she waited for him to begin their next round. "Just like I dinna want ye to feel forced into aught ye dinna like, I dinna want ye to feel like I'm doing this *to* ye. I want to do this *with* ye. If ye ever want to kiss me, ye dinna have to wait—"

Rose went onto her toes and pressed her mouth to his, opening and sliding her tongue past his teeth. It twirled and coiled with his as she arched her back further and wrapped her arms around his neck again. If their first kiss had been a bonfire, then this was a volcano erupting. Rose reached between them to push Blaine's sporran out of the way, bringing his length against her mound. He wrapped his hand around her right thigh and drew it to his hip, moving his thigh between hers. Hands on her hips guided her to move against him. They both knew how easy it would be to draw Rose's skirts and Blaine's plaid to their waists and out of the way. The temptation engulfed them, but a bird squawked in a tree, reminding them where they were.

He kissed the tip of her nose before pressing a series of soft kisses to her lips as their foreheads rested together. "We should go back inside before anyone questions where we went."

"I ken."

Neither moved as their racing hearts slowed. Blaine wrapped his arms around Rose once more, feeling her tremble in his embrace. She clutched his leine at his waist and sighed as she rested her head against his chest.

"Are ye well?" Blaine stroked hair back from her face as he peered down at her.

"Aye. I didna think we'd do that when we walked out here. I wasna prepared for how I'd feel."

"I ken, lass. I didna intend to kiss ye. I hoped to one day, but I didna think it would be this eve. I dinna regret it. Do ye?"

"Nay. But we only met a few days ago. We're still getting to ken one another. Arenae we still too much strangers for this to be aught but lust?" Rose loosened her grip and took a step back to look up at him.

"I dinna think so. Kyla, if it were just lust, I could seek attention elsewhere. If it were just lust, I would have told maself to stay away from Laird Hamish Sutherland's, the Earl of Sutherland's, maiden grand-niece. I wouldnae have told Thor that I wish to court ye. Do ye think it's just lust for ye?"

"Nay. If lust ruled me, I wouldnae still be a maiden."

Blaine's face became a thundercloud as his eyes narrowed. Jealousy unlike anything he'd ever experienced pulsated through him. "Who else have ye had yer eye on?"

"What? I didna mean that I have to control ma lust. I meant, I dinna want every braw mon who walks by. I dinna understand why ye just tensed so much."

"Because I was a jealous hypocrite." At Rose's confusion, he smiled guiltily. "I'm nearly seven-and-twenty. I obviously am nae a virgin if I thought to tryst with ye the other day. But I dinna like to think I'm nae the first mon to catch yer eye. I dinna like to think there might be competition here or at Dunbeath."

"Dinna forget Varrich. I visit there as often as I do here." Rose grinned and waggled her eyebrows. "There's nay one, Blaine. There never has been. I dinna want to think aboot yer past or—"

"Stop, Kyla. Dinna say present or future. There isnae anyone here or elsewhere now that I've met ye. I dinna have a leman, and I never will. I told Thor this too. I havenae had one in five years, and I dinna want one because they're too much trouble. But I willna stray, Kyla. Nae ever. I canna imagine how any mon would leave yer bed to go to another woman's."

"Ye dinna need a bed."

"Wheest, lass. Ye shall fill ma head with ideas that arenae appropriate for an innocent. I willna leave yer arms to go to another woman's. Even if I dinna marry ye and I must marry someone else, I wouldnae ever shame a wife that way. There are enough men in ma family who have done that to their wives. I dinna respect them for it, and I feel heartsore for the women. Even the ones who canna stand their husbands. It's humiliating for them, and I dinna wish to treat a wife that way. I'd rather be a monk than a mon with nay honor."

She sighed as she stepped closer once more and went back to leaning her head against his chest. She listened to his steady heartbeat as it lulled her. She wondered if one day she might fall asleep, sharing a bed with him and listening to it.

"I didna expect to talk so openly to ye aboot so much. Things are moving vera fast." Rose reflected how only half an hour earlier, she was convinced he only wanted her because her physique reminded him of a tavern wench. She knew that misbelief had come from her insecurity, but she hadn't felt such self-doubt since she first became a woman. She'd grown comfortable in her own skin years ago. She'd assumed the worst about Blaine because of something that was truly a mild misunderstanding. He'd already tried to make amends more than once.

"Too fast?"

"Mayhap a little."

Blaine understood how vulnerable Rose must feel because he'd laid his heart bare throughout their conversation too. "At least we understand each other moving forward. Ma intentions are true, Kyla."

"People are going to question why ye call me that. I like it, but it'll draw a lot of attention."

"Then we keep it private. Do ye wish for others to ken I'm courting ye?"

"Ye talked to Thor, but ye must talk to Uncle Hamish. It willna matter what ma brother says. While I'm here, it's Uncle Hamish's decision. Ye ken, if Thor hasnae already drafted a missive to ma da, ma uncle will."

"Aye. That I didna doubt. But what aboot other people? Do ye wish for the clan to think we're friendly, or do ye wish them to ken there's more?"

"Until ye speak to Uncle Hamish, there canna be

aught. Until we hear from ma da and grandda, we canna look more than friendly."

"Do ye think anyone would say nay?"

"I dinna think so, but—" Rose pulled her lips in between her teeth as she gazed up at Blaine. She looked at the ground between their feet before she continued. "It would be vera disappointing to get ma hopes up."

"We'll work it out, Kyla." Blaine dropped a soft kiss on her lips before they let go of each other. He moved her behind him before looking past the shadows. He was slow to move into the waning sunlight until he was certain no one looked in their direction. He reached back for Rose's hand but guided her, so she remained shielded by his larger frame. When they reached the garden gate, he leaned forward to look toward the keep's doors before peering at the postern gate, then up to the battlements. He spotted no one looking in their direction. He drew Rose around to his side. "Goodnight, lass."

"Goodnight, laddie." She flashed him one of her dazzling smiles and winked before she dashed to the steps. Much like the first day, Blaine watched her gather her skirts and pull them forward to avoid tripping as she took the steps two at a time. He had a clear view of her backside, which made him want to groan. Having a chamber to himself had already come in handy. He suspected he would keep seeking privacy until they decided whether to marry.

Chapter Four

"They are naught more than opportunists," Blaine declared as he followed Hardi into Hamish's solar. A messenger arrived ten minutes earlier with a missive from Blaine's second-in-command. Clan Gunn raided the Keiths a fortnight after Blaine arrived at Dunrobin. The Gunns made it obvious that, not only did they know Blaine was traveling, but they'd waited until he was gone to strike. The rider had set off immediately after it happened and arrived as winded as his steed.

"We all ken they took advantage of yer absence. But they assume our alliance isnae strong enough to bring the Sinclairs and Sutherlands into the matter."

"Is it?" Blaine forced himself not to cross his arms. If Rose hadn't caught his attention, it would frustrate him even more that Hardi hadn't committed to an answer one way or another. He still didn't know if the laird would mediate, let alone send men. He would force Hardi's hand now that the raid resulted in five dead warriors and more than fifty head of cattle stolen.

43

"Aye, it is. Do ye ken why I've waited to give ye an answer?"

"Aye. Ye've been testing me. Ye want to ken whether I'll abuse our alliance and whether I'm worth risking men for. It's aboot me as a leader and a mon, never mind ma people who suffer in the meantime. I can appreciate ye needing assurance, even if it's insulting. But if ye arenae willing to help, then say as much. I canna waste time here if it isnae going to help ma people."

"So courting Lady Rose is wasting yer time." Hardi's brow lowered as his eyes narrowed.

"Right now, it's the only reason to stay. As much as I want to, I canna stay to court her if I canna rely on yer help. I must consider ma clan, and if I canna get yer support, then I must look elsewhere. I dinna want to leave Rose, but ye arenae giving me much choice." Blaine realized he and Rose hadn't been as discrete in their interest as they believed. If Hardi noticed, then surely so did almost everyone else at Dunrobin.

"She's nae a passing fancy, then."

"She's a lass ye make yer wife. Ye dinna dally with a woman like Rose."

Hardi's scowl eased. "Who do ye want us to deal with first? The Gunns or the Murrays?"

"I must deal with the Gunns maself, and I must do it immediately. But I would still ask yer help to mediate with the Murrays. I'd prefer missives to work, but it may mean riding out to them to meet face-to-face."

"Ye dinna think they'd take that as an act of aggression? We show up on the doorstep with warriors with us."

"We take enough to guard us, but we dinna go with an army." Blaine tried not to think about the days spent waiting for Hardi to decide. Missives could have already arrived with the Murrays. They could already be on their way to peace, or he'd know a war was imminent. Hardi may have wanted to test Blaine, but Sir Robert de Keith, the Great Marischal of Scotland, still led Clan Keith. Blaine believed Hardi should lend his support based on that rather than whether he thought the Keiths' tánaiste was worth his salt.

"Blaine, I ken ye feel like I've neglected our alliance by nae giving ye an answer. And what I tell ye now will probably make ye think I've deceived ye. But ye arenae the only one who must think aboot what's best for his clan. I must consider ma own. We arenae without troubles from the Mackintoshes, the Chattans, the MacBains, and the MacThomases. I sent riders to Clan Murray. I told them to observe from outside the wall for three days, then to deliver a missive to the laird. I said naught aboot ye seeking ma help, but I offered to mediate. I said it was in ma best interest for ye to come to a truce. If the Murray isnae willing to agree, then we ken there's nay point in trying to solve things peacefully. Ma men and I will ride with ye and have our swords at the ready."

Blaine smirked. "I already kenned ye did that. Yer men arenae as stealthy as ye think. It wasna hard to notice two missing, and ye have some men whose voices carry in the barracks. I wondered when ye were going to tell me. I dinna appreciate that it took so long. But I am relieved ye havenae been ignoring me. Ye want me to prove I'm worthy. It goes both ways,

Hardi. If I canna trust ye to lend aid, then we dinna have an alliance. We have naught. Ye ken the Keiths would come to yer aid, even if it's with hesitation. I canna keep this from ma father, and I willna forget it once I'm laird."

"Are ye threatening me?"

"Nay. I'm being honest. I have naught to gain by nae letting ye ken where I stand. I want our alliance to continue. If it doesnae, then I want ye to ken why. I dinna like those types of surprises, so I wouldnae do to ye what I dinna want others to do to me."

Hardi assessed Blaine as they stood together in the solar. The Keiths had a storied history. Not only had Blaine's father accompanied King David to France when the English forced the young king to flee and then into exile, but Blaine's cousin—not the one to start the feud with the Murrays—accompanied Robert the Bruce's heart back to Melrose Abbey after the great leader died. Hardi sensed Blaine had the potential to be a superior leader to even his father. But Hardi didn't want to put his faith in only a suspicion. He'd needed time to be sure. He'd trusted his clan council when he inherited the lairdship, and they'd nearly killed him and Blair while bankrupting the clan. His trust no longer came easily.

"It'll be a few more days before we hear from ma men. It gives ye time to sort things out with the Gunns. Will ye return home?"

"Nay. But I will visit the Gunns."

"By visit, do ye mean raze some of their fields?"

Blaine shrugged. If he told no one but his men what he planned, then no one else could be held to blame. He needed to consider his course of action rather than react while still angry from the missive and frustrated with Hardi.

"I shall go for a walk on the battlements and clear ma head before I decide aught. I willna react in haste." Blaine opened the solar door and let Hardi pass through before him. They went their separate ways, and Blaine made his way outside. As he did every time he left the keep, his gaze scanned the bailey for Rose. He knew it was just as likely she was somewhere inside, but he searched, nonetheless.

"Blaine?"

He turned to find Rose on the top of the keep's steps behind him. "Aye, lass."

"Thor said a messenger arrived with a missive for ye. He said it was a Keith. Is everything all right or was it just a regular report?" Rose shielded her eyes from the sun before Blaine returned to the top step and stood in front of her. She lowered her hand and gazed into familiar gray eyes.

"The Gunns burned some crofts and stole two-and-a-half score of cattle. Five clan members died."

"Bluidy hell." Rose gazed beyond the wall as though she could see all the way to Gunn territory before shifting her eyes as though she might also see the Keiths' land. "What will ye do?"

"I havenae decided. I just met with Hardi. I planned to go for a walk on the battlements to think."

"I dinna mean to keep ye. It worried me when Thor said the messenger arrived on a lathered horse and looked like he hadnae slept in days."

"Kyla, I may need to leave for a few days to sort this out. I may even need to go home, but I will come back as soon as I can. If I go, I dinna want our courtship to end. I dinna want ye to forget aboot me."

Rose's eyes trailed over him from head to toe and back up again before they lingered on his lips. "I dinna think ye'll be easy to forget."

"If ye look at me like that again, I might ride off with ye." Blaine grew serious and shook his head. "But I canna until I'm certain it's safe to bring ye to Ackergill Tower."

Rose nodded and looked back toward the wall. "I ken ye havenae decided, but what do ye think ye'll do?"

"Visit the Gunns."

Rose shook her head. "Nay, Blaine. Ye have a score of men with ye. Ye canna go razing their fields or burning their crofts with so few men behind ye, so far from home. I ken ye willna ask Uncle Hamish or Hardi for men to do that. Please dinna go without more men."

"Why do ye think that's ma solution?"

"Isnae that always the solution? The Sinclairs, Sutherlands, and Mackays have had generations of trouble with the Gunns. It's how it always gets solved, but it never lasts. The difference is we can retreat to our homes, and we have powerful armies. Ye are far from home with vera few men. Please dinna do this, Blaine."

"I havenae decided, Kyla. That's why I wanted to go for a walk. This isnae just a neighborly spat. By now, they're nearly home with ma cattle. If they didna kill them just out of spite. It's nearly a day's ride from here to Clyth Castle, but I need to plan now rather than on the way."

"I must go back inside and help Auntie Amelia with the candle making. I wanted to be sure ye were all right."

"Thank ye, lass. I suppose it'll all come right. I just need to ruminate on it." Blaine reached out and gave Rose's hand a quick squeeze before they turned in opposite directions. Rose opened the door but peered back outside, watching Blaine take the steps two at a time up to the wall walk. She made her way back to her aunt, who had the candle molds spread across one of the long trestle tables in the Great Hall. As she worked alongside Amelia, her thoughts distracted her. She feared Blaine would give the situation plenty of thought and still opt for a hot trot that could get him killed.

When the ladies finished, Rose hurried to her chamber and opened her chest. She withdrew an ink pot, quill, and a piece of parchment. She had them to write missives to her parents on behalf of herself and her siblings. But she wasn't writing to Callum or Siùsan. She considered her message before she began writing.

Squirrel,

Did ye ken the fox struck again? He left his warren and went far away. What shall we do?

Rabbit

When the ink dried, Rose sealed it with a dollop of wax, but she didn't add the Sinclair crest to it. She needed anonymity for this to work. She tucked it into her pocket before she made her way down the servants' stairs to the scullery and out to the laundresses' area. She looked around before she strode across the bailey. She squinted as though the sunlight once more blinded her. It was no accident when she bumped into a Sinclair guard. She passed him the missive without a word. Henry glanced down and frowned. Rose knew he disapproved, but she also knew he would deliver the message. He was the only man she trusted to accomplish this mission while at Dunrobin.

"Ma lady," Henry whispered. "This isnae a jaunt where I can go and come back in a day. Clyth Castle is a day's ride from here. Someone will notice I'm gone."

"I ken. Pick a fight with Thor, then say that ye're going hunting to cool off. Everyone kens ye're the best tracker and hunter among the Sinclairs. As long as ye come back with something—even a hare—then it's worth it."

"And if Thor doesnae agree?"

"I'll make sure he does."

Henry inhaled as he dropped the missive into his sporran. "Dinna get any ideas aboot riding out to meet her."

"Ye already ken that I will. Grandda and Da havenae figured out how the information aboot the Gunns arrives, but it's saved lives in both clans. It will probably save plenty this time, too."

"Vera well, ma lady. Just dinna ride out alone. I ken this is yer second home, but the distance is too great to go without a guard."

"I promise I willna do aught without ye."

"Let's get on with it then." Henry huffed as he turned back to the lists. Rose watched from the entrance to the lists as Henry made his way to Thor. When the guard stopped, he placed his fists on his hips. Rose couldn't hear what Henry said, but he pointed his fingers and gestured toward the battlements. She watched him shake his head, put his fists on his hips again, then spin toward the entrance, his plaid swishing around his legs. She watched him appear to storm off the training field.

"What did ye say?" Rose whispered.

"I said he'd better nae expect us to join the Keiths' fight just because we're staying here. I said I would ride for Dunbeath and speak to the laird. I said ma job isnae to fight another mon's war. It's guarding the laird's family, and I wouldnae be the one to tell the laird the second in line to inherit died for naught."

"What did Thor say?"

"I didna give him much chance to say aught. He wanted to ken how I got the idea the Sinclairs would join the fight."

"How did ye get that idea?"

"We're here, and it's obvious Blaine came for Laird Cameron's help. If the Camerons join the Keiths, then the Sutherlands join. If the Sutherlands join, then we join. I ken Laird Sutherland and Laird Cameron would never have any of the Sinclairs leave ye and Shona without members of yer clan here, but I wouldnae be able to stop Thor if he rode out and Laird Sutherland agreed. I just exaggerated a wee. Ye can say ye tried to calm me down, but I decided time hunting would cool ma temper."

"And if Thor thinks ye're really riding home because ye dinna come back tonight?"

"Like ye said, ma lady, I better bring something back." Henry grinned before heading to the stables. Rose stood alone until Thor joined her.

"Did he tell ye what got him so upset?"

"He doesnae think any of the Sinclairs should ride out on the Keiths' behalf without Grandda's permission."

"And I agree. I told him that, but he said he heard voices in the barracks saying I already planned to ride out, which meant our warriors would feel obligated to join me. I didna even ken what he was talking aboot since I dinna ken why a messenger came. I havenae seen him so angry before. He's usually one of the calm ones."

"The Gunns traveled all the way to the Keiths, then raided cattle and killed five people. Henry said he's going hunting. Let him calm down. He'll be back tomorrow eve or the next day."

"I dinna like him being away from the keep that long and alone. I should send someone with him."

"Nay. Let him be. He willna want a nursemaid. Ye remember how he was when his da died. He did the same thing. Give him a little time." Rose prayed Henry made the journey to and from Clyth Castle with nothing going amiss. He would have to skirt Dunbeath to get there, so she prayed he didn't encounter one of their clan's patrols. Second thoughts about being too selfish plagued her. But she knew her connection in the Gunns could save lives. She just wasn't prepared to tell anyone who it was.

"I pray ye're right. I dinna want to explain to Da and Grandda why we lost one of our best warriors. He better come home safe and sound." Thor and Rose watched as Henry led his horse from the stables, his bow and quiver of arrows attached to his saddle.

"I just need to cool off. And we havenae hunted aught for the Sutherlands since we arrived. Giving them something to make up for the food we've eaten, even if they're yer kin, is only proper. I'll be back in two days." Henry didn't wait for permission, nervous Thor would stop him if he didn't hurry. He mounted and spurred his horse.

"Ye have a few more hours to train. I'm going to

help in the kitchens. Dinna get hurt because I willna have any sympathy."

"When do ye ever, sister?"

Rose giggled and slid her arms around her brother's waist for a quick squeeze before she dashed inside. She told herself not to worry until there was a reason to.

Chapter Five

As much as Blaine wished to ride out immediately, he knew he and his men needed time to calm their tempers after the initial spike of rage and bloodlust. His men knew he wasn't rash and always had several plans before he rode out. It's why he'd lived into his late twenties when his cousin died on what became known as Keith's Pot, or Keith's Stone. He wouldn't lead his men to certain death since there were so few of them.

Blaine was on the battlements the second evening after the messenger arrived. He would set off for the Gunns in the morning. He noticed a rider approaching the keep with a deer tied to a makeshift litter behind his horse. The Sutherland guard near the gate announced it was a Sinclair arriving. From where Blaine stood, he watched the man pass under the portcullis. He noticed Rose leaving a storeroom, headed to the kitchens, but she veered toward the Sinclair guard when she spotted him.

Blaine's brow furrowed when he noticed how close they stood beside the horse's head. He was certain the man passed something to Rose that she crumpled in her hand. They couldn't have exchanged more than a dozen words before Rose headed back to the keep, and the Sinclair guard led his horse to where the deer would be butchered. Blaine debated whether to follow Rose or the guard. He opted for the latter. When he reached the man, he grinned.

"Successful hunting trip. Well done. She's a healthy size."

"Aye. She was alone and didna notice me in time. I was far enough away that I couldnae tell just how big she was. Once I approached her, I worried she might have been carrying. She's just well fed."

"Did ye have to go far?" Blaine kept his tone relaxed and conversational, but he noticed a flash of wariness before the guard answered.

"I probably rode out too far, but I had a spat with Thor and needed time to settle maself."

Blaine wondered if the wariness came from admitting he'd fought with his leader or something else. "I'm certain Thor will appreciate this. Mayhap it'll mend whatever caused the rift."

"I hope so. If ye'll excuse me, I must see to this and get clean before the evening meal." Henry nodded before turning to unfasten the animal and stretcher from his horse. A stable boy took the steed while Henry hoisted the deer over his shoulders. Blaine decided he would find Rose next, but she was nowhere to be seen when he entered the Great Hall. People were already gathering for the evening meal. He assumed she would be down soon, but she didn't appear by the time everyone sat on the dais.

"She was outside too long today and doesnae feel well," Shona explained as she leaned across Rose's empty chair. "She'll be right as rain by morning. She's so fair that sometimes the sun can be too much. She's taking a tray in her chamber."

Blaine debated whether he could sneak to her chamber and check on her since they were the only people staying on the third floor. He knew he wouldn't sleep if he didn't. The meal couldn't have been slower.

Rose hurried to her chamber after receiving the missive from Henry. She'd crumpled it in her hand to keep anyone from seeing. She knew people watched them, so she wanted no one to see her shove something into her pocket. Now that she sat on her bed with her chamber door locked and barred, she smoothed the parchment out on the mattress. She recognized the neat script, but the message disheartened her.

Rabbit,

The fox knew the bear and its cub were not at home. The fox wishes to prove its strength and canniness to those around. It thinks this success means other trips away from his warren will now be successful. The fox wishes to draw attention to one target while moving on to its next. The fox thinks those who would hunt it will go to its warren. But the fox will not be there. The fox will be at another warren ready to strike. The fox thinks it can make its hunters chase it.

The fox's plans have not worked in the past. I do not know why they would work this time. I think the fox believes it is timing. I fear the fox and its friends will be away from its warren, and its hunters will destroy the warren to leave the fox with naught. Or the

*hunters will make the warren their own. I do not think
they will chase it. The fox believes its solitary and does
not concern itself with those who might suffer.*

*The fox has an eye on a new mate. The fox thinks
this will prove its power and impress this potential
mate's father. The mate cannot decide for themself because its father is a bigger fox than those near it. They
underestimate that each hunter has more than one
arrow.*

*The squirrel and rabbit need to make haste to
watch from the woods beneath the oak.*

Squirrel

Rose stared at the missive. It amazed her how the
Gunns survived at all with one rash and useless
leader after another. They harassed the Sinclairs,
Mackays, and Sutherlands frequently and lost more
than one laird because of it. They believed they were
the wronged party, but there would have been no
feud if Thomas Gunn hadn't killed Laird Liam Sinclair's younger brother, Daniel, because he and
Thomas's youngest sister, Ceana, fell in love. The
hostility grew when Thomas's brother, James, decided he wanted Rose's mother for himself and tried
to steal her from Rose's father. Thomas met his fate
when he rode out with men who intended to kill
Rose's aunt Brighde after she fled to the Sinclairs and
married Rose's uncle Alex. Thomas's illegitimate son,
Beathan, was the only living male connected to the
laird's family. When he took control of the clan, he
tried to steal Arabella from Lachlan when his betrothal to Arabella fell through.

They raided the Mackays for sport at first, but
when the Mackays allied with the Sinclairs through
Mairghread Sinclair's marriage to Laird Tristan

Mackay, that brought the Sinclairs and the Sutherlands to the Mackays' aid. The Gunns couldn't accept that graciously and cried foul, as though they were the wronged party. Liam, Hamish, and Tristan kept the Gunns at bay, but the time was rapidly approaching where skirmishes and raiding each other wouldn't be enough. It would come to war. The Gunns would lose, and Rose's friend would likely die. Rose wasn't prepared to accept that.

She waited until well after the sun set, and she heard the Great Hall grow quiet. It was summer, but she pulled her cloak from her chest. The older Sinclair generations insisted that anyone who traveled off Sinclair land have a cloak to disguise them if it wasn't safe for someone to recognize their plaid. With her strawberry-blonde hair, Rose knew it was doubly important that she be incognito.

She put her ear to the door, and when all she heard was silence, she opened her door. She looked down the passageway in both directions, her gaze lingering on Blaine's door. She knew he would disapprove and that he would worry if he discovered she left the keep. She knew he would be angry when he learned after the fact that she had ridden out. But they weren't married. They weren't betrothed. They didn't even have an agreement that they suited. Until there was a signed contract, Rose convinced herself she wasn't accountable to Blaine.

She eased down the servants' stairs and out to the bailey. She remained in the shadows until a man and horse appeared. The portcullis was already closed, so they would have to leave by the postern gate. She wondered how Henry would convince the guard to let them out. It would be obvious that it was either she, Shona, or Tira who left. Lachlan and Arabella had no daughters, but Blair and Hardi did. There was no doubt Arabella, Amelia, and Blair would never leave in the middle of the night.

Rose stepped into place on the far side of the horse, her hood already up. She kept her head lowered as they approached the gate. She peeked from under her lashes at the Sutherland guard who stepped in front of the gate.

"The laird kens ma intentions with the lass, but we arenae ready for everyone to ken."

Bluidy hell. Now nay one can ever find out it's me. People will think I'm trysting with ma guard.

Rose kept her head down, praying the guard, who she sensed stared at her, would let them pass. A moment later, the gate swung open to let them through. As soon as they were away from the gate, Henry helped Rose onto the horse. She slid back to make room for Henry, so she could ride pillion. She held her hood beneath her chin to ensure it didn't blow off and reveal her hair.

Fortunately, it was a cloudless night with a brilliant moon and stars to light the way. They rode for four hours before they came to a forest. She could already see a lone figure standing beneath the oak tree near a loch. They were far closer to Dunbeath than Rose preferred, but this was their usual meeting spot. While Rose stayed at Dunrobin, it was roughly halfway. She dismounted while Henry drew his sword and sat guard.

"Greer, ye risk a lot coming here. What if yer da finds out?" Rose hurried to her friend, Greer Gunn, the oldest daughter and only legitimate child of Laird Edgar Gunn.

"He'd likely kill me. But ye willna be without trouble if yer family finds ye back on their land."

"But I dinna fear dying for this. Nae unless yer father finds me with ye."

"He returned with the Keiths' cattle then left. He's visiting the MacDonnells. He has his eye on the laird's daughter."

"She's younger than us!" Rose recoiled in disgust. Edgar Gunn was nearly fifty, and the girl in question was barely five-and-ten. "What if she doesnae bear him a son?"

"I worry she willna have a long life if she doesnae. He's getting desperate. His bastards are all lasses. I dinna have a brother on either side of the blanket."

"When do ye think he'll strike next?"

"Likely a fortnight since he'll need to spend some time with the MacDonnells. But he willna want to wait too long. I ken he worries the Keiths will strike back while he's away. He's doubled the guards."

"Who's next?"

"I think the Mackays, but I dinna ken for sure. I dinna think he's told anyone, nae even his second."

"Rider, ma ladies. Into the trees." Henry spurred his horse to engage the approaching rider farther from the women.

"Kyla!"

Rose spun around. Only one person called her that, and he sounded irate rather than excited to see her. She muttered, "Shite."

"Is that Blaine Keith?"

"Aye. We're courting. I didna tell him or anyone else where I was going. Henry pretended I was a servant who didna want anyone to ken aboot our relationship. If Blaine only got the last part of the explanation, I can only imagine what he thought."

"Why didna he stop ye on the road?"

"He obviously wanted to see where I was going and kenned I wouldnae have told him. Have ye met?"

"Aye." Greer muttered.

"It didna go well?"

"I'm a Gunn. He's a Keith."

The women walked toward the men, who trotted to the tree line. Blaine swung down from his saddle and stalked over to Rose. He leaned forward to whisper. "Ye will explain the entire reason ye left the keep at night with one guard, pretending to be his mistress, to meet Greer Gunn, the daughter of ma latest enemy. Dinna miss a single detail, Kyla."

Rose nodded. There was anger in Blaine's eyes, but there was also fear. She wondered if it was for her safety or if he feared she was involved with Henry. Or worse, conspiring with the Gunns.

"I met Greer years ago at a Highland Gathering. I kenned ma clan didna get along with hers, but we were ten summers. I just kenned I met a nice lass who liked the same things as me and made me giggle. We've been friends ever since. For a long time, we only saw each other at Gatherings. It was the only place the Gunns dared show their faces when ma family was around. But for the past few years, Greer has been giving me information aboot her father. I've been secretly giving it to ma da and grandda. They dinna ken where it comes from, but they've learned it can be trusted."

"Ye could both be dead. Edgar would kill ye without hesitation, and I dinna doubt he'd kill his own daughter if he believed she crossed him."

"That's why we meet at night and away from our keeps. It isnae that hard since Clyth and Dunbeath are much closer than Clyth and Dunrobin."

Rose and Blaine turned to Greer, whose teeth bit into the underside of her lower lip. When she noticed them watching her, she drew her top lip between her teeth. She shifted nervously. Everyone there knew Blaine would never hurt her, but that didn't mean he didn't intimidate her.

"I sent Greer a missive. That's where Henry really went. He brought one back. Greer asked me to meet her here. The only way to do that was to make people think I retired early then sneak out."

Blaine wanted to believe Greer would never deceive Rose and lead an attack or kidnapping. But he trusted no Gunns, and he feared for Rose.

"Blaine, ye have nay reason to believe me." Greer didn't have to guess hard to know what Blaine thought. "But I've been friends with Rose for three-and-ten years. I wouldnae suddenly betray her. I could have years ago, just like she could have done the same to me. All I want is for ma clan to live in peace with our neighbors. That isnae what ma father wants. If I can help the Sinclairs and their allies to keep ma father from getting ma entire clan killed, then I will. We canna risk a siege or a full-scale attack on Clyth. We wouldnae survive."

"Tell Blaine what ye told me in yer missive."

"Do ye send missives back and forth often? What if someone intercepted them?" That idea didn't sit well with Blaine.

"We call me rabbit, and Greer goes by squirrel," Rose explained. "Laird Gunn is the fox. Any other laird is a bear, and the laird's tánaiste is the cub. We dinna use any real names, and we try to never write he or she either. We dinna use our signet rings to mark the wax. Only Henry delivers the missives for me. He meets a Gunn guardsman, Albert, and they exchange them."

"Albert's aboot a mile north, scouting. He'll warn me if anyone followed me." Greer swallowed as she watched Blaine.

"Even with a code, ye must ken how dangerous this is." Blaine spoke to both women, but he looked at Rose. He slid his hand into hers before changing his mind and wrapping his arm around her waist. He pulled her against him and kissed the top of her head. He lowered his voice once more. "Ye truly scared me, lass."

"Then why didna ye try to stop me?" Rose shook her head. "Ye wanted to see where I was going, and who I would meet."

"Aye. I didna want to endanger ye if anyone watching ye found out I followed ye. I would have ridden to yer side, but I didna wish to tempt fate."

Rose nodded before twisting to see Greer. "Tell him what ye told me."

"Ma father thinks he can outsmart all of ye. He thinks he can reive one clan and draw out the Sinclairs, Sutherlands, and Mackays. He's certain they would chase him, but he thinks he can remain one step ahead and attack each clan before they realize where he will strike next."

"Each clan is strong enough to defeat him on their own. They only ride together as a sign of unity. The Sinclairs, Mackays, and Sutherlands dinna need each other, even if they each wished to lay waste to yer clan."

"I ken that. Ye ken that. Everyone bluidy well kens that, except for Laird Edgar Gunn. He wishes ma next stepmother be Laird MacDonell's daughter."

"Which MacDonnells?" Blaine forced himself not to tense since Rose continued to lean against him.

"Of Loch Boom. They're the closest to us, but ye ken they're a bluidy spider. Between their other branches and their ties to the MacDonalds, they can reach anywhere. Nay laird from a larger branch would consider him, but if he secures that alliance, then he has the potential for one even larger than what the Sinclairs and Sutherlands created."

"What did ye think Rose would do with this information?" It already felt strange to Blaine to call her anything but Kyla.

"Tell Laird Sutherland and her grandda. If the clans thwart his plan, then he willna prove himself to Laird MacDonnell. There will be nay marriage. Ye'll also ken nae to ride out to chase him if he strikes. The clans can prepare. I think the Mackays are his next target."

"Ye're a traitor to yer clan." Blaine hoped it sounded more like an observation than an accusation.

"Some might say that. But any of yer clans could have laid siege to Clyth already. They could have attacked and destroyed ma home and ma people. Instead, each clan was able to stop ma father before he did too much damage. He's nae the only one who does all of this for the betterment of our clan. I dinna agree with him aboot aught except for protecting our people and trying to bring them security and prosperity. He thinks that'll come from triumphing over most of the northern Highlands. I think it'll come from nae having the most powerful alliance in Scotland wind

64

up on ma doorstep. We dinna need the Camerons, MacLeods of Assynt and of Lewis, the Mackenzies, and the Frasers of Lovat joining the Sinclairs, Sutherlands, and Mackays."

"Ma lady," Henry interrupted. "We canna linger much longer if we're to be back before dawn."

"Ye've given me much to think aboot, Lady Greer. I have only one question. Will yer father come back to ma land?"

"Most likely. I just dinna ken when. It wouldnae surprise me if he tried to stir more trouble between ye and the Murrays."

Rose pulled away from Blaine and embraced Greer. "Be careful. I'm always so scared for ye, especially when ye meet me. I dinna want aught to happen to ye."

"The same to ye. I hope yer ride back to Dunrobin is vera boring." Greer tightened her hold before letting go. Rose watched Henry help her mount before Greer waved, then she was off.

"Ye ride with me, Kyla. We have much to talk aboot."

"Henry, give us a moment, please." Rose took Blaine's hand and drew him deeper into the darkness of the trees. When she was certain Henry wouldn't hear them, she turned to face Blaine. "Did ye believe I was sneaking off to a lover?"

"I feared that, aye."

"How did ye ken I left?"

"I was coming to check on ye before I retired. I saw ye go to the servants' stairs just as I got to the landing. I followed ye. Yer cloak made it obvious ye werenae sneaking to the kitchens for something to eat. When I spied ye leaving with Henry, I got ma horse and followed ye. It took me a little while to catch up. I expected ye to stop somewhere nearby. When ye didna, I became more curious than suspicious. I kenned if I stopped ye, ye wouldnae tell me aught. Ye might even accept coming back to the keep. Kyla, ye arenae a daft woman. Ye understand the dangers. Ye left Dunrobin for a reason, whether it was a tryst or something else. I needed to ken why."

"Ye didna trust that I would come back in one piece, and ye didna trust that I would tell ye the truth if ye asked."

"People only sneak out at night when they ken they're doing something they shouldnae. It makes it hard to trust someone who purposely courts danger or breaks such a serious rule."

"Fair. What aboot ma friendship with Greer?"

"I dinna think it's wise, but it's obvious ye're close. I dinna want ye getting hurt or caught in the middle of a battle. That terrifies me. But I willna ever dictate who ye can and canna be friends with." Blaine opened his arms, and Rose stepped into them. She wrapped her arms around his neck as his went back around her waist. She tilted her head back to see what she could of his face in the darkness.

"I am nae interested in any other mon, and I dinna have a past with any mon. I kenned ye would be upset if ye found out, but I thought I'd have time to confess."

"Ye would have told me?"

"Aye. If ye truly want me to marry ye and help ye lead one day, then I canna keep secrets from ye. I liked how honest we were in the garden. I never imagined having such a conversation, especially only days after meeting someone. I'd prefer to tell ye these things in advance, but I kenned ye would try to stop me. And if we dinna suit, I didna want to give away a secret I've kept from everyone—even Thormud—for three-and-ten years. I havenae ever kept aught from him. I canna because he always guesses, and other than this, I've never wanted to."

"Are ye angry that I didna trust ye and that I followed ye?"

"I could be. But I didna act in a trustworthy way, so I canna fault ye."

"Kyla, I dinna trust ye any less than I did this morning. I admit I was angry, scared, and hurt at first. But I understand now."

"Are ye going to tell ma family?"

"Nay. I willna reveal aught ye dinna want made public. As laird and lady, and as husband and wife, I'm certain there are things that only ye and I will ken. At least for now, this is one of them."

Rose went onto her toes as Blaine pressed her against his body until there was no space between them. Their kiss was as fiery as it was in the garden. It drew on until a birdcall interrupted them.

"Henry's getting impatient."

"It's a good thing he reminded us, or I might have ravished ye." Blaine pecked her lips before they walked to the horses.

"I'm glad we talked in private. Henry kens much of this, but I preferred to tell ye alone."

"I hope ye ken I'll always be yer confidant. Come to me aboot aught."

"Will I be yer confidante?"

"I wasna just coming to wish ye goodnight. I wanted yer opinion. But now I must rethink things aboot the Gunns. I'd like yer advice in the morning."

"I'll do ma best."

Blaine helped Rose onto the horse, positioning her so he sat behind her in the saddle. His arms held her tight against him. His hand slipped beneath the cloak and massaged her breasts. When they both hovered on the edge of frustration, Blaine slid his hand to Rose's belly. It felt possessive and protective to the perfect degree. She wasn't eager for another four hours on horseback, but Blaine made up for it as she dozed off in his arms.

Chapter Six

Rose, Blaine, and Henry rode in silence the entire way home, stopping once to water the horses. No one wanted to draw attention from any nearby patrols. It wasn't until Dunrobin came into view that they whispered to one another.

"What did ye tell the guard when ye rode out, Blaine?" Rose could only imagine what he might have revealed to the postern gate guard, but she had faith he didn't reveal her identity.

"I said I was meeting one of ma men who was to return that night from scouting the Gunns. I didna want to alarm ma men, so I was meeting the scout away from the keep."

"Ye ken I'll have to ride back in with Henry. I dinna think it would be wise if we all arrive at the same time. It's almost dawn. If I'm a servant, then I need to be ready for work in an hour. Hopefully, whoever is at the gate willna ask any questions. Do ye want to go ahead of us?"

"Nay. I dinna want ye outside these walls in the dark with only one guard. I trust Henry, and I ken we're close to the keep. But I still dinna like it."

They stopped long enough for Rose to switch mounts before she and Henry set off ahead of Blaine. He watched as they reached the gate, and he grew anxious when it didn't open immediately. But it was only a few minutes before Rose, Henry, and his horse entered the bailey. Blaine waited another five minutes before emerging from the trees where he waited. He had no such trouble getting into the bailey, which made him worry again. Had the guard recognized Rose? He wouldn't know until he could find her. He didn't have to wait since her chamber door stood ajar as he passed it. He rapped softly on it before pushing it open. Rose stood beside the window embrasure and looked toward him as he shut the door.

He crossed the chamber and drew her into his arms as their mouths collided. Their hands explored each other as need coursed through them. Blaine's fears about Rose's actions and safety eased, and her fear that he would be angry or disappointed in her lessened. Instead, relief and longing made them cling to one another. Blaine's hands tunneled into Rose's hair as he held her head in place as they ravaged each other's mouths.

When he could stand it no longer, Blaine tugged at Rose's kirtle, nearly ripping the laces from the back. She pushed it down her arms before he pushed the chemise down to follow it. His hands kneaded her heavy and aching breasts. He couldn't get enough of her, loving how there was always more of her to discover no matter where his hands roamed. He spun her away from the window embrasure and backed her against the bed poster as he pulled her skirts higher.

Rose couldn't keep her eyes open as previously unexperienced sensations assailed her. She reached back to wrap her hands around the poster, using it to keep her upright as her legs threatened to buckle. When she felt Blaine kneel, her head fell forward, and her eyes snapped open. She watched in stunned silence as he pushed her skirts to her waist. Without thought, she let go of the bed with her left hand and gripped the material as Blaine's head disappeared beneath them. His tongue flicked along her seam before his teeth grazed her pleasure center. She truly thought she would no longer remain upright when he sucked the nub into his mouth and kept it there as his tongue slid side to side over it.

"Blaine." It was hoarse whisper at she succumbed to the pleasure that tightened her core and spread throughout her body. When she could breathe again, she tugged at his shoulders. He rose, and her hand dove beneath his plaid. She wouldn't be deterred, and his single groan spurred her on. It only took a dozen strokes before he coated her hand with his seed.

They sagged against each other, savoring the moments of euphoria. When the heightened emotions faded, they leaned apart before releasing each other. Blaine helped her right her clothes. While their cheeks glowed with the bloom of satisfaction, longing for more remained in their eyes. Blaine took a step back, and Rose would have if the bed weren't behind her. They knew remaining too close would only lead to more, which wouldn't be prudent.

"If anyone catches me here..." Blaine wouldn't object to marrying Rose if anyone found them together in her chamber, but he wished it to be her choice as much as his.

"I ken, but ye said ye wished to talk to me before

71

ye retired. I'd like to ken what ye plan to do with what ye learned."

"Greer is yer friend, and she risked much. Ye already have a system that works for ye. How will ye let yer uncle ken without telling him ye saw her?" Blaine gestured for Rose to sit on the window seat.

"Uncle Hamish kens Grandda and Da have someone who leaves missives for them in their horses' stalls. I time it for when I ken they're riding out. If Uncle Hamish finds one tomorrow, he should guess what it means."

"But then he'll ken it's either ye, Shona, or Thor who's the spy."

"He's likely to assume Thor, and when ma brother denies it, Uncle Hamish will try to figure out which guardsman it is." Rose shrugged as she looked up at Blaine.

"Nay. Yer uncle is more likely to come to ye and Shona before he goes to Thor. Yer family kens how canny the lasses are. It's nae that the men arenae intelligent, but the women are far more subtle. Ye have an aunt who spied for King Robert the Bruce. Dinna ye think yer uncle will assume ye and Shona learned something from her?"

"Then I need to think aboot how to get him the information without revealing Greer or I left our keeps."

"Why canna ye reveal yer secret yet? Do ye fear yer da and grandda?"

"Nay. I've never had a moment's fear from either of them. But they wouldnae support me sneaking out of the keep to meet Greer. There's nay way for her to come to Dunbeath for a good nab gash. Even if they allowed me to leave at night, they would insist on more men than just Henry. That would draw far too much attention and defeat the point." Rose turned her gaze toward the door and inhaled. She'd considered telling her parents and grandfather many times, but she worried that their good intentions to keep her safe would keep her from getting the information Greer smuggled to her.

"Who does Greer think is next?"

"Uncle Tristan."

"Then ye canna dillydally telling Hamish. If he needs to send a messenger to the Mackays, then the mon should leave soon. Even if the Gunn will be away a couple more sennights, Tristan still needs time to plan. Yer da needs warning too in case Greer guessed wrong."

"I ken. I dinna think there's much for it. I'm going to have to tell Uncle Hamish the entire truth, which means he'll tell Da and Grandda, too. Or he'll make me do it. I dinna ken which is worse. I wish ye could come with me, but we canna have anyone ken ye followed me or that we decided aught tonight. They'll want to ken when we talked."

"Do ye think it can wait till morn?"

"It can, but I think it'll go worse for me if I admit that nae only did I leave the keep to meet someone in secret, I did it hours earlier and just waited until I thought it convenient to tell. I should wake Uncle Hamish and Lachlan. But that means waking Auntie Amelia and Arabella too. I feel badly aboot that."

"Lachlan has watch at dawn, so vera soon. He's probably already awake."

"I'll look for him, then he can decide if he or I should wake ma uncle and aunt." Rose stood from the window seat and stepped into Blaine's embrace. "Are ye sure ye arenae angry at me?"

"I'm nae pleased. But it isnae anger. I ken I'm nae yer husband or even yer betrothed, but I hope to be one then the other vera soon. I dinna like the idea of ye taking such risks. I admire ye for yer resourcefulness and yer courage. I just want ye to be more careful. Mayhap ye felt ye had to do this alone, but I think Thor would have understood. I dinna understand why ye've kept this from him. Wouldnae he have supported ye?"

"If it were anyone but the Gunns, mayhap. But he lost his best friend in a skirmish the first time they rode out. They were barely five-and-ten. Thor and Jamie got separated from Da and Uncle Magnus. Thor did what he could, but Jamie bled to death before anyone could help them. He held Jamie in his arms while his friend died. It was Edgar's second who did it. Thor hasnae forgiven the Gunns yet, and I dinna ken that he ever will. Ma brother wouldnae hold this against Greer, but he also wouldnae trust her. He definitely wouldnae agree to me leaving the keep at night to possibly be kidnapped or killed by one of Edgar's men if he found me. He'll be hurt when he finds out. That's part of why I've kept it a secret for so long. I dinna want to deal with how I ken he'll react."

"Do ye wish for me to be with ye when ye tell him? Do ye think he's less likely to get upset if I'm there?"

"He'll only find me later." Rose sighed and scrubbed her face with both hands. "I think I'd better tell him at the same time I tell Uncle Hamish and Lachlan. But, aye, I'd like ye to come. Ye're yer clan's tánaiste and have already been the Gunns' victim. And I'd like ye at ma side."

"Ye wake Thor, and I'll find Lachlan."

"I should rouse Uncle Hamish, too. Ye and Lachlan can meet us in Uncle Hamish's solar."

Blaine slid his arm around Rose's waist and titled her chin up. "We'll get through this together, *leannan*." Sweetheart. It was the first endearment either spoke. It warmed Rose to the tips of her toes. She embraced Blaine, resting her head against his chest as she squeezed.

"I suppose this is one way for us to learn if we suit. Naught like a crisis to either bring people together or push them apart. I'm glad I am nae doing this alone, *mo ghràdh*." My darling.

Blaine brushed his lips against hers before they released each other, both knowing that anything more would only lead to distractions they couldn't afford. When they reached the second floor, Rose turned toward the family chambers while Blaine continued downstairs. She crept to her brother's chamber and prayed he would wake and not one of her cousins. She didn't want to explain to Tira's brothers why she disturbed them. She knocked in a pattern she and Thor had used since they were young children. She did it twice before she heard someone moving within.

"Rose?" Thor opened the door enough to stick his nose out. She could tell he only had his plaid wrapped around his waist. "What's the matter?"

"I need ye to meet me in Uncle Hamish's solar. Blaine's gone to fetch Lachlan. I'm going to wake Uncle Hamish."

"What's happened?"

"Naught, but there's something that I canna wait

to discuss. Will ye step out here for a moment. I dinna want to say this through a wee crack." Rose waited until Thor pulled the door almost closed. "I'm going to share a secret with ye and the others that I've kept from everyone for three-and-ten years. I have never felt guiltier than right now because I didna tell at least ye. But I hope ye can understand and forgive me for why I didna. I can tell ye honestly that I have never kept aught else from ye. Nae ever."

"Did something happen to ye? Did someone hurt ye, Rose?"

"Nay. Naught like that. Nay one's ever touched me. I've been friends with someone ye wouldnae approve of, and I've seen her many times over the years. That's all I can say now. Please dress and meet me belowstairs."

"Rose, even if what ye tell me angers me, I'll always be yer other half. Naught changes that. Ye look like ye fear me disowning ye as ma twin."

"Ye might." A lump rose in her throat as she fought the prickle behind her eyelids that forewarned tears.

"Never. It's been us together since the vera beginning. It'll be us together until the end, Sister. Dinna fash."

"Thank ye." Rose bounced onto her toes to peck Thor's cheek before she turned toward the laird and lady's chamber, trusting her brother would dress and make his way belowstairs. She drew a fortifying breath before she knocked. She heard the bed creak immediately and the sound of a sword being drawn. She tried not to be too loud when she spoke. "Uncle Hamish, it's Rose."

A moment later, the door opened wide enough for

Rose to see her uncle was similarly clothed to how Thor was when her brother opened his door. Her aunt sat up with the sheets tucked beneath her bare arms. It embarrassed her to disrupt the older couple. She'd seen her parents in the same state countless times, but her grandfather was a widower who'd never looked in another woman's direction. She'd never knocked on his door and witnessed something so intimate as the laird and lady in their chamber.

"What's the matter, lass?"

"Uncle Hamish, I need to talk to ye in yer solar. I already woke Thor, and he's getting dressed. Blaine went for Lachlan. Auntie Amelia, will ye wake Arabella, please? I think ye should both be there too."

"I'm awake." Rose turned to find Arabella standing in the passageway, wrapped in her robe. "I heard the knocking then voices."

"Why is Blaine going for anyone at this hour? Did ye wake him first?" Hamish's eyebrow nearly touched his hairline.

"He was already awake, but I'm nay waking ye to tell ye we need a priest or that we've handfasted. It's naught like that, I promise."

"All right, lass. Give us five minutes, and we'll be down." Hamish closed the door as Arabella returned to her chamber. Rose hurried belowstairs and reached the solar as Blaine and Lachlan did.

"What's amiss, Rose? Keith wouldnae tell me aught. Why are ye and he awake together at this hour?"

"Ye may as well call me Blaine."

"What the bluidy hell did ye do to Lady Rose Kyla?" Lachlan boomed.

"Shh! He didna do aught. Go inside, Lach." Rose

77

pushed her father's cousin into the chamber. He was nearly the same age as Callum and could easily be her father. But she didn't want him caterwauling for every person sleeping in the Great Hall to hear. She followed Lachlan inside, and Blaine followed her. "Ye ken Blaine's courting me. It seems everyone in our family kens, even if we havenae said aught. He's also Hardi's ally. He's given ye leave to call him by his Christian name, and I dinna think this is the first time. Do ye nae trust Blaine?"

"I trust him, assuming ye are in the same state ye were when ye arrived. Yer da will run me through if ye arenae." Lachlan's dark eyes and dark hair already gave him a brooding appearance, but his deep scowl made him menacing.

"This has naught to do with ma *state*. I'm just as I arrived." Rose had no chance to say more because the solar door opened, and Hamish, Amelia, Arabella, and Thor trooped inside. Hamish made his way to the head of the table while Lachlan sat at the other end. Amelia went to her seat at Hamish's right hand, just as Arabella went to Lachlan's right side. Rose sat to Hamish's left, and Blaine sat beside her. Thor sat across from Rose.

"The roosters are still rubbing their eyes. I dinna make a habit of rising so early anymore, lass. What's this aboot?"

Rose glanced at Hamish before locking eyes with Thor. "Three-and-ten years ago I met Greer Gunn at a Highland Gathering. We became fast friends even though we kenned our clans canna stand each other. We used to meet in secret every year. Thor, didna ye think after a while that it was odd that I always had ma courses at the same time as the Gatherings?"

Thor flushed deep red and muttered, "I dinna like to think aboot that when I think of ye."

Rose knew it was the wrong time to laugh at her brother, but his embarrassment was almost adorable. He looked like he had when they were twelve, and he learned about a woman's monthly cycle because he'd barged into Rose's chamber and nearly fainted at the sight of blood on linen strips.

"Aboot five years ago, Greer and I happened to ride out to the same loch where Uncle Daniel would meet Ceana. Henry was ma guard that day, and Albert Gunn rode with Greer. After that, we started meeting in secret once a moon. Three years ago, Greer told me the first secret I wrote down and hid in Grandda's saddle. Since then, we've met regularly for her to pass information to me aboot the Gunns' plans. I'm the one who's been leaving the missives for Da and Grandda."

Hamish leaned forward over his steepled fingers, his hands resting on the table. "Those missives show up in the early morning. They're always tucked into whoever is riding out first. That must mean ye're leaving the keep in the middle of the night. Yer da and grandda often wonder who outside the family kens their schedule. They've suspected Thor or one of the other lads, but they've never been able to catch any of them."

"That's because none of them moves with an ounce of stealth when they're within the keep's walls. I dinna ken how they hunt or fight if they're that obvious." Rose observed Thor as she spoke.

"We dinna think we need to hide from anyone at home," Thor countered. Rose knew he was angry. "How could ye trust a Gunn, Rose. Even if it werenae

Greer to betray ye, how could ye believe ye were safe? How'd ye ken nay one followed Greer?"

"Greer's da doesnae worry aboot her at all. I think he'd likely be happy to have his legitimate daughter die. Then he'd never have to pay a dowry for her."

"And he'd be the one to do it." Thor's hands fisted on the table. "And when he did, he'd kill ye too."

"Thor, what's done is done. Obviously, I willna be meeting her in secret now that all of ye ken. But that doesnae matter right now. Henry didna leave to hunt because he was upset with Thor. He used it as a ruse to deliver a missive for me. He returned with an answer last night. I didna feel ill. I lied, so I could retire early, then sneak out to meet Greer. Henry took me, and Blaine followed. Thor, before ye thrash Henry, remember he canna tell me nay if I insist."

"Bollocks. I ken ye didna have to twist his arm that hard. He would protect ye like ye were his own lass. At least, ye had him. He's the only one outside our family I'd trust. Why'd Blaine follow ye?"

Rose looked at Blaine, who waited for her to speak. She nodded before she looked at Hamish and Amelia and waited for Blaine to explain.

"I worried aboot Lady Rose being poorly. I also wanted her counsel aboot what I'd decided to do. I trust her advice, and if she's to become ma wife, then she needs to ken the state of ma clan. Just like her mother essentially became Lady Sinclair because Laird Sinclair's a widower, she will do the same for ma family. Ma father is in France, and ma mother is dead. We will lead as though we're already Laird and Lady Keith." Blaine shifted his gaze from Hamish and Amelia to Thor. "I planned to visit her chamber, but only to talk. I will do naught to compromise Lady

Rose. If she agrees to marry me, then we'll stand before a priest before we do aught."

A collective snort filled the chamber, and Rose ducked her head. Blaine looked at her questioningly, but it was Thor who answered.

"I canna think of a couple in our family that hasnae handfasted because they canna wait long enough to walk to the kirk. Uncle Hamish and Grandda started it."

"It wasna me. I learned from yer grandda and ma sister." Hamish winked at Amelia.

Blaine had never witnessed such an intimate family conversation. It was unlike anything he'd experienced with his father, mother, or cousins when they all lived together at Ackergill. He watched the older couple for another moment before continuing his story.

"I caught sight of Lady Rose leaving her chamber as I approached. She didna hear or see me, so I followed her down the servants' stairs. I watched her meet a Sinclair guard in the bailey. She had on her cloak and her hood up when they approached the postern gate. I couldnae believe it when I saw them pass through. I kenned the Sutherland guard couldnae have kenned it was Lady Rose. I saddled ma horse and rode after them.

"Rose, what did ye tell that guard?" Lachlan asked.

"Henry pretended he was courting a servant. He said Uncle Hamish kenned his intentions and that we didna want anyone to ken yet. I kept ma head down until we passed through the gate. Then I kept ma hood up once we mounted."

"I told the guard that I had a scout returning from

the Gunns, and I didna want to alarm anyone, so I was meeting him at night and away from the keep." Blaine finished explaining and looked around the group. It appeared like everyone accepted his reason for being with Rose during the middle of the night, but he could tell Thor wasn't through questioning him. When Thor remained quiet, Blaine knew it was likely to continue in the lists.

"Uncle Hamish, Henry and I rode almost to Dunbeath. We were back on Sinclair land when we met Greer. She'd already sent a missive that told me Laird Gunn intends to lure our clans away from home. He plans to attack us and the Mackays, hoping he can lead ye on a merry chase. According to Greer, he may start with Uncle Tristan and Auntie Mairghread. He thinks he can lead his second attack while the Mackays, Sinclairs, and Sutherlands rally to chase him. He believes all three clans will leave their keeps vulnerable, so ye can try to catch him."

"Daft bugger," Hamish muttered. "He kens each of our clans could ride out with over a hundred warriors and still have enough to defend our people and our keeps. He kens we dinna need each other to win. We fight together because we're family and nay one threatens any of us without getting all of us."

"I think he counts on our family ties to draw all three clans into pursuing him for that vera reason. He must ken each of our clans can defend itself, but he believes we'll always want to prove how mighty our alliance makes us. He thinks he can defeat us with our pride." Rose sat back, uncertain if she should have done more than pass along the messages. Blaine's shoulder brushed hers as though by accident since his

82

back was so broad. But his forearm pressed against hers as they each rested on their chair's arms.

"I think ye have the right of it, Rose." Amelia smiled at her grandniece. While Rose looked like the spitting image of her mother, except for her eyes, she reminded Amelia of her long dead sister-by-marriage. Kyla Sinclair, Hamish's younger sister, had been a force with which to reckon, but she'd still been uncertain of herself when Amelia and Hamish married. Kyla and Liam hadn't even been married a year when the women met. Amelia arrived as Hamish's bride, and Kyla was adjusting to her position within the Sinclair clan. She'd been observant and astute like Rose. But she'd worried that she spoke out of turn when she made suggestions to Liam and his father.

Amelia sensed Blaine would be the silent support Rose needed to gain the confidence Kyla developed. Kyla became a formidable force as Lady Sinclair, Countess of Sinclair. Amelia was certain Rose would be the same once she became Lady Keith. She didn't doubt the young couple would marry. She'd already wagered with Hamish about how much longer they'd have to wait for the couple to handfast. She estimated a moon, but Hamish said it would be longer since Rose wouldn't dare marry without her parents there. Amelia hadn't withheld her laughter, reminding him that the couples in their family liked the privacy of a handfast.

"Isnae Tristan in Orkney right now? We need to send someone to warn him there and to alert Wee Liam." Arabella spoke with the assurance of someone who'd been part of the laird's council for decades. Theirs was an unconventional family since women had equal voices to the men in the Sinclair, Mackay, and Sutherland clans. Lachlan reached for his wife's hand and squeezed.

"If ye want to go sailing because Blair got to, then just say so." Lachlan grinned. "I'll take ye to Orkney." Everyone knew if Arabella joined Lachlan, it wouldn't make his arrival appear so urgent. It wouldn't set the tiny archipelago abuzz with gossip and suspicion.

"We need Hardi and Blair to join us." Thor looked at Blaine. "What are ye going to do? Do ye ride with us when we deal with the Gunns, or do ye ask Hardi to ride with ye to the Murrays?"

"He sent a messenger to the Murrays. The mon should return soon. I suppose it depends on what the Cameron warrior says. I'd rather sort out the Gunns first, since they are our most recent menace. But I may nae get a choice."

"Ye both must be exhausted. Why dinna ye have forty winks, then we can all meet again once ye're rested?" Amelia noticed the shadows darkening beneath Rose's eyes. Blaine would easily survive many more hours without sleep, but Rose's fatigue was obvious. The younger woman nodded and moved to push back her chair. Blaine rose and helped her.

"Hardi and Blair will be awake soon. Shouldnae we tell them right away?" Rose worried.

"We can wait a few hours," Hamish assured. Rose nodded before she turned to the door. When she reached it, she turned back.

"I'm sorry I've deceived everyone for so long." Rose looked at her brother. "I wouldnae have done it if I'd thought there was a better way. I did consider alternatives many times over the years, but naught ever seemed better."

Thor shot her a tight smile and jerky nod. Rose supposed it was the best she could hope for under the circumstances. Blaine opened the door for her, but he didn't follow her. She glanced back over her shoulder and knew he would wait for the sake of appearances. It seemed pointless, but she appreciated that he tried not to flaunt their burgeoning relationship. She made her way to her chamber and stripped off her kirtle, having chosen one with ties on the sides so she could manage alone. She climbed into bed and was asleep within moments.

Chapter Seven

Blaine retired to his chamber after Rose went to hers, but his mind wouldn't settle. He laid in bed for two hours before he abandoned his hope for sleep. He decided fresh air would do him more good than tossing and turning. He wished Rose was in the bed beside him. He'd envisioned her there every night since they met, but he also wished to continue discussing the situation with her. He looked forward to a day when they could lie side-by-side and share the events of their day and plan for their clan together. He didn't want to get too far ahead of himself in case Rose decided she didn't wish for them to marry, but he felt confident she would.

He joined the men in the lists and sparred for another three hours before he made his way toward the keep. He wondered if Rose was awake yet. He assumed she'd fallen asleep since she appeared exhausted by the time she left Hamish's solar. He hoped she stayed abed as long as she needed.

"Royal messenger approaches," a Sutherland guard announced. It was as though everyone in the bailey held a collective breath. Did that mean a mes-

senger from the exiled King David or one from the
English King Edward III, the false king of Scotland?
Blaine watched a man pass beneath the portcullis.
The insignia appeared subtle, announcing he arrived
on behalf of King David. If he'd worn anything like
Robert the Bruce's royal livery, the man would be a
target for anyone who supported the English.

"I'm looking for the Keiths' tánaiste," the messenger announced as he entered the bailey.

"I am he." Blaine changed course and met the
man beside the winded horse.

"A missive from His Majesty King David." The
man handed a battered missive and a scroll to Blaine.
He didn't doubt it passed through several hands while
on its journey from France.

"Is a reply expected?"

"Aye. But I was told to give ye a day because there
would be arrangements to make."

"Arrangements? Is ma father dead?"

"Nae that I ken. It's nae ma place to ken what's in
the missive."

Blaine's heart pounded as he gave the man a silver
coin before taking the steps up to the keep three at a
time. He pried the wax seal open and unfolded the
parchment as he entered the Great Hall. He skimmed
the message before halting at the base of the stairs up
to the bed chambers. He couldn't believe what he
read.

*It is by royal decree, Blaine Edward Keith, tá-
naiste to Clan Keith, will marry Lady Eliza Mary
Irvine on 1 September in the year of our Lord, thir-
teen-thirty-seven. The bride's dowry has already been
negotiated and accepted by Lord Robert de Keith on
behalf of his son, Blaine. The groom will sign the be-*

*trothal agreement and return it to Laird Irvine within
one sennight from this missive's arrival. This marriage
forms an alliance between the Keiths and Irvines,
ceasing all hostility between the clans. The Irvines
will lend aid to the Keiths against any foe, just as the
Keiths will do the same for the Irvines. This marriage
is ordained by the Grace of God and His Majesty King
David II.*

Blaine stared at the missive and the royal seal at
the end. He feared he might be ill. His hand trembled
as he looked up the stairs, as though he could see all
the way to Rose's chamber. This was not what he
wanted or planned. He couldn't pretend as though he
didn't know since the royal messenger delivered the
missive and contract directly to him.

"Blaine?" Hardi approached, concerned by the
younger man's paleness. It appeared as though all the
blood leeched from his face. The laird could see
Blaine's hands shaking. It unnerved Hardi to see
Blaine so shaken.

"Aye?"

"Ye look like ye need a stiff drink. A dram or five
of some Sinclair whisky will set ye to rights."

"I dinna think so, but I willna turn it down."

"What's happened? Ye're white as a sheet."

"I dinna wish to discuss this where anyone can
hear."

"Come up to ma chamber. I have a jug in there."
Hardi led the way as the men walked in silence. It
was late enough that no family member remained in
bed, but the servants hadn't begun their rounds yet.
Hardi left the door ajar, unconcerned that someone
would interrupt them. He poured a healthy portion of
whisky and handed it to Blaine, who finished it in two

gulps before thrusting his arm out for more. Blaine drank this cupful slower.

"The royal messenger delivered this to me." Blaine handed the parchment to Hardi. He wouldn't unroll the contract until he absolutely had to. As long as he didn't read it, he could pretend none of this was real. He watched Hardi's eyes move as he read the letter twice.

"I'm betrothed. Lady Eliza Irvine is to be ma wife. Ma father's already agreed to and likely already accepted the dowry. The banns have likely already been read. I'm as good as married." Blaine felt like part of him died as he spoke the words aloud. He stared at the floor for a long moment before he continued. "Ma father didna bother to tell me himself. He let the king tell me through a missive the boy-king didna even write in his own hand. Some scribe likely did it. Ma father could have just as easily sent me the news, but he kenned I would argue with him."

"Have ye read the contracts yet?"

"Nay. I'd rather burn them than read them. This canna be happening. Five minutes ago, I thought I'd be talking to the woman I really wish to marry and asking her opinion aboot what we should do next for Clan Keith. I canna stand Eliza Irvine. She's vapid and lazy. She is the least desirable mate for me. I dinna ken what ma father is dreaming aboot to think she should join our clan. He has the influence over the king to dissuade him from this. But ma father couldnae be bothered to send me a letter in his own hand to explain why I should agree to something so ludicrous."

"Do ye think kenning ye wish to marry Rose would change yer father's mind?"

"Nay. If he'd wanted to refuse the king, he would have done it already. He must wish for this too. His chance to argue against it, if it was the king's idea, has come and gone."

"Blaine, how badly do ye wish to marry Rose? Do ye think ye could love her one day?"

"Aye. Without a doubt. I'm on the way to it already."

"Do ye ken the Sutherlands' and Sinclairs' connection to the Bruces?"

"Both lairds fought alongside the Bruce from the vera beginning. Lachlan and his cousins even fought in some of those battles. They continue to fight under Andrew Murray's command. We all do. I dinna like the bastard because of his clan, but I respect him as a military leader."

"That's all true, but do ye ken what else connects them?"

"Nay. Is there more?"

"Och, aye. The Bruce and Queen Elizabeth de Burgh were Blair, Lachlan, and Maude's godparents along with Callum and his siblings. Hamish, Amelia, and Liam are King David's godparents. The Bruce couldnae and wouldnae decide between Hamish and Liam, so he asked them both. If ye really wish to marry Rose, then ye need to ask Callum's permission sharpish. Liam will send a missive on yer behalf, but ye canna dillydally if ye want to change the king's mind before ye're forced to the kirk to marry the woman ye dinna want."

"What if I'm already married?"

"Ye mean handfasted?"

"The Irvines are Highlanders too. They'll have to respect the sanctity of it since they understand it.

Canna we say Rose and I handfasted last eve, before I got the missive?"

"That shall seem mighty suspicious timing."

"Aye, but Rose slept late this morning as far as anyone kens. Wouldnae that make it convincing? A bride—her wedding night—I—"

"Haud yer wheest, lad. I ken yer meaning. Ye dinna need to trip over yer tongue." Hardi chuckled, and Blaine glowered, which only made the former laugh harder.

"I need to speak to Rose, then I need to find Hamish. I'll ride for Dunbeath as soon as I've spoken to them both."

"Ride off and leave yer bride? Nay. Thor can go."

"But I dinna want to completely insult Callum and Lady Siùsan. I should be the one to tell them."

"Under normal circumstances, aye."

"Vera well. I'll find Rose, then Hamish, then Thor. I wish I could just burn the lot of this."

"Nae yet. Hopefully, soon."

Blaine and Hardi parted ways in the passageway. Blaine ran up to his chamber and hid the contracts in his locked chest before he went to find Rose.

Rose heard Hardi and Blaine's voices as she made her way belowstairs. She wondered if Blaine was telling Hardi what they'd shared with the rest of her family several hours ago. She prepared to knock, even though the door was partially open. Her arm froze in the air as Blaine's words floated to her ears.

"I'm betrothed. Lady Eliza Irvine is to be ma wife. Ma father's already agreed to and likely already accepted the dowry. The banns have likely already been read. I'm as good as married."

Rose felt as though someone kicked her in her belly. She wrapped her arms around her waist and sagged against the wall. The ringing in her ears kept her from hearing anything else. Tears streamed down her cheeks as she stumbled away. Halfway down the stairs, she wiped her cheeks dry and pushed back her shoulders. She straightened her spine with a deep breath. With her chin held high, she entered the Great Hall. No one paid her attention, so she hurried outside. When she reached the lists, she whistled for Thor. His head swung in her direction, and he was sprinting to the entrance, waving away Sinclair guards.

"What's happened? What's wrong?" Thor's hands cupped Rose's shoulders. Each member of the laird's family had a birdcall that was their own. But Rose used the one they'd devised as children when they needed each other and wanted no one else. They'd felt guilty at times because it excluded Shona, but they couldn't deny the unique bond they had as twins. They didn't love their sister any less, but it wasn't the same connection.

"He's already betrothed. He's played me for a fool all along. I kenned it. I kenned he didna want aught more than a tumble. He doesnae think of me as more than a wench to tup."

"Slow down, Rosie." No one but Thor called her that. It made her think of how only Blaine called her Kyla. Her eyes watered at the memory. "How do ye ken he's betrothed? And to whom?"

"Lady Eliza Irvine. I heard him talking to Hardi. I heard their voices as I came downstairs. I thought

Blaine might be filling Hardi in. I was aboot to knock when he told Hardi he's betrothed."

"Did he say aught more?"

"Something aboot the banns already being read."

"Aught else?"

"Nay. I dinna think so."

"Rosie, ye must nae have heard it all. Hardi would beat him to a pulp if he learned Blaine kept this from ye, from all of us. He'd kill him for mistreating ye. Blaine kens I'd kill him if Hardi didna. Ye must have misheard."

"Dinna patronize me, Thor. I ken what he said. He's betrothed. He thought I was a maid he could swive. When he realized he couldnae have me in the stables or the scullery, he tried to seduce me. He never wanted me as his wife. He just wanted to bed me like a whore."

Rose pulled away from Thor and looked around. She lifted her skirts and ran toward the postern gate. Thor easily kept up with her until they passed through the portal. Dunrobin sat on a rocky headland, so there wasn't far for them to walk before they reached the cliff. They stood together, watching the waves crash until Thor wrapped his arm around Rose's shoulders, and she turned toward him.

"Rosie, why do ye think he only wants to toss yer skirts? The mon I saw in the solar this morning is a mon who admires and respects ye. I think he may even be falling in love with ye. I could tell from the way he watched ye, how attentive he was when ye spoke. Naught made me think he merely wants to bed ye and move on. I thought ye both cleared up the misunderstanding."

"I thought we had too. But clearly, I was vera

wrong."

"Why didna ye ask him? Why nae confront him with Hardi there? He would have spoken the truth if for nay other reason than Hardi being there."

"I didna want to hear lies. If he's been telling me falsehoods this entire time, then he would lie in front of Hardi. I feel like such a fool. I kenned it was too good to be true."

"That he wanted to court ye?"

"Aye. Men like him dinna marry women who look like me."

"What the hell does that mean? What's wrong with the way ye look?"

"I'm nay slender like Shona, or Tira, or Saoirse, or Maisie. I'm nae like any of our cousins. I look like a tavern wench who managed to cover her tits and arse. I should have kenned."

"Ye are nae making any sense."

"Because ye're nae a woman."

"If this is how ye lot thinks, then it's just as well. What does ye nae being slender have to do with Blaine being too good for ye?"

"A braw mon like him wants a bonnie woman for his bride. One he can be proud to have welcome his guests and run his keep. People are more likely to think I'm his leman than his wife if we married."

"Rosie, have ye felt this way aboot any mon who might court ye?"

Rose bit her bottom lip before she shook her head. "Nay one else has ever paid attention to me besides a few impolite comments when men didna realize who I am."

Thor gritted his teeth. He would find each of those men and bury them beneath his horse's hooves.

"And their comments make ye worry aboot how ye filled out?"

"When we were younger, a little. I hadnae really thought aboot it in ages. I dinna mind the way I look. I accepted that I'm nae like our sister or cousins. But that was all right until now. I ken it doesnae make sense. I can barely reason it out maself."

"Do ye think Blaine's too good for ye?"

Rose pressed her lips between her teeth before she nodded her head.

Thor held her tighter. "Why?"

"He's so handsome and charming. He's intelligent, and people respect him. Anyone can tell he'll be as great as his father once he's laird. I'm scared even if he could marry me, he'll regret it and willna want people to ken he married a woman who doesnae look like a lady."

"Rosie, listen to me, please. Everything aboot ye announces ye're a lady. The way ye carry yerself, the way ye walk, the way ye speak, the way ye lead women with barely a word. Ye can read and write, and ye can do sums better than me. Ye speak Gaelic, Scots, English, French, and Latin. Ye read them all too. Nay tavern wench can do that. Aye, ye've filled out a wee sooner than the others. But Auntie Amelia and Maude are just like ye. Mama isnae as slim as she was before she had us. None of our aunts are as slender as when they married. Do ye see Da or any of our uncles upset by it? Grandda says they're worse than when they were newlyweds. He says it reminds him of when he used to chase Grandmama, even after Da and our uncles and aunt were born. There is naught wrong with how ye look, Rosie. Ye're bonnie and elegant. Blaine's lucky a woman so fine as ye even glanced in his direction, let alone wants him to court her."

"Kyla! Kyla! Thor!"

"It's Blaine."

"Why's he calling ye that?"

"He—it was special." Rose turned away from Blaine as he hurried toward them.

"Kyla, what's wrong? One of the laundresses said ye were crying, and Thor was chasing after ye. What happened?" Blaine took a step back at Rose's withering glare over her shoulder. He looked at Thor, whose gaze wasn't quite scathing, but was filled with suspicion.

"Go away, Blaine." Rose pulled away from Thor and walked closer to the edge before turning her back on Blaine again.

"Kyla, come away from the edge. Ye're too close."

Rose heard the fear in Blaine's voice, and it spurred her to continue walking as she was. She knew she was needling him, but it felt like a victory, albeit hollow.

"Thor, make her stop. She's going to fall."

"We've been walking along these bluffs since we were in leading strings. Ye're more likely to go over the edge than she is."

"It's windy today. Please." Blaine wanted to yank Rose back to where he stood with Thor. She wasn't close enough to the ledge to tumble over, but he feared the wind off the water might make her stumble. He envisioned her going over the side, her body battered on the rocks below. Rose turned back to look over her shoulder, seeing his distress and relented. She moved farther from the edge, but she continued to walk.

"Ye have some explaining to do. Why didna ye tell ma sister the truth?"

"Aboot?"

"Aboot yer betrothal," Rose answered. All three voices carried on the wind.

"Kyla, how do ye ken aboot that?" Blaine's heart sank. Hardi couldn't have told either of them yet. Who had?

"Ye dinna deny ye're betrothed." Thor's shoulders went back, expanding his already massive chest. He crossed his arms and widened his stance until his feet were hip-width apart. Every warrior in Scotland likely knew the Sinclair stance. It foretold ill tidings for whomever stood in front of a Sinclair man. Before joining the Sinclair family, Deirdre Fraser called it the Odin stance when she met Magnus. The men became immoveable, almost god-like figures who intimidated even the most hardened soldier. With the exception of the red hair he inherited from Siùsan, anyone would know he was a member of Liam Sinclair's family.

Blaine looked at the man he'd hoped would soon be his brother-by-marriage. They were the same height and nearly the same size, but he knew Thor weighed nearly a stone more than him, and it was all lean muscle. He would hold his own if it came to fisticuffs, but he wouldn't walk away without injury. He prayed it didn't come to that.

"How do ye ken, Kyla?" Blaine ignored Thor.

"I heard ye talking to Hardi. I came to see ye when I heard yer voice. But just as I was aboot to knock, ye—" Rose tucked her chin and looked at the ground before she whispered, "—ruined ma world."

"Is that all ye heard?" Blaine no longer waited for

Rose to walk back to Thor and him. He strode to her side and pulled her another ten feet from the cliffs. He was careful not to hurt her, but he would have hauled her over his shoulder if he had to. "Could ye stay away from the bluidy edge? I canna think straight while I picture ye plummeting to yer death. It makes it hard to breathe."

Rose scoffed. "Hard for ye to breathe? How do ye think I felt to learn ye've made a fool of me? That I was right all along."

"Thor, yer sister and I are going for a walk. We'll stay where ye can see us, but I'm nae having anyone else hear what I have to say. There's been enough overhearing and misunderstanding." Blaine slid his hand into Rose's and looked down at her, softening his tone. "Please, Kyla. I came to find ye because I wished for yer counsel on how to handle this. It isnae what ye must think. I didna lie to ye. I just found out. Ye can ask Hardi when we get back."

Rose's lips pursed, but she nodded. Blaine reached into his sporran and retrieved the missive he'd jammed in there. As they walked inland, he handed it to her. She looked at him questioningly until he nodded. She opened it and scanned it, her pace slowing with each word until she stopped. Her mouth fell open before she clapped her hand over it. Once more, her eyes filled with tears as she looked up at Blaine.

"I was so quick to judge, to assume ye'd wronged me. I'm horrible. I'm so sorry."

"Kyla, if ye only heard the part where I told Hardi I was betrothed and nae what I said after, I canna fault ye for assuming the worst. And I canna blame ye for nae sticking around to hear more."

"Dinna absolve me, Blaine. I assumed the worst of ye in the beginning, and I was far too fast to do it again."

"Then why?"

"I dinna ken exactly." Rose frowned as she pushed wispy hairs from her eyes. "Ye ken what I believed in the beginning. I went right back to that without asking ye for the entire story. I dinna usually mind how I look. I dinna ken why I'm bothered by it now. I just fear ye'll regret marrying me when people mistake me for yer leman rather than yer wife."

"Who the fuck would do that?" Blaine's voice carried, and he noticed Thor rushing forward. He shook his head and waved Thor away. "I mean, who would mistake ye for anyone other than a lady? And who would think I would be unfaithful to a Sinclair woman? Why would any mon look elsewhere if he were so fortunate as to marry a Sinclair? And how could any mon be daft enough to believe he could say such and live long enough to tell the tale? And who the bluidy hell would have a death wish strong enough to call ye ma leman rather than ma wife?"

Blaine's voice rose with each question until he was practically yelling. His hands were on his hips, and he realized how intimidating he must appear because Thor reached for a dirk. Blaine took four steps back and turned toward Thor.

"I'm nae angry with yer sister. I'm nae bellowing at her, but I'm getting frustrated." Blaine looked back at Rose. "*Mo ghràdh,* there are a number of reasons why people wouldnae confuse ye for a mistress. Anyone who kens me, would ken I married a Sinclair. Anyone who kens of the Sinclairs and saw yer hair would ken ye're Siùsan Sinclair's daughter. Nay one would mistake ye for aught else but the future Lady Keith."

"Mayhap they'd ken I'm yer wife and a lady, but that willna stop people from thinking ye could have married better. That I dinna look fitting to be a clan's lady." Rose knew the arguments sounded weak, but in her own mind, they'd taken hold. Part of her knew they were irrational, but her emotions had too tight a grasp on these ideas for her to let them go.

"Kyla, I ken this matters to ye. I ken ye feel strongly aboot this. But nay one else sees it as ye do. Nay one else looks at ye and sees a whore. Anyone who looks at ye sees the bonniest lass who's kind-hearted, hardworking, devoted to her family and clan, thoughtful, and intelligent. Ye dinna walk around looking like ye want a tumble, nor do ye go around offering one. Naught aboot ye when I first saw ye made me think ye were offering. I hoped I'd be lucky enough ye'd say yes. Please dinna let ma blunder make ye think anyone would treat ye poorly for becoming ma wife."

"Ye deserve—" Rose looked down at her feet.

"What do ye think I deserve?"

"It'll sound so superficial and childish if I say it aloud."

Blaine took both her hands in his and brushed his thumbs over the backs of hers. "I dinna care how it sounds. If it's troubling ye, then tell me. We'll sort it out together."

"I dinna feel good enough for ye. Ye're a braw mon, and I see how other women look at ye. People will expect ye to marry someone..." Rose shook her head. It sounded so lame to her own ears, but it felt so real within her mind.

"Ye are good enough for me or any mon so lucky as to have ye for his wife. Ye ken arranged marriages arenae based on looks. Most noble marriages dinna happen for love. Look at the mess ma father's gotten me into. Aye, yer looks got ma attention. But it's who ye are that's stealing ma heart. If it were yer looks alone, I would have stopped pursuing ye once I learned yer name."

"I dinna understand why this is bothering me so much. I guess I dinna want to be disappointed if ye dinna feel for me what I feel for ye." Rose watched Blaine's thumbs as they moved over her hands. It was soothing and tender.

"Kyla, we're still getting to ken one another, but I already think we're going to agree we suit. We ken more aboot each other than most couples when they marry. I ken I've never considered marrying any woman before I met ye. Ma father's hinted, even suggested, but I've always refused. I hope we fall in love and remain that way until our last breath. I want ye to have what the other couples in yer family have. But even if ye never love me, I would still love ye. I would always treat ye well and be the best husband I can. I dinna want Eliza or anyone else. Only ye."

"Ye think ye could love me?"

"Lass, I'm more than halfway there." Blaine cupped Rose's cheek and brought the tip of his nose to brush against hers. "Could ye love me?"

"Aye. With ma whole heart."

"I am nae going to declare aught because I ken it's too soon. I dinna want ye to think I throw the phrase around lightly. I dinna. But I want ye by ma side, Kyla. To have and to hold, forever. I want us together, so we can fall in love. I want us together because I trust ye and seek yer advice. I want us together because it's our children I'd see ye carrying when the clans come together for the Gatherings. I dinna want to see ye with another mon. It would break ma heart."

"It's nae that ye make me feel badly aboot maself. I do that on ma own. When I'm with ye, I feel heard. I feel like what I want matters. In a family as large as mine, sometimes ye get lost in the crowd. Ye make me feel needed and wanted. I dinna want ma foolishness aboot ma looks to get in the way."

"It isnae foolish if that's how ye feel. It's real to ye, and it's something making ye unhappy."

"I dinna expect ye to solve it for me, Blaine. I dinna want ye to think I'll need yer attention and compliments all the time."

"I would give ye both all the time if I could. Mayhap we can try to solve it together."

Rose smiled for the first time since she overheard Blaine and Hardi talking. "Thank ye for being patient with me while I work through this. I think it's really aboot me fearing being disappointed. It's an easy excuse to use ma appearance rather than having to accept there might be something deeper aboot me that ye dinna want."

Blaine leaned forward to whisper in her ear, even though they both knew Thor couldn't hear. "I want all of ye, lass. Inside, outside, and everything in between. I would marry ye this eve to show ye what I want to do with ye in our chamber. But I'd marry ye even if I could never touch ye. It might kill me, but I'd do it if ye were by ma side."

"That's where I want to be. Now we just have to figure out how to defy the king and keep our heads."

Chapter Eight

"Hamish, I willna marry Lady Eliza. Nae just because I wish to marry Lady Rose." Blaine sat with Hamish, Lachlan, and Hardi in the laird's solar. "Have ye met her? She doesnae say much, but she makes her wishes kenned to her father. Those wishes are vera expensive. She can spend coin as though it were water through a sieve. But she canna save it to save her life. She will bankrupt ma clan within a year. She's also a horrible chatelaine. Ye've all been to the Irvine keep. Her mother's bedridden, and Lady Eliza canna be bothered to supervise the servants. I willna have ma home falling down around ma ears. I need a wife I can trust to lead our clan when I must ride out. I would never want to leave if I kenned she were in charge. I would come home to naught. I willna marry her."

"I've heard ye—both times." Hamish held up his hand. "I ken this is upsetting to ye. Do ye think Rose is ready to at least handfast?"

Blaine inhaled as he looked at Hardi. "She overheard us, but she only heard the first part of what I

103

said. Understandably, it upset her." Blaine shifted his gaze to Lachlan, then back to Hamish. "We've talked it out, but she's feeling unsure aboot herself right now. She's afraid things willna work out between us, and she's trying to shield herself from disappointment. In her mind, she tried to convince herself that she wasna the right type of woman to be ma wife. I think we've moved past that—or at least are getting there—but I dinna want to rush her. I want her to ken she's safe with me, and I will support her. But if it's nae enough, and she'd be miserable as ma wife, then I dinna want her trapped, even if it's only for a year and a day."

"Ye need Liam and Callum's support against yer father. I will send a missive today, but I'm only the lass's great-uncle. Ye need the request to come from her father and her laird."

"I ken. I would ride to Dunbeath today if it would help. When Hardi and I spoke, we thought we might tell everyone we handfasted last night. But like I said, now I dinna want to rush her. It means I could leave without it looking questionable that I've abandoned ma bride. I canna dally because I'm supposed to re- turn the signed contracts to the Irvine within a sen- night of receiving them. That willna even be long enough to get a missive to the king. I fear what the Irvine will do if I dinna sign them. He'll ken some- thing is amiss."

"I think ye're only choice is to see Liam and Cal- lum. The Irvines dinna have many allies, but the one they have is the reason ye're in this situation. They've been loyal to the Bruces since nearly the beginning. Laird Irvine must have pressed for this, and yer father saw yet another way to connect the Keiths to the

Bruces. And he could create peace between yer clans to boot."

"I ken. But an alliance with the Sinclairs is far more powerful than one with the Irvines. Everyone kens that. I hope a letter from Laird Sinclair will be enough to sway the king. With the alliance we already have with the Camerons, we're already indirectly allied with ye and the Sinclairs. Marrying Rose would solidify it and align us with ye from two directions. Is that what ye wish, Hamish?"

"Aye. I wish Rose to be happy and loved. If it's with a mon who leads a clan I can support, then all the better. I support ye, Blaine, and I support the Keiths. They arenae the same thing, but ye should ken I will ride out for either cause."

Blaine smiled at the older man, wishing for the umpteenth time since he arrived that Hamish could have been his father or grandfather. He looked at Lachlan, knowing that one day it would be his choice whether to continue the alliance.

"Dinna fear, lad. I can make up ma own mind, but if Da says he supports ye, then I ken it's a wise decision. I willna end the alliance."

Blaine nodded before shifting to meet Hamish's gaze. "Thank ye both. Do ye think I should set off for Dunbeath today?"

"Nay. I dinna like it, but I say wait a couple days. I want to ken where bluidy Edgar is before sending ye north. I dinna trust that weasel. While ye wait, I'll send out scouts, and I'll send a missive to France. While Lachlan and Arabella sail to Orkney, I'll have ma other best sailors take a missive by sea to Edinburgh. A royal messenger will take it by sea the rest of the way to France. Ma men ken what to do. It willna be the first message delivered this way."

"Then I'll follow yer lead. I'd like to find Rose and share what we've discussed. She was upset, so I wanted to give her time to feel more composed. But the next time we meet, I'd like her to be with us." Blaine wasn't sure if he was making a declaration so much as asking permission. He knew Amelia, Arabella, and Blair would be there if their husbands asked. But he wasn't certain whether the men would welcome Rose since she and Blaine weren't even betrothed.

"Do ye wish for her to hear what we discuss, so she doesnae feel left out?" Hardi wondered.

"Partly. But I also want to hear her thoughts. I ken how unusual ye each are as leaders. Most men wouldnae involve their wives in aught. But it canna be a coincidence that yer clans prosper, even in times of strife. Only the Gunns remain foolish enough to ride on any of yer clans. Even when ye are away, nay one dares approach any keep where a Sinclair or Sutherland woman lives. Men dinna want to face yer wives, and to be honest, I think they'd rather face the men of yer clans on a battlefield before confronting the women during a siege. I admire that. That's what I want with Rose. Before meeting her, I thought it was a nice idea to have what all of ye have, but I didna think aboot whether I would try to have it. Now that it seems possible, I canna think of aught else."

Blaine was forthright by nature and saw no point in being otherwise if it weren't strictly necessary for diplomacy. But he'd revealed more of what he thought and how he felt in the short time he'd been at Dunrobin than he had in his entire life. It unnerved him to discuss his emotions and private thoughts amongst any group of men, but he didn't fear these men thinking less of him for it. He wondered if they might respect him more for it.

"Rose is likely in the kitchens at this hour. She told Arabella she'd help preserve the summer fruit." Lachlan grinned. "I may go with ye. See if I can filch aught or at least steal a kiss from ma bonnie bride."

"Just one this time, lad. I expect ye back out in the lists."

"And will ye make it there, too, Da? Or do ye need Mama to look at something in yer chamber again?"

"Wheest, ye cheeky devil. I didna find that funny when ye were a wee stripling, and I dinna find it funny now." However, Hamish's smug expression said otherwise. Like father, like son.

"Ye two are as bad as each other." Hardi shook his head.

"Ye're one to talk. That's ma wee baby sister ye canna stop pawing. It's disgusting." Lachlan scowled, but mirth brightened his dark eyes. "Ma sister is likely with Tira in the orchard."

"Ye dinna need to tell me how to find ma own wife and daughter." Hardi smirked. "Beside I need only walk outside, and Blair will find me."

"I shall tell her ye said that!" Lachlan crowed.

After such a serious conversation that left Blaine feeling exposed, the banter among the men of the family lightened the weight that settled onto his shoulders with the first line of that fateful and dreadful missive. When the men left the solar, Hardi and Hamish went in opposite directions, but Lachlan and Blaine made their way to the kitchen. Just before they reached the door, Lachlan stopped and turned toward Blaine.

"We respect ye for what ye've said aboot Rose and what ye wish for yer future together. I dinna think Callum and Siùsan will disapprove of the match, but I want ye to ken they may nae seem eager. It isnae ye. It's Rose is their first daughter who will leave the clan. They've kenned all along that she and Shona will marry lairds or heirs. It's inevitable as the daughters of the future laird. But that doesnae mean they're ready for it."

Lachlan looked toward the keep's main doors as though he could see his sons in the lists.

"I would never see having a lass as aught less than a blessing, but I willna lie and say I'm nae glad ma lads will never leave Dunrobin. Be patient with Siùsan and Callum. It wasna easy for Alex and Brighde. They should have said all along that dreading their daughter leaving their clan was why they didna support Saoirse and Magnus Óg. But I dinna think they even realized it at first. Siùsan left her clan to join the Sinclairs, so she understands, but that willna make it any easier for her. Callum and his brothers were like lost puppies when Mairghread married Tristan and made Varrich her home. Alex still has a hard time talking aboot Saoirse nae being at Dunbeath anymore. Callum willna be any different. Dinna take it personally if nay one seems as excited as ye hope."

"Thank ye for the warning. Should Rose come with me?"

"Aye. But nay one wants her riding out again, especially nae when we dinna ken where Edgar lurks. If she goes back to Dunbeath, then it would be better if

Thor and Shona went back too. Then ye could have all yer men, all the Sinclairs, and some of our Sutherlands ride with ye. They're an earl's granddaughters and beautiful women. They will be Edgar's targets if he catches sight of them."

"I'll ask Rose what she wants."

"Smart mon. She might make a good husband out of ye after all." Lachlan clapped Blaine on the back, once more lightening the suddenly serious mood. The men went into the kitchens, and Lachlan made directly for Arabella. Blaine averted his eyes when Lachlan wrapped his arms around Arabella and squeezed her backside. With floury hands, she cupped her husband's backside and gave him a smacking kiss. Lachlan twisted, trying to see the handprints left on his plaid. Arabella giggled and shook her head.

"Can we talk again, *leannan*?" Blaine whispered as he moved to stand beside Rose. When she nodded, she grabbed a linen cloth and wiped her hands before she stood on her toes.

"Mayhap one day ye'll be the one with flour on yer arse."

"God, I hope so, lass." Blaine waggled his eyebrows. They left through the kitchen door and stepped into the bright early afternoon sun. Rose led them to the gardens and looked around. Like the last time they sneaked in together, they moved into the darkest shadows. Blaine reached out and spun her around before backing her against the wall. Without hesitation, Rose's arms wrapped around his neck. He pushed his sporran to the outside of his hip before pressing their bodies together. He couldn't help the groan that escaped as his hands settled on Rose's voluptuous backside. When his rod pressed against her mound, he steeled himself not to maul her.

"May I kiss ye, Blaine?" Rose tensed, afraid she'd been too brazen.

"God, I hope so, lass."

"Ye said that already." Rose giggled.

"I've been praying a lot since I met ye." Blaine leaned forward, but before Rose could reach his lips, he paused. "Kyla, ye dinna ever have to ask. I would accept yer kisses and touches anytime if they're freely given."

"But what aboot..."

"Kyla, anytime. I trust ye to ken when it is or isnae appropriate. But ye dinna ever have to ask."

Rose arched her back as she lifted her chin. She had a moment's hesitation about being so bold, but kissing Blaine was all she wanted. Her lips brushed his before she opened to him. The moment their tongues touched, she lost all inhibitions. She channeled her fingers into his short blonde hair as he held her without a hair's breadth between them. It was as though they'd fasted for days and now were offered a feast. Both knew the kiss was without finesse, but neither cared. They're already reassured one another with words when they spoke on the bluff. But this was a soul-deep connection they were forming as they each gave of themselves without reservation. It transcended words as they hinted at the joy they would find when their bodies became one. The silent communication of their willingness to give and their gratitude when they took bonded them. It was several minutes before they pulled away from each other.

"How do ye feel, *leannan*?" Blaine brushed hair from her temple and tucked it behind her ear.

"Better than I did. I'm sorry for being so ridiculous."

Blaine didn't care for the embarrassment and shame he heard in Rose's tone. He drew her against his chest, and he felt her relax as her ear rested over his heart. "Kyla, ye werenae being ridiculous. I dinna want ye to feel badly for it. Aye, we had a misunderstanding, but it also meant we cleared the air. Ye are nae the only one who fears being disappointed if they engage their heart, and they are the only one who does."

Rose leaned back to look up at Blaine. "Do ye fear ye will care aboot me more than I care aboot ye?"

"Aye. I have more experience than ye. I ken enough of life to ken that I havenae ever met a woman like ye. I admire ye, and I ken I dinna want anyone else. I could have married before now, but I never wanted to. I ken what is out there and that I've found someone and something precious. Ye dinna have that experience. What if ye think ye can care for me because ye dinna ken any better? What if ye realize that ye only cared because ye didna ken anyone else? Ye have naught to compare me by."

"So ye only appreciate me because ye believe I'm different from the other women ye've bedded?"

"Nae. I ken many more women than just the ones I've bedded. I'm aulder and I've traveled more. I—"

Rose snorted. "Why do ye think ye've traveled more? Ma family *is* the northern Highlands. I've gone to almost every Highland Gathering since I was born. I've been to the Lowlands and to court. I may nae have bedded a mon, but I ken plenty of them. Even if I hadnae traveled much, think aboot how many men are in ma clan without considering the ones I'm indirectly related to. There are hundreds of Sinclair men across ma family's lands. I ken many of them. Then there are the Sutherland men, the Mackays, the MacLeods of Lewis and of Assynt, the Mackenzies, and the Camerons. Never mind the ones I'm actually related to. I have as many male cousins as I do female. I havenae lived in a nunnery, Blaine. I dinna have to tup a mon to ken what men are like. I'm drawn to ye because ye arenae like the other men I've met. It's like an instinct. I can tell ye the things I admire aboot ye, but there's something more elemental." Rose shrugged. "I dinna have another way to describe it."

Blaine gave a jerky nod, but Rose felt how his arms tightened around her. She arched her back to lean far enough away to see him when he held her close.

"Blaine?"

"I'm nae feeling so magnanimous aboot ye kenning so many men and aboot understanding them."

"Do ye mean ye're jealous?"

"Aye."

Rose waited for him to say more, but Blaine remained silent. She chuckled and squeezed his waist as she settled her head back against his chest. "We are a pair."

"I meant what I said the other day. I willna ever tell ye who ye can and canna be friends with. But that doesnae mean I willna have moments when I feel jealous. I'm nae that type of mon by nature, but I ken I have something precious with ye, Kyla. I willna let ye go without a fight."

"Ye can hold on as long as ye like, *mo ghràdh*. I dinna want to go anywhere."

"As much I wish to kiss and never stop, I need to

talk to ye aboot what ye wish to do. I met with Hamish, Lachlan, and Hardi again. Hamish thinks I should speak to yer father and grandfather, but he advised I wait a couple days before I set off. He will send scouts to see if Edgar is nearby."

"I ken ye should speak to them, but I dinna like the idea of ye riding toward Edgar, wherever he might be."

"And I dinna want to leave ye, so I wondered if ye should come with me to talk to yer family. Lachlan thinks that if ye return to Dunbeath, then Shona and Thor should go, too. That way we can have all ma men, all the Sinclairs, and some Sutherlands with us. But I dinna want to force ye to end yer time here early, and I dinna want to end Shona and Thor's visit either. I can see yer parents and grandda on ma own."

Rose shook her head. "It's nae that I think they would deny ye just because ye went alone. I'd like to be there when ma family learns that I wish to be courted."

"Is that what ye want, Kyla? I ken we only met a short while ago."

"True. But we could have an arranged marriage and meet on the kirk's steps. We arenae saying we'll wed tomorrow. But ye should have ma da's permission to court me. I canna think of aught that would keep him from saying aye, but he'll want to ken it's what I wish."

"Do ye think Thor and Shona are ready to return home?"

"Nay. But they'll understand." Rose offered him a reassuring smile.

"If that's the case, do ye wish to tell both of them?"

"Ye want to speak to Thor, dinna ye? I'll speak to Shona."

"I dinna want yer brother to think I bullied ye into this when we were by the cliffs."

"He doesnae think that. He kens I canna be bullied, and he also kens that if any mon tried, I'd tell him. Then the mon would die. Clearly, ye're vera much still alive." Rose's saucy smile enticed Blaine into another kiss as his hands once more gripped her backside.

"I'd still like to be sure things are right between us. Do ye think Shona will object to me?"

Rose blushed as her lips pressed between her teeth. She shook her head. "Shona's been encouraging me and teasing me aboot ye since ye arrived. I think she'll say it's aboot time."

"Aboot time? It's barely been more than a fortnight."

"Aye, well, she'll tease me aboot dillydallying. It wasna a smooth path for our parents when they met, but it didna take long for them to realize they were meant to be together. Originally, they were an arranged marriage, but by the time they got to the kirk, they wanted to marry each other and had already handfasted. Ma da calls Mama his bonnie Highland temptation even after all these years. Shona will say that there's nay reason to drag our feet if Da could realize Mama was the perfect woman in less than a moon. Da's a wee hardheaded." While they'd hinted at falling in love, Rose was careful not to say her parents had. She didn't want Blaine to feel pressured, nor did she want him to believe she was already in love with him. She wasn't sure what she was, and she wasn't ready to give away anything until she was sure how he felt.

"I'm glad to ken at least one of yer siblings might welcome me."

"Thor will. I dinna have to explain it to him. He'll just understand."

"Because ye're twins?"

"Aye. We ken each other better than we ken ourselves. It's nae like I can read his mind or he mine, but we understand what's important to each other. And we want the best for each other. If I say that's ye, then he'll support us."

"I'd still like to talk to him. If he and Shona are willing to go back to Dunbeath already, we can leave in three days. That should give yer uncle's scouts long enough to tell if Edgar and the Gunns lurk along the way. He also said he would send a missive to King David to lay a path for us. But a letter from yer da and grandda is necessary."

As their gazes locked, time ceased to matter. Now they moved slowly as they came together for another cataclysmic kiss. Blaine's hand slid over Rose's hip, then over her ribs before cupping her breast. She pressed the mound into his palm, her fingers digging into his back when he squeezed, then massaged the ample flesh. Blaine feathered kisses along her jaw and from her collarbone to her ear.

"Lass, I wish to do far more than kiss ye. At least more than kiss just yer lips. I wish to touch ye and bring ye pleasure."

"Blaine, I may never have coupled with a mon, nae even kissed one, but I understand what ye're saying. I ken there is plenty a couple can do without joining."

"Do ye wish to do any of those things with me?" Blaine tried not to squirm as he asked and waited for her answer.

"I wish to do all of those things with ye."

Blaine gathered her skirts in his hands until he could dip them beneath the yards of material and cup the bare skin of her buttocks. He slid his palm down the back of her thighs, using his right hand to hold up her skirts while the left trailed around to the front of the juncture between her legs. His fingers brushed her curls, and she shivered. He wondered what he would find the first time he glimpsed his personal promised land. He inched his fingers lower until he could press them between her thighs. Rose shifted to give him more space, but he was careful to ease his fingers between her dewy netherlips. He pressed the tip of his middle finger into her as his thumb rubbed her pearl.

Rose's breath hitched as she rested her forehead against his chest, focused solely on his hand between her legs. His slow movements soothed her for only a moment before pushing her arousal toward a crescendo. When his lips pressed a kiss behind her ear before he flicked and nipped at her earlobe, she felt her knees wobble. When his warm breath wafted over the shell of her ear, she couldn't help her shiver.

"Does this scare ye, Kyla?"

"Nae at all. Dinna stop, Blaine." She realized she'd been gripping his leine on both sides of his waist. She glided her palms up his chest until she could cup his cheeks. She went up on her toes, bringing her mound against his cock. She felt his rod pulse when her fingernails grazed his scalp. Blaine pressed her back against the wall as he drew her thigh over his hip.

"I would watch ye come apart, kenning I'm the mon ye hold in yer arms."

Rose nodded, at a loss for words until her mind finally fired thoughts that made sense. "I'd like to hold part of ye and give ye the pleasure I'm aboot to feel."

Her suggestion should have shocked Blaine, but she was a Sinclair. Nothing would surprise him. He realized that while Rose may have never done anything, she wasn't without knowledge. He found that intrigued him. That they could share mutual pleasures that were new to her but might not repulse or terrify her.

When Blaine said nothing to her offer, she decided not to take it as a rejection but as a challenge. She knew he mulled over something, but she wouldn't give him the chance to doubt their actions. One hand slid back down over his chest and washboard abdomen before it dove beneath his plaid. He twitched when her hand brushed his length, and he thought he might expire when she wrapped her palm around it. He fought to maintain even an ounce of control when she stroked him. He felt her hesitance, but he appreciated her curiosity and willingness to explore.

"Am I doing it right?" Rose watched Blaine, thinking he enjoyed her ministrations. But his expression was somewhere between agony and ecstasy. She wasn't sure how to interpret it.

"Aye, Kyla. Ye're doing it almost too right. I dinna want to embarrass maself and make ye worry that I'll always finish so fast." He redoubled his efforts as he swirled his thumb over her pearl. His free hand pressed against her bottom and guided her to rock along the thigh he slipped between hers. She rode his leg as she stroked him. Her head fell back with her eyes closed. The long expanse of creamy skin from her chest to her jaw begged for his attention. He grazed his teeth along the slim column of her neck before his tongue flicked along the heated flesh at her entrance. Their mouths fused once more, and he swallowed her scream as her first release tore through her, weakening her knees until she sagged against him. But she was determined not to forget her own task. She worked his cock until she felt it twitch several times, and her hand grew wet.

Blaine rested his forehead against hers as he wiped her hand clean with his plaid. He needed to sort through his rushing thoughts. He felt a tenderness that he'd never experienced with any of his previous partners. He felt physically satisfied in a way he'd never imagined. And what he wanted most was to spend the rest of time watching the magnificent sight that was Rose climaxing in his arms.

Rose's heart continued to race as her overheated and overstimulated body cooled. As Blaine ran his hand up and down her back, she felt her eyes drooping. She laid her head against his chest as she tried to collect herself, but she wanted nothing more than to curl up and go to sleep against him.

"Ye're practically purring like a kitten."

"I feel like one. Ye're warm, and I could curl up against ye like I'm sitting before the hearth."

"I pray one day soon we're curled up together."

"But nae today." Rose sighed and looked in the lists' direction. "I have to speak to Shona, and ye need to find Thor."

"I ken. Just a moment more." Blaine inhaled

Rose's sweet scent of heather and violets. He had never wanted to simply hold a woman before. His mind was constantly abuzz with his duties and each new crisis. Rose's embrace was his sanctuary that he wasn't ready to leave. Neither of them moved until voices drifted far too close.

Chapter Nine

"Thor." Blaine hurried to catch up with Rose's twin as he walked toward the postern gate. He held his leine in his hand, so Blaine suspected the younger man headed to the loch to refresh himself.

"Aye." Thor waited for Blaine to join him. "Have ye been with ma sister?"

Blaine heard the accusatory note, but he ignored it. "We just spoke. She's going to find Shona while I came to find ye."

"Ye spoke? From the expression on yer face, ye did more than just speak. What the devil did ye do to ma sister?"

"What expression?"

"The one a mon wears after he's had his release. What did ye do?"

"How do ye ken I didna just do it maself?"

"Uh-uh. A mon doesnae look that satisfied with his own hand."

"I willna share intimate details aboot Rose and me with anyone. But I didna compromise yer sister. She will be ma wife, and I respect her."

"Ye didna when ye met her." Thor crossed his arms and widened his stance to hip-width apart.

"Do ye wish to have it out, then? I thought ye accepted ma misunderstanding, and we'd moved on."

"We had until I see ye looking like a mon who's just tupped a woman. I ken ye have the good sense nae to look elsewhere while ye're here, but I dinna think ye have the good sense to keep yer hands to yerself."

"Look elsewhere? Thor, I hope vera soon that ye will be ma brother. I dinna have any, and I respect ye. But let me be vera clear. I made an arse of maself thinking I might have a tumble with a woman I thought was a maid. Since then, I've gotten to ken Rose, and I admire her for more than her beauty. I have nay need nor desire for any other woman. The thought of breaking her trust, the pain I saw in her eyes when she thought I'd lied to her—I never want to see that again. I want to be a mon she can love and willna regret marrying."

"Ye assume ma da will say aye."

"Are ye going to tell him he shouldnae?" Blaine crossed his arms too. While he was an intimidating size, he didn't have the same *je ne sais quoi* about his posture that the Sinclairs had. It didn't strike fear into Thor's heart like Thor's threatening demeanor did to anyone who saw him. Blaine would never admit it, but he feared marrying into a family of men who were just like Thor.

"For ma sister's sake, I willna speak against ye. But I will kill ye if ye hurt her. I'll be sure I'm at the front of a vera long line of angry men."

"The last thing I want to do is that. I asked Rose if she wishes me to go to Dunbeath alone to speak to yer parents. She'd rather come too. She wants to tell yer parents in person that she wishes for me to court her. Lachlan believes it would be best if everyone travels together, so that means ye and Shona would return too. Rose and I want to be sure ye and Shona are all right with that. I dinna want to cut yer visit short, but if we travel together, then all ma men, all yer men, and some Sutherlands can protect Rose and Shona."

"Why do ye call her Kyla?"

Blaine was unprepared for the drastic shift. "We both come from large clans, and if she becomes ma wife and Lady Keith, there will be plenty of people always vying for our attention. It's something that we can share with nay one else. It's something special."

"Why doesnae she call ye something besides Blaine?"

"She said she likes the name."

"So ye dinna like Rose?"

"I didna say that. I merely want something that can be private and shared only with ma wife."

"And that's important to ye?"

"Vera."

"Then I'm ready to return to Dunbeath." Thor grinned at Blaine. "Ye dinna understand why I asked ye all of that."

"I dinna."

"Da will expect ye to explain why ye wish to court ma sister. Ye didna say it outright, but it's obvious ye nae only think ma sister is special. Ye wish to show that ye will set her apart from everyone else. Ye will make her a priority. If ye didna care and thought she was nay more important than any other woman in yer clan, having something that's just between the two of ye wouldnae matter so much."

"I suppose I should say thank ye."

"Aye. That'll do. When do ye wish to ride out?"

"Three days. Hamish will send scouts to ensure Edgar isnae lingering in the area. Then we'll travel to Dunbeath." Blaine looked north toward Dunbeath. "Do ye think yer da and grandda will react as well to the news aboot Greer as Hamish did?"

"They willna care so much aboot it being Greer as they will aboot Rose sneaking away. Unlike each Gunn laird, we dinna hold our grudge against those in the clan who canna decide. It's against the lairds who continue to harass us. Ma great-grandda didna take issue when his son, Daniel, fell in love with Ceana Gunn, despite their rivalry. The woman didna control her brothers. Greer has nay control over her father. But it will alarm ma parents Rose has put herself in danger so many times. Their pride will be just as strong, but their fear will be louder."

"I ken the Sinclairs' reputation, but tell me the truth, Thor. Do I need to worry that yer father will mistreat her when he punishes her?"

Thor observed the concern written on Blaine's face and the resolve in his gaze. He would let no man harm Rose, be it her father, brother, or a stranger. "Ye willna have to step between them. Mama might have her cleaning garderobes until ye leave, but nay one will strike her."

"Will anyone disavow her for being friends with Greer? Anyone from yer clan?"

"I wouldnae go that far, but they may nae agree with it. But that doesnae need to go beyond the laird's family."

Blaine's shoulders lowered, and he realized how poised he'd been to go on the defensive. As the tension eased from his body, he understood he would have done anything to protect and defend Rose. Not that he thought she couldn't manage her family on her own. He simply didn't want her to have to. He would shield her if he needed to.

"Let me refresh maself, then we can see if Rose made any progress with Shona. Ma little sister is a wee hellion who gets away with murder here. She isnae interested in going home where Mama is far stricter than Auntie Amelia or Arabella."

"Neither of them strikes me as being indulgent."

"They arenae, but Shona isnae their daughter, and she kens it. She doesnae take advantage, but she also doesnae keep completely out of trouble." Thor led the way to the loch, where other men had already arrived to get clean before entering the Great Hall for the midday meal. "Mama can throw knives just as well as Auntie Mairghread, but she isnae competitive in the same way because Mama doesnae have four aulder brothers. Even though it was her brothers, Seamus and Magnus Óg, who taught her, they're younger. Rose and Shona ken how to wield them and throw them because Mama taught them. Rose is like Mama and is content to ken she can defend herself. Shona is competitive, like Auntie Mairghread. She doesnae mind showing up the lads and then having a good laugh with the other lasses. She and Rose both love to ride far too fast and are far too daring, but unlike Rose, Shona doesnae care for ma tender feelings when I tell her I fear she'll break her bluidy neck. Auntie Amelia willna let her ride out far enough to cause trouble. Mama willna let her ride out, and when Shona tries to, she winds up with the laundresses for a fortnight."

"Ye ken one day a mon will fall in love with that wild streak."

"God help us all." Thor knelt beside the water's edge and ran a bar of soap over his torso before dunking his head. Cleaner than before, he allowed the sun to dry him as they walked back to the keep. Shona and Rose met them at the bottom of the steps.

"Ye missed a spot." Shona waved her hand up and down toward Thor's torso. She grinned at her brother before turning a more serious mien to Blaine. "Ye wish for us to all return home in three days. Rose says ye're worried I willna wish to end our visit so soon. Dinna fash. I look forward to Mama and Da realizing Rose is all grown up. A wedding will keep Mama's attention on Rose and nae me."

Blaine looked at Thor, who smirked and shrugged. Shona was a wee hellion, and Blaine didn't envy the man who fell in love with her. He prayed the man would never try to change her, but he hoped the man might also slow her down. He foresaw battles of will, but he could also recognize that streak in Shona would make her a fine laird's wife who could manage a keep when her husband was away.

"So ye can be ready to leave in three days?" Blaine asked.

"Aye. None of us have much to pack."

"Thank ye for understanding." Blaine turned to Rose and nodded. He knew she wondered if things had gone as smoothly with Thor as they now did with Shona. When Rose smiled, it was as though he'd emerged from a dark tunnel. She shifted closer to him, so he wrapped her arm around his. He wanted nothing more than to wrap his arm around her waist, but they were in a far too busy area for him to do that when they weren't even betrothed.

"Hopefully, naught happens between now and when we can leave. I wasna ready to go home a fortnight ago, but now I look forward to seeing our family." Rose rested her free hand on his forearm. "I ken ye've met Grandda and Da before, but I ken ye dinna ken each other well. I think ye'll remind them of Wee Liam, which will reassure them. Ye'll fit it in just fine."

Blaine prayed she was right.

Lachlan and Arabella set sail for Orkney with Tira, and their sons, Dougal and Finian, the next morning. At the same time, another boat pushed away from the shore, bound for Edinburgh with a message on its way to the king in France. The keep felt quiet with five fewer people, but Rose and Blaine knew people talked more about them every day. It seemed many people already considered them as good as betrothed. Neither admitted how much that pleased them.

Three days after the disastrous missive and his conversations with the men in Rose's family, he set off north with his men and a full contingent of Sinclair and Sutherland guards. Since they headed to Dunbeath, Thor led the party while the women rode in the center. Blaine was torn between taking his place beside Thor and riding beside Rose. Finally, he opted to ride toward the rear, where he could be a shield to Rose if anyone approached from behind. He could see her and easily pull her onto his horse if anyone approached from another direction.

They set off at dawn, so it relieved him to see the keep come into view midafternoon. The bells rang as they entered the village. Five heads of chestnut hair appeared on the battlements next to the portcullis. Thor, Rose, and Shona waved to their family, and Blaine inhaled a fortifying breath. When they rode into the bailey, four stunningly attractive women walked down the steps together. The strawberry-blonde hair made it easy to recognize Siùsan. Blaine knew the woman with white-blonde hair was Brighde, Alex's wife. The woman with honey-colored spiral curls was Magnus's wife, Deirdre. The woman with the light brown hair was already wagging her finger and winking at a man jumping down the last five steps from the wall walk. He knew that must be Ceit since Tavish made his way directly to her and whispered something in her ear that made her grin and nod.

"Mama, Da!" Rose pulled her horse to a stop and swung her leg over the saddle. Blaine hurried to dismount and help her from her horse, but an older man with gray hair at his temples raised his arms and lifted her down. Blaine hung back, realizing it was just as well that Callum assisted Rose. He would have made a scene that might not garner him a warm welcome.

"Ye're de Keith's son, arenae ye?"

Blaine turned toward a deep baritone voice. He knew immediately that he stood before Laird Liam Sinclair, the Earl of Caithness. It was the title the laird had gained when he became the Earl of Sinclair *and* the Earl of Orkney. If he weren't standing close enough to see the lines around the man's mouth and eyes were slightly deeper than Callum's, he could have sworn Liam was a fifth brother, not Callum and the other men's father.

"Aye, ma laird."

"What brings ye here? Dinna tell me Edgar is causing trouble again."

"That's part of it."

"Grandda, mayhap Blaine could dismiss his men, and we could visit with ye and Mama and Da in yer solar." Rose walked over with her parents. From the corner of his eye, he watched the four brothers tense. Within a synchronized heartbeat, Liam, Callum, Alex, Tavish, and Magnus stood with their arms crossed and feet hip-width apart.

Bluidy fucking hell.

Blaine plastered a smile on his face and nodded before he turned to his men and told them to find the captain of the guard to request bunks in the barracks. When he turned back, the four women stood beside their husbands, trying not to laugh. Shona rolled her eyes before she embraced her parents and hurried into the keep, calling to another young woman ahead of her. Thor clapped Blaine on the shoulder and squeezed. When he winked, Blaine knew it was more out of support than anything else. It was a silent wish that things go well. However, it hardly reassured him that Thor felt the need to offer it.

"Are ye handfasted?" Callum didn't budge as the others turned toward the keep.

"Nay, Da." Rose shook her head. That only made Callum narrow his eyes and take a menacing step forward.

"Should ye be?"

"Da!"

"Nay. I havenae done aught to shame Lady Rose.

I never would. But ye've made it clear there isnae much point in playing bashful. I came for several reasons, Edgar included, but the most important one is to ask if I may court Lady Rose."

"Court?" Callum huffed. "I dinna think ye're asking that. I think ye're ready to ask for Rose's hand."

"We are still deciding if we suit. Until Lady Rose tells me she wishes for me to propose, I am nae asking for aught but yer permission to spend time with Lady Rose."

"Da, can we please do this in private? I dinna wish for the entire clan to hear what's happening until ye have." Rose's imploring gaze made Siùsan nudge her husband. Callum glanced at Liam before looking at his brothers. Finally, he nodded. Everyone but Thor turned toward the keep. Rose and Blaine already stood apart from one another, but without a word, Callum, Tavish, Alex, and Magnus moved to form a circle around Blaine.

This isnae fucking intimidating at all. I get their message. I doubt I'll have a minute alone with Rose until our wedding night, and that assumes she doesnae change her mind now that she's home. Mayhap she willna wish to leave Dunbeath and her family. Mayhap she'll realize she doesnae want me when she compares me with her relatives.

Blaine couldn't look over Alex's head, and he didn't dare lean forward or backward to see Rose, so he kept his eyes forward. Callum walked in front of Blaine, with Siùsan to his right, and led the group alongside Liam. The other wives walked in a group with Rose. The women chatted quietly, but none of the men spoke. Blaine grew irritated rather than nervous. He understood what the men did was intuitive to them, but he didn't appreciate it. He didn't want any of the Sinclairs to believe they could easily cow him, so he kept his chin up and shoulders back.

Much like with Thor, Blaine was the same size as the brothers, and he had a similar build to Callum and Alex. Tavish shared Liam's more barrel-chested physique, and Magnus was simply a mountain. But all the men were the same height—Magnus a hair's breadth taller than the others. They all possessed the same broad shoulders, but Blaine's build was leaner than the Sinclair men, so he knew they each likely weighed at least a stone more than him. The only man Blaine knew who truly rivaled any of the Sinclairs was Laird Brodie Campbell. He was a bear of a man. The only one in the group who didn't seem intent upon isolating Blaine was Liam. The man didn't need to try to intimidate anyone. He *just was* intimidating—a legend on and off the battlefield.

Chapter Ten

Blaine soon realized that everyone intended to enter Liam's solar. That was the last thing he wanted. As people took seats around the enormous oblong wood table in the center of the chamber, Rose slid next to Blaine. He pulled out a chair for her, then took the one next to it.

"Grandda, Da, Blaine has much to discuss with ye aboot the Murrays, Irvines, and Gunns. *Then* we will talk to ye and Mama." Rose's whisky-brown eyes locked with Callum's, the challenge ringing in the air. Her father nodded before turning his attention to Blaine, who waited for Liam to speak. When the older man didn't, Blaine assumed it meant he had permission to address the group.

"The Murrays continue to harass us. They canna accept their victory graciously. They ken that victory was their one moment of glory. They willna succeed again and havenae before that lone time. I rode to Dunrobin to see Laird Cameron. It was ma hope he could mediate and prevent a war between the Murrays and Keiths. During that time, the Gunns raided a Keith village. I spoke to Laird

Sutherland, Laird Cameron, and Lachlan aboot it. I planned to return home, but other events got in the way. I still must act against the Gunns, and we resolved naught with the Murrays. The Cameron sent a messenger to discover whether the Murrays would be open to mediation, but the mon hadnae returned before we left."

"And ye felt it too dangerous for ma grandchildren to travel without the extra guards?" Liam sat back in his chair, appearing relaxed. But Blaine knew the man watched him like a hawk. Inevitably, he would have to mention courting Rose, but he didn't want that to be the focus of this conversation.

"It is dangerous, but I dinna doubt the Sinclair and Sutherland guards could easily vanquish anyone so daft as to attack them. I intended to speak to Callum and Lady Siùsan, so I asked Lady Rose if she wished to be here, and she does." Blaine shifted his focus to Rose, who looked up at him. He saw the trepidation in her eyes, but she nodded. "Lady Rose also has information aboot the Gunns that ye all need to ken. She may vera well be able to help us end this before it escalates further. I offered to be with her when ye discussed it."

"Ye wished to ask if ye could court her." Siùsan observed the couple. Except for Rose's brown eyes, it was like looking at her own reflection. Her daughter had always reminded Siùsan of herself, but even more so now. She knew she shared the same private communication with Callum as she witnessed between Rose and Blaine. "Ye talk aboot wanting to ken if ye will suit, yet ye look to her for permission to share her news, and she looks to ye for reassurance. Rose, if ye wish for Blaine to tell us what ye ken, then we'll all listen. But I dinna want ye to fear telling us what's happened."

Blaine shifted, so his shoulder brushed against Rose's. He peered down at her as her teeth bit into the underside of her lip. He recognized it as her nervous habit. He longed for nothing more than to pull her into his embrace and give her the reassurance she sought. But he couldn't even hold her hand.

"Da, Grandda, ye ken the missives ye receive just before something happens with the Gunns? Those are from me." Rose waited, but no one appeared surprised. Her brow furrowed. "Ye already kenned that."

Callum's expression softened as he looked at his daughter instead of Blaine. "Rose, we've kenned from the beginning. But we didna say aught because it was obvious ye didna want us to ken. We werenae sure at first if ye acted alone or if someone gave ye the information, and ye wrote it down. I recognized yer script."

Liam leaned forward. "A guard noticed Henry leaving with a woman two nights in a row aboot a year ago, and that's when we realized ye werenae just the scribe. Ye kept us in the dark aboot that for two years. But when ye sneaked out a third time a sennight later, I followed."

Liam watched his granddaughter, and it was like he saw his long-deceased wife. While Rose looked like her mother, Liam felt so much of Kyla's spirit in her. His heart never recovered losing his soulmate, but he found solace in Kyla's spirit being in all of his grandchildren. He knew his one great love was still with them. He smiled at Rose as he continued.

"I recognized Lady Greer immediately. It terrified me that a Gunn followed her like I had with ye. I rode a wide arc around half the loch, keeping ye within view. I ken Henry was never beyond arm's reach. Once I was certain ye were safe, I remained in the trees and watched. Ye embraced each other like sisters at the beginning and end of yer conversation, so it was obvious ye are close friends. Ye rode past me, even though ye didna see me. I witnessed the sadness ye felt having so little time with Greer. But I also saw worry, then resolve. I kenned ye must have discussed something serious."

"Did ye always follow me?" Rose wasn't certain how to she felt about that secret coming to light, but she couldn't fault someone following her, then not telling her. She'd kept this secret from her family for years.

"Nay. Neither did anyone else. Yer da, uncles, and I took turns being on watch the nights we kenned ye left. It didna take long to learn yer routine and estimate how long ye would be away. As long as naught changed, and as long as we kenned ye didna go farther than the loch that separates our territories, we let ye have time with yer friend."

"How'd ye ken that we didna go beyond the loch or somewhere else?" Rose swept her gaze over the rest of the family. No one appeared surprised by any of this. Her temper flared, but she reminded herself that she was an enormous hypocrite for being offended that they kept something from her.

"As I said, ye had a routine. Ye couldnae have ridden farther and been back at the same time each night ye sneaked out." Liam reached out his hand to Rose, who sat beside him. He squeezed it once she slid her much smaller one into his.

"Keith, how'd ye ken aboot this? Did Rose tell ye?" Alex was the second oldest brother, and the most reserved. He observed and assessed people before he spoke, rarely giving away any of his thoughts, and only when he wished.

"I planned to ask Lady Rose's counsel on a matter. I saw her slip out to the bailey and leave on horseback with a mon. I admit ma jealousy. I followed her, keeping a distance to nae draw attention. I discovered her talking to Lady Greer."

Rose took over the explanation while still holding Liam's hand but shifting her gaze to Blaine. "I explained how Greer and I met at a Highland Gathering when we were ten summers. We became friends and would sneak away each year. I told him how three years ago, Greer started sharing information aboot her father's plans. She doesnae agree with him and how he runs their clan. She fears he will do far more harm than good for their people. She wishes to prevent any of our family from slaughtering hers."

"Lass, ye sneaked nay where. I kenned where ma children were." Siùsan cocked an eyebrow. "Greer isnae her father or any of the other worthless men in her family. Ye had fun together, and I kenned she had few friends. It was obvious. I was proud of ye for seeing her for who she is. Nae the name she carries. I am nae pleased with ye thinking ye could deceive us. I understand why, and I agreed with yer da to allow it. But now that it isnae a secret, ye and I shall find ye a few garderobes."

Rose looked over at Blaine, who tried not to laugh. Thor shared his prediction while they rode home. She looked back at her mother and nodded. "Thor warned me."

"Dinna ye worry. I have a bone to pick with yer

brother aboot a couple jugs of summer ale I canna find. He'll be peeling vegetables until it snows."

"What is yer latest news?" Tavish asked. The most laidback of the brothers, his arm appeared to drape lazily around Ceit's shoulders, but it fooled no one into thinking he wasn't attentive and astute.

Once again, Rose peered at Blaine, but this time it was Blaine who nodded his chin in encouragement. Rose was certain she heard a soft sigh of resignation from Callum.

"Greer learned the attack on the Keiths willna be an isolated incident. Laird Gunn plans to attack either the Mackays, Sutherlands, or us. Greer believes it'll be the Mackays first, so Uncle Hamish sent Lachlan, Arabella, and the others to Orkney to find Uncle Tristan and Auntie Mairghread and warn them. He also sent a messenger to Wee Liam." There was nothing "wee" about the oldest grandchild, but the family gave him the moniker as an infant to prevent confusion between him and his namesake, Laird Liam Sinclair. "The Gunn thinks he can lure the Mackays from Varrich and bring the Sutherlands and us to their defense. Once men leave all the keeps, he'll attack someone else. He thinks he can move from one castle to another, always ahead of ye. He wishes for ye to chase him, so he can raid with nay one stopping him."

"Daft bastard," Callum muttered.

"That's what Greer and I think. She doesnae understand how her father believes he can attack our family while any of the lairds would keep the castles unprotected. Everyone kens the Mackays, Sutherlands, and Sinclairs can ride out with full armies and still leave an army behind to defend our homes." Rose shook her head and shrugged. The idea was utterly ludicrous to her, and from the expression on everyone else's faces, they felt the same. However, that did nothing to stop Edgar from attempting his plan.

"Does Greer ken when Edgar intends to launch his first attack?" Magnus drummed the fingers of his right hand on the table while he held Deirdre's hand with his left. Rose could see how they took turns running their thumbs over each other's hands. It appeared synchronized after more than two decades.

"Nay, she doesnae. I hope the next time I meet her, she kens."

"Nay." Callum's piercing brown eyes bore into Rose. "Ye're nae riding out while Edgar is roaming our lands. It's too great a risk that he will stumble upon ye and Greer. Ye'll both be dead."

"How are we to get any information aboot his plans if I dinna see Greer? We arenae sending someone else in ma place. She willna trust anyone else, and if the Gunn did see her with anyone but me, he would most certainly believe she's a traitor. There's a slim possibility he might think we're merely foolish lasses."

"Ye absolutely arenae riding out, Rose. It isnae open for discussion. And if I must station guards outside yer door and under yer window, then I will." Callum crossed his arms as he sat back in his chair. It was clear the man was used to issuing orders, and his demeanor spoke of a man who would one day lead a powerful clan. Rose glanced at her mother, but she knew Siùsan would side with Callum. Not just because they were married, but because she was no more willing that Rose should endanger herself than Callum was.

"I will ride out with Lady Rose," Blaine inter-jected. "Lady Greer met me the last time she had a rendezvous with Lady Rose. We bring half a dozen Sinclair men who remain in the trees like Laird Sinclair did when he followed Rose. They're nearby if we need them, but nae obvious. Anyone who sees me with Lady Rose will ken she isnae as vulnerable as they thought."

"Ye dinna get to decide aught." Callum glared at the younger man. He would admit it aloud to no one but Siùsan, but the notion that his oldest child was ready to marry and leave their home hurt. He'd known since the day his twins were born that Rose would one day leave Dunbeath and likely marry a laird or an heir. It had been the only moment of sadness that day, but it had grown no easier to accept as Rose grew into womanhood. Now the time had arrived, and Callum would hold on to the remaining days with a death grip. He'd met Blaine before and knew the young tánaiste by reputation. He had no reason to doubt Blaine would make some woman an excellent husband. He was just unconvinced that Blaine—or any man—would ever make a good enough husband for Rose or Shona.

"I think it's time Blaine and I spoke to Grandda and ma parents alone." Rose glared back at her father. She would never disobey him, but she wouldn't let her father deter her. She understood she had to prove to her family—even if they never demanded that she did—that she had the gumption to one day help lead a clan. It was the only way they would agree she could leave Dunbeath with a husband. Right now, that meant standing up to her obstinate father. But she understood behind her father's resistance was a heart that beat for Callum's family. They were everything to him, and he would defend every member, but particularly his wife and children, to his very last breath.

She understood the idea that she would become another man's responsibility was something both her parents would need time to accept. Her heart ached, knowing that if she and Blaine married, she would go months, if not years, without seeing her family. She knew her parents were acutely aware of the same, and her father was doing his best to keep his wee lass his for as long as he could.

"We look forward to hearing aboot yer visit at the evening meal. Tavish, I need help with something." Ceit rose, and her sisters-by-marriage followed suit. Their husbands wrapped their arms around their wives' waists and silently filed out of the solar. No one spoke until the door closed.

"Laird Sinclair, Callum, Lady Siùsan, ye ken I wish to court Lady Rose. I hope ye allow me the chance to prove to ye that ma intentions are true, and that Lady Rose is vera special to me. If ye dinna want Lady Rose to only ride out with me, then someone else comes, too. But I am nae remaining here and waving goodbye. Ma mind understands any Sinclair warrior will protect her to his death, but ma heart willna be at peace if I dinna see it for maself." Blaine prayed he didn't sound like a fool making such a declaration. He perceived the fine line he stood upon that separated good intentions and sounding like a lovesick pup. He didn't wish to come across as though he issued anyone orders, but he also wouldn't back down. He kept his gaze locked with Callum's as he spoke.

"I will ride out with ma daughter."

"Ye can, Da. But ye willna be with me when I

meet Greer. Ye will scare her, and she will feel betrayed. Even if she understands, ye dinna exactly carry a welcoming air aboot ye. One look at ye, and she will think ye're judging her. Greer kens how our family is. I ken she longs to have what I do. But, because she doesnae, she canna understand, in truth, why ye would never harm her but canna remain behind. Please, Da. Even if I never gain another piece of information from her, I love her nearly as much as I do Shona. She's a kind and brave woman, but she's one who's spent her life being mistreated. She doesnae need to face a warrior who looks like the Devil on horseback."

"And ye believe she'd accept Blaine riding with ye. Why?"

"For starters, just the fact Blaine is blond and doesnae scowl at everyone who isnae family. He doesnae look like he's riding to kill anyone in his path. I dinna doubt he could, and I feel as safe with him as I do with ye or Grandda or any of ma uncles. She also kens that I wish Blaine to court me and that since he's still trying to earn ma hand, he's less likely to kill, then ask questions."

"Ye think I would kill yer friend, a lass?" Callum sat aghast.

"Nay. I ken ye wouldnae. But that's what I mean. Greer kens the Sinclair men dinna harm women. But that doesnae mean after a lifetime of her father threatening and bullying her, she willna fear ye. She kens how her father acts. She will likely always fear that any father could treat his daughter as Laird Gunn treats her."

"Rose, just how bad is it for Greer?" Siùsan's voice remained even, but her family knew the simmering rage that brewed beneath the surface. Her father disowned her for the first ten years of her life, despite her being his legitimate child. He blamed her for her mother's death during childbirth. He resented that his father forced him into a second marriage to Edgar's aunt, Lady Elizabeth Gunn, eventually making her Lady Mackenzie. When he finally acknowledged Siùsan and allowed her to move into the keep with his wife and two sons by his second wife, he treated her as a servant. He was oblivious to how James Gunn obsessed over her and eventually attacked her.

She'd come to terms with her father years ago, and she'd broken all ties to him when she married Callum. He died several months ago, and her younger brother, Seamus, was now the laird. But she would always be protective of anyone, particularly a woman, with a father who mistreated them. Rose appreciated her mother's protectiveness, and she knew Siùsan would talk to Callum later and remind him Greer was no more the enemy that she'd been when she arrived to marry Callum. But Rose also knew her mother was likely to ride into battle to slay any man who mistreated her children. On second thought, Rose didn't doubt her mother could sneak into any keep and into any bed chamber to kill a man where he lay. She'd wake him just before she plunged her dirk into him.

"Nae as bad as ye had it, but he yells at her a lot when he isnae ignoring her. He's struck her a few times." Rose shifted her gaze to her grandfather. It wasn't a secret that her grandmother arrived to marry Liam with lingering bruises from her abusive father. She'd spent a lifetime on the receiving end of her father's hand and belt. Liam didn't ride into every battle

141

these days, but he'd ridden out more than once in the past two years. Her father and uncles gained their intimidating bearing from Liam's training over the years. What hadn't been nurtured was nature. No one doubted Liam would join this fight if it meant ending someone's suffering that mirrored his beloved Kyla's.

"Rose, ye and Blaine will arrange another meeting with Greer." Liam decided for everyone. "I will send scouts out the day of, and if there's even a hint that Edgar is nearby, yer da, uncles, and I will ride along. We will fan out around the loch. We will have other men with us, but they will remain half a league away. If there's nay reason to believe Edgar or any Gunn could attack, Blaine and Henry will accompany ye to yer meeting place. Half a dozen men will remain in the trees on our land. Ye dinna cross into Gunn territory, Rose. Even if that means ye canna embrace Greer, ye dinna give any reason for Edgar to cry foul."

"Aye, Grandda." Rose smiled at the man who'd carried her on his shoulders. When his grandchildren were very little, they would hang from the mountainous man's arms and wrap themselves around his legs as he stomped around the Great Hall as though he were the monster they wrangled. She could remember how she would squeal with laughter and cling to him until they would all collapse near the hearth, and he would tell stories until they were nearly all asleep. "Can ye live with that, Da?"

Everyone knew Callum would normally never gainsay Liam's edict, but everyone also knew Liam would always respect his children's right to parent as they saw fit.

"I can live with that. I wish to speak to Blaine

alone. Dinna fash, lass. He'll survive with nae a scratch nor hair out of place."

Rose darted her eyes to her mother, whose nod was nearly imperceptible. Liam rose, and Siùsan followed. As she came around the table, she stopped behind Rose's chair and leaned forward to kiss her daughter's temple. "Ye can come with me, and we'll decide where ye'll start cleaning." Siùsan squeezed Rose's shoulders with a chuckle.

Chapter Eleven

Once Blaine and Callum sat across from one another in the otherwise empty solar, the two men assessed each other. After a stare-off that lasted only a minute, Callum relented.

"Ye havenae kenned Rose long, but I can see as easily as anyone else that ye care for her. Ye havenae relaxed once since Rose began defending ye and yer wish to court her. I ken ye dinna fear I'll ever harm ma daughter, but ye dinna like her being at odds with her family. It's clear ye're ready to come to her side. It doesnae take having the gift of second sight to understand ye'll marry, whether it's only at the kirk or with a handfast to start. Why?"

"Yer daughter is undeniably beautiful. I admit that's what I noticed first, but I thought she was a servant because she wore a St. Birgitta's cap. Ma thoughts were nay ones to have aboot a maiden. I willna hide that from ye because if ye're going to learn aboot ma misperception, then I would have it be from me. We didna start off well since she thought I only wished to tup her, even once I learned she was a lady. I believe I've proved to her that, while I find her beautiful, I wish to marry her for more than a tumble. I watched how people love her, and how big-hearted she is to everyone she kens. She works harder than most people I've seen. But I admire her most when she asserts herself."

Blaine paused for a breath to consider whether what he said would snooker his chances or bolster his explanation.

"Before I met Lady Rose, I never gave much thought to the woman who would become ma wife. I kenned I would marry eventually, but I hadnae met anyone I wished to pursue or ask ma father to arrange a match with. Lady Rose is a woman whose advice and counsel I already seek, and I dinna doubt that she is the Lady Keith ma clan needs and deserves. Watching and listening to her today confirms she's meant to be a clan's lady. She can manage a keep full of servants, and she will defend her clan to her last breath. I dinna fear anyone will think our clan and our home are vulnerable when I ride out. I wish to marry yer daughter."

"Our. Ye sound certain she will ask ye to propose or that she'll say aye when ye do."

"I am hopeful. I think she'll accept when the time comes, but I dinna want to rush her. She kens how I feel, and I will wait until she's ready."

"And if ye must go home before then?"

"Then I will return as soon as I can. If we must exchange missives in the meantime, then we will."

"Ma Rose is exactly as ye describe her. I could tell how much ye wished to touch each other, even if only to brush against each other. I've never seen her act that way around anyone, much less a mon. She trusts ye, which makes me want to trust ye. I ken yer reputation. There are many who believe ye'll be a finer leader than yer father. I understand why people predict that. I wish to see ye together for a while longer before I consent. If ye wed and ye find ye canna treat her as ye promise, if ye'd both be better setting her aside, bring her back to Dunbeath. If I ever find out she's miserable with ye and forced to stay, she'll set ye aside, and I'll set ye in a grave."

"I understand, Callum. But there is a matter that complicates this. I'd hoped Lady Rose and Lady Siùsan would be with us, and preferably Laird Sinclair, too. Can we ask them to come back?"

"What kind of matter?"

"A matter ma father arranged without ma knowledge or agreement, and the kind the king agreed to." Blaine's grim expression made his implied meaning clear. Callum nodded and went to the door. He spoke to a servant quietly, then went to fill several mugs with drams of Sinclair whisky.

It wasn't long before Rose, Siùsan, and Liam returned. When Rose stepped inside the solar, she went to Blaine's side as he stood. Her questioning gaze broke Blaine's willpower to keep from touching her. He took her hand in his and covered it with his free one. He gave it a quick squeeze before he forced himself to let go. But Rose wasn't ready for them to separate. She entwined their fingers and stepped closer to him.

"Did things go badly?" Rose whispered.

"Nay, lass. He agreed to let me court ye. But I wanted both yer parents and grandda to be here when I explained the problem with the Irvines."

Rose inhaled deeply and was slow to release the breath. She'd wondered when the matter would come up. She wanted to be present for the conversation, but she assumed that once she left the solar, it would take place without her. She twisted to see Liam and her parents, who watched them intently. She released Blaine's hand when he moved to pull out her chair once more. He adjusted his, so it touched hers. Since no one objected, he took Rose's hand again.

"As if the matters with the Murrays and Gunns werenae bad enough, a missive arrived from the king just before I planned to ride here to ask yer permission. I received a command to marry Lady Eliza Irvine. I ken the woman, and there couldnae be a poorer choice to become ma wife. The woman isnae suited to be the lady of any clan, even if her mother supposedly trained her. I ken ma father maneuvered this for the alliance. I'm certain he believes that nae only will it end our sporadic hostilities with them, it will deter the Murrays from continuing to bait us. Once ma father learns of the Gunns' attack, it will further convince him that an alliance with the Irvines is for the best. He's willing to overlook what Eliza will likely do to our clan for the opportunity to gain her father's support. Except, we'll be bankrupt and have naught to defend if she becomes Lady Keith. Ma mother has been dead for more than a decade. Even though ma father is fit and will probably live for at least another two score, she would be in charge of the keep and all household accounts. He will regret the decision, but I'll be the one at Ackergill sorting out the mess."

"Ye come here and tell us ye wish to court ma granddaughter, *then* ye tell us ye're already betrothed. How am I supposed to consider ye honorable when I learn of this duplicity?" Liam's tone remained mild, as though he truly wished to understand.

"Laird, I'd already made ma intentions kenned to Lady Rose when the missive arrived. It wasna much of a secret by then. Laird Sutherland, Lady Sutherland, Laird Cameron, Lady Cameron, Lachlan, Arabella, Shona, and Thor all kenned ma interest in Lady Rose. I think half of Clan Sutherland kenned, too. The missive directed me to sign the contracts and return them to the Irvines within a sennight. That was four days ago. Laird Sutherland has already dispatched a messenger to the king advising against the match. But he rightly said missives from the Earl of Caithness and the Clan Sinclair's tánaiste would be more influential since ye're Lady Rose's laird, and ye're her father. He believes they will carry more weight. I'd like to think the alliance would please ma father, and that he'd see the benefits to allying with the Sinclairs and yer extended ties. But I canna be certain."

"And once we're allied, what will ye expect of us? What will yer father expect?"

"Likely more than I will. I still hope Laird Cameron hears from the Murrays that they're amenable to Laird Cameron mediating a peace between our clans. He's already pledged to support ma clan if he canna talk the Murray into abandoning his mission. I think the Camerons' support will be enough to either deter or defeat the Murrays. Kenning the Sinclairs, Sutherlands, Mackays, Mackenzies, and the MacLeods of Assynt and of Lewis might also ride to our aid is likely to keep anyone from even sniffing in our direction. I wouldnae ask ye to bring men to fight unless I truly need them.

We've done well defending ourselves in the past and will in the future. I asked Laird Cameron's help because I desire naught more than to avoid further bloodshed. I dinna want to lose another mon to prove ma point."

"As yer father-by-marriage, ye ken I would lead men to yer defense for nay other reason than to ensure Rose's safety. Are ye so certain of yer victory that ye wouldnae accept ma offer?"

"I would be the world's greatest fool ever to decline the Sinclairs' support. But I am nae asking to court, then marry, Lady Rose for yer army. Lady Rose could be from a tiny sept of a tiny branch of a tiny clan, and I would still wish to marry her. Ma clan doesnae live in constant conflict, but I do wish for a strong partner to help keep it that way." Blaine would repeat the same verse over and over until he turned blue, but he was growing tired of explaining why he wished to marry Rose. He kenned the reasons were obvious to him and everyone else, and he understood her family wished to be certain he knew them, but he didn't want to have to keep justifying his interest.

"So ye wish for me to send a missive, telling the king to change his mind." Liam cocked an eyebrow and grinned.

"Laird Cameron explained yer family connection. I believe ye could be of greater influence than ma father. I canna deny the convenience that brings to ma wish to marry Lady Rose. But I would hope the king would see the merits of the match without ye being his godfather. While I hope ye all believe I am nae marrying for the prestige or position allying with the Sinclairs will undoubtedly bring, I hope King David and ma father see it as just that since they willna care how I feel aboot Lady Rose or how I hope she will feel aboot me."

"Will feel?" Rose interjected. "Do ye believe I dinna care aboot ye yet? Or that I dinna care as much?"

"I willna put words into yer mouth, Kyla." Blaine froze, and Rose's eyes widened. They looked at Liam.

"Why do ye call ma granddaughter that?" Liam's shock radiated from him. Callum and Siùsan appeared as taken aback.

"Lady Rose," Blaine thought it better to revert to her proper name and title, "explained that Lady Siùsan and Callum always intended for people to use her full name, but over the years, everyone shortened it. It's nae that I think there is aught wrong with the name Rose. I admit I wish to have something that is just between us. Something we dinna need to share with anyone else. It may nae always be appropriate to call Lady Rose by any other endearment."

"And what does ma daughter call ye?" Callum tilted his head and looked at Rose.

"I havenae come up with aught because I like the name Blaine a great deal." Rose rested her free hand on top of their clasped ones, which sat on his armrest, before they let go of each other. Neither wanted to antagonize anyone after his blunder. "But I'm sure I will come up with something."

"If the contracts are due with the Irvines in three days, then that doesnae leave time for a missive to reach the king in France." Satisfied with the explanation, Liam brought them back to the real topic. "I willna write to him and ask to end a betrothal if I am nae certain things will progress between ye. I willna risk causing a feud with the Irvines over what turns out to be naught."

"Lady Rose and I can handfast. If she doesnae wish for a lifetime with me, then she can repudiate the agreement. But it will allow Lady Rose time to decide, and it doesnae completely close the door on the Irvines if Lady Rose wishes to end our arrangement." Blaine prayed that no matter what, he didn't end up with Eliza.

"If Laird Irvine realizes ye handfasted to avoid marrying his daughter, he may believe ye chose Rose out of convenience. He could push for ye to repudiate Rose and honor the agreement." Liam spoke aloud what Blaine already knew.

"Laird Sinclair, as I see it, we have a few choices. We tell them Lady Rose and I handfasted before the missive arrived. She slept late the morning after she visited Greer. If anyone at Dunrobin questions a handfast took place, we say it was private the night before. Nay one here has spoken to anyone—"

"Shona and Thor might have," Rose interrupted.

"Shona might, but Thor willna," Blaine countered. "He encouraged me to approach ye, and he understands the situation. Our other choice is to handfast now that we're at Dunbeath and hope that the Sinclair name is enough to keep anyone from speaking against us."

The room fell into silence as everyone considered what to do next. If they claimed they'd handfasted nearly a sennight ago, it meant perpetuating a lie. If they did it now, they risked the Irvines calling foul and arguing they handfasted merely to allow Blaine to avoid fulfilling his duty. Blaine turned in his chair to look fully at Rose. He felt rude continuing to whisper to her in front of the others, but he had few choices.

"I havenae asked if this is what ye want. If ye arenae sure, then we dinna have to do aught more than continue as we are. If ye want to handfast but would prefer to make it a marriage in name only, I willna pressure ye for more or hold our abstinence against ye."

"Is that what ye want?"

Blaine leaned farther forward and kept his voice so low Rose strained to hear him. "To abstain from sharing a bed with ye? I think ye ken that answer, Kyla. But I will wait as long as ye wish to be sure ye're ready. If we do, and ye decide to repudiate the handfast, it will make it harder for ye to find a real husband."

"And if I want the marriage to be real and then confirmed in a kirk?"

"Then we marry in a kirk three sennights after ye tell me that's what ye wish."

"Blaine, all the couples in ma family share a chamber. If I said I wish to wait, it would appear odd if we had separate chambers."

"The couples in ma family dinna share. We could easily say I'm the one who doesnae want to. But ken the truth, Kyla. If we wed, and ye wish for it to be a true marriage, we will share a chamber. I willna have ye sleeping anywhere I dinna. Ye always have the right to tell me nay. I willna ever force ma attentions upon ye. That will never change ma wish to be near ye every night for the rest of ma life."

Rose looked at her grandfather and parents. They appeared to ignore the couple, even though both Rose and Blaine knew they could likely hear bits and pieces of their conversation.

"Ye seem vera sure for a mon who didna ken me three sennights ago. Ye're giving me the chance to decide, but ye seem to have already made up yer mind."

"I grow fonder of ye every day. I dinna ken what the future holds for how we'll feel aboot each other. But I've already told ye how I see things. "

"Then I'll ask again, do ye think yer feelings are stronger than mine?"

"I dinna ken." Vulnerability coursed through Blaine as Rose watched him.

"I am nae entirely sure of ma feelings yet, but I dinna want ye to believe they dinna exist or that they may never develop into more than admiration and fondness. I think they could."

"I think mine could too. What do ye wish to do, Kyla?"

"Handfast." Rose realized she'd made up her minds days ago that she wanted a future with Blaine. During one of the rest stops, Blaine shared Hardi's suggestion about handfasting. She discovered she liked it from the start. It eased her fear that she was being impetuous about her decision. Blaine nodded.

"Mama, Da, Grandda, Blaine and I have decided to handfast. I dinna ken if we should say it took place today or while we were at Dunrobin, but we wish to make our intentions kenned and share it with the world."

"If ye believe ye will want to marry before a priest, ye'll have to wait. If we try to post the banns, and anyone outside our clan learns of it, the Irvines will have reason to object. We canna give them any power to prevent yer marriage going forward. We'll have enough trouble with the king." Siùsan turned her head to look at her husband, but Callum said nothing.

Liam observed his oldest child and his first daughter-by-marriage. He recalled how their relationship started. Callum couldn't have made a bigger mess of their introduction if he'd tried. He couldn't have botched his courtship more if he'd tried. But despite his piss-poor welcome to Siùsan, they'd fallen in love and handfasted while away from the keep. He'd handfasted with his own wife after his cousin threatened her safety, and he defended her honor. He'd fallen deeply in love with Kyla within days of meeting her. Even though she'd now been gone longer than they'd been together, his feelings hadn't dimmed.

He prayed Callum and Siùsan could see the similarities between how their love developed and what was happening with Rose and Blaine. He hoped they didn't object like Alex and Brighde had when Saoirse wished to marry Magnus Mackenzie, Suisan's younger half-brother. They had no blood relation, but he was much older than Saoirse. Age might have been their excuse, but Liam had known all along the pain his second son and second daughter-by-marriage suffered at the idea that their oldest daughter would leave them.

"How long will ye stay here?" Callum inquired.

"Longer than I should, to be honest. I ken I need to get home, but I willna travel so far with Rose while we dinna ken where Edgar lurks. I dinna like it, but I will go back to Ackergill alone if I must. Then I'll return for Lady Rose. Until I'm certain it's safe for ma wife to be on the road, I willna risk it. But I canna leave without kenning whether I will have a wife to return for."

"Callum?" Liam's whisky-brown eyes met ones that were a replica of his, even down to the topaz ring around the pupils. They'd silently communicated with one another for years, understanding each other's thoughts as only a father and son, laird and tánaiste could. Callum turned to Siùsan and remembered the day someone had attacked them in the woods, and how she'd protected him after he injured his shoulder. He remembered how he could think of nothing more than making her his wife despite all that remained unresolved between them and issues with her clan and the Gunns. He tucked hair behind Siùsan's ear, just as he'd done since the very beginning. He knew the answer she would give. He dropped a kiss on her forehead before wrapping his arm around her shoulders.

"Do ye wish to handfast alone, or would ye like any witnesses? Rose, I'm certain Mama could arrange a feast soon. It's yer decision as a couple what ye wish the world to ken."

"Will our handfast be official from the moment we make our promises? Or will we say it happened at Dunrobin days ago?" Rose looked at Blaine.

"It will be official the moment we pledge ourselves, but it wouldnae be a bad idea to say it already happened. We should make sure Thor and Shona havenae said otherwise to anyone."

Rose leaned in to make sure no one heard her. "Ma bed isnae vera wide. Ye will take up much of it. I suppose I'll just have to sleep on top of ye."

Blaine's hand fisted beneath Rose's, which now laid on top of his. He was glad they were Highlanders, so his sporran hid his visceral reaction to Rose's suggestion. If they were Lowlanders, no one would doubt how much he desired his bride.

"I will endeavor to ensure ye're vera comfortable all night, ma bonnie bride." Blaine murmured next to her ear. "When do ye wish to make our pledge? And do ye wish for it to be private?"

"As soon as we ken what ma brother and sister might have said, and I'd rather it be private. A wedding in the kirk will be for our families, but this is for us."

Blaine spread his fingers and curled them around Rose's once she laced hers with his. "Lady Rose and I would like to handfast privately today."

"Then I suppose I'm Liam to ye now, lad."

Blaine watched the older man beam at his granddaughter before turning a kind smile to him. He and Hamish were similar in so many ways that Blaine already wished Liam was his grandfather, too. As he shifted his eyes to Callum, he wondered if Callum would ever look upon him like a son.

"Welcome to our family, Son."

Blaine grinned and nodded as Callum moved around to his side of the table. When Callum extended his arm to Blaine, they clasped arms in a warrior handshake. Blaine expected Callum to squeeze as a warning, but his grip was firm without hostility.

"Thank ye, Da." Rose stepped into her father's embrace, leaning toward her mother when Callum wrapped his long arms around them both. "Thank ye, Mama."

"I will find yer sister and learn what she has or hasnae told anyone."

"I'd like to take Blaine to the lady's garden.

Grandda, would ye mind if we used Grandmama's corner?"

"She would like that, lass."

Liam kissed Rose's cheek when Callum released her. She chuckled as his beard tickled her, just as it had when she was a child. She wrapped her arms around him and rested her head against his chest. "Thank ye, Grandda."

Chapter Twelve

Rose led Blaine out of the solar and down a seldom used passageway that opened into the lady's garden. Once upon a time, Rose's grandmother maintained the area and made it thrive, and Siùsan brought it back to life when she arrived. There was a corner tucked away amongst a patch of violets and lavender, two of Kyla's favorite scents. Only Liam spent time in this area, visiting almost daily now that Callum shouldered many of the leadership tasks that used to take Liam away from the keep. The laird often came directly from training in the lists. Everyone in the clan understood implicitly that he was not to be disturbed when he was there.

"Grandda carved that bench for Grandmama when Auntie Mairghread was born. Ye'll see the woodland scene he carved on his chamber's doorframe as a wedding gift."

The seat was in the shade amongst the flowers. There was a stag and doe with five fawns between them. Liam had carved trees to each side of the animal family, but he'd encircled them with beautifully crafted scrolls and vines. The picture sat directly in the center of the top surface. Despite its age, it was clear the bench was well maintained. Rose stood before it, gazing at the scene that so accurately depicted the importance of family to all the Sinclairs. She leaned forward and ran her fingers over the carving before turning to Blaine. He slid his arms around her waist, and she stepped closer.

"I didna think I would have a moment alone with ye until we wed. I didna ken if that would ever happen," Blaine admitted.

"I dinna ken what our future holds, Blaine. I dinna ken if we'll build a life together forever, or we'll part ways within the year. But I can guess. I wouldnae agree to this if I didna think it was for good. I dinna ken why God has smiled upon ma family, near and far. When we find who we're meant to be with, there is nay doubt. It's as though God reaches down with both hands and pushes the couple together. Mayhap it's the Holy Spirit whispering in our ears. Nay one in ma family has ever regretted the mate they chose. The Lord has truly blessed us."

"I ken God smiled on me the day our paths crossed." Blaine hesitated a moment. "Kyla, we havenae talked aboot what life will be like for ye at Ackergill. Arenae ye curious?"

"Of course, I am. But I ken how to run a keep. Mama has trained me since I was auld enough to peel a carrot. I ken yer mother's been gone for a long time, so yer housekeeper has likely figured out her own system. I willna arrive and suddenly change everything that has run smoothly for years. There may be a few things I discover I'd rather we do differently, but I hope to blend in and nae cause too much disturbance."

"I want ye to feel like it's yer home, Kyla. I dinna want ye to fear ye must do things because that's the way it's always been. Martha, our housekeeper, is a kind woman. When ma mother died, she took care of me, even though I was nearly a mon. She became like a second mother to me. She's assertive and has a way of doing things, but she also kens that a chatelaine governs her domain, nae a housekeeper. She will work with ye and make ye feel welcome."

"Is there—are there—" Rose didn't want to ask about Blaine's past. She knew he didn't keep a leman and didn't believe in them. But she also knew the story of how her parents relationship began, and a ghost from her father's past refused to stop haunting them.

"Aye, Kyla. There are women from ma past in the keep and the village. But there arenae many, and none that held any importance."

"Do they ken that?"

"Aye. They ken what was between us was never serious and never meant to happen again once it ended."

"They may ken ye said that, but do they believe that?" Rose's insecurities threatened to push themselves to the surface. Would the servants look at her and respect her? Or would they think she appeared nothing like a lady and would mock her? She assumed she was nothing like Blaine's mother. She wondered if she would live up to the inevitable expectations.

Blaine drew her closer, his hold gentle as he ran his hand up and down her back. "Kyla, I have never shared aught of maself but ma body with anyone else."

"And a far too fine one at that. Blaine, they already ken ye in a way I dinna. They've been in yer life far longer than I have."

"Are ye jealous, or are ye scared?"

"Both." Rose's chest burned as she admitted it aloud, even though she was certain Blaine already knew the answer.

"Kyla, if I'd wanted aught more than a casual encounter now and then, then I would have a leman. At the vera least someone to bed regularly, or possibly someone to share ma life with. But I dinna have that, and I havenae for many years."

"Ye did. What if that woman—"

"She's married with two bairns, Kyla. And nay, I am nae sad or hurt over that. And nay, they arenae ma bairns either. I dinna have any bastards."

Kyla nodded. She appreciated they were clearing the air, so there would be no surprises, but it didn't make hearing any of this easier.

"*Leannan*, do ye worry aboot what people will think of ye?"

"Of course. I would even if I were the most confident woman. Everyone will judge me, for better or for worse. It's natural. But I admit ma fears are coming back, even as I try to stop them."

"Stand up to me the way ye stood up to yer da, and nay one will doubt ye're a lady capable of running a keep." Blaine grinned.

"I didna do that to ma da in public, and I would never, ever do that to ma husband in front of his people."

"They'll be our people. I trust ye to never insult me or ma position, but that doesnae mean ye must agree to everything I say or do. It may nae be possible to have a private conversation, so we might have to

161

talk in front of others. I dinna want ye ever to fear telling me yer thoughts."

"And if ye dinna agree with ma thoughts?"

"That may well happen. But I will never shame ye for having them, and I will never tell ye nae to think them. I will nae order ye aboot, and I dinna take ye for the type to henpeck a husband."

Rose tightened her hold around Blaine's waist, and he bent to kiss her. It was tender and languid. Neither hurried, and a wealth of emotion passed between them. It solidified what they'd already shared and hinted at more to come. When they pulled apart, their gazes met, and neither could help but smile. Blaine released her and unpinned the extra length of plaid from his shoulder. They clasped hands and bound their wrists with the wool.

"Rose Kyla Sinclair, I promise ye all that I am and all that I have. Ye will become bone of ma bone, and flesh of ma flesh. Ye will have ma whole heart and all that I can offer ye. I will be yer shelter from life's storms and the safe harbor where ye can rest yer head. Yers will be the last eyes I look into before I sleep and the first smile I see when I wake. I ken we pledge this handfast kenning it might only be for a year. For as long as we are together, ma promises will never waiver. I will respect ye, care for ye, and honor ye always. I wish to make ye ma wife, just as I wish to be yer husband. I plight thee ma troth."

"Blaine Edward Keith, I promise ye all that I am and all that I have. Ye will become bone of ma bone, and flesh of ma flesh. Ye will have ma whole heart and all that I can offer ye. I will make our home one ye wish always to return to. I will offer ye the first bite of our repast, and the first sip of our wine. I ken we pledge this handfast kenning it might only be for a year. For as long as we are together, ma promises will never waiver. I will respect ye, care for ye, and honor ye always. I wish to make ye ma husband, just as I wish to be yer wife. I plight thee ma troth."

The couple stared at each other, both too emotional to speak further. As though they both wished to prolong the moment, they eased into their first kiss as husband and wife. Blaine pushed his sporran out of the way before his steel arm wrapped a band around Rose's waist. She was certain she could feel his heartbeat in her own chest. While he held her firmly, she never felt trapped. There was the same tenderness as when they kissed before they handfasted. His other hand cupped her cheek, and his thumb grazed her cheekbone.

Blaine cleared his throat. "Ye are so precious to me, Kyla. I meant every word. I dinna want ye to ever regret binding yer life to mine. I want to be worthy of yer heart and yer faith."

"Ye are. Ye make me feel cherished in a way I never imagined I needed. Ye're patient with me and dinna mock ma fears. I pray I can overcome them, so they dinna become a barrier between us."

"*Leannan*, I ken why ye're scared. Ye're leaving all that ye ken to come to a strange home with strange people. There will be times when ye feel lonely and mayhap intimidated. I hope ye will come to me when ye need me. I ken I took strength in having ye by ma side today. Yer family isnae aught to take lightly. Ye bolstered me when I feared floundering. I am nae ashamed to admit that I needed ye and that yer family intimidates me."

"They intimidate everyone. I dinna see ye as weak

for admitting that. I'm glad to ken I made ye feel better, and I'm glad I can turn to ye without fearing ye'll think less of me for nae managing on ma own."

"I dinna want ye to feel like ye must do it all on yer own, even if I ken ye can."

Rose cupped Blaine's jaw with both hands. "Are ye this thoughtful by nature? Or did yer mother or Martha teach ye to be mindful of others' needs?"

"Truthfully? I am nae just saying this to win yer favor, Kyla. It's ye. I dinna think I am this thoughtful to anyone else. I try to be mindful of ma clan's needs before ma own. But I dinna think I've ever cared aboot a single person and what's best for them as much as I do ye."

"Ye're a good mon, Blaine."

Their lips melded together as they sealed their commitment with another kiss. It drew on as their tongues slid against each other and tangled in a hint of what would come when they were truly in private.

"Kyla, I want to make love to ma wife. I dinna want to wait until this eve and after everyone retires. I want to strip ye bare, kiss every inch of ye and watch ye come apart in ma arms again. It feels like it's been years, nae days since I last touched ye. I want to be inside ye when I spend. I desire ye more than ma next breath. I want to show ye, nae just tell ye, that I will honor and care for ye."

"We can go down to the beach. Nay one should be down there right now. The fishermen willna be back for a few hours. I doubt any of ma cousins are there either since they have other responsibilities. They're in the lists or seeing to their duties."

Rose made to take a step away from Blaine, but he wasn't ready to let go. He pulled her close again for a kiss that left them breathless. She took his hand and led him to the garden gate, but they drew apart as they stepped into the bailey. No one outside her immediate family knew why Blaine was there. She didn't want to answer questions before they announced their marriage to her cousins, and then to the entire clan. People would already wonder why the Keith warriors arrived and why Rose left the keep with Blaine. There would be plenty of speculation—some of it even accurate—but they didn't need to fuel the gossip.

Once they were beyond the loch that lay outside the postern gate, they laced their fingers together. When they reached the top of the cliffs overlooking the North Sea, they stopped.

"That cave has a tidal pool that's also heated by a hot spring. With the hole in the top of the rocks allowing light in, it looks as though the pool glows from beneath the water. Ye can only access it when the tide is out. If anyone is there when the tide comes in, they'll be trapped and drown."

"Have ye explored it?"

"All the time." Rose grinned. "When we were weans, nay one could go unless there were at least four or five of us. That was never a problem since it was usually me, Thor, and Shona with our cousins Blake, Maisie, Tor—"

"Thor and Tor? Bluidy hell."

"Och, aye. Ma brother was named for ma mother's grandfather, Thormud MacLeod. Uncle Magnus and Auntie Deirdre liked the name Torquil. Saoirse and her sisters, Nessa and Mirren, would join us. They're Uncle Alex and Auntie Brighde's lasses. Blake and Saoirse are the closest to ma age, along with

Tate. He's Uncle Tavish and Auntie Ceit's auldest. Shona, Nessa, Mirren, Tor, and Maisie arenae that much younger, so they soon came along with Wiley and Ailish, Uncle Tavish and Auntie Ceit's other two."

"Good God, there's a lot of ye."

Rose laughed. "That doesnae include Wee Liam, Hamish, Alec, and Ainsley. They're Auntie Mairghread and Uncle Tristan's brood. They always come with us when they're here."

"Just how many of ye are there?"

"Dozens." Rose held up her fingers as she counted. "Five siblings and five mates, so ten from the aulder generation, plus Grandda. That's eleven. Auntie Mairghread has four, so that's five-and-ten. Mama and Da have three, so that's eight-and-ten. Uncle Alex and Auntie Brighde have three, so that's one-and-twenty. Mmm... Uncle Tavish and Auntie Ceit have three, so four-and-twenty. Then there's Uncle Magnus and Auntie Deirdre with their three, so seven-and-twenty. Wee Liam, Blake, and Saoirse are married, so that's thirty. Wee Liam's wife, Elene, brought her younger brother and sister with her when she arrived from Orkney, and they've had a bairn. That puts us at three-and-thirty. Blake and Cerys have a bairn too, and dinna say a word to anyone, but I think Saoirse might be with child. She hinted at it the last time they visited. That would put us at five-and-thirty. And now we have ye, too. Six-and-thirty. Like I said, dozens."

Blaine had met most of the Sinclairs over the years, so he knew the names, if not the people. But they'd always just seemed like a giant family without him giving any thought to just how many made up the laird's family. Except for Mairghread and Tristan's family and Saoirse's now that she was a Mackenzie, Blaine realized he would meet the rest at the evening meal. They would all stare at him. He suddenly understood every insecurity Rose had on an elemental level.

"Dinna fash. They'll all love ye. Though, ye might take a wee thrashing in the lists tomorrow."

"Nae tomorrow, lass. Ye and I willna be leaving our chamber for at least a day." Blaine winked. His brow furrowed at Rose's grin. It was as though she knew something he didn't.

"If ye really want to fit in, then we dinna reappear for a sennight. Our family is—prodigious—" Rose giggled, "—for a reason."

"Come teach me, *leannan*." Blaine tugged her toward the path that led to the beach.

"The tide is in, so we canna go to the cave. Besides, I ken that's where Saoirse and Magnus Óg went when they handfasted. They can keep that as their spot." Rose led them toward a collection of boulders that she knew would keep anyone from seeing them from overhead or from the path. No one could approach by any of the other directions. If she'd known the family history among those rocks, she might have abandoned it like she did the cave.

"Kyla, yer family doesnae expect a bedding ceremony, do they?" Blaine knew the answer from her disgusted expression.

"Nay mon in this family would ever countenance such a thing. And the women in this family would gut any mon who suggested it. Any woman daft enough to think she can cast her gaze on a groom would find herself without her eyes."

"What aboot the sheet?" Blaine sighed and ran his hand through his hair. "Kyla, I have to have it. Ma clan will expect it. They'll want to see it flown from our bedchamber window."

"Ye ken I'm a maiden, and I dinna think anyone in ma family would doubt that. Either we use chicken blood, or I'll cut ma finger. We can make a sheet to air from yer—our—window. But I dinna want to go back right now."

Blaine sighed a second time. "It doesnae feel right to create so many lies aboot us. I hate that we canna just be honest aboot all of this, but I ken we dinna have much choice. We must maintain appearances. I dinna want to go back right now either. I want to make love to ma wife for the first time without kenning people might hear us." Blaine waggled his eyebrows. "I might make ye scream later, so everyone kens ye're mine. But for now, I dinna want to share."

"And if I make ye scream first?"

"Then I havenae done a good job if I finish before ye, lass. And I willna scream. I will roar."

Rose tickled his ribs, uncertain whether he would react. He squirmed away before he caught himself, which only made Rose do it again. Blaine swept her into his arms as they crossed the sandy beach. When they reached the rocks, he perched her on top of the lowest one. He stepped between her legs as she reached for his belt. He drew the scabbard from his back and propped the sword within reach. He would never leave Rose unprotected. He feathered kisses over her cheeks and along her neck as he plucked at her laces. He felt the belt loosen around his waist, catching it and his plaid as the latter unraveled. While he set the belt beside his sword, Rose pulled the rest of her laces loose.

"Would ye let me undress ye?" Blaine whispered. Rose nodded as she stared at the man before her, clad in only his leine, stockings, and boots. She wondered if he would take off the shoes.

"I'd like that."

Blaine removed her riding boots before sliding his hands beneath her skirts. His palms ran from her ankles, over her calves, and up to her thighs. She was unprepared for him to kneel before her like he had in her chamber at Dunrobin and push her skirts high enough to duck beneath them. She gasped when his tongue skimmed her inner thigh as he rolled down one, then the other stocking. She pulled her skirts back further when his tongue flicked her netherlips. Blaine breathing cool, then warm air against her seam had her yanking her gown out of the way, so she could watch Blaine as she rested back on her elbows.

His hands gripped her hips as his tongue delved into the dew collecting at her entrance. His thumb swept over her pearl before rubbing in slow circles. When his lips drew her sensitive bundle of nerves into his warm mouth, and his tongue flicked it, she moaned as her head fell back. She sensed Blaine moving, but he didn't cease his ministrations. She knew vaguely that he must have been toeing off his boots and stockings, but she could concentrate on nothing beyond the sensations he created and her impending release.

"Blaine, more. I'm close to how ye made me feel the last time we were alone."

Blaine sucked hard as his fingers ran along the entrance to her core. He watched her expression as she laid back with her eyes closed. She fumbled to push her gown down her arms, then he plucked her chemise's ribbons loose at her shoulders. She pressed her feet against the boulder to lift her hips as her climax tightened all her muscles.

"Blaine!"

"Aye, *mo chridhe*."

Rose's eyes flew open, and she reached for him. She cared not that she could taste herself. She needed to kiss him, to pour out all the emotions that roiled in her. She pushed her gown and chemise beneath her breasts and drew his hand to cover her heart.

"Ye're ma heart, too." She cupped his jaw before she kissed him again. With her right hand, she nudged him toward her breasts, which felt full and heavy. Her left hand offered him the mound he gladly latched onto, suckling like a famished babe. His teeth teased her nipple until it became a puckered dart he swirled his tongue around. With each moment of teasing, she grew more restless. She maneuvered her clothes past her hips, and Blaine shifted to let them drop to the sand. "Blaine, please. I ache for ye so much it hurts. It's painful how much I need to feel ye inside me. I dinna ken what's happening, but I ken ma body is begging for ye."

Blaine stood up and whisked his leine over his head. Rose sucked in a whistling breath as her gaze roamed over Blaine's chiseled body. She sat up and trailed her fingers over his chest and abdomen before sliding them over his back and down to his buttocks. She noticed how his cock leaked.

"Do ye see how I want ye just as badly, Kyla? I've never been so hard in ma life. Ma bollocks feel like they're going to explode. I fear I'm going to be too rough with ye. I willna couple with ye on these rocks. Wait while I spread out ma plaid."

Instead of listening, Rose slipped from the rock and helped him lay his plaid out on the beach. He eased her to the fabric before following her down to rest between her thighs.

"I ken it will likely hurt, and I ken ye dinna mean for it to happen. But I think I might cry if I have to wait any longer. I feel so unsettled."

"Wheest, wee one. I'll do all I can to make it better."

Rose grinned and looked between them. "I can hardly call ye that."

"Cheeky." Blaine slid his hands beneath her and cupped her backside, giving it a tight squeeze. His mouth once more found her breasts, and he flicked her nipple as he brought the head of his cock to her entrance. He teased her, sliding the tip in before withdrawing. He matched the rhythm of his hips to how he sucked on her breast. When she pressed his head to her and arched her back, he surged into her.

"Argh!" Rose's fingers fisted his hair as pain coursed through her core, making her toes curl.

"*Leannan*, I'm so sorry. Do ye wish me to stop?"

"Dinna ye dare. I ken neither of us is done. The pain will end, but if ye pull out, we'll both be miserable." Rose eased her grip and rubbed her fingertips over where she realized her nails scraped his scalp. She widened her already bent knees and exhaled. "It doesnae hurt anymore, but would ye stay still for just a moment? I want to—I like—" Rose feared she was going to make a bigger deal of their coupling than what Blaine felt.

"Ye like how we're one?"

"Aye. And how full ye make me. It's vera arousing, even though ye arenae moving." Rose clenched her core, eliciting a groan from Blaine. She did it again, and he rocked his hips. Slowly, they moved together. Blaine didn't thrust yet. He continued to rock his hips, circling them to rub her pearl.

"I'm content to stay as we are. I'm fighting nae to spill. But if ye're ready for more, I would show ye."

"I'm ready."

Blaine drew back before he thrust into her, watching for any sign that he was too forceful. Rose's cheeks flushed as she panted, but her hips rose to receive his every movement. He lifted her leg and wrapped it over his hip as he rested on one forearm.

"Ye are so bonnie, Kyla. I dinna ken if I'll ever drag maself from yer arms. I could remain like this for the rest of ma days."

"That might be a wee impractical when ye train or when ye must hear clan members' grievances."

"Nay mon is seeing me buried in ma wife while I pleasure her. I could stay with ye here always. Or I'd wrap us in ma plaid and have us ride away somewhere nay one can find us."

"I'd ride ye before I ever rode another horse." Rose couldn't believe the brazen things she said, but the way Blaine increased the force of his thrusts, she trusted he liked it. Blaine rolled onto his back, so he could oblige Rose's suggestions. She braced herself with her palms on his chest as she tested how to move. She leaned forward, moving her forearms beside his head, so they could kiss. His hands on her backside guided her, but he kept the pressure light.

"I'm doing all that I can nae to spill yet, Kyla. I

dinna ken that I can hold out much longer. I willna finish before ye."

Rose leaned back and ground her mound against his pubic bone as she found the pace that brought her to release again. Blaine watched as her nipples tightened further with her climax and the cool breeze. He sat up to kiss her as she continued to ride him.

"Fuck," Blaine muttered. "I'm too close."

"Show me what ye really want, Blaine. I willna break."

He rolled them, so Rose lay beneath him. "I willna let maself lose control, despite the temptation ye are. I'll hurt ye, and ye willna feel well by morning. But dinna doubt I wish to devour ye. I wish to pound into ye until I canna see straight. Ye feel so bluidy good."

"A dip in the sea and then a hot bath will cure it all. Blaine, show me."

Blaine increased his pace, pistoning his hips as he drove his cock into her core over and over. As her nails clawed at him, then dug into the taut flesh of his backside, he let go of all but the last few strands of his control.

"More, Blaine. I willna break." Rose watched Blaine's expression as he concentrated. Something dark passed into his gaze, and she didn't understand it. "Blaine?"

"Wheest, *leannan*. Naught is wrong. Ye feel unlike aught I ever imagined."

"Is that good? Is it what ye want?" Rose felt another release tightening her core. "Ye're going to make me climax again. Dear God!"

"I want to make ye need me so much that ye canna think of aught else because that's what ye've done to me. I want ye to crave feeling me inside ye because this is where I belong. Ye're mine, Kyla. And I am only yers. It's ma seed that will take root in yer belly. It's our children ye'll birth. Now that I've been inside ye, felt what it is to have ye hold me, to watch ye shatter kenning it's ma cock ye're squeezing, I willna ever let another mon near ye. I willna ever look at any woman but ye. I ken what a possessive monster that makes me sound like, but right now, I dinna care."

"Blaine, look at me." Rose's voice rang with command. "I have a brother and slew of male cousins, so I ken words I shouldnae. I'm going to use some now. I willna ever speak this way except for when we're alone. I pray I dinna disgust ye."

Rose's words piqued Blaine's curiosity and drove him wild. "Tell me now, Kyla."

"I want ye to fuck me until I see stars. I want yer cock inside ma cunt because I am the only woman who will *ever* touch ye again. Ye are mine, and I dinna give a shite what any other woman ever thinks. I dinna share. Only ma quim gets yer seed, and only I will bear yer children. I am as possessive as ye, and I dinna want either of us to change. I want to feel yer seed on ma thighs as we walk back to the keep. I have something nay other woman can. A mon might think leaving his seed in a woman brands her as his, but me taking yers brands ye as mine. Spend in me, *mo chridhe*, and make me spend too."

With a roar, Blaine thrust hard and fast. Rose met each surge, encouraging him with her whispers and her tight hold on his buttocks. When she went stiff and screamed, his roar matched hers as jets of his seed filled her. They were both breathless and drenched in sweat by the time they stopped moving together. They stared at one another before they shared a passionate kiss that would have sparked another round if either of them had the energy.

"Kyla?"

"Mmm?"

"Are ye well?"

"Mmhmm." Rose nodded, her eyes closed. "I could curl up and blissfully go to sleep right now."

"Did I hurt ye?"

Rose opened one eye. "Kiss me again, please."

Blaine was tentative, waiting for Rose to take the lead. This one was affectionate as she ran her hands over his back. They finished with a series of pecks. "Kyla, what I just said—I meant it. But I ken how demanding and controlling it sounded. I willna ever force ye."

"Is that how ye feel? I mean, even when we're nae like this?" When Blaine hesitated, she continued. "What aboot what I said? For all ma fears aboot people mistaking me for a tavern wench, I didna speak like any lady should. Are ye put off by that? Was I too possessive for a wife?"

"Couldnae ye tell that every word ye said only made me need ye more? Nay woman has ever talked to me like that, and I would let nay other try. But hearing ye like that while we couple is beyond arousing. I never imagined I would like it, but I do. And aye, that's how I feel whether we're coupling or nae."

"I like it too."

"Ye dinna fear I will treat ye like an object, like a belonging rather than a person?"

"I never thought that. I felt like the most special person in the world to ye at that moment."

"Ye are, and I felt the same. I told ye what I want, Kyla. But that doesnae mean I'm reneging on what I promised. If ye decide ye wish to leave, if ye decide it would be best if we're careful and ye dinna conceive yet, then I will always respect that."

"I dinna doubt ye, Blaine. Dinna fear that, please. This is who we are and what we like when we're coupling. Should we be ashamed?"

"Nay. Never. What we do together is our business, *leannan*. There is nay shame in a mon and woman enjoying their marital rights. I dinna want bedding me to feel like a chore to ye."

"Me bedding ye? I've never heard a mon put it that way. Does that mean I can ask for it when I want?"

"Of course. This is something we do together. It isnae something I do to ye. Just like I've said I willna ever force ye if ye dinna wish to couple, I welcome ye letting me ken if ye want to join."

"If?" Rose snorted. "I think I proved *if* is nae a question. It'll be when and how often."

Blaine rolled onto his back once more, bringing Rose with him. He threw the yards of loose plaid over them. Rose settled against his side as he held her. They shared several more pecks and slow caresses. Blaine watched as her eyes drifted closed. He knew she wasn't asleep, but they both enjoyed the feel of being cocooned together.

When the sun shifted behind the rocky headland, Rose sighed and sat up. "We have to go back soon. The evening meal isnae long off."

They stood, and Blaine kept the plaid wrapped around Rose. He didn't care if anyone saw him naked, but he didn't enjoy thinking of Rose being so vulnerable. She swiped her chemise from the ground before helping to hold the plaid out of her way as they walked to the water's edge. Nothing prepared him for Rose to shed the fabric, drop her chemise, and wade into the surf with ease. She skipped through the water, clearly used to the waves. He followed her until the water was chest deep for her. It was frigid, but she seemed not to notice. Blaine struggled to hide his chattering teeth. His cock and bollocks had surely shriveled and hidden within him in fear they would freeze and snap off.

"It's a wee chilly. I ken. I'll only be a moment." Rose sighed as the freezing seawater eased the discomfort setting in. She wouldn't change how they coupled for the first time, but she knew Blaine's warning had been fair. She would be in pain by the time they returned to the keep. She prayed there was enough time for a hot bath, too. When they waded back to the shore, Blaine wrapped her in his plaid again, rubbing her dry. She donned her chemise as they hurried to their clothes. They helped each other make themselves presentable. She squeaked when Blaine lifted her into his arms again.

"Walking across the sand and up the cliff side willna be easy. I saw yer winces, Kyla. I dinna want ye in further pain. Do ye wish to take a tray for the evening meal? Yer mama is nay fool. She kens what we're aboot. I'll ask her for the tub with plenty of hot water. Ye can soak as long as ye need."

"Will ye scrub ma back?"

"I'll wash whatever ye tell me to." Blaine waggled his eyebrows, but Rose could see recriminations beginning in his mind.

"Husband, I couldnae have asked for a better way

to become yer wife. Both in the garden and on the beach. Ye ken how large all the men are in ma family, and ye ken how wee the women are in comparison. Wait until ye see our tubs. They must fit men like Da. I'm a wee smaller than ye, just like Mama and ma aunts are smaller than their husbands." Rose cocked an eyebrow, hoping Blaine got her gist.

"Do ye wish to share yer bath with me, lassie?"

"Vera much." Rose wrapped her arms around Blaine's neck as he trudged up the path. She rested her head against his shoulder and sighed. "Blaine, I ken there is undoubtedly trouble coming. And I ken things havenae been easy yet, but ye make me happy. Thank ye."

"That's all I want, Kyla. I want to be a good husband to ye and for ye to be happy with the life we'll build." Blaine kissed her as he set her on her feet at the top of the path. She leaned against his side as they walked back to the keep, arm-in-arm.

Chapter Thirteen

Blaine and Rose entered the castle and made their way to a back stairway after Rose asked Sorcha, Dunbeath's housekeeper, to send up a bath to her chamber. They were nearly to her bedchamber door when Siùsan called out to them.

"It nearly killed yer da, but he and yer uncles already switched yer bed to a larger one."

Rose's face was aflame. She grimaced and nodded. "Thank ye."

"That's the same look Da had when I told him what needed doing. Go easy on the auld mon tonight. Tavish, Magnus, and Alex werenae kind. At least, Alex wasna until Da asked how he thought Saoirse was doing since we all think she's carrying a bairn. I thought Alex might faint. Such large men brought to their knees by their wee lasses." Siùsan shook her head as she laughed.

"There's naught discreet aboot four men moving those beds. Now everyone will ken what we are aboot. How many people do ye think already ken I'm married?"

"Dinna fash, lass. Yer da and yer uncles were vera

179

quiet when they were moving the furniture, despite how large they and the beds are. Some people may have noticed, but nay one kens the details. Shona didna tell anyone aught before I found her. We'll announce yer handfast at the meal. Did ye order yerself a bath yet?"

"Aye, Mama. It's on its way now. Blaine and I will be belowstairs in time for the meal. Can someone, please, bring his saddlebags up to ma chamber?"

"It's already there."

"Mama! Now all the servants will ken a mon is coming to stay in ma chamber. They'll all be gossiping aboot it by now." Rose looked toward the landing that overlooked the Great Hall, where she could hear voices floating up to the rafters.

"Auntie Deirdre brought it up for ye. If ye would rather have a tray this evening, then we can do that. I think it would be best if we introduced Blaine with all the family together to support ye. But if ye arenae up to having that much attention, then ye can retire early, and we can do the introductions tomorrow. Which do ye prefer?"

Rose glanced at Blaine, who nodded his head. He would do whatever Rose wished. He worried she would be too exhausted after riding for a day from Dunrobin to Dunbeath and after what they did together on the beach. He worried that a hot bath wouldn't be enough to ease the soreness that must already be setting in. If his wife wanted a quiet night in their chamber alone, he certainly wouldn't object. But he would stand tall and proud beside her if they joined the rest of the family for the meal. He didn't fear being introduced to the rest of the Sinclair clan as much as he had feared meeting her family. In fact, he looked forward to everyone knowing he was the fortunate man who got to call Rose his bride.

"We will join ye for the meal. Give us a little while to refresh ourselves, and we will be down in plenty of time."

Servants arrived with an enormous tub—the largest Blaine had ever seen—and a trail of buckets with steaming water. Rose opened the door to her bedchamber and stepped aside as the troop of servants entered her chamber and prepared the bath. When they all left, Rose looked at her mother. Once more embarrassed that anyone would know what she and Blaine were going to do in that chamber once they were alone, her mother gave her a quick hug and turned away, not wanting to prolong her daughter's agony. It amused Siùsan that after living in such a family her entire life, Rose would suddenly feel so modest. But Siùsan understood it felt different to be the one who was the focus of all the attention, rather than being the one paying the attention.

Alone in the chamber, the couple stripped before Blaine tested the water to be sure it wouldn't scald Rose. He stepped in and offered her his hand, then sat with his legs apart. Rose settled between his thighs and leaned back with a sigh. Blaine had to admit that the steam felt marvelous as it seeped into his weary bones and fatigued muscles. They remained silent for several minutes as Blaine glided his right hand up her arm until he could massage her shoulder and neck. His left arm wrapped around her waist. He felt Rose's body go lax, and he thought she might have fallen asleep until she stroked his shin.

She twisted to look back at him before resting

against him once more. "Are ye worried aboot meeting ma family?"

"I've met many of them before at various gatherings. I look forward to meeting the rest and getting to ken some better. If I lived to tell the tale after the first time I led ma men out, I can do this. I remember fearing they wouldnae trust me nae to get them killed. They'd kenned me ma entire life and seen ma father train me. But it was vera different when I kenned they relied upon me, nae someone else. If I survived that, I can survive this."

Rose chuckled. "I dinna ken. They can be a fierce lot."

"Aye, all three dozen of them. At least I think I have yer aunts and uncles on ma side."

"Ye do. I can tell." Rose soaked a linen square and lathered it with soap before lifting Blaine's right arm over her shoulder. She turned to face him and kneeled between his legs as she ran the sudsy cloth over his arms and chest. Then she playfully tugged his shoulders to make him sit forward. The moment she leaned against him to reach his back, he lifted her until she straddled his hips. She'd felt him grow hard as they lay in the tub together. He looked at her and waited. But it only took a second for her to nod.

He eased her onto his length, and they both sighed. Rose rested her head against his shoulder, bathing him already forgotten. Blaine's hands rested on her backside as he held her tight. Neither of them was in a hurry to move their coupling along. Instead, they savored the moment of their bodies being joined. Soon, however, that stillness wasn't enough. As they moved gently together, the lapping water around their chests felt erotic. Instead of the forcefulness from the beach during the first time they coupled, this time was sensual and unhurried.

"I could stay just as we are for the rest of time." Blaine kissed along Rose's jaw until he came to the creamy skin behind her ear. He pressed soft kisses as he moved around its shell until he nipped at her earlobe before sucking it.

She shivered as a wave of arousal coursed through her. She rode him, rising and falling on his length as he kneaded her sore backside. She hadn't realized how the muscles ached, but it made sense after hours on horseback and their first vigorous joining. It surprised her that such differing sensations could create a powerful need to couple along with a sense of comfort and tenderness. It wasn't long before they crested together as their bodies tensed with euphoria.

"Now I understand why newlywed couples hide away for a honeymoon for a sennight, if nae an entire moon." She swirled her hand along the water's surface. "I dinna wish to get out of this water any time soon or join the rest of the world. Taking a tray up here this eve sounds more and more appealing every time I think aboot it, but I understand it would be best for us to join everyone."

"We dinna have to dally there long, *leannan*. We can retire once we finish the last course, unless ye wish to stay and mingle with yer family and clan, or mayhap dance if there are musicians. We can come abovestairs whenever ye wish. If ye get too tired to last throughout the entire meal, then we will retire early."

"If we do that, *mo ghràdh*, then everyone will guess why we came abovestairs. They'll believe we canna wait to couple again."

"We can do that as often and for as long as ye

wish. But if ye are too tired or too sore, then there's always later. I am nae going anywhere."

Despite Blaine's reassurance, they knew they needed to hurry. They ran the soap over each other before they washed each other's hair. Blaine supported Rose as he poured fresh water over her head to clear away the soap, then he leaned forward, so Rose could do the same. Much like he had on the beach, Blaine ran a drying cloth over Rose's body, rubbing her arms and legs to keep her warm.

He wrapped a drying linen around his waist and watched as she moved across the chamber to her armoire. He wondered how great an effort Rose made to walk around their chamber bare. He recognized from the stiffness in her shoulders that it wasn't easy for her, but he certainly appreciated the view. He knew it took courage on her part since he sensed she still had some uncertainty about her appearance, despite how they'd enjoyed one another twice that day.

Now that he had seen her naked, he hoped she understood how much he enjoyed every part of her, inside and out. As he watched her hips sway as she walked towards the wardrobe, he imagined leaning her across the bed, standing behind her, and entering her. He would hold her waist and watch as her backside jiggled with each thrust. The more he pictured holding onto her ample bottom and squeezing it as he plowed into her, the more aroused he became all over again. He turned away and rummaged through his saddlebag lest Rose notice he was ready for a third coupling. He pulled a fresh leine from his bag, along with clean stockings and a spare plaid. He didn't realize she watched him until he stood up.

Rose held a gown in her hand as she returned to

the foot of the bed. She glanced at the discarded plaid on the mattress, then the one in Blaine's hand. "I ken that is far too large for me to wear as an arisaid, but I look forward to the day when I can wear yer clan's pattern."

Blaine opened the other side of his saddlebags and withdrew another plaid. He'd had this one freshly laundered when he was at Dunrobin. He pulled a knife from his belt that rested on the bed beside his sandy plaid. Rose watched in stunned silence as Blaine shook out the clean plaid, then cut a sash from it. It horrified her once she realized what he was doing.

"Ye dinna have to ruin yer plaid for me." Rose rested her hand on his forearm, even though it was too late to stop him.

"It isnae ruined, *leannan*. Even with the sash cut off, I ken it's too long for a proper arisaid. But ye could fold it enough to work. It's too warm for one now, so the sash will do. I wish to see ye in ma clan's plaid. I'm proud to have everyone ken ye're wearing the laird's family pattern because ye're ma wife."

Rose accepted the swath of material and laid it on the bed beside her gown before she opened a chest and withdrew her undergarments. While she donned her stockings and chemise, then combed her wet hair, Blaine pleated his plaid. She watched him, having seen plenty of men do the same thing, but never having appreciated the intimacy of a wife watching her husband. Once he had it belted in place, he helped tie her gown's laces. She carried the sash with her to her dressing table, where she looked in her jewelry box and withdrew a brooch that had been her mother's mother's. It was one of the few pieces Siùsan had from Rose MacLeod, and she'd given it to her daughter Rose on her eighteenth saint's day. She fastened the sash to her shoulder, tucking the ends beneath her girdle.

"Ye're the bonniest lass this side of the Highlands."

"Ye're a rather braw mon yerself. I will have to fight off the lasses with a pitchfork."

They laughed together as they made their way to the main stairs that would take them to the Great Hall. Blaine wrapped Rose's arm around his as they reached the bottom stairs. It took little time before they garnered people's attention. Rose watched as her clan members leaned together and whispered, some even pointing to the plaid she wore then the one Blaine had wrapped around him. They made their way to the dais, where other members of her family already gathered.

Thor and Shona stood together, but they both opened their arms to Rose. The two sisters and brother tightly embraced, just as they had throughout their entire lives. Thor kissed Rose's temple and squeezed tighter.

"I'm happy for ye, Sister. He's a good mon, and he will love ye beyond measure."

"Shh. Dinna say that. I dinna ken how he feels aboot me. It may never be that, so dinna tempt fate or embarrass him."

"Thor's right." Shona kept her voice much lower than her brother had. "The way he watches ye, and the way he is when he's beside ye. I'd say he's besotted, but it's more than that. More real. He isnae infatuated with ye, Rose. Mayhap it isnae love yet, but it's far more than just puppy love."

"Ye ken all that from watching us walk across the Great Hall?" Rose tilted her head as though her siblings were the foolish ones.

"Dinna be daft. Of course nae. I ken it from watching ye for nearly a moon."

Rose shifted so she could see Blaine from the corner of her eye. He tried not to be obtrusive, but she could tell it was uncomfortable for him to stand alone while so many people watched. "I still dinna want either of ye talking aboot it. If he ever feels that way *and* wants to tell me, he will. Dinna stick either of yer nebs where they dinna belong."

Shona released an aggrieved sigh as she rolled her eyes. "At least dinna deny ye're well on yer way to being in love."

"Shh." It was Shona's turn for Rose to shush her. "I dinna need him to hear that either. I'm nae sure how I feel. And I dinna want to be played a fool if he doesnae feel like I do."

"Rosie," Thor whispered as he shot Shona a warning glare. "Nay one will say aught. But it seems like ye two are the only ones who canna see what the rest of us do. Mayhap ye should both look in a reflecting glass together. There's nay rush to decide how ye feel or to tell anyone, but I think ye'll both see what's there if ye look." The right side of Thor's mouth lifted in the half-smile he'd given her so many times. She nodded before stepping away from her siblings and returning to Blaine's side as Liam approached.

"Are ye ready for me to make the announcement now? Shall we say ye handfasted back at Dunrobin?"

"Aye, Grandda. Please say that we pledged ourselves five days ago."

Liam nodded. "I think it is for the best that we stick with that story. If ye say yer vows before a priest, the contracts will state that date as the beginning of yer marriage. Regardless of whether it was today or five days ago, ye're already as good as married to everyone else. They'll wish ye happy and enjoy the excuse to celebrate. I dispatched a missive from yer da and one from me to King David. I think I was vera persuasive."

The couple followed Liam onto the dais and to the front, while the clan members took their seats at massive trestle tables. Liam waited until the crowd quieted before he reached out a hand to Rose, who took it and stepped beside Liam. He wrapped his arm around her shoulders while she slid her hand into Blaine's.

"Sinclairs, today is an occasion to celebrate. Nae only have Thor, Rose, and Shona returned with our men, we have a new family member to welcome. Ma auldest granddaughter handfasted with Blaine Keith, Clan Keith's tánaiste. They met while they both visited the Sutherlands, and he's returned with Rose, so we might all share their joy. As Laird Sinclair, a proud grandda and leader of our clan, I welcome ye, Blaine, to our family."

With only a few well-chosen words, Blaine gained the acceptance of hundreds of people and the sworn support of an entire army.

"Thank ye, Grandda." Rose's voice carried as people cheered. "I will always be a Sinclair. Naught can ever change that. It's who I am and who I always will be. But I canna say aught has ever made me happier than becoming Lady Rose Keith."

"Kiss, kiss, kiss!" The crowd chanted before

erupting in applause as Liam released Rose, and Blaine encircled her in his embrace. The couple intended it to be an appropriately chaste kiss, but as was usually the case, it soon ignited into more. Breathless when they pulled apart, they rested their foreheads together.

"I didna exaggerate for their sake, Blaine."

Blaine kissed Rose's forehead before turning his head toward the crowd. "It's an honor to marry into the Sinclairs, but it's a privilege to marry Lady Rose. There is nay mon luckier than me. And I ken I have at least—" Blaine paused as he held up six fingers, one at a time as though he counted. "—six men who will try to convince me otherwise in the lists. But I ken the truth."

He peered down at Rose and kissed the tip of her nose.

"I dinna care what yer grandda, da, uncles, or cousin says. I am the luckiest mon, and I'll gladly fight anyone who says otherwise."

Rose went onto her toes to whisper in his ear. "There is only one sword ye'll be swinging to prove how lucky ye are, and it isnae the one ye use in the lists."

As she settled back on her feet, the crowd howled. Rose leaned back to see Blaine's cheeks had deepened to a dark red. She had no idea he could blush so profusely. His arms dropped from around her, but he took her hand. She looked over her shoulder to follow his gaze, joining the crowd's mirth. Ten men stood with their arms crossed and feet hip-width apart. Nine grinned like naughty schoolboys, and one scowled so deeply Rose feared the lines would become permanent on her father's face. She laughed as she led him to the chair next to hers.

The meal progressed with good natured teasing from everyone, and eventually Callum relaxed as he watched his daughter with her groom. Only a fraction of him felt the dismay he projected, and that came more from obligation than truth. He was happy for his little lass, and he could tell Blaine would treat her well.

"His introduction to the clan is going far better than mine did," Siùsan whispered. "Despite that disaster, I still fell in love with ye. And I havenae stopped loving ye since. He reminds me of ye, ye ken. He's a good mon, *mo chridhe*. He will treat her just as well as ye've treated me since we married. She made a good choice."

"I ken, *mo neach beag*." My little one. Callum had called her that since the beginning. "I dinna let a day go by that I take yer love and our life together for granted. I pray he's as wise."

"Wise? That might be a wee much." Siùsan ran her hand underneath her husband's plaid and up his thigh. She would have done more, but the keep's doors swung open, and a guard practically dragged a young woman into the Great Hall. She stumbled and would have fallen if the guard didn't have his arm around her. It became obvious that he was holding her up rather than pulling her against her will.

"Greer!" Rose's chair shot out behind her, but it was Thor who leaped from the dais and sprinted to the unexpected arrival. He swept her into his arms and scowled at the guard.

"We dinna tug women along with us. Ye carry a weakened woman or ye get help." Thor spun on his heel, his plaid swishing around his legs. He brushed hair back from Greer's face and spied the bruises and what was likely a broken nose. He headed toward the stairs, but he had to stop when Rose stepped in front of him.

"Greer?" Rose kept her voice low.

"He kens." Greer's hoarse voice scratched her throat and made her wince. She curled toward Thor's chest and shut her eyes. He felt her relax as he tightened his hold. He didn't know what possessed him to rush to her aid, but he'd never seen a woman in a worse state.

"Mama?" Thor looked at Siùsan as she joined him and Rose as they watched Greer. Blaine came to stand beside Rose and eased her out of Thor's path.

"Bring her upstairs. I'll get a chamber ready for our guest. Lass?"

Greer shook her head and burrowed closer to Thor. He looked at Rose, unsure what to make of his feelings or Greer's implicit trust in him. They'd met several times, but it was rarely cordial. He followed his mother and sister up the stairs, his aunts and Blaine following. When Siùsan continued to the second flight of stairs to reach the third-floor guest chambers, Thor turned away. He marched to his chamber and shouldered open his door. He drew back the covers on his bed and eased Greer onto the mattress. He eased off her slippers and pulled the covers over her before he went to stand by the fireplace.

"Thor, she canna stay here." Siùsan shook her head.

"I ken, Mama. But what am I supposed to do while we wait for ye to make up the chamber? I canna hold her when it's obvious she needs to lie down. She doesnae look like she could sit up for more than a breath. I'll take her to the chamber once it's ready."

"Ye have an unwed sister and five unwed cousins. Ye could have taken her to any of their beds," Brighde spoke up. She chuckled when Thor scowled at her. "Ye look like yer uncle when ye glower like that. It didna intimidate me when I woke in Alex's bed after sennights of being poorly more than a score ago, and it doesnae intimidate me when ye do it. I changed yer raggies."

"And Uncle Alex kenned ye were in danger of freezing to death. He didna think ye would survive waiting for Hagatha to ready a chamber for ye. I dinna think Lady Greer will die, but I thought she would be more comfortable on a bed. I dinna go bursting into ma sister's or ma cousins' chambers. I learned nae to when Rose and I were twelve. I'm never doing that again." Thor crossed his arms. His aunts laughed as his mother left to ready the guest chamber.

Rose perched on the edge of the bed and rested her hand on her friend's shoulder. She couldn't care less who carried Greer or where they lay her. She just wanted to know if her friend was in worse condition than she looked.

"Greer? It's me. Are ye awake?"

"Aye, Rose. Everything hurts. I need to speak to Laird Sinclair or yer da. I rode here to see them. It's urgent."

"I'll get them," Blaine offered from near the doorway. With a collective warning glare at Thor, the three aunts Deirdre, Ceit, and Brighde, followed Blaine from the chamber. Thor approached and stood beside Rose, but then he thought better of it and crouched beside the bed.

"Lady Greer, did yer da do this to ye?"

Greer's eyes fluttered open as she looked at Thor, then Rose, then back at Thor. "Aye. He found out that we're friends, Rose. He caught me preparing a missive. I wouldnae tell him what it meant or who it was for. He guessed Albert would ken since he's always ma guard." Tears slid down Greer's dirt-smeared cheeks. "He ordered Albert to appear before him and demanded to ken everything. Albert, God bless him, remained silent. Ma father took the lash to him, and Albert still didna betray me. I couldnae bear it after the third strike and broke free from the guards holding me back. I stepped in front of him as he brought the lash down a fourth time."

Greer shifted on the mattress to pull apart her arisaid. Thor and Rose thought they might be ill. The front of Greer's gown was shredded and saturated with blood. There was a livid welt that surrounded an open cut from where the lash struck her. She must have stood very close to Edgar when he landed the whip. She would need stitches and would likely always bear a scar.

"I told Father that I'd made a friend in a neighboring clan and sometimes went to visit. The Oliphants and ye are the closest that I could easily ride to. He guessed I made a friend here. He raved aboot how the women in our clan are naught but whores for the Sinclairs. He assumed ma friend is a mon. He beat me for it. He doesnae ken it's ye, Rose. And Albert lived. That's all that matters to me."

Rose and Thor watched as Greer's eyes slid closed again, and they knew she struggled through the pain. Thor reached out and stroked her hair as he looked at Rose. Never in all the years since he'd first ridden out had he felt so utterly useless as a man. There was nothing he could do to fix Greer or her situation, but it tore at his heart to see his sister's best friend in such a state. He hadn't agreed with Rose when he learned about her secret friendship, but he hadn't begrudged her having a friend who was a Gunn. No question that friendship had cost Greer, flinging her into this dire situation, but it relieved him to know she trusted the Sinclairs enough to come here. He backed away when someone knocked on the open door. He watched Liam and Callum enter.

"Laird Sinclair?" Greer's eyes remained closed. Both were blackened, but they hadn't swollen shut. However, they looked painful, so no one thought less of her for speaking to the earl with her eyes shut.

Rose moved out of the way, and Liam took her place then answered softly. "Aye, lass."

"Father isnae going after the Mackays first. By now, he's attacked the MacLeods of Assynt. This happened yesterday. I was unconscious when he rode out. He had me locked in ma chamber, but a maid let me out just after nightfall."

"Yesterday! Bluidy hell." Thor pushed past Rose and eased Greer onto her back. He gentled his tone. "Greer, yer wounds need tending sharpish if they're already a day auld. They'll get infected. May I show Grandda what yer father did?"

Greer nodded and lifted her hand to move her arisaid, but she was too weak to do it again. The little energy she'd had, she'd spent during her mad dash to Dunbeath. Thor eased open her arisaid and looked at Liam, then Callum. Both men appeared horrified as

Thor let go of the material. He made to step away, but Greer's hand rested on his wrist. He slid it into his.

"I ken ye dinna approve of me being friends with yer sister. If ye did, she would have told ye. Why are ye being so kind to me?"

"Because ye may be a Gunn, but ye are ma sister's friend. I dinna have to think yer friendship is wise to accept that ye're important to Rose. And nay one deserves this kind of treatment from their father." Thor shook his head in disgust and disbelief. He couldn't imagine any Sinclair man ever treating his child like a criminal. There were times when his parents likely wanted to skelp him, and he'd been on the receiving end of his father's hand across his backside more than once as a child, but Callum had never beaten him.

"Rose?" Siùsan entered the chamber.

"Aye, Mama. Greer, can ye make it up the stairs if we move ye into a different chamber?"

"Nay." Thor insisted. "I'll take the guest chamber. Lady Greer can remain here until she's well enough to walk to the other chamber on her own. Until then, she can use this one." He opened a chest and withdrew a satchel. He filled it with clothes and slung it over his shoulder. "Lady Greer, there is nay need to rush. Rest and let Mama tend to ye."

"Thank ye, Thor. I feel badly aboot taking yer chamber, but I appreciate nae having to move again. Lady Siùsan?"

"Aye, lass."

"I think I may need yer healer."

"She's on her way. Rose, tell the servants to bring the tub in here. Callum, Da, step out, please." All the sisters-by-marriage began calling Liam "Da" not long after they each married into the family. It felt natural

195

from the start. None of the women had healthy relationships with their own fathers, so they'd all welcomed Liam's paternal kindness. "Thor, we prepared the chamber above this one."

When only Siùsan and Greer remained in the chamber, Greer did as best she could to help Siùsan while the older woman undressed her. "Lady Siùsan, ye dinna approve of yer son giving me his chamber. I'm sorry."

"Ye have naught to apologize for. It's history repeating itself, that's all."

"Lady Brighde said something aboot that, but I didna understand."

"It's naught to worry aboot and a story for another day."

"I still appreciate his offer. I dinna ken that I'm up to aught more than just getting undressed. Ma lady, everywhere hurts. I didna ken I could be in so much pain and still be breathing."

They fell silent as servants arrived and Rose returned. Once the three women were alone, Rose and Siùsan helped Greer to the tub. Siùsan bathed her as gently as she had her own children when they were infants. Rose helped by pouring clean water over Greer's hair after she scrubbed the locks and gingerly massaged her friend's scalp. Siùsan and Rose kept their expressions studiously blank in case Greer should open her eyes and see them, but they exchanged looks many times. Livid and swollen bruises covered Greer's body. Some were clearly from fists, others were likely from boots. Fingerprints marred her throat and upper arms. The wound from the whip troubled Siùsan, so it relieved her to see Matilda slip into the chamber.

The woman took over the position as the clan's healer when Saoirse married and left Dunbeath. She hadn't been the clan's official healer for long, but she'd helped Saoirse and her predecessor for years. Siùsan was confident in the woman's skills. The three able-bodied women dried Greer and eased her back into bed before Matilda tended to the various wounds. She brewed willow bark tea and used a yarrow-based salve on the wounds after she sewed the deep cut shut. By the time Greer drank the tea, and Matilda finished her ministrations, Greer was fast asleep.

Rose answered the door when someone knocked twice. She opened the door to find Blaine on the other side. She stepped into the passageway as Siùsan and Matilda tidied the chamber.

"Is she all right?"

"Matilda says she will be. Blaine, it's terrible. She's covered in bruises, and it took Matilda a long time to stitch the lash wound. It was even deeper than it appeared. If she develops a fever or it weeps more puss, Matilda is worried we might lose her."

Blaine held Rose as she shuddered against him. He stroked her hair while she clung to him. "Do ye wish for me to sit with ye?"

"This is our wedding night."

"And it's one night out of many more to come. I ken how important Greer is to ye, and ye wouldnae enjoy aught because ye'd feel guilty. I will keep ye company, and mayhap ye can doze while I keep watch."

"Ye're a good husband. I dinna think most men would be so understanding."

"Kyla, there will be times when I canna put ye first nay matter how much I want to. But I can do that

Celeste Barclay

now. I spoke to yer da and grandda. Can we talk for a moment out here? I dinna want to disturb Greer, but I also dinna want her to hear. I fear it'll upset her, even if she chose to come here rather than remain with her clan."

"How is she?"

Blaine and Rose turned toward Thor who strode down the passageway. He'd been part of the meeting Blaine took part in. All the laird's family had except for Siùsan and Rose.

"It's grave, Thor. Things must have been far worse than she ever told me. To endure the pain she must have felt, tells me she built a tolerance for it. I ken ye saw the gash, but there was nary an inch of her nae covered in bruises and marks. She'd been punched and kicked. Someone—assumedly Edgar—tried to strangle her."

"Is she sleeping?" Thor looked at the door.

"Aye. Matilda gave her some willow bark tea. Mama and I will take turns sitting with her tonight."

Thor's jaw worked from side to side. Rose had never seen her brother react the way he had tonight. He'd tried to appear casual once he realized the attention he drew by taking Greer to his chamber, and he attempted to appear unaffected now. But the tick in his jaw gave away his true feelings.

"I hope she gets some sound sleep tonight and that she's soon on the mend." Thor spoke, but he looked at the door rather than Rose or Blaine. He nodded as though to assure himself before he turned to Rose. "Ma felicitations, Rosie. I'm happy for ye and Blaine. I ken this isnae the wedding night most couples would wish for, but I still wish ye well." He'd already hugged his sister before the evening meal, but

198

he gave her a quick embrace again. He stuck out his arm to Blaine and grasped the older warrior's forearm. "It's aboot bluidy time I got a brother."

They embraced loosely, pounding each other on the back before releasing their grips. Thor made his way to the stairs, but Rose and Blaine remained in the passageway.

"The meeting was brief," Blaine explained. "But we are all in agreement that we're riding out as soon as everything is organized. Edgar's violence toward Greer speaks to his desperation. He lashed out because things arenae going according to his plan. We need to take advantage of that."

"I figured ye would. I ken better than to ask when ye'll return or to ask for a promise that ye will. But be careful, Husband. I dinna wish to be a widow when I've just become a wife."

Rose and Blaine slipped inside the chamber. Blaine arranged a chair beside the bed for Rose and angled another near the fireplace for himself. Rose whispered quietly to Matilda and Siùsan, listening to their instructions before they left. The couple settled themselves into their chairs, prepared for a long bedside vigil.

Chapter Fourteen

Rose woke to the rise and fall of a boulder beside her head. She blinked open her eyes at the same time she inhaled. She immediately knew the rock-hard surface against which she rested was her husband's chest. *Husband.* She repeated the word to herself and smiled.

"What's made ye so happy this morning, *leannan?*"

"Waking in ma husband's arms is a rather fine way to start ma day."

"And holding ye was a fine way to spend ma night." Blaine grinned as Rose tried to stifle a yawn.

"I dinna remember coming to sit in yer lap."

"Ye didna. Ye were dozing off in yer chair. When yer head bobbed for at least the tenth time, I decided ye should rest against me."

Rose's lips pursed, then chuckled. "Ye make a fine pillow. Soft in all the right places."

Blaine glanced at Greer, who slept like the dead, but he still lowered his voice. "Ye ken exactly which place is hard. Yer arse has kept me up for hours."

Rose grinned at the double entendre. She shifted,

which only made Blaine groan, but he helped her sit more upright. "Thank ye for holding me while I slept. I guess I needed the rest even though I thought I could stay up all night. Has she woken?"

"Nae once. She's barely moved. Just enough for me to ken she's alive. She hasnae been sweating either, so I dinna think she has a fever."

Rose stood and shook out her skirts, smirking at how Blaine's plaid now tented over his rod. He tugged his sporran back into place and swatted Rose's backside as she turned toward Greer. She made her way to her friend's bedside and laid the back of her hand against Greer's forehead. It was cool to the touch, which pleased Rose, even if it was a little clammy.

"Greer?" Rose gingerly rested her hand on her friend's shoulder.

"Aye, I'm awake. I never imagined ye snored."

"What?" Rose's eyebrows shot up, and she glanced at Blaine, mortified.

"Just jesting." Greer's eyes opened a crack, but she flinched at the early morning light peeking around the fur window hangings and the candlelight from the bedside table. "I dinna ken if ye do. I just woke. I dinna remember much from last night."

With an agonized moan, Greer shifted and tried to sit up. Blaine rushed forward to help Rose adjust Greer. Blaine supported her torso while Rose shoved pillows behind her. Sweat beaded Greer's forehead when she rested back against the pile.

"This isnae yer chamber, is it?" Greer looked around. "This is Thor's. He brought me here?"

"Aye. He thought ye needed to lie down and didna think ye would last while Mama made up a guest chamber. Ye can stay here until ye're well enough to move upstairs."

"Nay. I have to go home. I only came to warn yer grandda and da. I canna leave ma people." Greer half-heartedly pushed at the sheets. She wore one of Rose's nightgowns that a servant brought when the tub and water arrived the night before. She looked tiny within the voluminous linen, even though she wasn't that much smaller than Rose. It made her vulnerability starkly obvious.

"Ye're nae going anywhere, Greer. Ye're too poorly, and if this is what yer father already did to ye, then I'm nae letting ye go back for him to finish ye off."

"The MacLeods will retaliate, and the Lord only kens where ma father is now. I must go home to ma people."

"Lady Greer, dinna fash. Laird Sinclair sent men last night to scout near yer home. If Torrian or Michail lead troops to Clyth, the Sinclairs will intercept them. They'll tell the MacLeods to come here first."

"And if the damage is already done?" Greer shook her head and tried to swing her legs over the edge of the bed.

"Greer, stop. Ye'll do yerself a mischief. Ye simply canna travel. Ye shouldnae get out of bed. Listen to me, please. If ye push yerself now, ye willna be any good to anyone soon. Ye need to rest and heal. Ye canna help yer people if ye're dead."

"I'm nae dying, Rose. But ma people might if someone isnae there to protect the keep."

"Lady Greer, ye canna do that single-handedly. Yer clan's warriors ken what to do to defend yer home. Lady Rose is right. Ye willna make it to Clyth as ye are now. Give yerself a day's rest at least. If ye're up to it tomorrow, I'll take ye by wagon maself."

"Why?" Greer's eyes had swelled more during the night, so she could only open them a slit. If she weren't already squinting, she would have narrowed her eyes at him. "Wouldnae it be better for ye if I fell from ma horse and broke ma neck?"

"Ye are ma wife's friend. I dinna wish ye harm even if our clans dinna get along. It's obvious ye wish a vera different future for yer people than yer father does. I canna fault ye for defending yer people. And I dinna wage ma wars against women and children."

"Wife?" Greer turned toward Rose.

"Aye. There's plenty for me to tell, too. Blaine and I handfasted."

"Felicitations." Greer turned her hand over and slid it toward Rose, who perched on the bed. Rose took her friend's hand and held it. "Keith, why havenae ye ridden on ma clan yet? It's been more than a sennight since ma father raided yer village. I dinna understand why ye've waited. Is it because ye were courting Rose?"

"I didna want to act in haste. I planned to retaliate, but yer information made me reconsider. Other matters have come up that complicate this, but I will nae act alone. It's a matter of deciding how best to handle this."

"Does that mean the Sinclairs, Mackays, and Sutherlands will ride out with the Keiths? Ye will annihilate anyone who crosses yer path."

"We havenae decided yet, Lady Greer. Yer father must be stopped, but that doesnae mean massacring yer people. Who stands to inherit once yer father is gone?"

"He'd planned to remarry and continue to try to beget an heir. There arenae any more men in the laird's family except for Seamus and Magnus Mackenzie, or Michail, Adan, and Edward MacLeod. They're all cousins of some sort. Seamus is already Laird Mackenzie, and Michail will one day be the MacLeod of Assynt. Until Seamus's son is auld enough to become the clan's tánaiste, Magnus canna go anywhere. Besides, I dinna think any of them would want to be Laird Gunn. Mayhap if I married a nobleman who wasna a laird or tánaiste, the mon could take the title. I truly dinna ken."

Seamus and Magnus Mackenzie's mother, Elizabeth, was Edgar's aunt on his father's side. Michail, Adan, and Edward's mother, Catriona, was Edgar's father's cousin. There was no male, legitimate or otherwise, left to inherit the lairdship. If none of these men or Greer's future husband took the position, the clan's council would vote in a new laird. The risk of further instability in the northern Highlands made that a highly undesirable outcome.

"Has yer father talked of marrying ye to someone?" Rose could think of no one in the Highlands who would wish to bind their clan to the Gunns because it would put them in opposition with an alliance no one could defeat.

"Nay. He's still praying he'll have a son. I think he intends to make me a spinster, so I will run the keep. If he marries the MacDonnell lass, she should become chatelaine. But I suspect he wants me to keep that position, so he can play with his toy whenever he wishes. He willna want her distracted by duties if he's trying to get her with child." Greer grimaced in disgust. The MacDonnell lass was almost ten years her junior. Greer couldn't picture the young woman knowing how to run a keep as well as Greer did after more than a decade as Castle Clyth's chatelaine.

"What do ye want, Lady Greer?" Blaine asked. "Would it be a husband who can lead alongside ye or one of yer cousins to take yer father's place?"

"Alongside me?" Greer shifted her gaze from Blaine to Rose. "Ye picked the right mon. He thinks like yer family. Keith—"

"Please call me Blaine. Ye're Rose's friend, so I dinna think we must stand on such formality."

"Vera well." Greer was slow to agree, but with a sigh she relented. "Ye should call me Greer then. Blaine, most men dinna want a woman alongside them for aught but bed sport. Nay mon is going to have me lead a clan as his partner."

"That's nae true, Greer." Rose attempted to appear reassuring. "We ken plenty of lairds and ladies who see each other as equals and whose clans respect that."

"And they're all somehow related to ye. Yer grandmother was a Sutherland, whose brother is married to a Ross, who is Lady Campbell's aunt. Yer mother's cousin is Michail of Assynt, who is married to Lady Blythe, whose sister, Lady Emelie, is married to Laird Campbell's brother. Their other sister, Lady Isabella, has lived here with yer clan since we were bairns. Lady MacLeod of Lewis is yer father's cousin. Her sister is Lady Cameron. They're both originally Sutherlands. I could go on and on, and ye ken it. Whether it's by blood or by marriage, everyone is connected through alliances except for the Gunns. Nay one will ever want to marry me."

"Would ye leave the Highlands?" Blaine assumed he knew the answer, but he asked, nonetheless.

"I may nae have a choice, but I dinna want to. I'd rather be a spinster with ma clan."

A knock interrupted their conversation. Rose helped straighten the sheets around Greer while Blaine went to answer the door. He found Siùsan, Callum, and Thor on the other side.

"I brought a tray for all of ye," Siùsan explained as Blaine opened the door wider for them to pass. Blaine watched Thor's eyes dart around the chamber before settling on Greer. He witnessed the flash of rage before Thor extinguished it. Greer appeared more rested than the day before, but with more sunlight filtering into the chamber, her injuries became more defined. Thor moved to stand beside the hearth while Callum followed Siùsan to the bedside. She placed the tray on the bed and pushed it toward Greer.

"Lady Greer, it's good to see ye awake. Is there aught our healer or Lady Siùsan can bring ye to make ye more comfortable?" Callum stood behind Siùsan with his hands cupping her shoulders. Greer watched the long-time married couple, and she felt even more keenly aware of her dire future than she had only minutes ago discussing it with Rose and Blaine. She glanced at Thor, who watched her from across the chamber.

"Nay thank ye. I'm feeling much better than last night. Lady Siùsan, thank ye for the tray. I admit I'm famished."

"Ye should eat. We can come back." Thor pushed away from the wall as he stared at his father. Something passed between them that Rose, Blaine, and Greer sensed but none understood.

"We'll leave ye in peace in just a moment," Callum countered, his harsh stare keeping his son from countermanding him. "Lady Greer, a messenger from Assynt arrived an hour ago. He'd ridden day and night. Yer father razed six villages in one day. The warriors scattered to the wind, riding only in pairs. The MacLeods couldnae chase all of them, and they never discovered where they reunited with yer father. Do ye ken where that might be?"

"I dinna ken. There is all of Mackay territory between them and us. They could hide there, and I dinna ken that land. If ma father already attacked the MacLeods, I dinna think he will attack the Mackays next, even though he will have crossed their land. It's too obvious. I think he will either ride on the Keiths again or go to the Sutherlands." Greer shook her head. "Nay, nae the Sutherlands. If he didna attack the Mackays or here, it's because he kens ye'd overpower him. The same is true for the Sutherlands. Mayhap the Camerons since the laird is with the Sutherlands. I fear he might try to lure the Camerons' enemies to help him. I heard him talking aboot the Mackintoshes, MacBains, and MacThomases a while ago. I ken things are still tense with the Chattan Confederation. I—I admit I listen to ma father's meetings with the council. That's how I ken what to pass along to Rose."

"That's what we suspected. We have scouts out. Missives were dispatched to Varrich and Dunrobin, so the Mackays and Sutherlands will ken soon." Callum offered a fatherly smile to Greer. "Lass, we ken this isnae yer doing. Ye've risked much for yer clan, so I can guess how eager ye are to return. I ken ye feel responsible for everyone, but ye canna leave until this is finally done. We will do what we can to spare the innocent, but yer father has declared war. I can guarantee nay Sinclair or any of our allies will kill ye, but I canna make that guarantee aboot yer father or his allies. Ye are welcome here indefinitely."

Greer's shoulders drooped, but she nodded. "Could I have a little while by maself, please?"

"Ye canna get out through the window, and there is nay way ye're making it out through the Great Hall or the kitchens, so ye can cease yer plotting and just stay put." Thor stalked toward the bed, stopping when he stood beside it. His gaze met Greer's, and he forced himself not to reach out and shake her, hoping it would knock sense into her. "I see ye glancing at the window. Ye'll break yer neck before ye make it out of here, so dinna bother limping over to look. Ye willna make it down a flight of stairs without falling and likely rolling to yer death."

"Thor!" Rose stared at her brother, but he paid her no attention. He was locked in a battle of wills with Greer, unlike anything Rose had witnessed from her brother or from her friend. She knew they had never been social or even pleasant to one another, but she couldn't believe how he acted.

"What? I'm nae standing next to ye while ye sob at her funeral. Dinna do that to ma sister, Lady Greer. She might forgive ye, but I willna."

Greer opened her mouth, then snapped it shut before opening it again. "I remember just fine how ye hold a grudge, Thor. I willna add to ma list of sins. All I wish is for a nap. I ken I canna do aught more without help."

"Gree—"

"It's naught, Rose. Thor, thank ye for allowing me to stay in yer chamber. I willna do aught foolish." Greer didn't look at Rose as she spoke, keeping her gaze on Thor. But she reached for the tray and grabbed the heel of bread. She bit into it and tore a chunk from it, cocking her eyebrow as though she dared Thor to argue against her eating.

"Ye're welcome." Thor nodded, his posture relaxing as he stepped back from the bed. His parents glowered at him, but he refused to heed their warning. He walked to the door and opened it, but he didn't pass through. He met Rose's gaze. She slid her hand into Blaine's and tugged his. They walked into the passageway and waited for Callum and Siùsan. Before shutting the door, Thor added, "Sleep well, ma lady."

"What was that aboot?" Rose hissed.

"I realized how ye broke yer wrist when we were three-and-ten at the Gathering the Gordons hosted. Ye may have fallen out of a tree, but ye were with Greer. Ye said ye'd taken a wager, but ye didna say with whom. Now I ken. Ye hadnae told me who, but ye said the person ye raced was a squirrel. Yer names for each other make sense now."

"So ye dinna trust her?" Callum asked.

"I trust her to do what she believes is best for her clan. That doesnae mean it'll be best for her. Keep yer eye on her, Rose. She will try to leave." Thor stalked away, taking the stairs down to the Great Hall. His family watched him before the two couples went their separate ways. Rose led Blaine to their chamber, where he unlaced her gown and helped her into bed.

Despite sleeping in Blaine's lap for much of the night, Rose had felt exhausted as they walked down the passageway to their chamber. However, now that she lay beside Blaine in bed, she found sleep wasn't what she craved. She trailed her fingertips along his collar bone several times before trailing them down his abdomen. His hand caressed her backside, marveling at both the feel and the knowledge that he would spend the rest of his life enjoying the sensation.

"Are ye tired, *leannan*? Do ye wish for more sleep?"

"In a little while. Nae yet."

Their mouths fused as their tongues dueled. They inched closer until their bodies were pressed together. But Rose pulled away, watching Blaine as she slid down the bed. She nudged his legs apart as she fisted his length. He couldn't tear his eyes off her as she kneeled beside him and leaned over. She swirled her tongue over the tip of his cock, flicking at the slit, before her hand released him. She licked him from the base of his rod to the bulbous head. She flicked her tongue again, this time against the ridge running along the underside. He twitched, and she grinned as she lowered her mouth onto him.

She knew as much as what Saoirse, Cerys, and Elene had told her over the couple years that her cousins had been married. Wee Liam's Orcadian wife, Elene, had struggled at first since her Gaelic wasn't fluent when she arrived in the Highlands. But by the time Cerys married Blake, she'd learned enough that she and Cerys enlightened several of the unmarried female cousins. Saoirse had offered even more insights after she married, so Rose had felt confident with what to do and how to pleasure Blaine, until she actually began. She prayed what she did brought him the same pleasure as his ministrations brought her.

When she glanced up at him, she found him watching her intently. One hand fisted the sheets while his other arm was bent behind his head, propping him up enough for him to see. His abdomen flexed with every labored breath as his excitement grew each time she drew him deeper into her mouth. She struggled a few times until she recalled she was supposed to relax and breathe through her nose. Once she mastered that, she took more of him into her mouth until she could handle no more.

"Kyla, I shall spend, and this isnae how I want to do it. I wish to be inside ye as ye climax and take me with ye."

She didn't wish to release him when he tried to draw her away, but she squeaked when he lifted her and practically tossed her onto her back with a growl. He rolled over her and hovered his body above hers as he rested on his forearms.

"Are ye too sore after yesterday? Do ye need more rest?"

"I'm only a wee sore, and it's more from muscles I've never used like that before. I'm nae in any pain. Unless ye count the way I ache for ye right now. Blaine, I need ye."

"Who am I to deny ma wife her needs?" Blaine lined the head of his cock with her entrance. "Do ye wish for me to be gentle?"

"Nae in the least. Maybe some other time. I want to show ye how much I desire ye, and I want to ken if ye—" Rose couldn't finish because Blaine swooped in for a passionate kiss that stole her breath. It was possessive and needy, and it matched how she felt.

"Ye want to ken if I desire ye as much as ye do me. Bluidy hell, Kyla, nay mon has desired a woman more than I want ye. It's nay possible. Ye've kenned I've wanted ye more than aught since the moment I saw ye." Blaine watched Rose, and he realized physical desire wasn't all she meant. His kiss was tender and languid this time. "I didna exaggerate yesterday. Ye have all of me. Ye ken I want more than a handfast, but I willna rush ye. There's never been a woman before ye who I wanted to spend ma life with. I want ye as ma wife for far more than just yer body."

"I believe ye, Blaine. I've never doubted yer word, but I think ye understand how I feel now. I was going to say, I want to ken if ye can keep up." Rose grinned as she flexed her hips and tilted them to invite Blaine's cock inside her. With a growl, he thrust into her, seating himself to the hilt.

"I shall show ye just how ye keep me up, and I will last as long as ye can. Dinna ye doubt that I will make love to ye for hours if ye want."

He surged into her over and over as she rose to meet each thrust. She gripped his backside as the muscles bunched beneath her palms. She encouraged him to piston his hips harder and faster. He shifted his weight to rest on one forearm as his other hand kneaded her breast and rolled her nipple. Her right hand moved to the back of his head, burrowing her fingers into his short blond locks. She pressed, and he obliged. Their mouths once more together. When they were breathless, Rose peppered kisses along his jaw, and he was certain the fire between them singed each place her lips brushed. Heat built within him as need consumed him.

Rose kept her moans quiet, but she already knew

Blaine enjoyed hearing them as much as she reveled in each grunt as he worked her closer to release. She shifted and sought the exact angle that would bring her bliss. He grasped her thigh, bringing it to his shoulder, changing the sensations as he slid deeper. It was almost too much for Rose, but she wanted to try any and everything with her husband.

Blaine shifted onto his knees, drawing her other leg over his shoulder as he slammed into her over and over. He had one thread of control left, and it rapidly frayed. He clung to it lest he lose all inhibitions and inadvertently hurt Rose. He was always mindful that she was new to coupling, and he was so much larger than her. But she was so responsive, and the temptation was so great. With her hair strewn across the pillows, her breasts bouncing, and her cheeks flushed, he couldn't help himself.

When she reached for him, he couldn't resist the invitation. He shifted her legs to wrap over his hips as he lowered himself once more. She coiled herself around him, her arms and legs encircling him.

"I'm close, Blaine. Just a little more...Aye...Like that...Aye...Oh!"

Blaine felt her entire body contract, and her core squeezed him as she held him in place. He couldn't stop his body's need. His seed squirted from him in hot jets as he pulsed over and over inside his bride. He hung his head, their foreheads resting together. When her arms tugged at him, he eased some of his weight onto her, knowing already how she loved the feeling of them being chest to chest. Their kisses were short and affectionate as their pulses slowed.

He rolled off when his arms shook too much for him to be certain he wouldn't crush Rose. He pulled her with him, enjoying how her waist-length hair spread over her back and onto his chest. He gripped her backside as they laid together in companionable silence. He glanced down at her when she couldn't stifle her yawn.

"Did I wear ye out?"

"Mayhap I wore maself out."

Blaine gave her backside a playful slap, then a squeeze. "Cheeky."

"Aye. But dinna lie. I saw ye fighting nae to yawn a moment ago."

"Mayhap a wee one."

They moved until they could draw the covers over themselves. Rose nestled closer as she dropped soft kisses on his chest. His hand stroked her back until he knew she'd drifted off. He followed her only a moment later.

Chapter Fifteen

Neither Blaine nor Rose had their wish for a sennight-long honeymoon. Greer's unexpected arrival meant they had responsibilities they couldn't overlook. Rose tended to her friend, keeping her company throughout the day. She read to Greer, or they chatted about what Rose feared when she left Dunbeath and began life as a keep's chatelaine. Greer slept off and on throughout the day, so while she napped, Rose returned to her usual duties. Blaine spent his time either in the lists training, or in Liam's solar with the laird, Callum, and Thor. He never discovered the younger man's reason for his disdain toward Greer. Blaine sensed it stemmed from far more than Rose's accident ten years earlier. Thor steadfastly refused to give away anything.

By the third day after Greer's arrival, they put a plan in place. Blaine agreed that the most immediate concern was tracking Edgar and his warriors. There was nothing they could do about the Irvines and the betrothal until they heard from King David. They'd practically forgotten the Murrays. Liam and Callum explained the content of their missives. Both granted Rose and Blaine their permission to marry. Callum reminded the king that one quality the monarch's father, Robert the Bruce, best admired about the Sinclairs was their unceasing loyalty to the crown and one another. The Bruce had often cited the Sinclairs as the reason why he fell in love with his first wife, Isabella of Mar, and why he'd developed tender feelings that blossomed into love for his second wife, Elizabeth de Burgh. Callum reminded him that such affection for the Sinclairs was why the Bruce named Liam one of David's godparents.

Liam's missive reminded King David that, as the Earl of Caithness, marriage into his clan was more than just advantageous for the couple. It secured the alliance that would support the Keiths, just as it did all the other clans bound to the Sinclairs. He noted that the Bruce's ultimate goal was a unified Scotland. The former king believed that uniting the clans was the only way to defeat the English, and it proved true. It was the unified clans under Andrew Murray that continued to beat back the new waves of English incursion. More clans allied to the Sinclairs meant greater peace and stability in the Highlands. It would allow the clans to continue their focus on defeating the English rather than each other. Without commanding the young king, Liam essentially gave his own edict.

"The scouts returned," Liam announced as he joined his family in his solar. He'd summoned them when the watch spied the men cresting the last hill. He met with them and heard their report. His grim expression told his family they wouldn't like the news. "Edgar attacked two of our border villages, but they were unprepared for farmers to have trained as warriors in their younger days. The village survived, and they told the scouts that the Gunns attacked in the dead of night. It made it difficult to track them when they fled."

"Did he attack at night, and that's why the Mac-Leods couldnae find him?" Tavish rested his elbows on the table as he leaned forward.

"Nay. He led that raid in full daylight. I think he wished for the MacLeods to ken just who they were." Callum's tone dripped with loathing.

"Where did he strike next?" Deirdre looked at her husband, and Magnus covered her hand.

"I dinna ken if he's been anywhere else. They havenae gone to the Frasers of Lovat as far as we ken." Liam offered Deirdre what little assurance he could. Her relationship had remained strained with her parents while they lived, but she held no animosity to her cousin, who now led the clan. They'd grown close during adulthood, and she worried for the people among whom she'd grown up. "Ma cousin would support ye if ye asked."

Deirdre silently worried that it was her family who would ask for aid if the Gunns thought to make their way to Cameron territory. The Gunns could easily pass through Fraser territory.

Rose knew the Gunns would have to cross the Mackays' entire southern territory from the Mac-Leods of Assynt and enter the Sinclairs' just to reach their own land. Then they would have to travel farther north to the coast to raid the Keiths again. It would be too easy for the allied clans to trap them. "I dinna think they'll strike the Keiths again if they already struck two of our villages. Were the ones they attacked on the border with the Mackays or Sutherlands?"

"It was where our land meets the Sutherlands and Mackays. He was making a point." Liam's lips flattened. "Ma guess is he'll aim for the smaller, northern branch of the Frasers. He might even raid the northern branch of the Munros. He kens Tristan willna ignore that, and it'll draw him into the fight. Lady Munro's father is Tristan's godfather. He'd truly be a fool to attack Cairren's clan. Innes Kennedy was a mercenary in France with Tristan's father before they both unexpectedly inherited their lairdships. Innes will come, and Edgar willna even ken the mon breathes the same air as him before he's dead."

"Would that be so bad?" Blaine would gladly accept Innes's stealthy tactics if it ended the bloodshed and ended the threat to his clan and his new family.

"Aye and nay. It would rid us of the Gunn, but it would heighten tensions with the Lowlanders. They willna think Innes acted alone to protect his daughter. They'll believe we're drawing them into our savage feuds. Worse, they'll think we needed a Lowlander to solve our problems. We dinna need to antagonize them more when we still have the English to deal with. We have to fight alongside the border lairds."

"Tristan kens the same things as Innes," Siùsan pointed out. "He trained Michail years ago, and Michail's had success with the tactics when the Gunns have tried to infiltrate their keep. Seamus and Magnus Óg learned too."

"Aye." Liam exhaled a frustrated breath. "We ken we have people in the Highlands with the knowledge, but it willna matter if Edgar targets Cairren or her people. Innes will come. Tristan sent a messenger that he's coming here tomorrow before he heads home to Varrich. We can strategize with him, but I think our best plan is to send warriors to our borders. If we include Seamus and Óg, and warn Montgomery, we could cast a net and trap Edgar in the center."

Montgomery Campbell inherited the Ross laird-ship through his mother, Laurel. His uncle and name-sake, Montgomery Ross, could never marry his partner or allow the relationship to be public. An injury provided an excuse for Monty the Elder to remain a bachelor. Monty the Younger just became Laird Ross the previous year. It bound the Rosses and Campbells twice over.

Siùsan's brothers wouldn't hesitate to lend their aid since they were devoted to their sister, who raised them when their parents were too indifferent to care. It also benefited them to cease the Gunns' aggression, since they could easily fall victim as Edgar made his rounds.

Thor remained quiet while everyone else spoke, but he had his own suspicions about why the Gunns attacked the Sinclairs next. "He must ken Greer came here. Our villages were our punishment for giving her shelter."

"Are ye suggesting we turn ma best friend out?" Rose's chest pinched as she stared at her brother. She couldn't understand why her twin and her best friend seemed to dislike one another so much. She'd never mentioned Greer to Thor, and she'd never truly complained to Greer about her brother. She never imagined their clan differences would matter to them as individuals, but she supposed they did.

"I didna say that, Rose. I gave an explanation for the situation. I wouldnae give a stray mutt to Edgar

Gunn, let alone the daughter he's already beaten within a hair's breadth of death. She isnae going anywhere near her father or her land until he canna harm her. I'm insulted ye would think I would ever turn her, or any woman—any person—away who canna defend themselves. Our family raised me better than that." Thor appeared genuinely hurt by Rose's accusation, and she felt appropriately ashamed.

"I'm sorry. I'm scared for her."

Thor sat beside his sister and tugged her hair as he had when they were children. "Besides why pick on her when ye are so much closer?"

They'd never remained at odds for long, and Thor saw Rose's embarrassment and remorse. He wouldn't make her feel worse. As she had when they were children, she pinched his rib in return.

"I agree with Thor." Magnus looked at his nephew and thought about his own sons. They were nearly a mirror image to him, and he was a mirror of his brother Callum. It meant Thor looked so much like him, except for the strawberry-blond hair, that Thor could pass for Magnus's son. He admired his nephew and knew one day he would make a fine laird. Thor could see the trees for the forest, and that was what the clan would need. Magnus's sons would one day follow Thor's lead and ride into battle without the older generation at their sides. He felt confident in Thor's judgement, and it made him worry less about his sons' futures.

"Who would ye send with our men?" Ceit looked at Callum, but the question was open to anyone to answer.

"I'm going." Thor stared at his father, unwilling to back down. It wouldn't be the first time he'd led men, but it didn't mean Callum was eager to watch his son ride away from the keep.

"Uncle Tavish, Uncle Alex, and Uncle Magnus will go with ye along with their lads. Ric and Kirk will go, too. Each of ye leads yer own band. That way ye can cover most of our borders." Callum didn't name himself because he had other plans. "I'm going to Clyth."

"If ye do that, Da, Greer will never forgive me or any of us. She came here nae only to warn us but to protect her people. If ye attack Clyth Castle, then her people will suffer."

"We dinna make war on innocents, and I dinna plan to start, Rose. But Edgar will have left men behind to protect the keep. They are our targets. We willna harm the farmers and villagers unless it's a choice between a Sinclair's life and a Gunn's. Edgar nae only needs to go, but so do any of the men who support him. A new laird needs putting in his place with warriors who support sound decisions, nae the insanity that seems to run in their family."

"And if that means ye have to kill every warrior and leave them defenseless?"

"Lass," Liam interjected. "Yer da kens what I do. If Albert took the lash for Greer, then there's at least one mon who doesnae agree with Edgar. Where there's one, there's many. People wish for peace and safety. While the Gunns, as a clan, may hate us, they still dinna wish to live in constant danger. We may nae change their opinion of us, but I can almost guarantee there are plenty who would gladly end the feud."

"Ma mission isnae to besiege the keep, Rose." Callum's tone reassured his daughter. "It's discovering who is for and against Edgar. Those who willna lay down their sword dinna need to carry one anymore. Those who wish for a different life from what they've had for more than two score years can continue on. But the real question becomes, who will their council vote in as laird? Unless Greer marries a mon who can lead, there is nay one left. None of the Mackenzies or the MacLeods of Assynt will do it."

"Do we ken for sure Adan or Edward wouldnae want to?" Thor looked around the table. "Torrian is in fine health, and I dinna think he's popping his clogs soon. Michail's son is just aboot auld enough to truly become a tánaiste if the time comes sooner than anyone wishes. That would allow Adan to step down as captain of the guards and consider a different path. Ward would be just as good a choice as Adan."

"Everyone can be part of that discussion once we have Edgar out of the way and Clyth secured. But what ye say makes sense." Alex smiled at his nephew. He never once wished he had sons rather than his three daughters. He had enough nephews to often feel like he had his own lads.

"When do ye ride out?" Brighde was the only person who hadn't spoken, and she asked what everyone wondered.

"The day after tomorrow." Callum drew Siùsan closer and kissed her head. The chamber grew quiet as wives made mental checklists of everything their husbands and the warriors would need in the way of food and bedding. The brothers knew they needed to assign the men to the various war bands and explain the mission.

Rose's hand squeezed Blaine's as though she might keep him from leaving if she held on long enough. While no one said where the Keiths would ride, it was obvious Blaine would join the Sinclairs. She looked up at her husband of four days and attempted to appear stoic, but she feared she would burst into tears.

"Come abovestairs with me. We have more to discuss. I ken ye willna want to hear it, but if aught happens to me, ye're already basically Lady Keith."

Rose nodded and followed Blaine in silence until they reached their chamber. Once the door was closed, Blaine pressed Rose against the wall. They clung to one another as their tongues twirled, and their craving for one another intensified. They fumbled with Rose's skirts until she lifted them above her waist. The next moment, Blaine's plaid flipped out of the way. He lifted Rose until she could wrap her legs around him. He thrust into her as she tightened her hold on every part of him she touched.

"Kyla, I need ye." Blaine gazed into eyes that were the rich brown of perfectly aged whisky. He would drink in every moment he had with his bride because he didn't know *when*—he refused to think of *if*—he would return.

"Harder, *mo chridhe*." Rose panted as her back bumped against the wall every time Blaine surged into her. "I need ye, too."

They moved together until pleasure radiated throughout Rose's body. Her core clung to Blaine's rod, threatening to squeeze it dry. Blaine gritted his teeth against the need to climax. He wasn't nearly done with his wife. When she relaxed, he walked them to the bed, withdrew, and spun Rose around. She bent forward, and he reentered her with a thrust that made them both groan. Annoyed with the layers of material in his way, Blaine pushed Rose's skirts higher.

"There isnae a finer arse in all the world, Wife. The things I wish to do to ye when I spy such a lovely sight." Blaine ran his hands over the voluptuous expanse of smooth skin as he surged into her over and over. He cupped what fit in his hands and squeezed before leaning forward to whisper in Rose's ear. "Every time I bathe, I will think of ye as I palm maself. I will miss every inch of ye and all the ways I wish to pleasure ye."

"I think yers is the finest arse, Husband. I could stare at it for ages, and I already have. Ye taught me how to ease ma need when we canna be together. I shall close ma eyes and picture trailing ma hands over ye as I walk around ye, enjoying the view." Rose looked over her shoulder as she spoke.

With a light swat, Blaine pulled out again. He lifted Rose once more until she slid onto his cock. He sat on the bed, allowing Rose to set the pace as she rode him. He yanked at her laces until they came free. He whipped the gown, then the chemise over Rose's head. He hungered to see all of her, to etch the memory of his wife making love to him into his mind forever. He supported her neck and back as he encouraged her to lean back. He kissed a trail over each nipple, tugging them with his lips before bending to kiss her belly.

The first time he'd done it, Rose shied away, embarrassed that she wasn't as trim as other women she knew. But Blaine had quickly put her fears to rest as he showed her just how much he preferred her generous curves. He'd kissed and nipped until he left love bites peppered across her middle. He'd climaxed faster than either expected once he eased into her. He'd planned a leisurely coupling that time, but he hadn't lasted after enjoying his exploration of his wife's body.

Now, he kissed her belly, swirling his tongue in her navel to make her giggle before he continued back up to her breasts. When she sat upright, his hands roamed over all of her. She tugged at his leine, forcing them to pause as he unpinned his plaid before he could remove his shirt. Once they were skin to skin, their passion erupted. Rose increased her pace, and Blaine guided her hips.

"I'm close again, Blaine."

"Good. I need to spill, and I canna wait much longer."

"Dinna wait. St. Columba's bones this feels divine." Rose's head fell back as her fingers clawed at his back. She was careful not to dig her nails in, knowing they would leave marks the other men would see. With a surge that nearly lifted him from the bed, Blaine's cock pulsed within Rose. His hand tangled in her hair as their kiss grew savage, both glad for the euphoria, but neither wanting their coupling to end. When they drew apart, Blaine flopped back onto the bed, and Rose followed. She rested her head against his shoulder as their chests heaved.

"That wasna why I wanted us to come up here, but I couldnae stop maself."

"I wanted the same thing, so I didna stop ye. I want to beg ye nae to go, but I ken I canna do that. I willna do it. But I hope ye understand how much I wish ye didna have to ride out. I'm scared."

"I ken, *mo ghràdh*. I dinna ever want to leave yer side, especially nae when we've had so little time together. But I'm doing it for the same reason as the other men are. To make our homes safe for our families. I willna take ye to Ackergill and pass Clyth Castle while we dinna ken what threat awaits us." Blaine sighed. "Unless something changes, I'm riding toward the Sinclairs' northern border near our land. I have to go back to Ackergill, Kyla. I must check on our people and learn exactly what Edgar did. I dinna ken if I'll have to wait until after we find Edgar, but I plan to do it first. If I canna, and it must wait until after we end his plan, then I will be away longer than the others. I loathe thinking that, let alone saying it. I dinna wish to be apart from ye at all."

"Haud yer wheest. What we want for ourselves never comes before what's best for the clan. While yer father is in France, ye are Laird Keith as much as I'm becoming Lady Keith. I might want to spend ma days and nights with ye and never be interrupted, but that isnae real life. Go to Ackergill, discover what's happened, do what ye must. I'm nae going to disappear. And I willna forsake ye because ye had to leave ma side. Ye arenae abandoning me, even if it takes ye sennights or moons to return. I understand."

"Ye're wonderful." Blaine blurted the thought, and it made Rose giggle.

"I think ye're mighty wonderful too." Rose waggled her eyebrows in imitation of how Blaine often teased. He rolled them over, making Rose squeak. He kissed her neck and behind her ear.

"Ye do things to me, lass."

"I ken. I rather like it." Rose turned her head and snared his lips for a smacking kiss. However, their amusement didn't last since they both knew there was more to discuss. "I need to ken what to do if ye dinna come back, Blaine. What if they dinna bring ye back?"

"If I die, then ma men will take ma body back to Ackergill. Our clan will bury me alongside ma mother and ma other family. If they canna bring me home, then they'll bury me where they can. Either way, it's nae how I want ye to arrive at Ackergill. A widow with nay one to introduce ye. Ye're a Keith, so ye can make yer home there. Since we've been married long enough to consummate the marriage many times—" Blaine closed his eyes and sighed "—blessedly—" before he opened them again— "so ye might carry ma heir. The clan council willna name ma successor until they ken if ye're with child. Even then, it will be ma cousin, who's ma second, who will fill the role until ye give birth. If ye have a lad, then he could likely foster with yer family, but ye would still be Lady Keith once ma father dies. Ye would have duties. If ye have a lass, then ye could come back here with nay one causing a fuss."

These were things they needed to discuss, but neither wanted to imagine a future where they weren't together. While they hadn't discussed marrying before a priest because of the uncertainty that loomed over them, they each knew that they wanted their lives to be one. Yet, even with that surety, neither hinted at how they felt, except for the terms of endearment and displays of affection. Neither wanted to be vulnerable, so Blaine would ride out in two days without either of them expressing their burgeoning love.

Chapter Sixteen

Rose stood beside her mother and aunts as the women watched their husbands ready their mounts and issue last minute orders to their men. Liam stood with his sons and grandsons, reviewing the plan one last time. Rose swallowed the lump in her throat as Liam embraced each son and each grandson, and his son-by-marriage twice before Callum, Alex, Tavish, Magnus, and Magnus's son Blake, and Tristan walked to their wives. The other grandsons gathered near the horses. Rose had watched the same scene countless times over her life, but this time felt infinitely more heartbreaking. She'd always feared for her father and her family, but never had she been the one to say goodbye to her life partner. She glanced at Blake with his wife, Cerys, as he kissed her, then their infant son. She turned her attention to her parents, who clasped each other and shared a prolonged kiss. She knew better than to watch Tavish and Ceit since they were positively shameless. Mairghread and Tristan, the first couple to marry, were no better.

"Kyla?"

Rose's eyes watered as she fought not to cry when

Blaine joined her at the base of the keep's steps. When he opened his arms, she fell into them. Never could she have imagined a little over a moon ago, she would meet a man and marry him so quickly. She certainly hadn't imagined developing such strong feelings for a man, then watching him ride off to battle.

"Be safe."

"Kyla, ye ken I canna promise ye I'll live. But I will promise ye that I will do everything I can to make sure I return to yer arms and our bed. To return to take ye for walks to the beach here and at Ackergill. To return to watch ye grow round with our bairns and to bounce them on ma knee." Blaine cupped her cheeks and brushed his thumb beneath her eyes, catching the single stray tear that fell from each before Rose mastered her emotions.

"I'll be here when ye return. I may have to fight Mama and ma aunts, but I will be the first one down the steps. Ma arms will be open before ye get off yer horse. I want all those things with ye too, Blaine." Kyla swallowed the words that nearly came out next. Speaking so far in the future implied they would marry. Neither wanted to consider how the Irvines and the king might interfere with that plan.

"I shall hold ye to that, lass."

"Hold me to whatever ye want as long as ye hold me." Rose attempted a half-hearted smile, hoping she might bring a little levity. Blaine tightened his embrace and lifted her off her feet. She knew they matched all the other Sinclair couples in the bailey. All the women were significantly shorter than their husbands, so the last kiss—when husband and wife truly clung to one another—always had the women's feet dangling against their husband's shins.

Rose's arms encircled Blaine's neck as their kiss rivaled any of the older generation's or Blake and Cerys's.

"With that invitation, I may never let go. I'll miss ye, *mo chridhe*. I'll be back as soon as I can." Blaine lowered Rose to her feet, but he didn't release her. Their eyes met, and Blaine couldn't let go without at least hinting at his feelings. "I didna think I could come to care aboot someone the way I do ye. Ye are the beginning and the end for me, Rose."

"I care aboot ye, Blaine. I dinna have any doubts that life's path led me to ye, and we're to walk it together from now on."

"Goodbye, Kyla.

"Farewell, *mo ghràdh*."

They let go of one another, and Blaine made his way back to his men. He mounted and waited for the Sinclairs and his men to do the same. He and Rose watched each other, neither interested in talking to anyone. Rose swallowed the lump that once more took root in her throat. Blaine hadn't cried since his mother died, and he'd only done that in the privacy of his bedchamber. He battled not to show any of his emotions now, but if he'd been alone, he would have wept.

Liam watched his sons, grandson, daughter, and granddaughter as they each said goodbye to their soulmate. He already knew Blaine and Rose were meant to forge a life together, even if they hadn't realized it yet. He expected some resistance from the king, but he had a few more arguments he could make, including being so blunt as to say he and his family rode to King David's defense only a year ago. Blake and Cerys discovered the plot to assassinate him, and

Liam and his sons followed the couple to France. Liam wasn't above calling in the debt.

As he said a final goodbye to his unmarried grandsons, he thought about his wife and how many times they'd shared the same ritual in the years they were married. It was before the alliance became what it was now. The Sinclairs and Mackays were ever hostile to one another, and they didn't get along with the Mackenzies either. While he didn't miss leaving Kyla behind, he missed having his best friend and his one great love beside him during times of trial and tribulation.

"They'll be home soon, Da." Mairghread waved to Tristan as she leaned against her father. While she shared many of Liam's features, much like her brothers, she resembled her mother more by the year. Liam wrapped his arm around his only daughter's shoulders.

"I ken, lass. I wish we could have had more time with ye and Tristan here together."

"Mayhap after this is done, Wee Liam and Elene can bring the rest of the family here. There might be a wedding to celebrate." Mairghread glanced at Rose before raising her eyebrows in question.

"Aye. I suspect by the time Blaine returns, they'll have figured out what they mean to each other. There will be a wedding, even if it means disobeying the king. That will be another mess to solve, but that is for another day. I'm glad to have ye here, lass."

"This is still home just as much as Varrich is. I miss ma weans fiercely, even if they are adults now, but I ken I canna travel over land right now. I may have to sail back though, Da. If this becomes protracted, I canna stay away from Varrich for more than another moon. Elene can run the keep without a question, but I have duties I canna ignore while the laird is gone. Wee Liam has done a fine job for the past moon, but he's still Tristan's tánaiste, nae our clan's laird."

"I ken. Yer mama is so proud of ye, lass." It was no secret that Liam often spoke to Kyla. Whether it was in the lady's garden or their chamber, which remained exactly as it had been when Kyla shared it with him, Liam drew strength from having his wife's spirit alongside him. His family believed she was with them as much as he did.

"Thank ye, Da. Ye ken what that means to me."

They turned toward the other women as Cerys's son wailed. She bounced him, but the child was inconsolable. "He misses his da already."

They all understood the sentiment. Once in the Great Hall, they each went in their own direction, but Rose felt lost. She had no specific chore she needed to do at that moment, so she felt purposeless as her sadness grew. She took the stairs to the second floor and made her way to Thor's chamber. She knocked and waited for Greer to bid her entry.

"They're gone now?" Greer patted the bed beside her. Rose kicked off her slippers and climbed beside her best friend. Before either woman could say more, someone rapped on the door. Without waiting for a response, Shona pushed open the door.

"I came to check on ye both." Shona shut the door and came to stand by the bed.

"Hop on." Rose curled her legs to make room for her younger sister. Since Greer arrived and needed much of her attention, Rose realized she'd neglected her sister. They'd still spent time together as they worked in the kitchens, but she hadn't sought Shona out in her spare time. She'd spent it either with Blaine or Greer.

"I thought ye might both need cheering up." Shona glanced at the door before she dug in her pockets. She produced a flask from one and something wrapped in cheesecloth from the other. She unwrapped the small bundle to reveal honey-coated treats. She removed the stopper and handed the flask to Rose before passing Greer the candy.

"Ye plan to get us three sheets to the wind?" Greer giggled.

"Nae three. Mayhap only two, or just one and a bit." Shona glanced at the door again. "Dinna let Mama ken."

"That's why ye brought the penydes. They're supposed to hide the whisky on our breath. Ye ken she'll ken. If Thor canna sneak even a sip of summer ale without her kenning, there's nay hope for us." That didn't stop Rose from taking a healthy sip. The heat coated her throat down to her belly. Another sip eased her anxiousness about being caught. And a third sip, before she passed it to Greer, lessened the ache in her chest from Blaine's departure.

Greer drank as much as Rose, but she did it in one healthy glug, grinning as she passed the flask back to Shona, who was no better. Shona put the stopper in the flask while Greer selected a dozen pieces of the candy for herself, then passed the cheesecloth to Rose. She picked out three pieces, then thought better of it and snagged seven more.

"Dinna hold back on ma account." Shona nodded toward Rose's hand as she looked at her sister and

Greer. "If ye give me that many back, I'll eat the lot of them, then be sick as a dog."

"That's cause ye dinna ken moderation." Rose smirked.

"And ye sound like Mama. Ye sound auld."

"Wheest. Ye ken she has a sense for when ye say such things. She'll appear from nay where, so dinna tempt fate." Rose grinned. While Siùsan had always allowed her children much freedom once they finished their duties, she had a knack for always knowing where they were. It shouldn't have surprised Rose that her mother knew when she sneaked away at the Highland Gatherings.

The three women chatted and ate their treats until the sun was nearly overhead. When Greer could no longer stifle her yawns, the sisters left her to nap. She improved daily, but she still tired easily. Many of the bruises were now yellow and green, rather than the livid blue and purple they'd been when she arrived.

In the passageway, Shona turned to Rose and stopped her. Keeping her voice low, she asked, "Are ye really all right?"

Rose looked around to ensure no maids or family members could see them before she shook her head. Shona took Rose's hand and led her to the chamber Rose now shared with Blaine. Once inside, Shona wrapped her arms around Rose as the latter burst into tears. The sisters held one another until Rose's tears abated.

"Thank ye. I didna want anyone to see me crying."

"I ken. I'd hoped the whisky might help a wee."

"It did, but nae for long. I ken this is life, but I

never imagined just how different it feels to watch ma husband leave rather than when ma father does. I miss Da already, and I worry for him and everyone else. But with Blaine—I dinna ken how to explain it. It's like half of me went with him. I dinna feel whole anymore, like something is missing. How do Mama and the others make it look so easy?"

"Practice. Dinna ye remember when we were weans, how they would take us to play near the loch or in the fields, but they would huddle together? I can remember them crying." Shona rested her head against her sister's. "I dinna think it got easier for them. I think they got better at hiding it. Havenae ye noticed that they always find some chore that allows them to be alone?"

"I suppose. I guess I'm nae as observant as ye." Rose shrugged.

"Ye really care aboot him, dinna ye?"

"I do. Some of it must be the excitement of it all being so new, but I believe ma feelings are genuine for him."

"Do ye think ye'll give the handfast a full year before ye decide whether ye wish to marry?"

"I wish to marry him now."

Shona watched her sister for a moment before she responded. "So ye love him?"

"I think I'm falling in love with him."

"Mama and Da always promised we can marry for love. They may have been arranged, but it worked out for them. Are ye sure ye dinna feel this way because Blaine's the first mon ye've let pay ye attention? What if this isnae love but novelty?"

"I've wondered that too. But either way, Blaine is a good mon, and he'll be a good husband."

"But is that enough? Dinna ye want what Mama and Da have?"

"I do, and I believe that's with Blaine. But what if nae all of us are destined for that?"

"Wee Liam, Saoirse, and Blake are proof we are."

"Three out of how many of us? Two dozen?"

"I'd like to think that one day I'll share something with ma husband like what Mama and Da do. I dinna want to think aboot settling."

"I'm nae settling." Rose scowled at her sister. This conversation rapidly moved in the wrong direction.

"I didna mean that. I meant, ye deserve to have a husband who loves ye as much as Da and our uncles love their wives. If it isnae with Blaine, then the right mon will come. But if ye're married before a priest, ye'll never ken. Just dinna rush."

"Do ye think we rushed our handfast?"

Shona inhaled before she slowly released the breath. "I think ye would have handfasted eventually, but I think this situation moved things along faster than it should have."

"Do ye nae approve of Blaine?" Rose's stomach knotted. While Shona was younger than her and often silly, she offered sage advice and her opinion mattered to Rose.

"I absolutely approve of him, Rose. I just dinna want ye to rush into aught that might make ye happy now, but miserable forever."

Rose's shoulders slumped. "I think I'm falling in love with him, and mayhap one day he'll feel the same aboot me, but I admit I have some of those worries too. We ken more aboot each other and have spent more time together than most noble couples before they wed, but I worry that once the excitement and newness wear off and we settle into our positions at Ackergill, things willna be the same."

"Aye. They might be better. But ye can always come home, even if ye wed before a priest. Blaine doesnae strike me as a mon to mistreat ye or treat ye like a possession."

"I ken. But I could never leave until I bear him a son, and I couldnae ever let ma children go. I ken how hard it was for Auntie Mairghread to let Wee Liam come here to foster, and how much Mama suffered when Thor went to Varrich. I pray that if I have a son, he can foster here. Blaine already mentioned it."

"He did?"

"Aye. We had to speak aboot what would happen if he doesnae survive."

"Och, Rose. I'm sorry. That couldnae have been pleasant, and here I've been questioning whether ye're making the right choice. Ye've already had to plan for if yer husband dies."

"Ye havenae said aught I havenae already thought. At least hearing it from ye makes me feel less guilty for thinking it. But truth be told, even though I have some hesitation, it feels like I should have them, so I do. In ma heart, I believe I've met the only mon I will ever love."

"How do ye ken?" Shona attempted not to sound too eager, but when Rose's gaze met hers, she knew she hadn't sounded as casual as she wanted.

"Have ye met someone, Shona? Or are ye eager to find yer own husband?"

"I havenae met anyone. But I see how Blake and Cerys are together, and I watched as Saoirse and Magnus Óg fell in love. Now ye're with Blaine. I wonder when ma turn will come. If it will come. As a future laird's daughter, I ken the expectation is I'll marry well. But if Da isnae going to arrange aught and will allow me to wait until I fall in love, what happens to me if that doesnae happen? Do I just become everyone's favorite spinster aunt?"

"Ye would be the vera best spinster aunt. Ye would get the weans into endless trouble, and they would adore ye for it."

"Do ye think I'm too wild to settle down and marry?"

"I think ye're too wild, but I dinna think that has aught to do with whether ye should settle down. I believe a mon will come along who loves ye for that wildness. Dinna choose a mon who'll try to tame ye."

"But would any mon want a woman who prefers to hunt and ride and swim and throw knives more than baking tarts and making candles?"

"Ye dinna have to like chores to ken how to do them well. Ye ken how to be a chatelaine, and when the day comes that ye take that role, ye're prepared for it. That doesnae mean ye canna do the other things too. Look at Auntie Mairghread. She may nae be outdoors as much as she was when she grew up here, but she still does all of those things. Uncle Tristan loves her more than aught but their children. He loves them equally, even if it isnae the same. But he couldnae be happier than when he's with Auntie Mairghread. They do many of those things together. Ye could find a mon like that."

"Aye, and he'd be ma cousin. I couldnae marry any of them. They're all too much like brothers to us. They're too much like Thor. I'd kill the mon I married if he were like Thor. Suffocate him with a pillow." Shona grinned. While she didn't have the twin telepathy that Rose and Thor shared, Shona and Thor were as close as the twins were. But Thor definitely tried to tame Shona, and she rebelled even more.

"Ye ken he's like that because ye scare the devil out of him. He's convinced ye will break yer neck, and he'll be the one who has to tell Mama and Da. That terrifies him even more. I ken ye're nae reckless just adventurous. But he fears ye'll go too far one day. If he didna love ye, he'd ignore ye and what ye do. It would certainly be easier for him." Rose elbowed her sister as they sat together on the bed.

They fell into silence, neither needing to talk to enjoy the other's company. Five minutes passed, with each of them lost in their own thoughts before Shona spoke again. "How long do ye think they'll be gone?"

"I dinna ken. Blaine's headed to Ackergill to check on the villages and to meet with his second. He said that if he couldnae go straight there because of the Gunns, then he would have to go after. It means he may be gone longer than everyone else. I expect all of them to be gone close to a moon. I think Edgar will make them chase him just as he planned. But I also think their plan to surround him and draw inward like a net will work. It's just getting him in the center that will take time. Uncle Tristan said Wee Liam sent a missive to the MacLeods and asked them to join Uncle Tristan and the men he had with him while they were in Orkney. Uncle Hamish is likely to send Lachlan with men. I'm certain Grandda's already written to him. Hardi is there still, so he'll ride with Lachlan. Mayhap he'll ride to Tor Castle and gather more of his men."

"Do ye think Magnus Óg will join them?"

"He may have to, even if he doesnae wish to leave Saoirse if she's with child. Mayhap Seamus will ride out instead. He is laird, so they might both join the fight. I dinna ken all the specifics. I just ken the plan they developed while I was in the meeting with everyone, nae the one they had with Uncle Tristan and Auntie Mairghread, too. I was a wee distracted yesterday and didna ask Blaine."

Shona snorted. "A wee distracted. Neither of ye came out of yer chamber until midmorning. Then Blaine went into that meeting and the lists. Ye retired with a tray sent up to ye. Neither of ye spent more than six hours out of yer chamber. Distracted indeed. Do ye think ye're carrying ma niece or ma nephew?"

"Shh." Rose's cheeks pinkened. She knew everyone was very aware of how she and Blaine spent their last hours together, but she didn't need her sister to point it out.

"Can I ask ye something else?"

"Of course."

"I ken how things started with ye and Blaine, and I told ye he's attracted to ye for more than yer looks. It actually surprises me that ye didna make time to talk aboot more of the mission's details. He clearly seeks yer opinion and respects yer advice. But do ye feel better aboot the things that upset ye before?"

"Aye and nay. We've had many long conversations." Rose shot her sister an irreverent expression. "Ye ken, when we come up for air. So, I ken he respects me and cares aboot me for more than just a tumble. I thought I'd be embarrassed the first time I was bare in front of him, but I wasna. I felt more confident than I ever have, and I ken it's because of how he looks at me. I wasna so confident the first time he kissed ma belly. I shied away because I didna want the attention there. But he's shown me he appreciates that there's more of me than of most women I ken."

"Do ye—mmm—think that's always been his preference?"

"I dinna want to ken. But there are women from his past that I'm sure to meet. I suppose I'll ken then. I am still vera nervous aboot what people will think of me when I get there. I dinna think that they'd object to a woman who's broader across the beam if she were as square as a brick. I may nae be lean through the middle, but I'm ample in places that draw the wrong attention. It's why I feared he truly did only want a tumble. I dinna want people to assume I was some type of wench that he lost his mind for and married."

"Why do ye even think that?"

Rose looked at the floor and clasped her hands until her knuckles were white. "When Greer and I were seven-and-ten, we hid our plaids behind a tree when we were at the Frasers of Lovat for a Highland Gathering. We went to the market and thought we could look around without too many people noticing us. I had a cap on, so no one could easily see ma hair. Obviously, I am nae the only woman in Scotland with reddish hair, but it's nae difficult to guess I'm Siùsan Sinclair's daughter. The only other woman with hair close to our color is Lady Campbell, and she only has lads. Arabella's hair is red but far darker."

Rose had already pulled her kertch from her head when the sisters sat on the bed. She began wearing the married woman's triangular head covering once she handfasted. Now she pulled her braid over her shoulder and held up the end. She shot her sister a look that showed she accepted her bright strawberry-blonde hair and knew there was nothing she could do to change it.

"Some men stopped us and separated me from Greer when they encircled me. They said things that a maiden should never hear. They wanted to ken when I'd be back at the tavern and how much it would cost to toss ma skirts. It was the things they described doing with ma skirts out of the way that Greer and I never should have heard. They talked a lot aboot how I looked. They were vera colorful telling me what ma tits and arse would be good for. Ever since then, I've been aware of ma appearance. Here and at Dunrobin or Varrich, I dinna think aboot it. I think I look fine. But there have been a few other comments made when we've been to court or to other clans. None like that time in the market, but it makes me self-conscious. I suppose I'm more sensitive aboot it than I realized."

"I had nay idea. I think ye have every right to be sensitive if that's how they treated ye. Why didna ye ever tell me?"

"Ye were too young at five-and-ten for me to tell ye such things. At least I thought ye were. Then it became something in the past. It didna seem worth bringing up again. And if I had, I might have had to reveal ma secret friendship with Greer."

"Thank ye for telling me now. I think Mama and the others would understand if ye wished to go for a walk or a swim. It's yer first time having yer husband ride out. Do ye want to leave the keep for a while?"

"That would be nice. Let's see if we can take a picnic to the loch and swim for a while."

The sisters left Rose's chamber arm-in-arm and spent the rest of the day together at the loch. They hadn't had such a carefree afternoon in years. Her mother's and her aunts' understanding expression let her know they sympathized and remembered when they were new brides saying goodbye to their husbands.

Chapter Seventeen

Blaine closed his eyes for a prolonged blink as his horse cantered toward Ackergill Tower. He was close to his home, but the sense of peace he normally felt when he returned was missing. It wasn't because he knew issues with the Murrays, Irvines, and Gunns remained unresolved. It wasn't because he'd already spent two days with the Sinclairs chasing Edgar and his men. He knew it was because he was returning home without his wife. He missed Rose more than he ever imagined. They'd barely spent five days as a married couple, but he'd already grown accustomed to sleeping with her pressed against his side or him curled around her.

He missed her heather and violet scent and the silky skin he longed to kiss. He missed telling her about his day, even though they hadn't been apart more than a few hours at a time. He missed planning the next day with her. He missed her company. He'd arrived at Dunbeath uncertain whether Liam and Callum would grant him permission to court Rose. What felt like a moment later, he was handfasted.

Then it felt like little more than a heartbeat after that he was riding away from Rose. He'd thought—albeit only briefly—that he would ride alongside Rose the next time he passed through the gates at his home.

Now he clattered into the bailey as the bells rang to announce his return. He swept his eyes over the familiar scene. He recognized people he'd known his entire life, but as he looked toward the keep's steps, the one person he wished could greet him was still at her family's home. He pushed aside the fear that he would return, and Rose would have changed her mind. He feared time apart would make her realize how impetuous they'd been and regret her decision.

As he dismounted, a voice greeted him he normally wouldn't have minded. Now it made him tense. "Welcome home, Blaine."

"Hello, Marcus. How have things been? I'd like a full report leading up to the attack and since."

"We expected ye back sooner."

Blaine turned to look at the man who he trusted above all others, even more than his father after the surprise missive about Eliza Irvine. "Much has happened besides the raid. I would speak to ye in private."

"The council is ready to meet." Marcus tilted his head toward the keep, and Blaine almost groaned. He wished to speak to his cousin before he had to address the group of senior advisors. They wouldn't be pleased about any of what he shared, and they were absolutely the ones who could never know that Blaine and Rose handfasted *after* he received the king's decree.

"Vera well." Blaine led the way to his father's so-

lar, which had become his during his father's prolonged absence. He looked around the room before
walking to the head of the table. It took him nearly a
year after his father departed for France with King
David and Queen Joan before he felt it was appropriate for him to sit in his father's chair. Now it came
naturally. He wondered how he would feel if he had
to return to his former seat at the foot of the table if
his father ever resumed his duties as laird.

"Blaine, it's good to have ye home. We're ready to
ride out in the morn. The bluidy bastards have had
plenty of time to enjoy their freedom." Douglan was
the senior-most member of the council and Marcus's
father. He was also a thorn in Blaine's side.

"We ride out in the morn to join the Sinclairs
along our border with the Gunns. The Sutherlands
and Mackays already have men at their borders with
the Gunns."

"How do ye ken?" Douglan demanded. The man
had always been surly, but he hadn't ceased his domi-
neering attitude toward Blaine, even when the
younger man took over leading the clan.

"Douglan, I will share what's happened, but I
dinna answer to just ye. I'm in nae mood to be treated
like a wean. We have more problems than just the
Murrays and Gunns. I will explain everything, so
dinna interrupt."

"Welp, I—"

"Leave," Blaine commanded. He pulled out his
chair and sat, dismissing Douglan without casting him
a single look.

"Ye canna—"

"Da, he can. He isnae Robert, but he still leads

our clan. Ye canna keep speaking to him this way." Marcus whispered to his father, but everyone could hear as they stared at Douglan. The older man scowled at Blaine, who pretended not to notice. He wasn't in the mood for Douglan's theatrics. He'd had plenty of time to consider the man and the other council members on his ride home. He wouldn't insist upon Douglan leaving, but he'd made his point.

"I found Laird Cameron at the Sutherlands, and he sent a messenger to the Murrays to discover whether they would consider him as a mediator. While I was there, I met Lady Rose Sinclair. I hand-fasted with her, and we now have the Sinclairs, the Sutherlands, and the Mackays to call our allies along with the Camerons. While I was still with the Sutherlands, a missive arrived from King David that announced I'm to marry Lady Eliza Irvine. It's clear ma father wants this alliance, but there'd been no time to inform him or the king that I'm already married to Lady Rose. I will nae set her aside, so dinna bother suggesting it. Nae only is she a far superior choice as ma wife and chatelaine, but an alliance with the Sinclairs exceeds aught we could hope for with the Irvines. The Gunns intend to harry one clan after another, hoping to lead everyone on a chase. While we, the Sinclairs, Sutherlands, and Mackays pursue him, he plans to attack other clans. He believes he can remain one step ahead of us, and we willna be able to stop him. He thinks that if he draws out one clan, we will all come. He doesnae realize that while all four of us, plus the Camerons, will fight, we willna chase. Each clan has warriors at their borders. We will squeeze him until he's trapped in the middle. We canna send the same size force as the larger clans, but we will send three score when I ride out tomorrow."

"If they are already set to capture him, then why send more men to die?" Douglan crossed his arms.

"Ye think that now that I have secured us an alliance with the Sinclairs that we should have them fight our battles for us? Ye wish us to look weak in their eyes and everyone else's? There's nay shame in asking for support, and that's why I went to see Laird Cameron. But to nay fight alongside them is lazy and cowardly."

"It's smart," Douglan countered. "Marrying the woman should be worth something more than just a dowry and a tumble."

Blaine realized he'd never spoken to Callum about Rose's dowry. He'd never even thought about it. The alliance that he now belonged to was dowry enough in his eyes, but he knew his councilmen wouldn't think the same.

"Ma wife's name is Lady Rose, nae 'the woman,' and what I do with ma wife in private isnae up for discussion. Dinna disrespect her now or when she arrives."

"Lady Rose? Isnae she Callum's lass? The buxom one?" Angus, the youngest member who was about five years Blaine's senior, wondered. Blaine glowered at him in response. Angus sat back and put his hands up in surrender.

"Ma wife is a beautiful woman, but ye'd do well to keep yer eyes on yer own wife." Blaine knew Angus meant no harm, but he wouldn't have anyone misunderstand and think he would tolerate any man discussing his wife's physique. She would lead beside him, and he expected everyone in his clan to treat her with the deference they had his mother.

"Has the Gunn struck anyone else besides us? Are the clans riding to our aid simply because ye wed Lady Rose?" Marcus brought the conversation back to the more important matter. It relieved Blaine that the men remained focused on that and not how the Irvines believed he was marrying Lady Eliza.

"He did. He attacked the MacLeods of Assynt, then he attacked two Sinclair villages on their border with the Sutherlands and Mackays."

"If he's away from the keep, then we should go to Clyth and besiege it. It willna take long for it to fall. The Gunn will have taken his best warriors with him, and ye said he thinks everyone will chase him." Marcus was a natural leader and a superior warrior who preferred a direct attack.

"I wouldnae underestimate him already thinking we'd do that. I think he will have plenty of fine warriors there to defend the keep. Callum and his men are there now. They split off when I did. He believes there are some within the clan who willna be excited to see a Sinclair at their door, but they will be happy to end the feuds. After all these years of constant strife, they'll want peace and the chance for prosperity over being wiped out. The only question that remains is who will take the lairdship? There are men in other clans who could claim a right, but I dinna ken that any of them wish to join the clan."

"What of Lady Greer? She could marry someone, even within her clan, and he could claim the position." Angus looked around the table.

"The lass kens. She—"

"Ye've spoken to her?" Douglan barked.

Blaine sat back in his chair, appearing relaxed as he surveyed the senior councilman. His dislike had always been tempered because they were family, and he was close to Marcus. But something about Douglan's demeanor particularly grated on his nerves during this meeting. He appeared to assess Douglan, but he'd already decided. He would convene the council without Douglan, and he would have them vote. He suspected even Marcus would vote his father out if forced. He prayed he didn't overestimate the other men's dislike. He would walk dangerous ground if he tried to remove Douglan, and no one else agreed. But he would take the chance.

"Aye." Blaine pushed his chair back and rose. "Marcus, decide which men ride out with me in the morning. I'm nae eager to leave home so soon after returning, but I canna help it. Ye remain in ma stead. The next time I arrive, ma wife will be with me."

"Aboot that. Dinna think I forgot ye said King David decided ye would marry Lady Eliza. Ye will set this woman aside and marry the one the king chose." Douglan rose and looked down his nose at Blaine.

Blaine walked around the table until he stood in front of Douglan. When he inhaled, his chest expanded to its full breadth. While Douglan was still in fighting shape, he was half a head shorter than Blaine and didn't have the same muscle he once did. Blaine locked eyes with Douglan, and with more confidence than he'd felt since he took on his father's role, he responded.

"Ma wife is ma wife. There isnae anyone else. I will always be loyal to this clan, and I will always put the clan's needs ahead of mine. But I willna put any mon before ma wife. Call her by aught but her name or ma lady, and I will challenge ye, Douglan. We both ken who will survive. I have many years ahead of me to lead with Lady Rose at ma side. Dinna confuse me for the lad I was when I entered the lists for the first time. Dinna confuse me for the wean ye used to intimidate and lie aboot to ma father. Dinna think I dinna ken what ye did for years. As I said before, leave. Everyone else stays."

Blaine was aware of how Douglan would speak ill of Blaine to his father, exaggerating any mistake he made. He tried to maneuver the clan council to his favor, insinuating Blaine was inept to lead and that he should have instead. Blaine stepped back, so Douglan could pass. The latter looked around at the shocked expressions, but none supported him. He looked at Marcus, but his son stared at Blaine. He stomped out of the solar and slammed the door.

Blaine retook his seat and looked at each man, one blond eyebrow cocked. He would wait to see if anyone came to Douglan's defense before he made his argument. His gaze finally stopped on Marcus. His cousin shook his head as his shoulders sagged.

"I ken what ye must do, Blaine. But he's still ma father. I willna vote, but I will live with yer decision." Marcus could offer nothing more.

"Do ye really believe it's necessary?" Martin, another member, asked.

"We all ken I am nae the true laird by title, but I am by necessity. He has gainsaid me since the beginning. He does it just to be objectionable. But I willna have a council member remain who canna support our clan's lady. He will undoubtedly tell everyone that I should set Lady Rose aside and marry Lady Eliza. But ye've all met Lady Eliza. She couldnae be a worse choice. Even if he speaks poorly of Lady Rose, and even if he says that I chose her over him and that's why he's nay longer on the council, the fact remains that *we* removed him. Between that and meeting Lady Rose, I believe people will understand why she's the best choice."

"Did ye marry her just for the alliance?" Marcus watched his best friend.

"Nay. I care a great deal for ma wife, and I married her because I dinna want a life without her. I feel that way nae only because she's beautiful, but because she's intelligent and will serve this clan till her last breath. I dinna fear riding out and having ye come with me if she remains. Anyone foolish enough to ride on a keep with a Sinclair woman to defend it deserves the death he gets. She'll be a fair lady of the clan, and she will treat our people well. I willna set her aside. If it were anyone else, I ken I would have to. The king wouldnae countenance me disobeying, and Father would be rightfully livid. But she's a Sinclair."

"Ye ken I meant nay harm with ma comment, Blaine. I just meant to tell her apart from her sister." Angus's regret filled his words.

"Next time, tell her apart by her hair. Lady Rose has red, and Lady Shona has brown." Blaine looked around the table. "Are we in agreement that Douglan steps down?"

One by one the men spoke their agreement. Blaine breathed easier, knowing that he wouldn't have to listen to Douglan during any more meetings, but he didn't fool himself into thinking it was the last that he would hear from the man.

"Marcus, pick the men. Martin, ye were the one to ride out to the villages. Tell me what happened."

Blaine spent the next hour listening to Martin and the others give him a full report of all that he'd missed during his nearly month-long absence. By the time he slipped into bed that night, he felt less anxious about being home. But he laid on his side and looked at the empty space beside him. No woman had ever spent an entire night in his bed. Certainly, none had merely slept beside him. He stretched his hand out and swept it over the spot that would become Rose's. If he had to trail Edgar Gunn across the Highlands and back, Blaine would make the man pay for taking him away from his bride. Then he would return to Dunbeath, collect his wife, and finally feel like he was at home at Ackergill.

Blaine glanced back over his shoulder as Ackergill faded from sight. He considered a conversation he overheard as he came belowstairs that morning. Douglan appeared to take the news of his removal well the night before, but he was in fine form that morning, raring to pick an argument with anyone who crossed his path. Blaine caught Douglan saying Marcus should marry Greer, then he would become Laird Gunn. Blaine had stopped and listened, keeping out of sight. He'd wondered with whom Douglan spoke. It didn't surprise him to hear Martin, the councilman who'd given a report on the attacked villages, respond. He replayed the conservation in his mind.

"If the bitch marries ma son, then our family will lead as it's always been meant to." At first, Blaine thought Douglan meant the Keiths would rise to a greater position. While they weren't the largest clan in the Highlands, they had a long and influential history. But Blaine realized Douglan specifically meant his son.

"Do ye really think Marcus could make the Gunns come to heel? I dinna think it would be so easy." Martin sounded as skeptical as his words.

"He'll have excellent advisors to ensure he kens what to do. Once he gets his wife with child, it'll secure the Keith line and the end of the Gunns'. She ought to be of more use than she is now. Even a kicked dog isnae as pathetic as her."

It was that line that made Blaine curious now. A kicked dog? Having seen how Greer arrived at the Sinclairs' and knowing someone had not only punched her but kicked her, it made that phrasing suspicious to Blaine. Perhaps it was a coincidence, but the more Douglan spoke, the more Blaine questioned. How did Douglan know enough about Greer to think her pathetic?

"I hear she does more for her people than Edgar does," Martin said "She quietly keeps the clan together while he claims to avenge one slight after another. The mon is barmy, a bluidy bampot. All the men in that family have been for two—nay, three—generations. Do ye want that insanity in yer bloodline?" Blaine only agreed with half of what Martin said. He didn't think insanity ran in the family's bloodline. He thought other people nurtured the misplaced visions of grandeur along with the perception that they were always the wronged party.

"She just needs to spread her legs and be as useful now as she's been in the past. If she opens her legs as much as she opens her mouth to speak, then Marcus will get her with child in a sennight."

"She doesnae strike me as a talkative one."

"She may nae natter away, but she does plenty of talking."

"How do ye ken?" Blaine appreciated Martin asking since he wanted to know the same thing. And what did Douglan mean about her being useful in the past?

"I've heard things."

The conversation had ended when the servants brought the last of the breakfast to the dais. Blaine had waited a couple minutes before he followed Douglan and Martin to the high table. He had said nothing about Douglan no longer belonging in the elevated position of honor. The dais was only for the laird's family and the clan council. Blaine shot Marcus a pointed look, who only nodded. Blaine was confident Douglan wouldn't make the same mistake once Blaine was back in residence.

As his men headed south to rejoin the Sinclairs, he wondered what and how Douglan heard about Greer. And he wondered whether he meant to place Marcus in the leadership position, so he could later encourage Marcus to use the Gunns' larger army to attack Blaine specifically. He suspected Douglan plotted to consolidate power between the two clans by doing away with Blaine. He might wait several years until Blaine's father died, then he would explain Blaine's death away as an accident.

Ye have a fanciful mind aboot a mon ye dinna like. He may be a burr in ma arse, but he isnae the devil. He's bluidy family. Father would skelp me if he kenned

I picture him as the villain in all this. But something aboot what he said just doesnae sit right with me. How does he ken aught aboot Lady Greer? What does he mean she talks a lot? Does he somehow ken that she's been feeding information to the Sinclairs for years? If he does, has he kenned what kind of information?

So many questions and nae a single answer. I dinna think Marcus would agree to any of it, but if he did, I'd like to think ma best friend wouldnae ever betray me. But then again, his father may betray his own cousin and kill his cousin's son. Nay. Marcus just wouldnae do it. Even if we werenae best friends, he wouldnae do something so dishonorable to our clan. But would Douglan? Ma gut screams aye, and that worries me more than I want to accept.

The morning passed, and it was just after midday when Blaine spotted Thor and Blake riding toward him. The men were riding hard, so Blaine spurred his horse. His steed ate up the ground as his men raced to keep up.

"What's happened?" Blaine had a sickening feeling that the men hurried to reach him because something happened to Rose at Dunbeath. He wondered if Edgar had the bollocks to attack near the castle.

"Naught. We saw ye and wagered who could reach ye first. We kenned ye'd recognize us." Thor pointed up to his hair. It wasn't only the man's reddish hair that gave them away. Blake had inherited his father's build, which made him one of the largest men Blaine had ever met. Magnus and Blake, along with his younger brother Tor, had thighs like tree trunks, and their shoulders were so broad that they almost always had to turn sideways to pass through doorways.

"So, everyone is hale?" Blaine directed his question to Thor.

"I havenae heard aught otherwise. Why?"

"Ye come barreling toward me, so what else am I to think than there was something urgent to tell me?"

"Ye thought something happened to Rose?" Thor frowned. "I didna mean to give ye a fright."

"Nay harm done." Blaine sat back in his saddle and breathed easier. He didn't want anyone to realize how strong the spike of fear that coursed through him had been. That something happened to Rose nearly paralyzed him. Then he couldn't get to her twin and cousin fast enough.

"We believe we ken where the buggering bastard is hiding." Blake's scowl deepened as he looked southeast. "I shall torture him, but it will be quick. I want to get home to ma wife and bairn."

Blaine couldn't blame Blake since he felt the same way. Thor merely rolled his eyes. The Keiths joined the Sinclairs as they rode southeast, back toward Dunbeath. They would pass Clyth Castle on the way.

"Have ye heard aught from yer father?" Blaine rode between Thor and Blake.

"Naught, but we're to join him at Clyth now that we've met up with ye. How did things go with yer council?"

Blaine shook his head and huffed. "I had to remove a member. He's—well, he was—the senior-most member, and he's ma father's cousin. His son is ma best friend and ma second. But he tries to naysay me at every turn. It's gotten worse since I've been away. I finally had to put a stop to it. I dinna envy Marcus being stuck with his father, but he understands why I had to do it." He considered sharing what he heard but decided to wait until after he'd pieced more of it together. He wouldn't accuse Douglan of anything until he had substantial reason, but he no longer trusted the man at all.

Chapter Eighteen

The Keiths and Sinclairs gathered a league west of Clyth Castle as the sun set. Blaine handed his reins to one of his men as he made his way to where Callum stood. Blaine looked in the keep's direction, even though he couldn't see it. Neither Thor nor Blake had information about what Callum had learned thus far. It made him curious.

"How are things at home?" Callum turned to his son-by-marriage as the younger man approached with Blake and Thor. The wariness in Blaine's gaze told him everything, but he waited for an explanation.

"Mostly all right. The keep isnae falling down around anyone's ears, and ma people are all well. But I disagreed with a council member which resulted in me finally removing him. He has never supported me, but he thought to question ma wife. I willna have Lady Rose arrive to aught less than every member of ma clan's leadership respecting and supporting her. He had to go."

"Did the council support ye?"

"Aye. It shocked them I called for the vote, but it

surprised none that it came to it. I dinna believe I've heard the last on the matter, but the council understands that Lady Rose is ma wife, and I willna set her aside despite how things stand with the Irvines and the king." Blaine glanced around, wishing to change the subject rather than have a private conversation in public. "How do things stand with the Gunns?"

"I sent a messenger two days ago, but he returned with nay news. Edgar's second-in-command wouldnae speak to him, even from the battlements. I sent another yesterday to inform them we would attack if they wouldnae cooperate. The mon claims we dinna have the forces to attack. He isnae wrong as things stand now, but Tavish and Alex are on the way."

"Do ye plan to besiege the keep after all?"

"I dinna think we'll have to once ma brothers and their men arrive. With the men I lead, along with yers, Thor's, and Blake's, we'll be enough to make them think twice aboot it. Ma brothers will be here by morn. This eve when it's dark, some of ma men will sneak to the river and put in a dam they built. It's nae that wide nor that deep aboot half a league from here. It'll only take a day before they run out of fresh water."

"That will make the villagers suffer more than the warriors," Thor pointed out.

"It will, but that will make them act faster. I dinna want to harm any of them if I can help it, but something must convince them to act sharpish. The keep has a well, so they willna be without water. But the purpose of the men who stayed back is to defend the castle *and* the village." Callum watched his son and knew something bothered him. He wondered if Thor doubted the strategies or took umbrage with depriving the villagers of fresh water. It was a common strategy, so it made Callum think Thor's objection was specific to the Gunns, or rather specific to Greer.

"If they surrender, do we leave men here to ensure they dinna change their minds?" Thor crossed his arms and stood with his feet hip-width apart. Blaine had come to realize that while the posture was intimidating to whom they directed it, it was the most natural stance to the Sinclair men. They did it without thinking. While it might have appeared oppositional if it had been someone else standing before Callum, it made Thor look at ease.

"Aye. We canna ride away and trust that they willna rally against us. Alex and his men will stay back. He's the only one with the patience nay to kill that turd Edgar calls his second. He had some choice words for ma messenger to bring back."

Blaine and Blake listened to father and son as the two men strategized. Blaine wondered why Blake didn't speak up. He'd heard about Blake's harrowing experience with Cerys when they met at court and discovered a plot against King David and Queen Joan, then their journey to the exiled court in France. He knew Blake had sound opinions and made wise decisions. Blake looked at Blaine and jerked his chin toward the very river men would block that night. Blaine followed him.

"Ye're wondering why I dinna speak up." Blake squatted to refill his waterskin.

"Aye."

"Did ye have aught to say? Aught to disagree with?"

"Nay."

"Neither did I. I dinna need to speak just to hear ma own voice. Ma uncle and cousin will listen if I have something to say. But I dinna disagree with them, so why waste ma breath and anyone's time if I dinna have to?"

"Fair enough. From what I can tell, yer father and Alex are the quiet brothers. Do ye take after yer father in more than just looks?"

"Both ma parents are quieter than most of ma family. Ma mama is a scholar. She doesnae have the time to read and translate like she did when she was a lady-in-waiting and had the royal library at her disposal. But she and Da still pour over auld tomes Grandda has in his solar. They enjoy discussing things from ancient lands. They always have. It's part of how they fell in love. I think I've grown more like Da and less like Uncle Callum or Uncle Tavish now that I've met Cerys. I prefer quiet evenings with ma wife and bairn. I enjoy ma wife's company because she's brilliant."

Blake's casual shrug didn't disguise the admiration and fondness in his voice when he described Cerys. It was hard to picture Blake being as jovial as Callum or Tavish, but he supposed he might have been before settling down. From what he understood, Callum and Tavish had been the wilder of the four brothers. Now they were outgoing but doting fathers and husbands. Blaine felt he must fall somewhere between Callum and Tavish, and Alex and Magnus.

"What do ye think of the plan? Ye didna say aught either." Blake shifted to let Blaine squat at the water's edge next.

"I think that it's the plan that will harm the least

amount of people. It's better than an attack that will inevitably kill innocents. Someone always runs into the fray or is accidentally caught between warriors. I think this will gain us what we need without betraying Greer's trust. I dinna want to be the one to tell ma wife's best friend that we slaughtered her people after promising to do our best to leave them untouched."

"I dinna want to tell ma cousin that, and neither does Uncle Callum nor Thor. But we all ken this is war, and so does Rose. Greer understands, too." Blake looked toward Thor and shook his head. No one understood why Thor and Greer continued to antagonize one another. Most assumed it was Thor's unresolved grief and anger over losing his best friend, Jamie. But that didn't explain Greer's reticence.

"I hope so." Blaine put the stopper back in his waterskin and followed Blake to the camp. The men built fires and hunted, then they waited until nightfall. Blaine watched the shadowy group of men carry the broad plank of wood they made from a tree they felled. Almost a score of warriors crept along the river until they reached the place where the wooden barrier fit. They were gone nearly an hour, and they all came back soaked. But they relayed their success to the group's leaders. Now it was a matter of waiting.

"Rose." Brighde spied her niece as she entered the kitchens. She tilted her head toward the larder, and the women stepped inside. Brighde kept her voice low. "A report just came in from Alex. Blaine is with him, along with Tavish, Callum, Thor, and Blake. They've blocked the village's fresh water supply, so now they're waiting until the people dinna have aught but the well inside the keep. Apparently, the Gunn's second isnae interested in parlaying with Callum. It isnae a besiegement, but it will gain our men control of the keep because the Gunns canna ignore their villagers' plight. Alex's message says they think it'll be over by the day after tomorrow. Two more days at most."

"Has there been any fighting?"

"Mayhap, but I dinna think any of it has been at Clyth. Alex didna mention it, and he would have. Da received updates from Magnus and Tavish, too." Brighde never imagined when she arrived in the dead of night during a storm that she would marry into the Sinclairs or how easy she would find it to consider Liam her true father. Her own father had plotted her death. "They've seen the Gunns' tracks, but they havenae encountered any. Tate and Wiley captured four Gunn scouts. They learned Edgar's moving south toward the Frasers. I have to tell Auntie Deirdre that." Brighde embraced her niece.

"Auntie, was there any word aboot Blaine or the Keiths?"

"He's with Alex. He arrived at Callum's camp yesterday, and Alex got there today. Blaine went to Ackergill and returned with three times the men."

"Thank ye."

"Lass, I ken how hard this is. It doesnae get easier, even if ye get used to it. Ma only advice is to learn nae to get upset until there is a reason to get upset. That doesnae make the fear go away, but it keeps the panic at bay. I canna tell ye how to get to that point, but ye must try." Brighde embraced her niece and kissed her temple. "Ye ken yer mama understands. Dinna hesitate to go to her or any of us. For all the years we've each been married, that first time our husbands rode out feels like yesterday. We love ye, Rose."

"I love ye, too." Rose returned her aunt's embrace. When Brighde went to find Deirdre, Rose debated whether to tell Greer the news. She decided it was better to tell her now than to keep it from her friend and have Greer discover Rose knew what was happening. She made her way to her brother's chamber and found Greer standing beside the bed. "Ye're looking in fine fettle. How do ye feel today?"

"Better than I have since before the last time I saw ma father. I ken Thor isnae here, but I really shouldnae remain in his chamber. People are bound to be talking. I'm well enough to move up a floor. I thought to tidy the chamber as best I could, then ask yer mother if I can move."

"Ye really dinna have to." At Greer's stubborn expression, Rose knew it was pointless to argue. "I can take ye up there. I ken which room she prepared."

Since Greer arrived with nothing, there was nothing to take. She'd borrowed gowns from Rose's cousin Maisie since they were closest in size. They made their way to the third floor and the chamber above Thor's. They angled chairs before the fireplace, even though it wasn't lit.

"Ye have news, dinna ye? There's something ye dinna want to tell me, but ye feel ye must."

"Aye. I just spoke to Auntie Brighde. She said a missive arrived from Uncle Alex with an update. Apparently, he and Uncle Tavish joined ma father at Clyth. Thor, Blake, and Blaine were already there.

They intend to flush out yer warriors by blocking the village's water supply. Ye ken the people willna last long without the fresh water, so the warriors will have little choice but to cooperate with ma da's commands. I dinna think yer warriors would leave the people to suffer."

"I'd hope nae, but I truly dinna ken. Nae all of them support ma father, but I dinna ken if they'd stand up to those who do. I'd like to think that nay matter what, they will all protect their fellow clansmen, even if it means giving in to the Sinclairs."

"I believe that's what Da and ma uncles believe, too. I think they ken Albert protected ye because he must nae support yer father. I think they understand that if Albert doesnae stand for yer father's actions, then others are like him. Is that true?"

"Aye. But again, I dinna ken if they will stand up to ma father's second and the men who obey him."

"We can hope. Is there aught to ken that might help? I dinna ken if a messenger has already left to return to Da, but mayhap there is something ye can think of that might make this easier for everyone."

Greer shook her head, then furrowed her brow. "Does yer family want a way to enter the keep?"

"I suppose only if it comes to a battle. They're trying to avoid that. Is there a way in other than the gates?"

"Aye. There are caves beneath Clyth. There's a sea gate set far back within the one farthest to the left if ye're looking at them from the water. It's locked at all times, but there's usually nay guard there."

"Does the tide rise and fall like in the cave here?"

"It does, but naught as dangerous as ye've described. Ye can still pass during high tide. But if ye stood on the ledges, ye would drown."

"I should discover whether the messenger already left. Either way, I need to tell Grandda." Rose looked at her friend and felt badly that she would rush off so soon, but she knew Greer understood. She embraced Greer and gave her a quick squeeze before gathering her skirts and hurrying to the Great Hall. When she passed a servant, she hailed her. "Have ye seen the laird?"

"Aye, ma lady. He headed to the stables nae five minutes ago."

"Thank ye." Rose rushed to the front doors and burst through them. She covered her eyes and scanned the bailey. She couldn't spot her grandfather, but she noticed horsemen beyond the portcullis. She recognized Liam with ease, and it was clear he wasn't riding out for pleasure or to even visit a local village. She looked around and noticed her cousin Nessa standing near the stables, talking to a village girl. "Where's Grandda gone?"

Nessa turned toward her. "A second messenger arrived from ma da. I dinna ken the details, but something's happened that made Grandda decide he needed to join the others. It must be something serious."

"Do our mothers ken what's happened?"

"Mayhap. I suppose yers does, and mine will soon."

"Thank ye. If ye see ma mama, please tell her I'm looking for her." Rose gathered her skirts once more and ran back up the keep's steps. She searched for her mother in the kitchens, the laird's solar, and finally her parents' chamber.

"I was just coming to look for ye, Rose."

At her mother's expression, she took a step back and shook her head. She covered her mouth as tears welled. "Is he..." She couldn't bear to ask.

"They dinna ken."

Rose's world crumbled as her heart shattered.

Chapter Nineteen

Blaine swung his sword at another Gunn warrior as sweat poured from his brow. He pivoted as he heard a sword swish through the air and barely lurched out of the way before the claymore swung past where his head had been a moment before. He raised his and slashed his opponent across the waist, nearly cleaving him in half. His foot shot out, and he kicked the dying man away from him. He looked around, separated from his men and the Sinclairs, before jogging toward Thor and Blake. The Gunns had successfully isolated him, drawing him from his men as they pushed the Keiths in the opposite direction from Blaine. He was nearly within shouting distance when something struck his head. He staggered four steps before he caught himself. He raised his sword as nausea assailed him. He wanted to vomit, but clearly this wasn't the time.

"Are ye fucking ma daughter before or after ye fuck yer Sinclair whore?"

With a roar, Blaine swung his sword backward as he turned to follow through. Edgar Gunn was prepared and had his targe raised. Blaine yanked a dirk from his belt, a weapon in each hand along with his targe on his left forearm. He rammed his shield at Edgar's chest, making the older warrior take a step backward. He swung it, attempting to smash it against Edgar's head, then draw his knife across whatever part of the man's face he could reach. He only landed a glancing blow, and the knife never made contact.

"Ye havenae said ye arenae."

"Ye're a vile bastard to speak of yer daughter that way, and ye willna speak aboot ma wife like that and live."

"Yer wife? How can that be when ye're already betrothed to the Irvine's daughter? I ken all aboot that. Do ye really believe the name Sinclair can undo contracts already signed and coin already exchanged? Yer father received the wee heifer's dowry, even if ye havenae returned the contracts. Ye're as good as legally wed, so a handfast willna matter."

While there were merits to Edgar's arguments, Blaine still had faith that the Sinclair name would triumph. He focused on defeating Edgar while the man continued to prattle. Little of it registered with Blaine as he worked to fatigue the pompous man. He saw his opening as more sweat dripped from Edgar's brow than it did Blaine's. He surged forward, several quick thrusts forcing Edgar to use both arms to hold the targe and shield himself. Just as Blaine lurched to the right to take advantage of Edgar's unprotected ribs, someone tackled him to the ground. He fought to roll over, but the weight was too great. It took only a heartbeat to realize that two men held him down. Searing pain at the base of his skull made him gag before everything went dark.

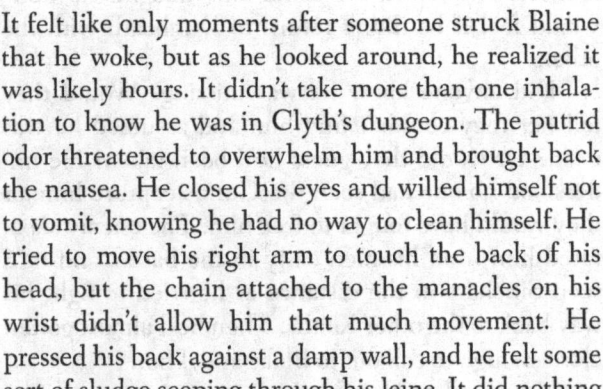

It felt like only moments after someone struck Blaine that he woke, but as he looked around, he realized it was likely hours. It didn't take more than one inhalation to know he was in Clyth's dungeon. The putrid odor threatened to overwhelm him and brought back the nausea. He closed his eyes and willed himself not to vomit, knowing he had no way to clean himself. He tried to move his right arm to touch the back of his head, but the chain attached to the manacles on his wrist didn't allow him that much movement. He pressed his back against a damp wall, and he felt some sort of sludge seeping through his leine. It did nothing to ease his sour stomach.

With his eyes still closed, he focused on regulating his breathing until his heart no longer hammered in his ears. His entire body ached, and the pain became more noticeable as the initial panic abated. When the Gunn warriors slammed him to the ground, they hadn't knocked the wind out of him, but they had bruised his ribs. He could feel pain diagonally across his back from where they'd pressed his scabbard into his muscles and along his spine. Able to master the pain, he opened his eyes once more and looked around. The light was too dim to see much, not that he needed to in order to know he was alone in the cell.

The door to his left had four metal bars two feet from the top. The slat that would open wide enough for someone to see in and hopefully toss a heel of bread was closed. He doubted anyone would be so generous. He was more likely to starve to death than he was to get out of the dungeon alive. That didn't mean he wouldn't do any and everything to escape and return to Rose. He could only imagine how she would feel if he didn't return to Dunbeath with the others.

Did anyone know he was missing? Would they tell her they couldn't find him and assumed he was dead? Or would they guess he'd been taken? He understood no one had seen the Gunns capture him, or they would have fought to free him. The enemy separated him from his men early in the battle, and he'd seen Sinclairs in the distance as he tried to fight his way back to the other Keiths. Then he'd almost gotten close enough to call out to Blake and Thor.

He considered what led to his imprisonment. The Sinclairs and Keiths knew their plan to divert the village's water supply was working because the Gunns' tánaiste rode out to speak to Callum from a safe distance. He'd been ready to broker an agreement for their capitulation. But it surprised everyone, including the tánaiste, when Edgar bellowed the Gunn's war cry, *"aut pax aut bellum."* Either peace or war.

Blaine and his men, like the Sinclairs, were mounted and mostly facing the keep. Edgar attacked from behind. Callum and Tavish spurred their horses and captured the tánaiste before anyone else could reposition themselves. Blaine was certain Edgar saw the brothers yank his second-in-command from the man's horse and hold swords to him, but he ignored his supposedly most trusted warrior's plight. He'd focused his attack on Thor, but he was already engaged with three Gunn warriors and making his way to fight back-to-back with Blake. The Sinclairs swore the key to their success was never their size and strength, though they agreed it helped. They asserted it was because they never fought alone. They remained partnered, so no back was ever exposed.

As Blaine sat within the dungeon cell, he realized just how sage that wisdom was. If he'd been fighting with Marcus at his back, he wouldn't be a prisoner in Edgar's war. It wasn't as though partnering wasn't part of the Keiths' strategies, but it was so ingrained into the Sinclairs that the warriors gravitated toward each other on instinct. He wished his second-in-command had been on that field with him.

It willna do me a lick of good to think aboot what I should have done. What is done is done, and here I am. What I need to think aboot is how the bluidy hell to get out of this fucking hole. If I'm alive, it's for a reason. Either Edgar intends to ransom me, torture me, toy with me, or let me rot. I dinna think it's the last one because it'll take too long, and he'll lose interest. He wishes to enjoy this. I dinna think he'll ransom me because he doesnae wish for me to survive and inherit ma title outright. So, it's toy with me or torture me. Most likely both.

He pushed to his feet, but the chains only allowed him to hunch over. He couldn't stand upright. However, they hadn't shackled his feet, so he could move them freely. His thighs were powerful from running, riding, and sparring. If he could get them wrapped around someone's throat, he didn't doubt he could choke them to death. But he didn't count on that scenario likely happening. He was stuck until someone released him. He also realized that the short chains that didn't allow him to touch the goose egg on the back of his head would also keep him from being able to eat or drink, if the Gunns were generous enough to give him anything.

He settled back to the floor, but he moved his legs as much as he could to keep the damp air from making him too stiff. He rotated his wrists in both directions as he drew his legs in and out. He continued his light calisthenics on and off for several more hours until he heard someone outside his cell. A key grated in the lock before the cell opened, and Edgar sauntered in.

"Ye look like shite."

Blaine wouldn't disagree. He felt like it and likely smelled like it, too. He watched Edgar as the laird lifted a torch to examine Blaine. He stood just out of reach of Blaine's legs, and Blaine assumed the man did it on purpose. Their gazes met as they assessed one another.

"What do ye want, Gunn?" Blaine wasn't interested in playing games. He would know his fate one way or another.

"Yer land for one. An end to yer new alliance for two. And ma traitorous daughter back for three."

"I can understand the first two, but what do I have to do with the third?"

"Dinna play dumb, Keith. I ken the little tart fled to Dunbeath. Ye've been there for days, so ye've seen her. She chose those marauding bastards over her own clan."

Blaine cocked an eyebrow. The Sinclairs had been called many things by many people, but Edgar made it sound as though they were still their Viking ancestors come to pillage and plunder the defenseless Gunns. Always the victim.

He wanted to tell Edgar that he shouldn't have

expected anything less when he beat his daughter to death's doorstep. But he wouldn't give away that he knew Greer's condition because that meant acknowledging she was at Dunbeath. Even if Edgar knew it to be true, Blaine would share nothing with Edgar. He would allow Edgar to get frustrated when his baiting didn't work. He sensed he would learn more that way than asking his own questions. The laird volleyed more demands for information, but Blaine prevaricated until Edgar slipped.

"Ye believe ye can outwit me," Edgar accused. "But ye all underestimate me. I am nae ma father or any of ma useless relatives. I havenae survived this long and led for a score of years without being smarter than the people around me."

Ye might still be alive, but how many times have ye tucked yer wee tail and run home? How many times have ye come within reach of yer enemy killing ye? They have sacked how many villages to retaliate against ye? How many men have ye lost? Certainly, far more than the other clans combined. The only reason nay one has wiped ye from the earth, despite how we endure yer constant hostility and antagonizing, is because it would have caused too much trouble with the Bruce, and King David wouldnae ken how handle such a situation, even if he were still in Scotland. It doesnae benefit yer enemies to kill yer entire clan. Instead, we suffer for it.

"I shall have fun with ye, Keith. Mayhap a cousin could deliver yer heart to yer father."

"It's good to ken ye think I'm worth such royal treatment. If such a journey befit King Robert, then I suppose I shall see it as a compliment."

"Fuck ye."

"I'd rather nae. I dinna ken that ye could find it in the dark. I hear it doesnae like to come out at night... or during the day. How long's it been since ye sired a bairn? Nearly a decade? And never a lad. Pity."

"I'll bugger ye up the arse, and ye can tell me what's come out of it."

"Och, so that's how ye get it to work. Nay wonder ye havenae sired a bairn in so long."

"Bastard."

"Dinna speak of yerself so harshly, Edgar. It's nae yer fault yer father didna marry yer mother until after ye were born. Still rather questionable how he legitimized ye years after ye came whimpering and flailing into the world. I'm nae so sure the Church sees ye as aught but a bastard. A pretender to the lairdship."

"Pretender, am I? Who's the one pretending to be laird but locked in a dungeon?"

"I'm certain this is only temporary."

"Ye're mad as a March hare if ye think ye're going anywhere but to yer death. That will hardly be temporary."

"Ye arenae going to kill me that soon. Ye canna collect a ransom if I'm dead."

"I dinna need yer clan's money."

"Ye need some clan's money. Isnae that why ye're considering the MacDonnell's lass? That and ye're still hoping to have a lad. So many women and yet nae a lad among them. One would think the only thing that's the same in all those situations is ye. I think ye canna do it."

"I'd rather ye were dead. I've been patient, but the time has finally come when all is in place."

Blaine kept his expression blank, but Douglan's words came back to him. Except Douglan said

Marcus would lead the Gunns if he married Greer. As Blaine remembered what he'd heard, he realized Douglan said nothing about who led the Keiths. Blaine had assumed he would continue to lead in his father's stead. Could Douglan have meant Marcus would be laird of both clans? A sickening feeling that had nothing to do with his undoubted concussion settled over him. He had no proof but what he'd heard eavesdropping; however, he knew he wasn't wrong about Douglan. Would his best friend and second-in-command abandon him for the chance to lead?

Doubt burrowed its way into Blaine's mind. He didn't want to believe the man he trusted more than his own father would betray him in such a way. Now both men had disappointed him, but only one was likely to get him killed. He didn't want to assume the worst about Marcus, but he doubted he would live to learn the truth.

"Ye intend to torture me, then kill me. Ye wish to make me scream."

"Nay. I find I dinna actually care that much. I will make yer death slow, but I couldnae care less if ye suffer. In fact, it's time now to take ye to yer grave. Guards!"

Men appeared outside the door, which swung open. Five men entered and surveyed Blaine as they considered how to approach him. Two carried shackles, and a third held a key. The last two men drew dirks in each hand as the one with the key unfastened Blaine's current restraints. He could attempt to fight his way out, but he knew it would be to no avail. He submitted to the men, but he smirked at Edgar the entire time. It was false bravado, but it was the only weapon he could wield.

He'd felt the *sgian dubh* that he wore at the small of his back as he leaned against the wall. While he knew the dirks in his boots and his belt, and the ones strapped to his thighs were gone, no one had searched hard enough to find that one. The short blade was deadly sharp, and the only one he always carried in a sheath. If he could get to it, he was likely to not only kill anyone who came within reach, he could probably open any lock.

But when the men led him along a dank passageway that took them farther into the keep's bowels rather than a torture chamber or out to the bailey for a public execution, they dashed much of that hope. As they approached a gate, he heard the waves lapping just beyond. The sound grew louder, even though the darkness remained. A guard held up a torch when they reached the portal. The one who'd held the key to unlock his manacles also unlocked the gate. Blaine was certain it was Edgar who pushed him forward.

They entered the cave, and Blaine could see the entrance out to sea thanks to the torchlight. It was early afternoon, and the tide was out. The light flickered against the walls and cast eerie shadows that made the men appear like goblins. They filed farther into the subterranean alcove until they came to a rotting wood post.

"Face the pole," Edgar commanded. A guard yanked Blaine until he had Blaine positioned with his back to the cave's entrance. Blaine knew this was its own kind of torture. He wouldn't be able to see as the tide rose. He would only know how quickly death approached by the water's height against his body. He tried to convince himself that not being able to see was actually mercy. He wouldn't watch in dread. The guard with the shorter chain forced his arms around the pole and fastened the wrist shackles. The other guard held a pair of manacles with a much longer chain. He wrapped it around Blaine three times before encircling his ankles with the shackles.

Edgar stood back and surveyed the men's work as though he'd done it himself. He jerked his head toward the gate, and the men left. Blaine watched him but said nothing. He wouldn't beg for mercy from Edgar. He was too busy saying his prayers that the Lord would protect and strengthen Rose after his death. He prayed that if they'd created a life together, that mother and bairn would be well. He knew Rose and Thor had an inexplicable way of silently communicating to one another. He wondered if such might be the case for a couple in love. He willed Rose to know that he loved her and regretted not telling her before he rode out. He tried to send thoughts of reassurance that all would be well, even if he didn't survive.

He was so deep in thought that he didn't hear Edgar's slew of curses before he stormed away, angered that he hadn't baited Blaine at the end. Blaine repeated his prayers over and over, trying to send Rose a telepathic message in between each round. He tried to convince himself one or the other would work, and someone would hear his last thoughts.

Chapter Twenty

Rose refused to open her door to anyone for the rest of the day and night. Her mother and sister knocked several times. Even Greer tried, but she wouldn't answer. She couldn't. Sobs wracked her body as regret that she'd never told Blaine how she felt tried to suffocate her. She knew if she could stop crying, she could breathe properly. But the tears wouldn't cease, and her chest hurt so much that she was certain the weight of grief would crush her.

Once the tears were spent, she fell into exhausted sleep. When the sun began to shine into her chamber and woke her, she dragged herself from the bed and splashed cool water on her face. She soaked a linen square and returned to the bed. She laid down and draped the cool cloth over her puffy eyes. She laid like that until pounding on her door shattered the moment of peace.

"Go away." Rose wasn't sure she spoke loud enough for the person outside her door to hear over their knocking, but she had no energy to be more assertive.

"Rosie, let me in."

"Thor?" Rose lurched upward, making herself see stars. She flung the cloth to the side and scrambled off her bed. She ran to the door and unlocked it. Hearing the latch release, Thor pushed the door open.

"Where is she?"

"Who?"

"Greer."

"She moved to the chamber above yers."

"I ken, and she isnae there."

"Ye went to see her first?" A fresh wave of hurt washed over her, but Thor pulled her into his arms.

"Aye, but only because I need to ken if there's another way into Clyth Castle besides the portcullis and postern gate. She's the only one who would ken."

"There is. She told me there are sea caves, and one of them has a gate that leads into the keep. Thor, is ma husband dead?"

"I truly dinna ken. They took him when Edgar surprised us. We thought he was marching on the Frasers, but he attacked us from behind at Clyth. The last anyone saw of Blaine was him fighting Edgar. Then he was gone. We looked once Edgar rode away in defeat. He fled from his own home."

"It wasna defeat if he captured the Keiths' tánaiste. He got what he wanted and saw no reason to continue fighting."

"That's only part of it. We killed more of his warriors than he did ours, and we took his second. He turned his back on his own tánaiste. The daft mon is still loyal to Edgar, even though he watched his laird ignore him while Uncle Tavish and Uncle Alex held swords to his throat. Uncle Magnus worked him over, but he willna talk. I rode here to see if Greer kens what her father might have done with Blaine."

Rose looked past her brother and into the passageway. "Greer?"

"Aye.

Thor spun round at the sound of Greer's voice, and their eyes locked. "I was finally hungry, so I went to the kitchens for an apple or cheese," she said. "I just came back up because yer mother said Thor was here and looking for me." She nodded to him as she spoke. He released Rose and moved to stand before Greer. She looked up at him, wariness filling her gaze.

"Ye look better." Thor's soft tone shocked both Greer and Rose.

"I feel better. But what has ma father done now? Rose, ye scared me when ye wouldnae open the door to any of us. Shona came to get me."

"I ken. I couldnae manage talking to anyone. I needed to be alone. But Thor came to find out if there's another way into the keep." Rose looked at her brother. "Do ye believe Blaine is in there? Or is this aboot attacking the Gunns?"

"Both. We want Blaine out first, but we will attack the keep. Greer, I'm sorry, but there is nay other choice. Yer father forsook his own tánaiste to save his arse. He has Blaine, and we learned from Ric and Kirk that Edgar already had four Fraser villages set ablaze. He's naught but a murderer sweeping through the Highlands. We believe he made his way back into the keep, and we must take him."

"I understand." Greer pressed her lips together as she looked at the floor. "Will ye burn the keep?"

"Nay. I dinna think it will come to that. We still

dinna want to hurt yer clan members, but that may be inevitable. Rose said there's a cave with a way into the keep. How?"

Greer looked at Rose then Thor. "I'll take ye."

"Nay. Just tell me. Ye arenae going back to yer father."

"I have to. Nae only am I the only who can get ye into the keep, I can ken where things are that Blaine needs. I also think I ken why ma father's doing this, and I think I ken where to find the proof."

"Just tell me what to look for. I'm nae taking ye onto a battlefield."

"That isnae yer choice, Thor. Take me, or I'll go maself. Ye willna ken how to stop me."

Thor marched forward and leaned to whisper in Greer's ear. "Ye dinna trust me again, and I understand why. But I am nae giving in to ye this time. Yer father nearly killed ye back then, and he nearly killed ye a sennight night ago."

"Just like back then, it wasna yer decision. Ye can either be on ma side this time, or ye can go against me again."

"I was never against ye, and ye'd ken that if ye werenae so stubborn."

Greer leaned back and glared at Thor. Rose didn't know what they were talking about. The snippets she caught made no sense, but they hinted at a past between her best friend and her brother that she knew nothing about. It seemed she wasn't the only one to keep secrets. She watched the standoff between them and grew anxious.

"Can ye two stop bickering? Every minute ye canna agree is another minute I dinna ken if ma husband lives. I just want Blaine back. Then ye can argue all ye want."

Greer and Thor turned to look at Rose, and they both nodded. Thor shifted to meet Greer's gaze again. "Ye dinna go anywhere alone. Ye take me into the keep, and ye keep me at yer side the entire time. Dinna test me, Greer. I'm nae in the mood to be so forgiving a second time."

Greer's eyes narrowed at Thor. "Forgiving." She snorted. "Yer memory is shite."

"I'm coming too." Rose didn't wait for her friend or brother. She rushed toward the stairs, but Thor grasped her arm and spun her around.

"I ken ye have a way of sneaking out of this keep, so ye can come. I dinna trust ye either these days. Ye stay with Da while Greer takes me into the keep. I'm nae losing one of ye because I'm trying to save the other." Thor released Rose and led the way to below-stairs. Siùsan met them as she came out of the laird's solar with a folded sheet of parchment.

"This is the missive yer da asked me to draft." Siùsan looked at her twins and shook her head. "Nay, Rose. Ye arenae going, and neither are ye, Greer. Tell Thor what he needs to ken."

"Mama, he's ma husband."

"And ye're still ma daughter. I dinna care that ye're an adult. It's hard enough to watch Thor leave. I'm nae sending ye off to war too. Nay."

Rose's shoulders drooped. "Mama, ye would do the same thing if it were Da. Please dinna make me disobey ye. Thor already kens I would sneak out. I have ways out I dinna think ye have figured out yet."

Siùsan swallowed as she looked at her children.

They were adults now, and she knew she had to let them make their own decisions. But if she had her way, she would hold on to them and let neither of them out of her sight. Rose spoke the truth, though. She wouldn't have been able to stay at the keep if something happened to Callum. She'd never had to go in search of her husband, but she knew she wouldn't have let anyone stop her if she had.

"I ken ye would, and I canna blame ye, even if I think it's ill advised. I'd rather ye be with yer brother than alone. But when ye get to Da's camp, ye listen to him and yer uncles. Yer grandda should be there already, too. If any of them tell ye nae to even twitch an eyebrow, ye dinna move." Siùsan turned to Greer. "Be careful, lass. I've grown too fond of ye to see aught happen to ye. I ken I'm nae yer mother, but I would protect ye as ma own. I'm nae so forgiving when someone tries to hurt one of ma weans. Mairghread may like to compete at the Gatherings, but she isnae the only one who can best all the men at knife throwing. It wouldnae be the first time a Gunn found himself at the end of ma blade."

Greer's eyes widened, and she glanced at Rose.

"That's a story for another day. Dinna do aught rash, either of ye." Siùsan embraced all three, holding onto Rose a moment longer than the others. She whispered to her daughter, "Remember what I taught ye. Dinna hesitate to use yer blade if ye think ye need it. Kill and run."

"Aye, Mama."

Siùsan watched as Rose, Thor, and Greer rushed out of the keep. She squeezed her eyes shut, only opening them when she recognized Shona as her younger daughter embraced her. They clung to each other, their heads resting together.

Greer reined in her horse, so Thor and Rose did the same as they rode along the North Sea's coastline. They'd followed the cliffs for the past two leagues, remaining precariously close to the edge. But they'd needed to watch for the fishermen who would soon return to the village outside Clyth Castle. They'd seen a few boats in the distance, but none had approached the shore.

"Do ye see the entrances to those three caves? It's the one on the left."

"How're we to get inside?" Thor watched the waves crash along the rocks. There was no beach, just sheer rock face. There appeared to be a path that only a goat would manage, but nothing else appeared to be a route to the water that wouldn't kill someone.

"The tides starting to come in now. The beach will appear when the tide goes out in aboot five hours."

"It'll be dark by then. We'd need torches, and that would give us away." Rose shifted in her saddle, eager to reach camp and any update about Blaine. She knew this reconnaissance was crucial, but she was impatient.

"There is nay 'we,' Rose. Ye and Greer are nae coming."

"I have to come," Greer argued. "I'm yer only way into the keep through that gate."

"Canna ye just tell me how? If ye're worried I'll learn some secret way to unlock the gate, that seems rather pointless when ye're leading me in. Do ye think ye need to keep it a secret, so I willna use it to attack in the future?" Thor watched Greer, and he saw that he spoke the truth. He respected her desire to protect her people and her home, but it seemed misplaced at this point.

"Ye need me to lead ye through the caves and into the keep lest ye find yerself lost and in need of saving." Greer shot him a smug look that made him grind his teeth.

"Is there aught else ye can show us, Greer?" Rose squinted to lessen how the sun on the water blinded her. She could see the mouths of the caves, but it remained difficult to make out any details. She wanted as much information as she could gather because she knew she faced a massive argument with her family once they arrived at the Sinclairs' camp.

"Aye. Inside, the caves connect, but only the one on the left will lead ye to the keep. It's fairly straight from the cave's sea entrance to the gate. But there are two places, one right after another where there are forks. Ye must stay to the left at the first one and the right at the second. If ye dinna, there is a sharp drop off a ledge after the first fork. It would be difficult to get back out of the water once ye're in. If the tide is high enough, ye can swim through."

"We should continue to the camp. I dinna like us sitting here so exposed with only three guards attending us." Thor continued to scan the area when he wasn't looking at the caves. They were far too easy targets in the open, and he feared the Gunns would have patrols even closer to the keep than usual. He didn't want to encounter any. He nudged his horse forward, and the others followed.

It took nearly another half an hour to reach the camp, and the sun passed overhead and inched toward the western horizon. Rose didn't like how the time raced by. It would make it difficult to enter the caves before the fishermen returned and could spot intruders. And waiting until after dark would make an already precarious mission utterly perilous.

"Rose?"

Rose rode toward her father and swung down from the saddle the moment her horse came to a stop. "Aye, Da. Dinna fash, Mama kens I came."

"And that's supposed to make me feel better aboot ma daughter riding toward the enemy?"

"Da, Greer kens the way in through the caves. She pointed out the entrance and gave us directions."

Callum offered a tight smile to Greer after he embraced Rose. He watched the fear in Greer's eyes as she swept her gaze over the more than one hundred Sinclair warriors who gathered in the wooded spot. The camp was too massive to keep hidden among the trees. No one fooled themselves into thinking the Gunns didn't know where they rested.

"What do ye recommend?" Callum's steady voice eased some of Greer's fears, but he could tell she continued to feel apprehensive. Thor turned toward her and nodded. Callum watched his son and the young woman, still as clueless about their history as everyone else. Some sort of truce appeared to have developed between them, but Callum didn't know how or when.

"If ye wait until after dark, ye can take one of the fishing boats and sail to the cave's entrance. The boat will be too big to take inside, but someone could get close enough to drop the anchor and jump down to the ledge that begins just outside the mouth. At this time of day, the ledge will be under about two feet of water."

"Can one person captain those boats?" Thor considered the boats the Sinclair fishermen used. Most were rowboats, but some were larger birlinns that a single person could captain.

"Aye."

"What happens to the boat once the person gets out? They're going into the keep through the sea gate. Willna it be suspicious if a boat's left bobbing so far from the shore?" Rose steeled herself for the inevitable argument that would come in just a moment.

"That's a risk ye would have to take." Greer turned an apologetic mien toward Callum and the other Sinclair brothers who stood nearby, listening. She seemed to shrink under everyone's gaze.

"What aboot when the tide changes?" Thor found it disconcerting to see Greer grow nervous around so many men after he'd watched her go head-to-head with him several times since she arrived at Dunbeath. "Ye said a beach would appear."

"Aye, but that's several hours from now. The beach doesnae extend far enough to walk all the way to the caves. It would make it easier to approach the boats without getting too close to the village, but you would still need them. It would be dark by then, which would mean torches on the boat. That would give away yer approach since fishermen wouldnae be out that late."

"There is only one way to enter the caves. Swim." Rose locked eyes with Thor, who immediately shook his head vigorously.

"Nay. Absolutely nae."

"Ye ken, just like everyone else, that I'm the strongest swimmer here. Auntie Mairghread taught me to swim in the sea. I can handle the cold better than most, and I ken how to swim with and against the currents. I've been climbing crags since we were weans."

"Ye'll freeze. Yer brother is right. Ye are nae going." Callum crossed his arms and spread his feet hip-width apart, but Rose didn't bat an eyelash. She'd seen her family stand like that too many times to be fazed.

"So, who is? Ye ken I'm the best choice. If ye dinna think I can make it, then nay one can. But I'm certain I can. Da, I'm going. Blaine's ma husband, and I'm the one who's most likely to succeed. I can hide far better than a warrior, too. Once Blaine is free, and we enter the keep, I can blend in. Any warrior will stand out in his plaid. It'll be bad enough that people could easily recognize the Keith plaid, but add a Sinclair one, and they'll ken an attack is imminent."

"What aboot yer hair? That's too recognizable. And how will ye hide if ye're soaking wet?" Thor wouldn't back down. He loathed the idea of his twin entering such a dangerous situation. He understood the hypocrisy of his fear since Rose contended with the same thing every time he rode out. He knew how much it upset her when he did. He knew she didn't sleep and rarely ate well.

"Greer, ye must give me directions for the tunnels, too." Rose kept her voice low, not wanting anyone outside her family to hear.

"Tunnels?" Thor's eyes narrowed.

"Aye. There are tunnels throughout the keep. One runs directly from the dungeon to the laird's solar in case the laird and his family must flee to through the cave. Another winds its way up to the laird's chamber, which is two doors down from mine. A third goes directly to ma chamber. Rose, ye could get fresh clothes from ma chamber and hide in there until everything is done. Nay one would think to search there since everyone must ken that I'm nae there."

"Dinna encourage ma sister," Thor snapped.

"Dinna be unreasonable," Rose countered. "If this is going to work, then it has to be me. I kenned that since before we left Dunbeath. It's why I came." She looked up to meet her father's gaze. "Ye ken I'm speaking the truth. Thor or someone else could try, but they willna do it as easily as me. They're more likely to fail. Ye may nae like it, but it's the only way."

Callum stared at Rose before he twisted to look at Tavish, Magnus, and Alex. All of their expressions were blank, so Rose couldn't tell what they were thinking. But she knew they communicated with one another as well as she and Thor did without speaking. After what felt like forever, the four men nodded.

"Nay. Rose isnae going alone." Thor shook his head and shot his father such a glower that it shocked everyone. "Ye may be fine sending yer daughter to her death, but I am nae all right with watching ma sister die. I'm going with her. Besides, if they hurt Blaine, Rose canna support his weight or carry him. I can."

Callum returned his son's glower and leaned forward, so only Thor could hear him. "Dinna ever accuse me of that again. Nae in public nor in private. Ye ken naught is more important to me than ye, yer sisters, and yer mama. If we dinna make a plan including her, she will go by herself. Dinna underestimate what someone will do for the person they love. Ye're willing to risk yer life for yer sister. Ye canna fault her for doing the same for her husband. Ye'll understand one day, and I dinna think it's that far off."

Thor's glower didn't lessen. In fact, it seemed to darken, but he nodded. Rose watched her father and brother, uncertain what passed between them, but they came to some sort of agreement.

"Rose, ye go, but Thor goes with ye."

"Nay. He's a strong swimmer, but nae like me. It's too dangerous."

"Either I come, or I will tie ye to a tree and make ten men guard ye. This is nay longer negotiable." Thor watched his sister assume the Sinclair stance as he issued his ultimatum. While her size was hardly impressive compared to his, the defiance and determination that she radiated would have made a lesser man back down. He muttered, "Ye are Mama's twin, nae mine."

"What's that supposed to mean?" Rose snapped.

"Ye look just like Mama. God help yer children. Ye'll be as scary as she is."

"Yer mama isnae scary." Callum chuckled. Everyone knew each of the mothers could terrify their children, nieces, and nephews with one look. But they were also the ones who offered their children and husbands comfort that no one else could.

"I shall tell her ye said that," Tavish chimed in.

"Dinna." Callum barked before grinning. The others couldn't help but smile, and it eased the tension, albeit for only a moment.

"Lady Greer, could ye lead the way into the

cave?" Alex shifted the focus back to the only Gunn among them.

"I could once we're there. But Rose is right. She is the best swimmer. I've seen her. She's won plenty of races at the Gatherings. And nae just against her family. She's bested lads and lasses from other clans, too. She's like a selkie."

"She is like Mama," Magnus pointed out. "She swims just like her, and it's nae surprise since Mama taught Mairghread, and Mairghread taught Rose. I dinna like the idea at all, but I canna disagree with its merit."

"Magnus is right." Alex nodded. "She's as good a swimmer as Mama ever was. I dinna like it either, but Rose really is the only one who can do it. Ye ken she's better with the cold than the rest of us. That's the only thing that would keep us from succeeding. Ye ken we're faster and have more endurance, but she manages the sea without freezing. We need her to get to Blaine and into the keep. She's the only way to accomplish both."

"Rose, when ye get to ma chamber, ye can take whatever clothes ye need. In the chest at the foot of ma bed is ma sealskin-lined cloak. Bundle into that too."

Tavish elbowed Magnus and grinned. The youngest brother scowled and rolled his eyes. At Greer's confused expression, Tavish laughed. "People used to call our mama a selkie because she could swim out toward the seals, and they would slap their flippers and bark. But they never ever threatened her. She never drew close enough to risk angering them, especially when there were pups. The cold rarely seemed to bother her, and she loved to swim along the coast in summer. When we were still vera young, Da gave Mama a sealskin-lined cloak. Magnus must have been aboot five or six, and he panicked that Da gave Mama back her selkie skin and that she would return to the sea forever. He cried for nearly a sennight straight and wouldnae leave her side until he fell asleep each night, completely spent."

"Dinna tease Uncle Magnus. I think that story is vera sweet." Rose cocked an eyebrow at Tavish, her arms still crossed, and her feet still hip-width apart.

"Yer brother is right, lass. God help yer children." Tavish wrapped his arm around Rose since he stood beside her. "Rose isnae wrong. She is the only one who can do this. Thor, I dinna think ye should go. The entire point of Rose going is because she's the one most likely to succeed. If ye go, it defeats the point. I ken ye dinna like it, and I dinna either. But we dinna have another choice. This is the one plan that is most likely to work without besieging the keep or a head on attack. This risks the least amount of lives and has the greatest likelihood of success."

"And if she canna move Blaine? If a guard catches her before she can open the postern gate? I'm going, too. As long as I follow her, and we get into the water as close to the cave as we can, then I can do it." Thor sent Rose a silent message, begging her not to go alone. As though she heard it, she nodded.

"Thor comes with me. He's right aboot Blaine. If he's too injured to walk on his own, I canna carry him. Besides, he might need someone to stay with him. If that's the case, then I canna sneak through the keep to unlock the postern gate. I couldnae do that if I hid, anyway. If Blaine isnae hale enough to sneak through the keep to the gate and fight off anyone who approaches, then we need Thor to do it." Rose stepped away from Tavish and came to stand in front of Thor. They looked at one another and nodded at the same time. It fascinated Greer, but everyone else in the family had seen the twin synchronicity since they were born.

"Greer, lead the way." Rose smiled at her friend as she prayed she wasn't making a mistake.

Chapter Twenty-One

The group mounted, and Greer led the Sinclairs to a path that led down the cliff, but it appeared to stop only halfway down. The rest was just sharp and uneven rocks. The waves crashed below, forming a white foam while whitecaps dotted the great expanse beyond the promontory within which the caves lay.

"Ye can take that as far as it goes, then ye'll have to jump. Be sure to time it to when the waves come in. With the way it is now, it'll be vera deep then. But when the waves recede, ye'll have to watch for rocks to the right. The beach isnae vera wide when it's exposed."

"What if we climb to over there?" Rose pointed closer to the rocks that jutted into the water and around which they would have to swim.

"The rocks'll be slippery. I dinna ken if ye'll be able to hang on. It would be an easier swim if ye jumped there, but I dinna ken if that's possible."

"If we make it and go in there, are there rocks beneath the surface?" Thor assessed their chances to make it as far as Rose pointed. They were slim.

"Nay. That's the safest place if ye can get there.

Ye wouldnae have as far to swim, and there is naught to land on but water."

"I lead. Ye follow. If anyone is going into the water first, it has to be me." Rose already knew Thor intended to say the same thing, but she was the stronger swimmer in this type of current. "Ye do as I do once we're in the water. If I dive, ye dive. If ye have to take yer eyes off me for a moment to do it, then that's what ye do."

Thor grimaced but nodded. He knew Rose was right. She'd always had a better sense of the open water than any of the others. Their aunt Mairghread taught her to read the waves the same way their grandmother taught Mairghread. Rose had understood their aunt's lessons intuitively while the others never quite got the hang of it. She would have made a fine sailor.

"I have to cut down ma chemise. I willna make it with the material around ma legs. Thor, ye should do the same with yer leine." Rose's chemise was floor-length and would tangle around her legs, making it impossible for her to swim. When the children were still young enough, they swam naked. Once that was no longer possible, the lasses had chemises cut to just above their knees. The lads would still strip but enter the water first. Everyone understood neither of them could be naked once they were inside the keep. It was the best they could do.

Greer took Rose's hands and squeezed. "Ye'll have to use a dirk to unlock the gate. Once ye're through it, there is a path that takes ye to the dungeon. There will be at least two guards there, but they willna expect anyone to enter from behind them. They keep the keys on a hook where the men will be sitting. Ye'll be able to get Blaine out of his cell. Ye can take the stairs up to a passageway that runs next to the kitchens, or ye can take a tunnel that leads to ma father's solar. Go that way. There's a latch aboot ma waist height, but there's also a peephole I can reach if I stand on ma tiptoes. Look through to be sure the solar is empty. Just past the gate, there's another path to the right. If ye take it straight, it'll wind up and through the keep until ye get to ma chamber. There's another path toward the end. If ye turn left where it starts, ye'll wind up at Edgar's chamber. Ye can avoid the dungeon if ye go that way."

Greer didn't release Rose's hands, but she shifted her attention to Thor, who watched the two women intently. He committed everything Greer said to memory.

"Ma father keeps correspondence that he doesnae wish even the clan council to ken aboot in his desk. The bottom drawer has a false bottom. There's a spot beneath the drawer ye press after ye pull it out. It releases the divider. I dinna ken what he's put there recently, but I ken there are missives from the MacDonnell chief, and he has missives he's written to himself with information from spies he has in other clans. As far as I ken, there arenae any in the Sinclairs, Sutherlands, and Mackays. But it wouldnae surprise me if he has someone in the Keiths, Oliphants, and Frasers. Mayhap even the Rosses and Munros. Rose, I've already told ye aboot spies he's sent to Assynt and the Mackenzies."

Thor began to unfasten his belt when Greer finished speaking. "I canna take ma plaid, but I must take ma sword and ma sporran. I can put all the parchments in there. I canna fight without a weapon."

Thor knew his sword would make it far more difficult to swim, and he knew that was one reason Rose didn't want him to attempt it. But it was impossible for him to defend her or Blaine without it. He supposed he could use Blaine's if the Gunns had injured the man too severely to use it, but he doubted it would be with his brother-by-marriage. He would lose time searching. It was inevitable he'd have to fight someone to get the postern gate open.

Greer released Rose's hands and took three steps back. She spun on her heels and whistled. A horse bumped the others as Greer ran toward it. "I'm going back in. I'll distract them."

She grabbed the reins she'd purposely tied when she dismounted and reached for the back of the saddle. She made to hoist herself into the saddle when two large hands plucked her from the air. She already knew who pulled her back.

"Ye are nae going back to that mad mon. Do ye wish to die?"

Greer spun around and snapped, "Aye."

Everyone froze and stared. No one had expected that answer. Thor gazed into eyes a color he'd never seen before meeting Greer. They were nearly violet, and they filled with tears. He strained to hear her when she whispered a secret she never planned to share.

"He does more than just beat me. And he allows his men ..."

Thor crushed her against him, his mind scrambling to make sense of what she'd told him. It wanted to reject the possibility, but he knew she would never lie about something like that. He looked at his family over her head and shook his. She'd told only him. He didn't know why she trusted him with such information, but she had. If she'd wanted others to know, she would have said it louder. He leaned to whisper in her ear.

"I will kill him and avenge ye."

She shook her head. "I dinna want ye to die for me. It isnae worth it. I didna mean to admit that."

"But ye did, and it's ma choice. I dinna doubt he's harmed other women, too. He doesnae get to survive for that alone. But ye're his daughter and ma sister's best friend, and I willna ignore what ye told me."

"I'm still nae—"

"Dinna ye dare finish that sentence. Ye and I have had a reckoning coming for a long time. If ye finish that thought, I will add it to what I've held against ye."

"That wasna ma fault. But this—"

"This I ken isnae yer fault. Dinna say it, lass."

Greer leaned back and swiped at the tears that streamed down her cheeks. "Ye'll never listen, and ye'll never believe me. Why'd I bother trusting ye?"

"I dinna ken either, but ye do. And I'm trusting ye nae to get ma sister or me killed. I willna repeat what ye told me. Nae even to Rose unless ye tell me I can. I willna forget it either. When I find yer father, and I will, I'm going to kill him. Can ye live with kenning yer best friend's brother did that? Will ye hold that against her?"

"Nay. Ye and she have always been yer own people." Greer swallowed. "If ye free me from him, I will be indebted to ye."

"There is nay debt, Greer. There's naught." Thor watched her eyes shutter as she pulled away, and he let her. "Ye're still nae going into that keep. Ma da will find another way to distract them. Rose willna be able to concentrate if she thinks ye're dying."

Greer sighed and looked toward the Sinclairs. She knew there was no point in arguing, and unlike her father, they wouldn't allow her to sneak away. She suspected she would have a guard to ensure she didn't.

"If Blaine is well enough for ye to wait, dinna open the gate until after sunset." Callum broke the tension by giving Rose and Thor instructions. "Thor, we'll be in place. Give us yer call when ye're ready."

Rose walked over, looking between her brother and her best friend. She understood now that there was a past between Thor and Greer that she knew nothing about, and it was far more serious than just them disliking each other because of their family name. It was clear neither wanted anyone else to know. It made her wonder if they would both take those secrets to the grave. That made her think about Greer offering to ride back into her father's reach and the mission she and Thor were about to attempt. The friends embraced.

"If ye ever wish to talk aboot what happened between ye two, I willna hold aught against ye. I willna judge ye ever." Rose didn't want to let go, and from the way Greer clung to her, her friend felt the same way.

"Mayhap one day. I dinna like keeping secrets from ye, Rose. But there are some things too painful ever to say aloud."

"I understand. I'm here if ye're ready."

The group knew there was nothing left to discuss, so Rose and Thor undressed. They both cut down the garments they still wore. Thor put his sporran back on but spun it, so it awkwardly rested beneath his sword. Rose looked at it skeptically but said nothing.

"When ye get to where the path ends, there's a chance the guards will see ye. Most arenae looking toward the sea because nay one has attacked us by water since the Norsemen raided this coast. Ye willna be in range for any arrows, but they may sound an alarm. We've had couples who werenae allowed to marry jump from the cliffs before, but it's been a few score years. However, it may make some guards come investigate."

Rose frowned at the morbid thought, but she pushed it aside as she embraced Callum. He wouldn't let go, even as she tried to lean away.

"Give me one more moment, lass. That was for yer mama. This is for me." Callum kissed the top of her head, then lifted her off her feet to kiss her cheek. "I love ye, *mo chailin ghrinn*." My sweet lass. He'd called her that since the day she was born.

She moved on to embrace her uncles, who lingered nearly as long as Callum. Her cousins were no better. She watched Callum and Thor grasp forearms before Callum pulled Thor against him. He held onto Thor as long as he had Rose. When Thor leaned back, they rested their foreheads together, and she knew her father fought not to cry. They'd done the same thing each time Thor rode out without Callum. It didn't embarrass their father to show his love for his family. He said it made their clan stronger to see that their leaders could love and hurt just like anyone else.

The twins made their way to the path, and the moment they were both on the shale, they clasped hands. They'd done it whenever they'd gone on what they'd called "adventures" as children. It had been when they did something scary or something likely to get them in trouble. They held hands until the path ran out, and it was time for them to scale the rocks. Rose put the handle of the dirk she'd pulled from her boot between her teeth. Thor did the same. They looked at one another and nodded.

Rose reached forward with one hand and pushed on the rock she grasped. When it didn't budge, she stretched her right leg as far as she dared and tested that rock, too. She looked back to see where she could place her left hand and foot once she stepped off the path. She continued to do the same thing as she inched along. Thor followed her; but more than once he had to find a different foothold because his greater weight broke off the rock and sent it skidding along the cliff to the water.

It took them half an hour to ease their way to the spot where Rose believed they could jump. The climb was already precarious, and her heart raced the entire time. When she twisted with her last step, so she faced the water, she was certain her heart stopped. She'd led them across and down, trying to get them close enough to the water that the impact wouldn't stun them too much or injure them.

Moving slowly, she took the dirk from her mouth and looked at Thor as he did the same thing. He'd made his last handhold the same as hers, so his fingers covered hers.

"Remember to follow me, nae just watch me."

"I trust ye in this life and the next. I love ye in this life and the next." The twins recited the pledge they'd formed when they were eight. It was when they dared each other to jump from the stable roof onto a pile of hay. They hadn't been able to sit comfortably for a day by the time Siùsan finished with them, but they'd taken the risk and the punishment together.

Rose nodded and leaped. The moment she surfaced, Thor jumped, landing where she had and coming up next to her. They put their dirk handles back between their teeth, and Rose began the trek. Thor mimicked her, setting his strokes to match hers, diving beneath the waves when she did. The water tried to force them back to the cliff or push them against the rocky outcropping. But Rose moved with ease, which meant Thor didn't struggle like he would have alone. The North Sea's water was barely tolerable in summer. They both felt the cold seeping into their bones, threatening to steal their breath and make their bodies sluggish.

Rose refused to give in to the numbing sensations that tempted her to pause and rest. She needed to get to her husband, and her brother trusted her to keep them from dying. She would let neither of them down. Thor pushed past the discomfort, refusing to leave his sister alone because he knew she would exhaust herself searching for him, and he knew she wouldn't be able to free Blaine alone. When they finally rounded the end of the rocks, they allowed the waves to wash them into the cave and push them several feet forward.

"Blaine!" Rose nearly lost her dirk when she called to her husband. He tried to twist to see her, but the chains were too tight. The water had risen to his mid-shoulders in the time he'd been chained to the pole. Rose knew if they'd waited until the tide went out, he would have drowned. She could tell it hadn't yet reached its highest point from the line where the smooth rocks ended, and the rough ones began. There was still several more feet before it crested.

She scrambled to pull herself onto the ledge, but she'd drained nearly all her strength. It shocked her when a hand pushed up on her backside and sent her sailing out of the water. She looked at Thor as he hoisted himself out and sat on the edge. She didn't know how her brother had the strength to get her out of the water with one push, then drag himself out.

"Kyla!" Blaine called over the crash of a particularly loud wave. Rose scrambled to her feet and hurried along the ledge, careful not to slip.

"Thor, is yer dirk thin enough to open these locks? We dinna have time to get the keys."

"Nay. The tip is too wide."

"I have a *sgian dubh* beneath ma belt." Blaine stretched his fingers to meet Rose's outstretched hand, but there wasn't enough rock for her to lean far enough forward. She was unprepared for Thor to jump back into the water. He treaded water as he freed the knife from between Blaine's belt and back. He inhaled deeply twice before he dove beneath the surface. He'd felt the chain wrapped around Blaine, and he was certain the lock was near his brother-by-marriage's feet.

The blade's deadly sharp tip fit into the lock, but the saltwater and sand that washed into it made it difficult to twist the dirk in the lock. Thor pressed, worried that he might snap the end of the knife. Just as he was about to surface for more air, the restraint gave way. He pulled the chain loose from Blaine. He kicked to the surface and handed the knife to Rose before pulling himself from the water a second time. His strength was waning. He knew he would have to rest before they attempted to enter the keep. He didn't doubt Blaine would need the same after having his arms at such an awkward height for so long. He came to his feet, and Rose handed back the knife. His height gave his arms more reach, so he could unfasten the manacles around Blaine's wrists.

Blaine's arms dropped lifelessly to his side as he grunted with pain. His shoulders had screamed in agony for hours, but the moment he stepped away from the post, his arms found the strength to wrap around Rose as his mouth descended to hers. Rose cupped his cheeks as their kiss drew on until it left them both breathless. They kissed along each other's cheeks and jaw until their lips met again in a series of short kisses before another long one. Blaine kissed her forehead before their gazes met.

"I love ye." They spoke at the same time, bringing a broad smile to both their faces.

"Kyla, what are ye doing here? Ye should be at Dunbeath." Blaine brushed back the hair plastered to her face. He didn't care for how blue her lips were despite their kisses. He reached up and pulled her left hand from his cheek and noticed her blue nails. He pressed her hand to his heart and covered it.

"I couldnae stay when I found out they had ye. Greer had already told me aboot these caves. I kenned I'm the strongest swimmer. I didna say aught aboot that until Thor, Greer, and I joined ma family just west of here."

"Thor made it. Ye didna have to risk yer life. Ye're freezing." Blaine pulled away and unpinned the extra length of his plaid before yanking the entire thing from beneath his belt. He wrapped it around him and Rose, pulling her back against him. He knew he had little heat to give her, but beneath the wool—even though soaked—they would grow warmer. He glanced at Thor, knowing the man was freezing too, but there was little he could do lest he invite the younger man into his embrace with his wife.

"Dinna even think aboot offering to hug me too." Thor shook his head and grinned. He stepped behind Rose and whipped his leine over his head. He wrung it out until no more water dripped from it. He donned it again, and Blaine realized what a good idea that was. Thor cocked an arrogant eyebrow as though Blaine should have thought of that. But Blaine had been too desperate to feel Rose in his arms to think about anything else.

Blaine helped Rose pull her chemise off before he removed his belt and sporran, so he could yank his own leine over his head. They wrung out their clothes as best they could, Blaine taking Rose's to squeeze more water from it than she could. When she put it back on, he realized how short the material was. He handed her his plaid.

"Make an arisaid before ye freeze to death."

Thor snorted. "That too. Ye dinna want anyone seeing ma sister's legs."

"Thank ye." Rose kissed her husband's cheeks before hurrying to fold the plaid. She had to modify the arisaid since she had no belt, and she wanted it to cover her legs. It wound up looking more like she wore it the way a man would. "Da said we should wait until after sunset before we do aught, but we canna all three stay down here wet for hours. Greer told me there's a tunnel that leads to her chamber, nae just the laird's solar or his chamber. If I go up to it, I can get clothes that cover me better. I may be able to sneak some Gunn plaids too. It would hide ye better."

"Nay. Ye arenae wandering the tunnels just to get lost and never found. Yer brother and I can take plaids from the guards." Blaine crossed his arms and spread his feet hip-width apart. Thor smirked and rolled his eyes. Rose launched herself at her husband. He wrapped his arms around her waist and lifted her off her feet.

She leaned to murmur in his ear. "Dinna do that. It does things to me. And I dinna mean it intimidates me. This isnae the time, and ma brother is here."

Blaine squeezed her bottom before he put her down. "We canna attack the guards until we're ready to enter the keep. If we do it too soon and men come down to relieve the ones already there, they will ken I got free."

"Ye canna shiver for the next four hours. It's that, or I find ma way to Greer's chamber, then find plaids. She told me there's a tunnel that leads up there that avoids the dungeon."

Blaine inhaled and nodded. He knew the soundness to her reasoning, and if she'd been a warrior, he would have agreed with far less hesitation. But the thought of sending his defenseless wife into the bowels of a keep he didn't know made him feel ill.

"Ye get clothes for yerself, and that's it. Thor and I will manage. We'll take the plaids from the guards."

"Ye keep saying that, but ye willna manage any better than I am. Ye're already freezing, and so is Thor. Dinna be daft. I ken ye dinna want me gone that long. I dinna want to be away from ye at all. But none of us will do one another or this mission any good if we freeze to death. We need to unlock the sea gate, then I can make ma way to Greer's chamber."

Blaine looked at Thor, who appeared as eager to refuse as Blaine felt. But Thor said nothing. He would let the married couple discuss it without interfering, despite how much he wanted to tell his sister no.

"I'll give ye twenty minutes. If ye arenae back, then I dinna give a fig aboot yer father's plan. I'm coming to find ye." Blaine softened his tone. "I love ye, Kyla."

"I love ye." Rose stretched for a brief kiss, then she led the way farther into the cave. Thor handed the *sgian dubh* back to Blaine, who worked the lock until it gave way. All three stepped through the gate and looked around. Rose spied the correct tunnel and made her way to it. Thor and Blaine stepped into the shadows as Rose raised her arms, with her hands out in front of her, and began her ascent.

Chapter Twenty-Two

Rose wanted to run, but she forced herself to make each step deliberate, lest she jam her foot or trip. Her hands moved side to side, often brushing the tunnel's walls. It didn't take her long to reach the end of the path and Greer's chamber. She felt around for a peep-hole like Greer said existed in the hidden door to Edgar's solar. She found nothing, so she put her ear to the door as she felt around for the latch. There was nothing to hear, so she pushed the door open a crack and waited. When no one sounded an alarm, she opened the door wide enough to enter the chamber. She looked around, shocked to find someone had ransacked the room. She was certain Edgar had done it, or at least ordered someone to. She wasn't sure if they'd done it to search for something or merely as a punishment if Greer should ever come home.

She covered her mouth to stifle her gasp when she spied wrist and ankle restraints on the bed. She forced herself not to imagine Greer being beaten while tied to the bed. She looked around and noticed the clothes strewn everywhere. Greer weighed far less than Rose, and her frame was smaller, but she searched for any gown that would work if the laces weren't pulled tight. She tried four before she found one she could get on completely. It tied on the sides, so it wasn't as noticeable that it didn't lace properly. She discovered one of Greer's plaids and a belt, so she folded it as an arisaid and shoved Blaine's back into the tunnel. She'd pushed the door nearly shut, but not all the way since she didn't know where the latch was on this side.

She crept to the door and eased it open a crack. She reared back when she heard laughter and Edgar's voice floating up from the Great Hall.

"They can sit and wait for as long as they like. Let them watch us and think their attack will come as a surprise. They must ken we see them and that we ken they're coming. By now, that bluidy Keith will be half dead. We'll send his body back to that Sinclair he's humping with our condolences." Men laughed. "I saw that worthless whore I'm forced to call ma daughter with them. Kill whoever ye need to, but I want her alive. That bastard Douglan Keith thinks he'll pry this clan out of ma cold dead hands by marrying his son to Greer. He doesnae understand it's the other way around. Once Blaine is dead, so is Douglan. He's given me all the information I need to make the Keiths a pitiful sept to the Gunns. Marcus will do as I say if he wishes to have Greer. Let him think he'll inherit the lairdship one day. In the meantime, the almighty Robert de Keith keeps babysitting that monchild king and his bitch of a wife. He canna come home while our poor little king hides in France. If Marcus doesnae come to heel, then Douglan's boasting aboot the secret ways into that keep will come in handy. I have enough men I'm paying inside Ackergill to ensure I have a warm welcome."

It stunned Rose to hear that a member of Blaine's clan had plotted against him by sharing the clan's secrets. It enraged her to discover that men had already betrayed him. She knew Marcus was Blaine's best friend and second-in-command. She didn't want to think he was a part of this perfidy, but it sounded like he already had his eye on Greer just to become Laird Gunn one day. She knew that if Blaine died without a son, Marcus would inherit the Keith lairdship too. Was the man that ambitious that he thought to lead two clans? Edgar sounded like he thought it was possible to do it himself.

Rose slipped out of the chamber and considered finding the laird's chamber. There would be clothes that fit Thor and Blaine, but it would mean wearing the laird's family pattern, which would make them stick out. It was already bad enough that she did with Greer's plaid. She swept her gaze down both directions of the passageway before noticing the servants' stairs. She crept down them and froze when she heard women's voices. She pressed herself against the wall, telling herself that she was a fool to test her luck.

Ye're a bampot to think ye can sneak through this keep and somehow find clothes for Blaine and Thor. Ye're more likely to wind up dead or in the dungeon, and nae before some mon forces himself on ye.

She ignored the voice in her head and continued down the last of the stairs until she found herself in the kitchens. With her hair still wet, it was nearly brown rather than strawberry-blonde. She darted her gaze around until she spied an open door that led to the bailey. She moved quickly, hoping to go unnoticed. It was too hot to justify pulling her arisaid over her head, and it even appeared odd that she wore one.

The door she stepped through brought her out beside the laundresses. It was her destination, and she'd found it without trouble. She sucked in a breath when men's leines flapped in the breeze in front of her. She snagged two of them and draped them over her arm, hoping that the cream shirts would hide some of the plaid she wore. The battle the day before sullied the warriors' clothes, so plaids hung to dry at the end of the lines. She walked behind the bedding that filled the space between the shirts and plaids. She glanced around before taking two down. She didn't linger, dashing back into the keep. She kept her head down as she passed through the kitchens again, saying a prayer of thanksgiving when no one stopped her.

She reached the top of the stairs and came face-to-face with Edgar Gunn. The man's shock matched hers. She tried to turn and run back down the stairs, but he grabbed her and lifted her off her feet. He pulled her back onto the landing and fisted her hair.

"Rose Sinclair. This hair and those big tits give ye away. And who else would dare wear ma daughter's dress? What are ye doing here? Ah, two leines and two plaids. Come to rescue yer husband? Too late. But who sneaked in with ye and how?"

Rose remained silent, even when he pulled her hair so hard she was certain several strands came out from the roots. He wrapped his hand around her throat and tightened mercilessly. Rose saw stars dance before her eyes, but she focused as her free hand felt beneath the arisaid for the pocket where she'd hidden her dirk.

She went limp, and Edgar's grip on her throat and hair eased. She slammed her bare foot down on his as hard as she could as she jammed an elbow into his belly and threw back her head. While none were enough to disable him, the combination surprised him into releasing her. She spun around and slashed the blade across his throat. It looked deep enough to kill, but he didn't immediately fall to the ground. His hands went up, as though he might staunch the blood. She aimed again, this time for his chest, but he grabbed her wrist with more strength than she expected. He forced her to drop the knife, but her knee went to his groin. He doubled over, and she swept up the knife. With both hands wrapped around the hilt, she stabbed upward at the base of his skull, embedding the dirk in his skull. She grabbed the clothes she dropped and dashed back to Greer's room, grabbing Blaine's plaid as she entered the tunnel. She didn't stop running until she shot past Thor and Blaine into the cave.

"Kyla!" Blaine wrapped his arm around her waist and steadied her. "The blood. Are ye hurt?"

"Nae mine," Rose wheezed. "The Gunn's. Stabbed him in skull—after—slashing throat. He has to be dead. I ran back to Greer's chamber and straight into the tunnel." By the end, Rose caught her breath enough to speak in complete sentences.

"How did he find ye? And these clothes? What did ye do, Rose?" Thor demanded.

"I slipped out of Greer's chamber and out to the laundresses' area. I found two leines and two plaids for ye. I was coming back to Greer's chamber when he found me. We fought, and I think I killed him." Rose looked up at Blaine, and her heart broke. "Blaine, I overheard him talking to men in the Great Hall." She closed her eyes and sighed before looking at him again. "I dinna ken the whole of it, but Douglan's been sharing yer clan's secrets with the Gunn. Marcus is supposed to marry Greer, so Edgar could make the Keiths a sept of the Gunns. Douglan thinks Marcus will one day lead both clans, but Edgar made it sound like that wouldn't happen."

Blaine stared at Rose, listening to everything she said. He felt number from the news than being nearly completely submerged. He'd suspected Douglan, but it made him wonder if Marcus conspired with his father after all. It was Blaine's turn to close his eyes. He inhaled deeply before looking down at Rose and nodding. He would deal with his clan as soon as he was free of the Gunns.

"We have to find Edgar and ken for sure he's dead." Blaine spoke to Thor, but he held Rose against him as she continued to tremble. She held out the clothes to her brother, and when he took them, she let go of Blaine and wrapped both arms around Thor. When Rose released Thor, Blaine kissed her head before sliding her hand into his. They all knew there was no time to waste. Someone would find Edgar and sound the alarm. With a prisoner in their midst, the Gunns would come to see if he'd escaped and killed their laird, and they would suspect the attack was imminent. Neither Thor nor Blaine faulted Rose for defending herself, but it complicated matters.

The men hurried to dress before she led them through the tunnel and into Greer's chamber. Both men looked around in the same stunned silence as Rose had. Thor ripped an ankle restraint from the bed and stared at it. The murderous rage Rose witnessed scared her. She'd seen no man look like Thor did. It made her fear what Greer whispered to him. He flung the cuff across the chamber so hard it bounced off the wall before it fell to the floor. He led the way to the door, flinging it open. He stopped short when he found Edgar's body still lying prone near the stairs. He marched to it and kicked Edgar's ribs. The body did nothing, so using his foot, he rolled Edgar onto his back. Thor and Blaine had already seen Rose's knife sticking out of the dead man's skull, and both knew that alone had been enough to kill him. They also knew that the slash to the man's throat would have killed him too, only slower.

Thor looked up at Rose as though she'd robbed him of something, but he nodded. "It doesnae matter who avenged her. He canna hurt her or anyone else ever again."

"We need to get to his solar and find the missives Greer mentioned. I need the proof that Douglan mutinied, and I need to see if there is any note aboot Marcus's role in all this." Blaine didn't flinch at the idea of Douglan hanging from the gallows, but his chest ached to think Marcus might swing beside his father.

"These stairs take us to the kitchens. We canna use them." Rose looked toward the main staircase and shook her head. "We canna walk into the Great Hall and think nay one will notice us. Do we go back down to the tunnels and go through the dungeon?"

"Nay. Blaine, take Rose back to Greer's chamber. I'm taking the stairs up to the battlements. I'm signaling Da. We canna wait any longer. Once I'm back, Rose, ye barricade yerself in that chamber. Ye dinna answer unless it's one of us." Rose knew he meant more than just Thor and Blaine. He included their father and any immediate family. She wouldn't answer to anyone claiming to be a Sinclair warrior. "We need to get ye a sword, Blaine."

"I dinna ken where they took mine, but his may be in his chamber." Blaine looked toward the door at the opposite end of the passageway. He sprinted down to it but inched the door open. He spied what he wanted, so he didn't linger once he grabbed it. When he returned to the twins, he held up the sword. "The bluidy bastard was going to use ma own sword."

"Be careful. I can go to Greer's chamber on ma own." Rose wrapped her arms around Blaine's neck and accepted the all too brief kiss before she wrapped her arms around her brother's waist. They watched her run to Greer's room and heard the lock click, then the bar drop. More furniture moved, telling them she barricaded the door.

Thor and Blaine took the stairs up to the battlements and cautiously opened the door. It opened to the side of the keep overlooking the sea, so there were few guardsmen nearby, and none looked in their direction. Carrying their knives, the men inched forward. They hid them in the folds of their plaids when guards caught their movement and looked in their direction. No one sounded the alarm, so they assumed the Gunn plaids they wore worked as a disguise. Thor looked over his shoulder at Blaine, then rolled his eyes up as though he could see his hair. Both had feared it would give them away. Blaine lurched forward and pushed Thor to the ground, following him, just as an arrow whizzed past where Thor's body had been a moment earlier.

"I guess it did give us away." Thor came to his feet as Blaine crouched beside him. They drew their swords, carrying them in their right hands while they held their dirks in the left. More arrows sailed over them as they slipped along the battlements. The crenellation allowed them to look toward the Sinclairs camp. "Blessedly, the wind blows in the right direction."

Thor whistled as loudly as he could, praying it was enough for his family to hear over the waves as the wind blew the sound toward the Sinclairs. He whistled four more times, but he could do no more when Gunn warriors rushed toward Blaine and him. They fought side-by-side, Thor switching his sword to his left hand to keep it from clashing with Blaine's and giving them a wider reach.

"Ye're going to need to teach me how ye do that. I havenae seen anyone wield a sword so well in their left hand." Blaine huffed as he spoke, and his focus was still on thrusting his weapon through the man who rushed toward him.

"Years of practice with five men who have the patience of saints when they're teaching but are ogres when they're correcting ye." Thor wiped his forehead during a momentary reprieve from the Gunn warriors. "Ye remember Wiley running laps around the lists a few days ago? Aye, he dropped the sword from his left hand. Uncle Tavish made him run with the sword in his left hand. His da said it would strengthen Wiley's arm. It would also remind him he didna want to make that mistake twice. Wiley loathes running. The mon's half fish."

"Girnigoe! Girnigoe!"

The Sinclairs' battle cry, harkening back to the Norse ancestors, carried on the wind. It reminded all Sinclairs of their roots at Girnigoe, a place their Viking forebearers once settled.

"That's Grandda!" Thor swung his sword, cleaving his enemy's head from his shoulders as Blaine withdrew his blade from a dead man's chest. Thor leaped over bodies of men they'd felled as he rushed forward to see Sinclairs pouring across the open expanse, Laird Liam Sinclair leading the charge. If there weren't still men ready to attack them on the battlements, Thor and Blaine would have watched in fascination. No one would ever guess the man with dark hair flying around his shoulders was well into his sixth decade.

With their swords drawn, four riders who looked like they could be the Four Horsemen of the Apocalypse raced behind their father. One lion mane rode beside a head of white-blonde hair. Dedric Hartley and his son, Kirk. Next to them, fanned out behind their fathers, were Tate, Wiley, Tor, and Blake. Thor didn't know how his grandfather, or his cousins Tate and Wiley made it. Liam hadn't been at the camp when he returned with Greer and Rose, and they had assigned Tate and Wiley to a different section of their border.

"We need to prove Edgar is dead. We have to go back." Blaine tugged at the back of Thor's leine. Thor nodded, and the two men ran back the way they came. They bolted down the steps and to Edgar's body. No one had found him since it still lay where Rose left it. Blaine's sword finished the work Rose's knife began. He grabbed a handful of the head's hair before leading the way back up the stairs.

By the time they reached the battlements, the Sinclairs were nearly at the gate. Blaine held up the severed head and whistled as loudly as Thor had.

"Put down yer weapons. Yer laird is dead. The Sinclairs didna come to kill ye, but they will if ye fight back."

When the Gunn warriors didn't listen, Blaine lifted the head high in the air shook it, dislodging tissue that fell from the bottom. Until a moment later, it was the most gruesome thing he'd ever done.

"Duck," he said to Thor.

Blaine swung the decapitated head in four circles high above the battlements, then released it into the bailey below. It struck a warrior who screamed and ran. The head rolled as people tried to back away from it.

"I am Laird Liam Sinclair, Earl of Caithness. Let me pass." Liam had lowered his sword, but his targe remained up to defend himself if needed. His horse walked forward until he passed beneath the portcullis. His family followed him into the bailey. "We arenae here to ransack yer homes or kill yer people. Those who wish for peace between yer clan and the rest of the Highlands, put down yer weapons. Nay harm will come to ye. If ye refuse because ye support yer dead laird, then ye will die by ma sword. Today ends the feud between the Gunns and their neighbors the Sinclairs, the Sutherlands, and the Mackays."

Thor stood where he could watch his grandfather, but movement outside the barmekin drew his attention. A solitary figure rode toward the keep. "I'm going to throttle the lass."

Thor hurried toward the steps that would take him to the bailey. When Gunn warriors didn't step aside, he barked, "Move." He reached the bailey as Greer rode beneath the gate. He caught her horse's bridle before he lifted her from the saddle. "Woman, ye could have been riding into a battle."

"But I didna. Put me down, Thor."

He hadn't realized he held her off the ground, so they were eye level. He practically dropped her but made sure she was steady on her feet. He shook his head and turned his back to her. He went to his father's side as Callum dismounted.

"We didna make it into Edgar's solar before—" Thor looked at Edgar's head that lay in the center of the bailey. "Rose killed him, but Blaine severed his head."

"Rose?"

"Aye. These women," Thor jerked his chin toward Greer before looking up at a window where he'd spied his sister watching, "dinna ken how to keep themselves from nearly getting killed. Rose was to get herself clothes from Greer's chamber. She sneaked through the keep and got clothes for Blaine and me. On the way back, she ran into Edgar. Cut his throat and shoved her blade up the back of his skull. She's barricaded in Greer's chamber. Blaine and I went back to get proof Edgar was dead."

"Da!" Greer ran across the bailey and into the arms of an older man who limped toward her. Thor and Callum watched as the pair embraced.

"That's Albert. The guard that would ride out with Greer to meet Rose." Blaine joined Thor and Callum before they and Liam walked to where the man held Greer's head against his chest.

"Ye kenned?" Albert asked.

"Since I was wee. Ye and I have the same birthmark on our arm." Greer pushed up her sleeve to reveal what looked like a cluster of freckles. Albert pushed up his sleeve and held his arm out next to hers. "Ye and Mama..."

"Aye. From when she arrived here as a bride until she died for her sins." Albert's shoulders slumped.

"He killed her, didna he? I always kenned."

"Aye, lass. He did. He discovered the same thing as ye and kenned." Albert looked up at the Sinclairs and Blaine before his gaze swept the bailey. People watched, but he doubted they could all hear. But those who could, would soon spread the gossip.

"Ye're still Lady Greer, daughter of Lady Gunn while she was married to Laird Gunn." Liam spoke with such certainty that Greer nodded. He continued louder, so the people throughout the bailey could hear. "I think ye have likely run this clan for many years and could do so in yer sleep. If nay one else takes up arms against us, we are at peace with yer clan. If ye wish to lead as laird, in truth, I support ye, ma lady."

Greer stared at Liam. Nothing had prepared her for him to say that. "Thank ye, Laird Sinclair. If it is ma people's wish for me to lead, then I will. If they'd rather a mon do it, then I will serve as I always have while the council votes in a new laird."

Six men stepped forward and approached along with the rest of the Sinclair family. Heads turned as a bolt of reddish hair flew past them. Rose rushed into Blaine's arms, but the moment she was certain he was safe, she pulled away and enveloped Greer in her embrace. The women clung to one another.

"I barricaded maself into yer chamber," Rose whispered. "I think I figured it out. Ye dinna have to stay here ever again if ye dinna want to. Come home to Dunbeath or come with me to Ackergill Tower. But if ye decide to stay, I will support ye to lead as the laird. It's yer right after what ye've done for this clan."

"Lady Greer will nae lead this clan. Nae now that her illegitimacy is nay longer a secret but also because she is a lass." Harold, the senior-most council member, stated. Liam stepped in front of Harold and drove his fist into the man's face. When Harold staggered backward, Liam threw another punch.

"I have waited forty-seven years to do this. Ye were the one who held ma brother down while Thomas killed him. Ye were the one who held Ceana while her brother nearly beat her to death while she carried ma brother's bairn. Ye've hidden from me like a sniveling wean." Liam smashed his fist into Harold's nose, driving the bone into his skull. The man collapsed to the ground, dead. Liam turned back to the rest of the council. "Ye have all been on this clan's council during one disastrous laird after another. Ye have done naught to lead this clan anywhere but to ruin. Step down gracefully, or as the Earl of Caithness —which includes yer land—I will sentence ye to death. I havenae exerted ma full will for the sake of keeping some semblance of peace. But now I do. The clan elects a new council today. They decide aboot Lady Greer."

Rose held Greer's hand and looked at her best friend. "Do ye wish to lead?"

"Until a proper laird is chosen. After, I—" Greer looked at Blaine, then back to Rose. "I'd like to come to Ackergill, at least for a little while."

"Ye are always welcome, Greer." Blaine smiled.

"Thank ye."

Blaine slid his arm around Rose's waist and guided them toward Callum as Liam continued to talk. Blaine kept his voice low. "I have to go to Ackergill. I must find out if only Douglan plotted against me. I willna take Rose with me until I ken it's safe for her, and nay one there is waiting for me to die."

"She'll be safe at our camp. We willna stay within these walls." Callum looked at Rose. "Do ye think Greer will want to stay in the keep? She will be safer at our camp."

"I'll talk to her." Rose stepped fully into Blaine's embrace. "Please dinna go alone. Take Thor and Blake, if nae all ma other cousins."

"I was going to ask yer grandda just that. I'll be back as soon as I can, hopefully by midmorning. I love ye, Kyla." Blaine tipped her chin up.

"I love ye." Rose pressed her lips to Blaine's. A whimper escaped as they pulled apart. "Take me to our home after this is settled."

"I will, *mo ghaol*." My love.

Chapter Twenty-Three

Blaine reined in his horse after passing beneath the portcullis at Ackergill. Blake rode to his left and Thor to his right as they entered the bailey. Behind them were Wiley, Tate, Tor, and Kirk. The seven strapping young men made an impressive sight as they dismounted. People stared as the new arrivals looked around. A few women batted their eyelashes at them, but none of the warriors took notice. They weren't there to idle away their time.

"Marcus." Blaine watched as his second stepped out of the keep. It shocked Blaine to see how much his friend appeared to have aged in the space of a few days. "What's happened?"

"Can we speak in yer solar? Everyone here already kens, but I'd rather explain the details in private."

"Tell me now." Blaine wouldn't budge until he understood whether he should fear a threat awaiting him if he trusted Marcus.

"Ma father is dead, and I killed him." Marcus's eyes locked with Blaine's, and there was such great sadness in them that Blaine's heart broke for his friend.

"Aye. Let's go inside." Blaine tilted his head toward the keep, and the Sinclair men, plus one Hartley, followed. It made Marcus pause, but he sighed and nodded. Once inside the solar Blaine had claimed as his own even though he still thought of it as his father's, he sat at the head of the table. The other men filled in the chairs. "Before ye tell me yer tale, ye should ken Edgar Gunn is dead. Ma wife killed him. I also read messages he recorded aboot yer father. I ken his treason."

"Ye likely learned of it when I did. When the Sinclairs rode on Clyth Castle, a messenger slipped away and rode here. Ma father ordered me to gather the men to ride out. But it wasna to come to yer defense. He ordered me to defend Clyth alongside the Gunns." Marcus scrubbed his face with his hands. His right hand slid over his mouth as his left hand dropped to his lap. He shook his head. "Ma father hinted to me many times that he wished me to marry Lady Greer. He told me that her illegitimacy meant I stood a chance to wed with her despite nae being a laird or a laird's son. I refused each time. She isnae who I want, even if she might be a fine woman."

"Since I didna see ye riding anywhere near Clyth, ye refused yer father. Did he expect ye to aid the Gunns and wed Lady Greer practically on the spot? Did he expect ye to kill me while ye were there? Did he want ye to kill Edgar? Or was he willing to allow the mon to die of auld age?" Blaine launched one question after another, but Marcus didn't react more than to look as despondent as he had since they entered the solar.

"He told me that if I killed ye, then I would rightfully gain ma place as Laird Keith. He wanted me to kill Laird Gunn once I wed Lady Greer and got her with child. He thought I would lead both clans, and that he could force the Gunns to submit to us."

"Why did he keep saying rightfully? I heard him say something similar, but I wasna sure what he meant."

"I didna ken this until ma last argument with him. Ma father wasna yer father's cousin. He was yer father's aulder but illegitimate brother. He was wed to ma mother when I was born. He believes that entitled me to inherit what could never be his. I've never wanted to be laird. I didna even want to be yer tánaiste while ye serve as laird. I was content to be yer captain of the guard. I want a croft with Ellie that we can fill with weans." Ellie...Blaine had seen the way his best friend's gaze had followed the miller's daughter. "I serve in yer place when ye tell me to, but it isnae what I've wanted. I loathe it. I loathe being forced to deal with the clan council and trying to be the voice of reason. I loathe hearing the pettiest complaints between farmers who should spend their time farming. I'd rather be outside than trapped in here going over ledgers and sorting yer correspondence. But I've done it without complaint because ye trusted me, and I ken ye dinna do that easily."

"What happened to yer father?" Blaine had suspected Marcus disliked the position, but he never realized how unhappy being his second had made Marcus. It also shocked him that Douglan and Marcus knew about Greer's paternity, but that was the least of his concerns during this conversation.

"When I refused to obey him and lead an army

against ye, he tried to rally men to his cause. Some actually agreed to ride alongside him. They're now in the dungeon awaiting yer decision aboot their fate. I tried to stop ma father as he mounted his horse. I reached for the bridle, but he made his horse rear. He would have had the beast strike me, but I dodged around the hooves and pulled him from the saddle. I pulled with more force than I realized, and ma father landed against the keep's steps. He cracked his skull and died as I towered over him."

"Then it was an accident." Blaine wouldn't accuse Marcus of anything if that's what happened.

"It was. But I didna feel any remorse when it happened, and I dinna feel it now. Tis a blessing to this clan that he's gone. He was ma father, and I loved him, I suppose. But he wasna a good mon. I went through his correspondence and discovered he's been selling information to the Gunns since before yer father went to France. He told the Murrays aboot our strategy at the Battle of Keith's Muir. That's why we lost. He wrote to yer father and suggested ye marry Eliza Irvine after her father paid him a pouch of silver to make it happen." Marcus shook his head. "There's much, much more. So much more."

Blaine sat back in his chair and listened to Marcus divulge his father's secrets for another hour. It left him speechless by the end. He sat and stared at his friend for several minutes before he nodded. "Does Ellie wish to marry ye?"

His question surprised Marcus. "Aye."

"Post the banns this Sunday. If ye'd rather be ma captain of the guard instead of ma second, then I will find someone else. But I dinna expect to be away from home as often now that things with the Gunns are through. Besides I have ma wife to bring home, and I wish to spend ma time with her, nae roaming the Highlands."

"Can it really be that simple?"

"Convince her father, then tell me whether it was simple. I dinna wish to make ye miserable, Marcus. Ye've proven to be true to yer oaths. I admit I've doubted ye when I grew suspicious of yer father. But yer actions have never made me question ye. I'd rather ye be happy, Cousin."

"Thank ye."

Blaine remained in the solar with Marcus and summoned the other council members. His family-by-marriage went to the loch to bathe. He spoke to his advisors for an hour as they discussed messages that had arrived that morning from Hardi and Hamish. They suspected it was what made Douglan so eager to ride out. Blaine read them, relieved to learn Hardi successfully mediated with the Murrays. It had required him to visit the clan, but he'd brokered a truce between the Murrays and Keiths. Hamish's letter informed him that King David relented and agreed to allow his handfast with Rose to stand as a real marriage. Blaine assumed a similar message likely awaited Liam when he returned to Dunbeath.

The hours and days were a jumble in his mind, but he counted down the minutes until he could ride out and join Rose at the camp. He knew it would have been wiser to wait until morning, but he was too eager to see his bride. Thor and his cousins understood, so they mounted their steeds and rode south to the Sinclairs.

It was a subdued evening as the Sinclair warriors built fires and roasted the meat they caught. Greer remained at the keep overseeing things as the transition was already taking place, and the council met to decide about the lairdship. Rose huddled beside Blaine until it was time to go to sleep. He'd gladly changed out of the wretched Gunn plaid and back into one of his before he arrived at Ackergill, having had to borrow one of his men's. He drew Rose close and wrapped her in his arms with the wool around them.

"I wasna sure ye would be able to return like ye planned. I thought ye might be away at least another day."

"Hell would have frozen over before I spent another night away from ye."

"I dinna like sleeping without ye, Husband."

"Dinna ye fash, Wife. I plan to be beside ye, under ye, and over ye every night for the rest of our lives."

They both knew that wouldn't be possible since he would have to ride out from time to time, but Rose's core ached at the sentiment. There were far too many people around them, especially since so many were directly related to her, for them to slip away for any privacy. They longed for nothing more than to strip each other bare and let their hands roam to their hearts' content. But that wasn't an option. However, they would make the most of the dark and Blaine's spare plaid covering them.

His hand slid down the front of her kirtle, which she'd gladly swapped for Greer's poorly fitting one. He palmed her breast before tugging at the laces along her back. He loosened them enough that, when he slid his hand back down her chest, he could pinch her nipple. She pressed a kiss to his lips as she pulled the plaid they used as a blanket higher around their shoulders. Her hand slid beneath the *breacan feile,* or great plaid, Blaine wore. She wrapped her hand around his length and stroked.

"Lass, when we're alone, I'm making a meal out of ye. I intend to kiss every inch of ye before I feast on ma favorite honey. I wish to watch her come apart on ma tongue and ma cock."

Rose's sheath ached with each tantalizing word Blaine whispered. She stroked him as he withdrew his hand and hiked up her skirts. He moved slowly to keep from drawing attention from anyone who might still be awake. The men on watch would face away from the camp, but he knew they would also glance back from time to time. He also didn't want Callum or any of the other laird's family to skewer him where he lay.

Rose's motions were slow for the same reason, but they teased Blaine to almost the point of agony. He slipped his hand between her thighs, squeezing the ample flesh that he looked forward to trailing his lips over. His fingers inched into her, and she stifled her moan.

"When we are alone, ye shall have to wait yer turn. I intend to savor every inch of ye." She tightened her grip to make her point. Blaine thrust into her hand as she stroked him. "I ken there is still much for me to learn, and I find I canna wait for ye to teach me."

They fell quiet as they continued to entice one another with their stealthy ministrations. Rose's free hand fisted Blaine's leine as she buried her face against his chest, practically disappearing beneath the top of their blanket. Her core spasmed around his fingers as her body tensed with her release.

"Roll over, *mo ghaol*. Face away from me."

While she didn't hurry, so it looked like she sought a more comfortable position, she couldn't wait to feel Blaine's rod pressed against her backside. He drew the tip through the dew that coated her netherlips. She pushed her hips back in silent invitation. Blaine's hand returned to her thigh as he positioned her and surged into her. They both froze as they reveled in that blissful sensation of their bodies becoming one.

Rose had never imagined how wonderous it would feel as a sword slid into her sheath. Blaine had never noticed the moment could be so tender and arousing at the same time. In the past, it had merely been a step toward his ultimate goal. Now it was something to savor.

He slipped an arm beneath Rose and wrapped it around her waist, holding her against him. Her hand covered his as he rocked into her. His palm caressed up the outside of her thigh until it could grip her hip. He eased her into a rhythm that matched his before sliding his hand down to her mons. His fingers explored as he heightened Rose's need. When his fingers circled her nub, she thought she might expire. Their slow movements tantalized them both until need consumed them. Blaine couldn't thrust into her as he wished, since everyone would know what they were about, and he'd likely die for it at worst, but it would humiliate Rose at best. But it meant they could draw out their joining until they joined each other in rapture.

Blaine did nothing to pull away from Rose once

they both climaxed. Instead, he pressed himself as close as he could along her back.

"*Leannan*, this isnae just for a year, is it?"

"It was never going to be for just a year, Blaine."

"Do ye wish to marry before a priest?"

"As soon as we can."

With a contented sigh from each other them, they drifted off to sleep as one.

Liam and Callum returned to Clyth the following morning to cement the truce and sign documents to codify it. While they were away, riders approached. Rose recognized her mother immediately. It wasn't difficult to recognize Brighde or Isabella Hartley, Ric's wife and Kirk's mother, since they both had white-blonde hair. Mairghread, Deirdre, and Ceit rode alongside the other women. Shona and her cousins weren't far behind.

"Mama?"

"Aye. It doesnae make sense for ye to return to Dunbeath just to say goodbye when I ken ye and yer husband need to go home. I wasna willing to accept a messenger telling me ye were fine, especially when he let slip something aboot ye swimming into a cave with yer brother. I'd like to see ye settled and happy before I let ma lass go for good."

"Thank ye, Mama." Rose inhaled her mother's scent as they embraced. It soothed her just as it had since she was a baby. The prospect of running her own keep crashed over her like the waves through which she'd swum only the day before.

"Wheest, *leannan*. Ye are ready for this, but I will

stay as long as ye need me." Siùsan stroked her daughter's head just as she had since the day she was born with hair that matched hers.

Rose looked at Blaine, who smiled and nodded. She loved they were already communicating silently, just as she'd watched her parents do countless times during her life. "Mama, we'd like ye and everyone to stay for the next three sennights while we post the banns. Blaine and I wish to marry before a priest. We decided last night just before we fell asleep."

Rose and Blaine had barely finished talking before they'd both fallen into the deepest sleep of their lives. The last thing either of them heard were Thor's light snores..

"We'd love naught more." Siùsan opened her arms and welcomed Blaine into her embrace. "I'm glad to have a second son. Mayhap ye can teach ma other one some manners."

"Mama." Thor's aggrieved voice came from behind them. Rose looked past Blaine to where Greer had just arrived with Callum and Liam. She heard her friend try to smother her laughter. Thor glared at Greer before helping her from the saddle. Rose couldn't hear their conversation, but Greer shook her head several times. Thor persisted with whatever argument he made until Greer relented. They walked away from the group, making it impossible for Rose to hear or see them. She supposed if either of them wanted her to know, they would tell her. She wouldn't ask—even if the curiosity might kill her. Her brother and best friend still couldn't seem to set aside their differences.

"It's time to go home, lass. Are ye ready?" Blaine's heart soared when Rose beamed at him. She nodded eagerly and hurried to her horse. Blaine followed her, laughing as they walked. Only a few minutes later, the entire Sinclair family and their guards were mounted and making their way to Ackergill Tower.

The next three weeks passed in a blur for Rose and Blaine as they settled into their new roles as husband and wife, and Rose became the lady of the keep. She adored Martha, the housekeeper, and the feeling was mutual. Siùsan guided Rose without being obtrusive, and it eased Rose's worries. Every Sunday, she and Blaine sat beside each other in the laird's family pew. Liam, Callum, and Siùsan joined them. They listened to the Mass, but both were eager for the service's end because the priest posted the banns. Greer remained at Ackergill once her clan refused to allow her to serve as laird during the interim, even though they hadn't settled on a new leader. The Sutherlands, Mackays, Camerons, and the MacLeods of Assynt and of Lewis, along with the Mackenzies, arrived a sennight before the momentous day.

The day of Rose and Blaine's wedding dawned with bright blue skies. Rose thought she might not survive her eagerness, knowing she had to wait until sunset. But the women in her family followed her abovestairs after the midday meal. They told stories from Rose's childhood as they helped her get ready. It was late by the time the summer sun set, but the moment Rose saw Blaine standing at the bottom of the kirk's steps, she knew it had been worth the wait.

Blaine's heart expanded to near bursting, and his bollocks ached when he spied Rose walking toward him with Callum beside her. He was grateful for his sporran to hide his reaction to his bride. He accepted her hand and kissed it. Before the priest wrapped their wrists with the Keith plaid, much like they had when they handfasted, Blaine whispered in Rose's ear.

"Ye are the finest of all roses in this land. Naught is sweeter than ye or bonnier. God granted me the greatest gift when He put me in yer path. I dinna want to imagine how empty ma life would be if we hadnae worked everything out. I love ye, Rose Kyla. Today, tomorrow, and every day."

"I almost missed the one great love of ma life because of ma own stubbornness. I thank God every day for bringing ye to Dunrobin. I might nae have realized what a good mon ye are if I hadnae pushed ye away. But never again. I will only ever hold ye tight. I love ye, Blaine. Today, tomorrow, and every day."

They recited the traditional wedding vows, but the pledges they exchanged before the ceremony began meant just as much, if not more to them. They sealed their love and their commitment with a kiss as the sun sank beyond the horizon. They endured the Mass that followed, but Blaine swept Rose off her feet and took the stairs by twos and threes once they entered the Great Hall. He slammed the door shut and barred it. They spent a sennight hidden away together, only accepting food and baths.

"It wasna easy to get to this point, but it amazes me how easily some matters settled. Fate kenned we were to love and make our life together." Rose smiled as they sat together beside their chamber's fire on the last evening before her family left in the morning.

"I pray all remains this settled. But when we face

the next challenge, I'm glad to ken we'll do it together. All I've ever wanted is to have ye by ma side."

"It's where I belong."

"I love ye, ma bonnie Highland Rose." Blaine kissed his wife.

Epilogue

"Get down." Rose flapped her hand before tugging Blaine's arm.

"What's wrong?"

"It's Thor. I dinna want him to see us." Rose scowled playfully as Blaine laughed. "It was fine spying Saoirse and her husband leaving the cave after their tryst yesterday. But I dinna need to see ma brother and his wife doing the same thing. Or rather, I dinna want him seeing me leaving after doing what we've been doing."

"Kyla, we've been married more than a score and have five children. They have six. I think it's obvious what we've all been doing." Blaine slid down to the sand behind the boulder where they'd coupled that day and the one before.

"Aye. And that's why we're here at Dunbeath for yet another wedding. But that doesnae mean I want ma brother to see me after ma husband just pleasured me."

"What if I dinna mind him seeing me after ma wife just pleasured me?"

"Of course, ye wouldnae mind. Ye'd strut like a rooster."

"I'll gladly show ye ma cock again if ye'll make me crow." Blaine pulled Rose onto his lap and yanked at her laces. She had no wish to fight her husband despite how she'd struggled to brush the sand from her body before putting her gown back on without exposing herself from behind the rocks. He put up no resistance when Rose pushed his leine up his chest.

Blaine still possessed the same muscular physique he had twenty years earlier, and Rose reveled in running her hands over it. Once he had his plaid spread beneath them, he guided Rose to straddle him. He lapped at her nipples before sucking her breast like a starved man finding an oasis. His hands traveled over her body, groaning as his bollocks tightened. He would never be sated with making love to his wife. He would always need more. He grasped her bottom and kneaded the flesh.

Five children had changed her body, broadening her hips and enlarging her bust. Her belly was fuller than it had been when they wed, and faint white lines proved she'd borne them several children. Throughout the years, their love deepened as they relied on one another, but there were times of discord, too. But never did Blaine's desire for his wife waver, just as she craved his touch as much as when they handfasted. He worshipped her body every chance he had, delighting in every inch.

When they emerged from their love nest after their wedding, Rose feared meeting women from Blaine's past. It inevitably happened during those early months, and she'd witnessed some of the women's jealousy and disdainful looks. She knew part of that came from the mere fact Blaine chose someone else, but she also knew the women couldn't fathom why Blaine chose her when she looked nothing like the ones from his past.

"St. Columba's bones, lass. Ye shall make ma heart give out." Blaine nibbled along her shoulder and up her neck until he kissed behind her ears. "That's— slow down, Kyla. I shall spend too soon."

"Dinna make me so eager." Rose giggled as Blaine rolled them. He thrust into her, showing her just how eager she made him too. Her hands roamed his chest until her body tightened around him. Her neck arched, and Blaine grazed his teeth along it as she trembled. Her inner muscles spasmed around him. He thrust three more times before he felt his own release.

Rose wrapped her legs over his as they lay panting together. His hands continued to roam over her, gripping her soft thighs. He rocked his hips and groaned as Rose clenched around him again.

"Do ye slip something into ma ale, Wife? I'm nae a young mon anymore, but I'm as randy as the day I met ye. I dinna ken how I'm able to keep up with ye."

"I'm happy to keep ye up. And nay, I dinna put aught in yer food or drink. I'm just a vera lucky woman to have such a virile husband."

"Ye have a body made to make me sin. I canna help it."

"Then dinna."

They basked in the autumn sunshine as they abandoned any thoughts about returning to the keep until the bells rang for the evening meal. They were even more in love and in lust than they had been all those years ago.

Thank you for reading
Highland Rose

Celeste Barclay, a nom de plume, lives near the Southern California coast with her husband and sons. Growing up in the Midwest, Celeste enjoyed spending as much time in and on the water as she could. Now she lives near the beach. She's an avid swimmer, a hopeful future surfer, and a former rower. When she's not writing, she's working or being a mom.

Subscribe to Celeste's bimonthly newsletter to receive exclusive insider perks.
Subscribe Now

www.celestebarclay.com

Join the fun and get exclusive insider giveaways,
sneak peeks, and new release announcements in
Celeste Barclay's Facebook Ladies of Yore Group

The Clan Sinclair Legacy

Highland Lion

Highland Bear

Highland Jewel (Coming August 2, 2022)

The Clan Sinclair

His Highland Lass **BOOK 1 SNEAK PEEK**

She entered the great hall like a strong spring storm in the northern most Highlands. Tristan Mackay felt like he had been blown hither and yon. As the storm settled, she left him with the sweet scents of heather and lavender wafting towards him as she approached. She was not a classic beauty, tall and willowy like the women at court. Her face and form were not what legends were made of. But she held a unique appeal unlike any he had seen before. He could not take his eyes off of her long chestnut hair that had strands of fire and burnt copper running through them. Unlike the waves or curls he was used to, her hair was unusually straight and fine. It looked like a waterfall cascading down her back. While she was not tall, neither was she short. She had a figure that was meant for a man to grasp and hold onto, whether from the front or from behind. She had an aura of confidence and charm, but not arrogance or conceit like many good looking women he had met. She did not seem to know her own appeal. He could tell that she was many things, but one thing she was not was his.

The Highland Ladies

A Spinster at the Highland Court

BOOK 1 SNEAK PEEK

Elizabeth Fraser looked around the royal chapel within
Stirling Castle. The ornate candlestick holders on the altar
glistened and reflected the light from the ones in the wall
sconces as the priest intoned the holy prayers of the Advent
season. Elizabeth kept her head bowed as though in prayer,
but her green eyes swept the congregation. She watched
the other ladies-in-waiting, many of whom were doing the
same thing. She caught the eye of Allyson Elliott. Elizabeth
raised one eyebrow as Allyson's lips twitched. Both women
had been there enough times to accept they'd be kneeling
for at least the next hour as the Latin service carried on.
Elizabeth understood the Mass thanks to her cousin
Deirdre Fraser, or rather now Deirdre Sinclair. Elizabeth's
mind flashed to the recent struggle her cousin faced as she
reunited with her husband Magnus after a seven-year
separation. Her aunt and uncle's choice to keep Deirdre
hidden from her husband simply because they didn't think
the Sinclairs were an advantageous enough match, and the
resulting scandal, still humiliated the other Fraser clan
members at court. She admired Deirdre's husband
Magnus's pledge to remain faithful despite not knowing if
he'd ever see Deirdre again.

Elizabeth suddenly snapped her attention; while everyone
else intoned the twelfth—or was it thirteenth—amen of the
Mass, the hairs on the back of her neck stood up. She had
the strongest feeling that someone was watching her. Her
eyes scanned to her right, where her parents sat further
down the pew. Her mother and father had their heads

bowed and eyes closed. While she was convinced her mother was in devout prayer, she wondered if her father had fallen asleep during the Mass. Again. With nothing seeming out of the ordinary and no one visibly paying attention to her, her eyes swung to the left. She took in the king and queen as they kneeled together at their prie-dieu. The queen's lips moved as she recited the liturgy in silence. The king was as still as a statue. Years of leading warriors showed, both in his stature and his ability to control his body into absolute stillness. Elizabeth peered past the royal couple and found herself looking into the astute hazel eyes of Edward Bruce, Lord of Badenoch and Lochaber. His gaze gave her the sense that he peered into her thoughts, as though he were assessing her. She tried to keep her face neutral as heat surged up her neck. She prayed her face didn't redden as much as her neck must have, but at a twenty-one, she still hadn't mastered how to control her blushing. Her nape burned like it was on fire. She canted her head slightly before looking up at the crucifix hanging over the altar. She closed her eyes and tried to invoke the image of the Lord that usually centered her when her mind wandered during Mass.

Elizabeth sensed Edward's gaze remained on her. She didn't understand how she was so sure that he was looking at her. She didn't have any special gifts of perception or sight, but her intuition screamed that he was still looking.

Pirates of the Isles

The Blond Devil of the Sea **BOOK 1 SNEAK PEEK**

Caragh lifted her torch into the air as she made her way down the precarious Cornish cliffside. She made out the hulking shape of a ship, but the dead of night made it impossible to see who was there. She and the fishermen of Bedruthan Steps weren't expecting any shipments that night. But her younger brother Eddie, who stood watch at the entrance to their hiding place, had spotted the ship and signaled up to the village watchman, who alerted Caragh.

As her boot slid along the dirt and sand, she cursed having to carry the torch and wished she could have sunlight to guide her. She knew these cliffs well, and it was for that reason it was better that she moved slowly than stop moving once and for all. Caragh feared the light from her torch would carry out to the boat. Despite her efforts to keep the flame small, the solitary light would be a beacon.

When Caragh came to the final twist in the path before the sand, she snuffed out her torch and started to run to the cave where the main source of the village's income lay in hiding. She heard movement along the trail above her head and knew the local fishermen would soon join her on the beach. These men, both young and old, were strong from days spent pulling in the full trawling nets and hoisting the larger catches onto their boats. However, these men weren't well-trained swordsmen, and the fear of pirate raids was ever-present. Caragh feared that was who the villagers would face that night.

The Dark Heart of the Sea **BOOK 2**

The Red Drifter of the Sea **BOOK3**
The Scarlet Blade of the Sea **BOOK 4**

Viking Glory

Leif **BOOK 1 SNEAK PEEK**

Leif looked around his chambers within his father's longhouse and breathed a sigh of relief. He noticed the large fur rugs spread throughout the chamber. His two favorites placed strategically before the fire and the bedside he preferred. He looked at his shield that hung on the wall near the door in a symbolic position but waiting at the ready. The chests that held his clothes and some of his finer acquisitions from voyages near and far sat beside his bed and along the far wall. And in the center was his most favorite possession. His oversized bed was one of the few that could accommodate his long and broad frame. He shook his head at his longing to climb under the pile of furs and on the stuffed mattress that beckoned him. He took in the chair placed before the fire where he longed to sit now with a cup of warm mead. It had been two months since he slept in his own bed, and he looked forward to nothing more than pulling the furs over his head and sleeping until he could no longer ignore his hunger. Alas, he would not be crawling into his bed again for several more hours. A feast awaited him to celebrate his and his crew's return from their latest expedition to explore the isle of Britannia. He bathed and wore fresh clothes, so he had no excuse for lingering other than a bone weariness that set in during the last storm at sea. He was eager to spend time at home no matter how much he loved sailing. Their last expedition had been profitable with several raids of monasteries that yielded jewels and both silver and gold, but he was ready for respite.

Leif left his chambers and knocked on the door next to his.

He heard movement on the other side, but it was only moments before his sister, Freya, opened her door. She, too, looked tired but clean. A few pieces of jewelry she confiscated from the holy houses that allegedly swore to a life of poverty and deprivation adorned her trim frame.

"That armband suits you well. It compliments your muscles," Leif smirked and dodged a strike from one of those muscular arms.

Only a year younger than he, his sister was a well-known and feared shield maiden. Her lithe form was strong and agile making her a ferocious and competent opponent to any man. Freya's beauty was stunning, but Leif had taken every opportunity since they were children to tease her about her unusual strength even among the female warriors.

"At least one of us inherited our father's prowess. Such a shame it wasn't you."